THE CROWN PROPHECY

MEG ACUNA

Cover design by miblart

To all the magical girls of lace and steel who are doing the work to unlearn their trauma and embrace self-love. I see you and I'm proud of you.

Lienoris
Formere

Valine
Moiaria
Falerin
Dyminian Pass
rias

PART ONE

Chapter 1

Leave it to my mother to equate baking a few croissants to committing a heinous war crime.

"For the love of the gods, please promise me this job you've taken is in a Mundane bakery at the very least. I can't bear the thought of my only child working for a *Wielder.*" She flung the word from her lips like a curse, a dirty thing unworthy of her enunciation.

I swallowed my irritation at her theatrics; this was not a good morning to let my temper get the better of me. On another day, I might have been sucked into the debate, but today I had more pressing things to worry about. Taking a measured breath, I reminded myself that I had prepared for this. Our two-bedroom cottage was no stranger to the sounds of our arguing, and anti-magic rhetoric was one of Mother's favorite tirades.

Tuning out her chorus of councilment, I focused on the warm, excited buzz in my chest that accompanied the thought of my new position.

Just as my hand made contact with the worn brass handle of the front door, I turned to face her. "I've made my decision," I said firmly, running through my well-rehearsed speech. "I don't expect you to agree, but you do need to respect it."

Not leaving room for argument, I swung open the cottage door and stepped out into the shy autumn sunlight.

The streets of Lilifel were bustling today, people weaving in and out of the various shops, arms laden with parcels. Children ran underfoot on the cobblestone streets, caught up in their worlds of make-believe.

Dotted amongst the Mundane stalls, a few Wielder vendors used small displays of magic to bring attention to their wares: the cobbler's shoes left glowing footprints on the ground as he advertised his new designs, the blacksmith's hammer clanged away at an anvil by itself, and the tailor changed the color of the dress on his form at will.

I watched as a young boy, perhaps five or six, pulled at his mother's skirts to show her an orb of liquid held in his palm. His water-wielding Gift must have been freshly manifested, because the sphere wobbled and splashed into a puddle on the stones before she could turn around to see it. The woman knelt and wiped his tears, encouraging him to try again. Resilient as children often are, he sniffled and went bounding off to the fountain for more.

The tender vignette brought a soft smile to my face as I twisted the copper curl at the end of my braid around my finger. The chilly air of the crisp, gold-touched season filled my lungs as I took my first deep breath in what felt like days, welcoming the peace that settled in my chest whenever I ventured into the city.

The decadent sugar-dusted vanilla and almond scents of the bakery district wafted through the air, beckoning me to follow them to a sweet reward. I looked wistfully down the road where my mother, Wilomena, assumed I had gotten a job at a bakehouse. Call it dishonest, but I hadn't corrected her. In fact, her assumption had been the perfect cover: innocuous enough to be believable and just far enough out of her way that she wouldn't stop by looking for me. It wasn't that the idea didn't have appeal; even now, my feet itched to follow their well-known route to my favorite patisserie, but I didn't have time for that today.

Steeling myself, I pivoted to the right and started toward the castle.

The palace gazed down at me imperiously, daring me to approach. The towering structure was made of a light polished sandstone with no fewer than seven peaks and over two dozen gleaming lattice windows.

The hair on the back of my neck rose as I counted the guards stationed outside the looming iron gate that surrounded the grounds. A portcullis guarded the entrance jealously, poised to drop at any moment. The Crown was notoriously secretive, and I had never known anyone who had been inside the castle until Mellie was hired as the Head Baker. Now, after months apart, the nearness of my friend made me giddy.

But five, then ten, then fifteen minutes passed as I stood waiting for her. Had she forgotten? I glanced down at her letter to make sure I had arrived at the correct time.

Quinn,

I've been given special dispensation to allow you commuting privileges from the village. Please reconsider accepting the Assistant Baker position and meet me at the Southwest gate in three days' time when the clock strikes nine. I miss you, Dumpling.

-Mellie

I stared down at the precise penmanship I had often seen on the receipts she wrote at her bakery, reassuring myself that I had remembered the details correctly. So where was Mellie?

Unwilling to miss my opportunity, I identified the most approachable guard, a young man who couldn't have been any older than his late teens, and advanced toward him.

"Hello," I started, shifting on my feet. "I have a note from the Head Baker. She was supposed to meet me here this morning to escort me into the castle, but I suppose she must have gotten caught up with something?" It came out as a question, and I kicked myself for letting my nerves show so plainly.

The guard took the note I was holding out, scanned it quickly, and shook his head, shaggy hair following the movement.

"Sorry, miss, but no one gets in and out privileges. Your friend must be mistaken." He turned back toward the guard station in a clear dismissal.

A lump of despair rose in my throat and I swallowed hard, my eyes prickling.

"QUINN PARRY, there you are!"

Tears of relief threatened at the sound of Mellie's voice. She walked toward us at a brisk pace, linen apron whipping against her legs as she moved. Her chin-length mousy brown hair was starting to grey, but her warm brown eyes held the same sparkle they always had.

"Apologies for my tardiness, Dumpling. I got caught up in all the contest nonsense–she cut herself short. "Mr. Ryden here hasn't been giving you any trouble, I trust?" She looked up at the guard with an air of authority that belied her short, stout frame.

"None at all, Permelia, ma'am," Ryden cut in before I could answer.

I stifled a giggle. I'd only heard her called by her full name a handful of times in the nine years I'd known her. She much preferred "Mellie" and had told me so the first time I'd wandered into her bakery in the village at fifteen years old.

"Good." Mellie waved him off curtly, ushering me toward the entrance.

She leveled her attention on the gatekeeper, who nodded and began to open it. I chuckled to myself. Four months here and she was already ordering the guards around.

Mellie linked her arm through mine and began to march us toward the castle.

"It's so good to see you, Quinny," she said, giving my elbow a squeeze with her free hand.

"Well, you haven't come to visit me since you moved here," I joked. "This seemed like my only option."

Mellie's steps stilled abruptly as she turned to face me with a heartfelt sincerity that made me regret my teasing.

"I'm so sorry, Dumpling," she said. "Truly. Palace staff are required to live on the grounds and the security here makes it difficult to commute back to the village. There aren't many opportunities for most of us to visit once we're stationed."

I raised an eyebrow. "I don't think I've *ever* known someone who has come back to the village from the palace grounds. This place seems so . . . insular."

Her only response was a cryptic nod, leaving me with even more questions. She moved to resume our journey to the grand double doors that led into the castle, but I held fast to her arm.

"Mellie, I have to ask . . . how did you get special permission for me to commute? That guard made it sound almost impossible."

The side of her mouth quirked up in a sly smile.

"Well you see, the queen . . ." she began.

"I knew it!" I barked a laugh, swatting her arm.

Even prior to her offer of employment at the castle, the whispers in the village square said that Queen Evalina had a soft spot for Mellie's cherry tarts. For as long as I could remember, royal carriages came by her bakery once every few weeks. The passenger, a hooded female figure, was always escorted into the shop by guards, and she kept her identity well hidden. Though I'd asked Mellie about it many times over the years, she always managed to evade the question or simply whispered, "I can neither confirm nor deny" with a twinkle in her eye.

"We need to be discreet about the arrangement, though," she warned seriously. "Everyone in the kitchen will be made aware, but there are certain people in the palace who might not take kindly to the knowledge that you're being treated differently than the rest of the staff."

Something strange lurked in her tone, but I couldn't quite place it, which was a rarity. After nine years of sneaking out to her shop whenever I could, I could usually read Mellie like an open book. She didn't give me much time to decipher it, though, as she tugged me along, chatting excitedly all through the courtyard and into the foyer.

"We're all Mundane in the bakery, but Jacques on the kitchen side has a Gift that allows him to stretch his body to fantastic proportions," she said. "It's a bit disconcerting, to be honest, but it certainly allows him to multitask. He can chop onions with one hand while the other puts something in the oven. The first time I saw it, I nearly fainted," she laughed.

"I can't wait to see that," I said, grinning. The thought of working so closely with a Wielder was strangely thrilling. Gifts had always fascinated me, but Mother made it clear that I wasn't allowed to associate with magic-users under any circumstances. It made my school years lonely, as half my classmates were Wielders and I found myself left out of almost every play group.

"Just last week poor Franc tripped over his leg halfway across the room," Mellie was continuing a few paces ahead, but I had stopped to gape at the extravagance of the palace.

Gleaming white marble floors covered with elaborate handwoven rugs drew the eye to the grand double staircase lit by golden candelabras; they held a dozen tapers each and must've been at least eight feet tall.

The ceiling was so high I could barely make out the details of the carved triangular panels, which each housed an intricate painted pattern. The result was lovely, reminiscent of an elaborate, gilded quilt. A crystal chandelier larger than my bed at home hung over the space, and I could see life-sized marble statues guarding the large doors at the top of the stairs.

When Mellie realized I was no longer following her, she doubled back to join me, smiling at my wonder.

"Beautiful, isn't it?" she asked. "They say the chandelier has been there for over two hundred years."

"How do you get any work done? I'll be hard-pressed not to spend all day staring at the art." Such extravagance was something I'd only read about in my favorite novels. Taking it in, I realized how little of the world I had seen outside our cottage.

"You get used to it," she dismissed with a wave of her hand. "Though I do thank the gods that I get to live and work in such a beautiful place."

I couldn't imagine getting accustomed to something so breathtaking, and I craned my neck to take in every beautiful detail as we walked.

We continued down the steps to the servants' passages as Mellie shared anecdotes from the last four months of living in the palace.

"You mentioned a contest?" I asked.

"We'll have our work cut out for us, that's certain," she huffed. "Over two dozen women are set to arrive next week. All Wielders. They'll be competing for the prince's hand." She waggled her eyebrows.

"Competing?" I scoffed. That was one prize I would be glad to let someone else win. "He certainly thinks highly of himself, doesn't he?"

"It promises to be a fierce fight, too." Mellie nodded solemnly, ignoring the latter half of my comment. "Any woman in the kingdom would be thrilled at the chance, I imagine. He's so *handsome,* Quinny!" She sounded like a schoolgirl despite being thirty years my senior, and her enthusiasm made me chuckle. "Dark, wavy hair, unbelievably blue eyes, and a jawline that could slice a loaf of bread, I'm telling you!"

I couldn't help but roll my eyes at that.

"Every story I've ever heard about the prince paints him as a vain, pompous ass," I said. I had little love for Prince Evander. Though I'd never met him in person, I'd heard enough whispers in the village to know that he was selfish, spoiled, and arrogant.

Mellie gave me a stern, reprimanding look that made me shrink down like the teenager I was when we met. "Be careful how you speak about the crown prince, Quinny," she warned. "He's respected here and I don't think there are many people in the castle who would take kindly to that sort of flippant criticism."

"Sorry, Mels." As usual, she was right. I didn't need to like my employer, but it probably wasn't the best idea to openly mock him in his own home. With any luck, I'd never even meet the man.

Mellie nodded in approval at my apology, launching into another story about the challenges of a new pastry she was experimenting with for the incoming guests. I swallowed as she described the difficulty she was having tempering the chocolate. The process sounded incredibly advanced. An ugly feeling of self-doubt came creeping in. Who was I to accept a position in the palace? My face heated, turning my freckled complexion tomato red.

Oblivious to my misgivings, Mellie opened the heavy wooden door to the kitchen, beaming with pride as she gestured broadly.

"*This* is where you'll be stationed!" she bubbled.

Looking around the vast space, I couldn't help but gasp. My eyes roved over the three connected rooms: the main prep and cooking area where we had entered, a pantry the size of Mother's entire cottage, and an enormous bakery space that made Mellie's shop in the village look like a shoebox. The L-shaped butcher block countertops along the back and left walls were laden with trays and trays of proofing pastries. Two matching rectangular islands in the center of the room were pristinely organized, and a row of wood-fire ovens on the opposite wall wafted the scent of baking dough toward the doorway. As I inhaled deeply, I felt the muscles in my shoulders relax.

"There are three ovens *just for bread,* Quinny!" Mellie gushed. "Working here has been a dream. The staff is so diligent, and I have all the ingredients I could ever need. Learning how to lead has been a challenge, of course; delegating has never been my strong suit. But it'll be so nice to have you around, Dumpling!" She beamed at me, slightly out of breath from her tirade.

I took both my friend's strong hands in mine and squeezed.

"Thank you, Mellie. Truly. I can't tell you what a relief it is to get out of that house."

"And your mother was amenable?" She quirked her brow knowingly.

"I told her I was going to work in a bakery," I grinned. "I didn't say where. And thanks to *you,* my brilliant friend, she'll be none the wiser when I come home in the evenings."

She scoffed. "It's a wonder she let you out of the house at all." Mellie made no secret of her disdain for my mother.

"Well, she wasn't thrilled." *That was an understatement.* "Of course she assumed you had some part in it, but I wasn't *technically* lying when I told her I wouldn't be working at your bakery in the village."

The negative opinion Mellie held of my mother was decidedly mutual. Mother had always resented the time I spent at the shop and I knew she was envious of our close relationship, so I wasn't any more eager to let her know who had hired me than I was to divulge where I was working.

"This morning, she switched tactics and asked me to promise it was a Mundane bakery," I continued. "I didn't even bother to answer that one. I'm a grown woman; her permission is irrelevant."

Try as I might to infuse confidence into my tone, the lie tasted bitter coming out of my mouth. Despite our fraught relationship, I hadn't figured out how to stop seeking my mother's approval in the last twenty-four years, a fact Mellie knew all too well.

"You shouldn't," she grumbled, opening a dark mahogany cupboard and pulling out a large bread bowl. "I don't understand why you continue to live with her, Dumpling. The way she tries to control you isn't healthy. She can't keep you in a box forever, monitoring your every move. That's not how love works."

Mellie had a point, but I couldn't explain the tangled emotions of my familial relationships to her. As ornery as she may be, Wilomena was still my mother, and I knew her overbearing nature came from a place of love. As she often told me, she only wanted to keep me from getting hurt.

Unwilling to argue after so long apart, I changed the subject.

"Are you sure this position shouldn't have gone to someone more qualified?" The kitchen was quiet now, but from what Mellie had said on our trek down, it seemed like she already had several bakers under her, inherited from the previous occupant of her position.

Though I didn't have a formal apprenticeship, Mellie had taught me as much as she could in the scraps of time we found during her bakery's slow hours. No other pursuit had ever matched my love of baking. The scent of cinnamon wafting through the air as I put all my frustration and worries into kneading the dough was its own kind of magic.

"Oh, tosh. I've taught you plenty." She dismissed my worries with a wave of her hand. "Besides, I've missed you, Quinny. We need someone with your spirit around here."

I wrinkled my nose, uncomfortable with the compliment.

"Now wash up," she said, tossing me a mustard yellow linen apron. "I'm going to start you on something easy. Try some rolls for supper tonight. All the ingredients are in the back right of the pantry." She gestured toward the storage room. "Just as I taught you, remember?" Her jovial wink made me feel lighter.

My nerves somewhat calmed, I wandered back to the pantry, selecting the ingredients I needed to begin prepping the dough and balancing them in my arms.

When I returned, I found the bakery filled with people, though I had only been gone for three or four minutes. Mellie was jovially giving orders to a thin man in his fifties who was pulling pastries from the icebox, a young blonde woman with her hair in a tight ponytail and sharp, shrewd eyes, and a young man about my age with the air of an overly-excited puppy.

"And this is Quinn Parry!" Mellie said, gesturing to where I stood, my arms awkwardly laden with ingredients. "She'll be joining us in the kitchen as my assistant."

"Four dozen rolls should be about right," she said, leading me to an empty workstation. "And be sure to make a few extras to take back to the village tonight."

"I'm sorry, but I must have misheard," the blonde woman snapped. "I thought you said *back to the village.*"

"Nothing is wrong with your hearing, Serena," Mellie said, her tone stern. "Quinn will be commuting home in the evenings. Special dispensation from the queen."

The young man's jaw fell open and Serena shot daggers at me with her eyes. Mellie leveled a disapproving look at her, silently warning her to drop the subject. She did so begrudgingly, muttering a few words that I couldn't catch under her breath.

Keeping my head down, I began to flour my work surface. How could I be so nervous to make a basic dinner roll? Even without Mellie's tutelage in the bakery district, I would've learned to make something as simple as this. Still, I had to stop to take deep breaths on more than one occasion as I found my mind spiraling with worries of somehow making rolls so horrid that the queen dismissed me.

While I waited for the dough to rise, I got to work making the puff pastry Mellie needed for the next morning's breakfast. Lost in the lamination process, my heart rate slowed and I entered the creative flow I often got into in the kitchen. Before I knew it, lunch was being taken upstairs.

We took a short break to eat our own meal, a more modest version of what was being served upstairs, and I did my best to ignore the holes Serena bore into the back of my head with her gaze.

The rest of the day passed in a blur of kneading and proofing, and I soon found myself back at the castle gate, clutching the basket of rolls from Mellie ("for believability," she winked.) Thankfully, this time she accompanied me and I didn't have any trouble with the guards.

My feet found their way back to the cottage without me, and I braced myself as I unlocked the door and stepped inside.

"Mother, I'm back," I called, wincing.

When I didn't receive a response, I wandered into the main living area, scanning the room to see if she was home. At last, I found her on the settee, but she barely lifted her head to acknowledge my presence. Her thin lips were pursed and her eyes, an identical hazel to mine, held no affection as she appraised me, tired and covered in flour.

Though her pale skin was beginning to show signs of age, her raven hair was as lustrous as ever. It was pulled back in a tight chignon tonight, which only served to make her look more severe. I waited for her to say something, but she just blinked at me and returned to her embroidery.

The silent treatment then. Fine. Anything was easier than rehashing the same old fight. Her prejudice against magic aside, I never understood why Mother was so insistent on keeping to ourselves. When I'd informed her that I was getting a job, she'd acted as if I were using her beating heart as hand pie filling.

By the time I reached the kitchen, I had given up hope of civil conversation and was surprised to hear her voice from the next room. "A letter from your father arrived today," she called.

"Oh?" I forced my tone to stay neutral even as my heart jumped. How long had it been since I had seen Father? Eight months? His work meant that he spent most of the year traveling to the port and back to meet with his suppliers and move goods. I missed him, but such was the life of a merchant.

"Apparently he's at the port in Lienoris," she remarked nonchalantly. "It's on the table if you care to read it."

I picked up the travel-worn envelope and fumbled to open it in my excitement. The majority of the letter was written to me, with a short postscript to Mother at the end.

Quinn,

I miss you very much, my darling girl. I have reached Lienoris and plan to head north from here. The post is few and far between in Dolende, so I may not be able to communicate as often when I reach the border.

I am writing to let you know that I am safe and thinking of you. Please be careful. The disappearances are increasing again in border towns. It seems to be mainly Wielders that have been targeted so far. I pray you'll be safe in Lilifel.

Sending all my love,

Father

P.S. Wilomena, I have seen to the request you made for new winter furs, though I'm unsure when I will be back to deliver them. Hopefully last year's fashions will be acceptable until I return.

"What do you think he would say if he knew about your *activities?*" Mother mused, still stationary on the settee. "It seems rather disrespectful of his hard work to seek out additional income that you can't possibly have use for."

I ground my teeth before replying. Truthfully, I didn't need the salary. We weren't rich by any means, but Father's work provided enough for us to live comfortably in our modest neighborhood. But the excuse to get out of the cottage and work with Mellie again was all the motivation I had needed to accept my position.

"I'm sure Father wouldn't mind me occupying myself."

She hummed in disapproval anyway.

"Did you read the bit about the Wielders? Good riddance, I say."

"Mother!" When I made my way back into the sitting room, I found her still concentrating serenely on her project as if she hadn't just said something horrid.

"The kidnappings are unsavory, to be sure," she raised one shoulder, "but I can't say I entirely disagree with Falerin's philosophy."

The acrid taste in my mouth didn't go away when I swallowed. The neighboring kingdom's years-long campaign for the extinction of magic was barbaric, founded on nothing more than ugly prejudice. Though most Mundanes lived peaceably alongside the Wielders, a select few, like my mother, held a disturbing nostalgia for the anti-magic rhetoric of the war.

Oblivious to my anger, Mother continued. "We should all be on equal footing." I almost laughed at that.

"Any advantages Wielders have over Mundanes are marginal at best," I pointed out. Though I'd heard their Gifts were stronger before the war, the magic of the realm seemed to have dwindled to almost nothing in its aftermath. All that was left were little cantrips, like the tricks shopkeepers used to draw eyes to their stalls. I failed to see how Mundanes were at such a disadvantage.

Though there was always a part of me that was raring for a fight, I was tired from my long day, and I knew answering would only result in an unwinnable argument, so I set the bag of bread on the counter a little too hard and headed for my room. Flopping down on my bed, I picked up the novel I was halfway through from my bedside table.

The next few hours found me lost in the pages of *The Eriargen Encounter*, my heart tight with worry when the heroine, Astrid, was captured by Gothresian soldiers and my eyes shedding tears when she lost her father. The romance in the story was passable, but the heart of the tale was the love that Astrid had for her kingdom and the lengths she would go to in order to save it.

Glancing at the clock, I sighed as I realized I had lost track of time again. The small iron hand alerted me that it was already well past midnight. Reluctantly, I blew out my lamp and resolved to get some rest. I had my own adventure to prepare for, and while I was sure it would be much smaller in scale, I fell asleep excited, for once, to greet the new day.

Chapter 2

MY FIRST WEEK OF employment consisted of testing out increasingly challenging pastries as I grew in both confidence and awareness of the kitchen workflow. While the baking itself was easier than I'd anticipated, my relationship with my coworkers remained uneasy.

Serena "accidentally" bumped into me on multiple occasions and once upset the mortar and pestle I was using to make the filling for some cardamom buns I had proofing on the counter.

"Soooooo sorry, 'Quinny,'" she crooned, enunciating Mellie's nickname for me like it was a slur. "Guess you'll just have to pop back into the village for some more cardamom." Never mind that we had a fully stocked pantry larger than most homes.

My blood boiled at her gibes, and there were many times I nearly failed in my resolution to control my temper for Mellie's sake. My hands shook in fury as I swept up the dough, and I felt my face heat as I thought of all the things I wanted to say to her– harsh, angry words she no doubt deserved to hear. But I refused to create more trouble for my friend. Not when she had gone to such lengths to secure me a place here. Instead, I blinked back my anger and focused on the sweet and peppery smell of the spices as I cleaned them off the floor.

Thankfully, the other bakers were easier to get along with, and though the atmosphere of the kitchen was charged, we found a tense truce amongst Serena's snide remarks.

I learned that the younger man's name was James, and though he would often shoot me apologetic glances after Serena's vitriolic comments, the two of them still seemed quite close and could be found at the dining table together every afternoon with a few other young people from the cooking side of the kitchen. He seemed nice enough, so I didn't understand why he put up with her snotty attitude, but I shrugged it off. I didn't need Serena to like me as long as we could get the pastries on the table. I had Mellie, and that was enough.

The other baker, Franc, was an older, silent fellow, and we quickly found an efficient rhythm.

Late one afternoon, between the hustle and bustle of lunch and dinner prep, I took tea with Mellie in her quarters, which were down the hall from the kitchen in the servant's wing.

The room was modest but warm and comforting, like Mellie herself. A single pine bed covered in a quilted bedspread stood across from a worn wooden table. The small stove used to heat the room also accommodated a small copper tea kettle with blue detailing on its porcelain handle.

"I don't think they like me," I confessed into my teacup, trying and failing to meet her eyes. As much as I wished it didn't bother me, I'd never been able to find peace in being disliked.

"They'll come around," Mellie said, waving it off.

"I suppose we don't know each other all that well." Not trusting my face to conceal my emotions if I looked at her, my gaze remained fixed on the chipped china in my hands, but my old friend saw straight through my forced air of nonchalance anyway.

The teacup she had been sipping from met her saucer with a soft clink. "Do you know Franc didn't speak to me for three weeks when I started here? And Serena was just as curt to me as she is to you, maybe even more so."

"Really?" I asked, my eyes widening in disbelief. Mellie seemed to have built up quite a bit of respect in the kitchen, and she held the mantle well. Even Helga, the head chef on the cooking side, seemed to listen to her advice and requests.

"Really," she nodded solemnly. The Head Baker before me had been here twenty-seven years. When he left, it was a hard blow to everyone."

I'd had no idea. Mellie seemed so at ease in her position here.

"So what did you do?" If she could change the staff's opinion of her, maybe I could as well.

"I kept treating them with kindness, but I was firm in my worth and my right to be here. It took a while, but we found a good dynamic in the end."

Curiosity was still niggling at me from our conversation on my first day of employment. "What happened to the previous baker? Did he pass?"

"Oh no, Dumpling," Mellie sighed. "He just got tired. Everyone does around here eventually. Living your entire life inside these walls is too much for a lot of people. From what I've heard, he bore it well for many years, but eventually he needed more, so he retired and moved back into the village."

That was the mystery I still didn't understand. She mentioned it so casually, as if it were a foregone conclusion, but I had yet to hear one good reason the palace staff was so sequestered.

"Why isn't anyone allowed to travel between here and the city? You said something about a security concern. Is it truly that dangerous?"

"Well," she hedged, "Falerin kidnapped so many Wielders during the war . . ." The far wall of her room suddenly became a very interesting thing that apparently required all of her attention.

Knowing Mellie as well as I did, it was easy to spot there was something she wasn't telling me. She'd never been a particularly good liar.

"Mels, there hasn't been any conflict with Falerin in almost thirty years," I pointed out, my brow raised.

The sigh she let out was deep and weary. "There's a lot you don't know about this place yet, Quinny. One of the conditions I agreed to in order to hire you on was not to share all the details, but there's a good reason they try to keep everything inside the castle walls." She gave me a pointed look I didn't quite understand.

"How do you handle it?" I asked. "I think I'd go mad."

"It's just part of the contract of working here for most of us. For me, the benefits outweigh the disadvantages right now. And there is a good reason, which helps me to rationalize it, but it is difficult. That's why Serena is so hard on you. She left a lot behind when she took her position five years ago. I haven't pressed her for the full story, but I know it eats at her that she can't go back."

The conversation was making me nervous. The more I pushed, the fewer answers I received.

"Mellie, you make it sound like the place is cursed." I hoped the teasing I tried to inject into my tone was light enough to hide my unease.

Mellie patted my hand. "Oh, nothing so dramatic, Dumpling. Don't you worry." I couldn't help but notice that she didn't quite meet my eyes as she changed the subject to the evening meal.

"It's time to start prepping for supper. We should go wash up." She stood and turned, hesitating a moment before facing me again.

"I wish I could tell you, Quinny. I really do. It's just one of those things, you know?"

I didn't, but I nodded anyway, not wanting to alienate myself from my only friend. Though I still had the distinct sense that she was keeping something from me, I swallowed the nagging feeling of betrayal and dropped the subject, turning my attention to the task at hand.

On my first day off since starting work at the palace, I slept in. My body hadn't yet adapted to the early morning hours of my new position, and I found myself in a constant state of fatigue. My tendency to stay up far too late reading, as I had last night, didn't help matters, but I hadn't been able to put down *The Eriargen Encounter*.

Glancing at the clock, I found I could barely call it morning. I stretched, sighing with contentment, and contemplated how I would spend my day. Though I was enjoying my employment, I had missed the village. Perhaps today I would venture out to the shops.

For now, though, I luxuriated in my warm sheets, watching particles of dust dance in a beam of sunlight from my open window. Pleasant chatter wafted in from the street, and a soft breeze blew the lace curtains gently.

When I finally extracted myself from my quilt, I found Mother sitting in the kitchen, sipping a cup of tea out of her favorite rose-patterned china.

"Good morning," I ventured.

To my surprise, she regarded me cordially.

"Good morning, darling. It's lovely to see you." There was a hint of passive-aggression in the latter half of her greeting, but I ignored it. This was the most civil she had been to me in a week.

Busying myself by preparing some breakfast, I debated whether I should invite her out with me today. If I didn't include her, I knew I'd likely get the same refrain that I wasn't spending enough time at home. Besides, with a planned activity to occupy us, and passersby to stimulate conversation, there was a chance we could make it through the afternoon unscathed. Maybe it would even be healing for our relationship.

"I was planning to go into the square today," I said, looking back at Mother, whose expression fell immediately, the corners of her mouth turning down. "Would you like to join me?"

She perked up at that, a small smile gracing her face. Guilt twisted in my gut at the sight. All my mother wanted was to spend time with me. Was that truly so horrible?

"Well, I do need a new pair of gloves," she mused. "We can make an afternoon of it!"

A short while later, we found ourselves in the crisp sunshine of Lilifel's town square. The oak trees were just beginning to don their autumn coats, burnished bronze and scarlet leaves drifting down like snowflakes.

A deep inhale filled my nose with the scent of the cinnamon apple turnovers being sold at a stand in front of the locksmith's. I hadn't seen this one before. It was likely a traveling cart, only in town for the season. I longed to try one of the pastries, but my heart sank as I watched the purveyor heat them with an open flame in his palm. If I purchased something from a Wielder in front of my mother, I knew it would start a fight.

Perhaps I should've come alone after all . . .

Reluctantly leaving the cart behind, I followed her down the street and allowed her to sweep me into her favorite tailor's shop. Like the bakery stand, the modiste on our own street was owned by a Wielder, so she made the trek to the square every time she needed to update her wardrobe.

As she selected a pair of kid leather gloves, I wandered the store, looking at the fussy, trussed-up gowns on the mannequins.

This year's styles are so stuffy, I thought.

In the far corner of the shop, though, was a sweet pink dress that was unlike most of the others in the shop. It was fitted through the bodice, with long bell sleeves and a flowing skirt. Turning the tag over, I noticed it was marked as discounted.

"Would you like to try that on?" a tailor asked. "The woman who commissioned it wasn't able to make the final payment, so it's looking for a new home. It isn't really the style this season, of course, but it's charming in its own way, I suppose. It looks to be about your size."

With a glance over my shoulder, I found that Mother was still occupied with the gloves. The attendant waiting on her was biting his lip nervously as she peppered him with question after question about their material and craftsmanship.

Surprising myself, I nodded to the tailor, who showed me to a small curtained section in the back of the shop. In the middle was a small pedestal, surrounded by three standing mirrors.

"Someone will be with you shortly to help you with the garment," the woman said. I didn't really need help donning the dress, but I nodded anyway, content to be waited on after a long week of caring for others.

As I ran my hand over the soft fabric of the dress I had picked out, the voices of two women carried over from the next pedestal.

"Even the crown prince would be taken with you in that gown, Fortunata! I'd wager he'd propose on the spot."

Her companion barked a laugh. "Unlikely. From what I hear, the man doesn't give a second glance to anyone he considers below his rank, male or female."

Mellie's words rung in my ears. He may be respected in the castle, but my initial criticism of him hadn't been baseless. Not that idle gossip in the modiste was a reliable source of information, but this was much more in line with what I had heard about the prince.

"That's only because he hasn't seen you in this dress," the first woman giggled.

Fortunata ignored her. "Royalty or not, I wouldn't want to be tethered to someone like that. I can't believe he still hasn't married and taken the throne."

"Perhaps he hasn't found love yet." The supposition was sweet and wholesome, and I imagined the young woman might be wringing her hands as she said it.

Her friend, however, wasn't so sentimental. Her tone remained resolute as she continued her admonishment of the prince. "Even if he isn't interested in romance, you think he'd do it for all of us Wielder subjects. How long has his mother been ruling alone? Four years? My father says that when there were two monarchs on the throne, his casting was twice as strong. Nothing like before we had to power the damn wards, but certainly better than the paltry excuse for magic we have now. If you ask me, the prince isn't too far from King Orobas."

My head shot up at that, and I was thankful for the cover of the curtains around me as I listened with interest. While I certainly wasn't one of the prince's adoring fans, comparing him to the Falerian king seemed like a stretch.

"Oh, you can't be serious, Tunie!" the first woman gasped. "You can hardly compare the prince not marrying to starting an entire war."

"I'm only saying that in a way, they're both acting against Wielders. Orobas may have been more antagonistic, but isn't the prince harming the kingdom's magic in his own way by refusing to take the throne? If Falerin ever breaches the wards, we wouldn't even have enough magic to defend ourselves."

"I suppose I can see your point, but being a bit spoiled and selfish doesn't make him nearly as horrible as *Orobas.*"

A being of smoke and mirrors, the Falerian king was only spoken about in frightened whispers. I'd heard many conflicting tales, but they all agreed on one point: the man hated magic with an unparalleled passion and was willing to go to extreme lengths to stamp it out.

"Nothing compares to evil like that," she continued, keeping her voice so low I had to strain to make out the words. "My uncle was captured during the war, and I overheard him telling my mother about what the Falerians did to him while he was a prisoner. They used some unnatural stone to cut him off from his Gift while they probed him for information about Enorias's wards. Orobas would've executed every last one of us with a drop of magic if he had gotten in."

"Thank the gods the shields held true then," her companion replied. Returning to a normal volume, she added, "I still don't like the prince though."

"I don't know, Tunie; his face might convince you to look past his faults," the first woman continued. "I caught a glance of him once as his carriage came through the city, and he was so stunning . . ."

Rolling my eyes, I tuned out the conversation. I'd heard enough of that from Mellie.

Where was the attendant? I was running out of time before Mother would notice I was gone.

I was about to give up waiting and try the dress on by myself when the woman bustled in, a tape measure draped around her neck.

"Apologies, miss. We have a very demanding guest up front and I was called in to assist with some of her more . . . pressing questions."

I stifled a laugh. I couldn't imagine who that could be.

The attendant helped me into the dress, closing it in the back with a line of fabric-covered buttons, and pushed the curtains aside so that I could see myself.

The sight made me smile, full and unreserved. The gown was lovely. It was flattering, easy to move in, and I loved the color. This would be a wonderful use of my first wages.

"Quinn! There you are!" Mother's voice came from behind me. I caught a glimpse of her in the mirror as her face turned sour.

"Oh, how horrid," she complained. "So plain. And that color clashes horribly with your red hair, don't you think? This one would be much more suitable." She fingered an elaborate baby blue gown on a mannequin near her and I swallowed the lump in my throat.

Well, the pink dress wouldn't be very practical in the kitchen anyway, I thought.

With the tailor's help, I removed it and emerged from the safety of the curtain wearing the plain clothes I donned before leaving the house. Glancing to the left, I saw the two women I had overheard talking about the prince.

True to her companion's gushing, the woman on the pedestal looked resplendent in the lilac floor-length number with a corseted waist that accentuated her form. Her friend clapped her hands together in delight, rising off the floor a foot or so as she spun around.

At the sight of her magic, Mother's face screwed up in disdain.

"We should leave," she ordered.

Too dejected to argue, I followed her, and didn't try on anything else for the remainder of the day.

The following morning, tension hung thick in the air of the kitchen. Helga, the head chef, shuffled around frantically, preparing to feed the large company the prince was entertaining for the contest. The carriages began rolling in last night and I was told they'd be staying for at least three months, so our workload wasn't about to lighten up.

Mellie and I worked side by side at a set of over six dozen miniature bread boules; While I may have thought three bread ovens a bit excessive when I first arrived, I was beginning to see the necessity.

I hummed to myself, taking care to score the top of each in a delicate leaf pattern. My lame dragged across the floured surface with ease and I admired my handiwork. Royalty always had someone to impress, it seemed, and I hoped that if anyone would enjoy the pretty detailing, it would be those used to luxury. Of course, it was also possible they would be so busy trying to hold up their massive heads that they wouldn't notice. Either way, I was enjoying the act of creating them.

These would hold a butternut squash bisque that I could already smell from the next room over, topped with dried cranberries, walnuts, and pumpkin seeds. My mouth watered just thinking about the blend of sweet and savory flavors.

Lost in my reverie, I didn't take notice of the door to the kitchens opening with a creak. Even if I had, I likely wouldn't have thought anything of it. With a staff so large, people were always coming and going as they worked towards completing the various tasks that were required to get a meal worthy of the royal family on the table.

Suddenly, though, the room became eerily quiet. Even the fire in the ovens seemed subdued somehow. The only noise I could hear was my o n soft humming, which I stopped sheepishly, raising my head to see hat had caused such a hush.

All at once, the air was sucked out of the room.

Standing in the doorway was a man with the most arresting blue eyes I had ever seen. My ego didn't even stop to chastise me on the ridiculousness of such a thought as I drank in his form: tall and barrel-chested, he took up a sizable portion of the doorway. He looked to be in his late-twenties and had the posture of someone who held themselves in high regard.

Prince Evander.

It was the fine brocade doublet that gave him away as royalty. The dark blue garment featured intricate golden embroidery that must've taken a team of seamstresses weeks to complete. The luxury extended down to his finely tailored pants and shiny leather riding boots.

True to Mellie's gushing, he had a strong jaw and dark hair with a hint of a wave as it swooped off his face. His penetrating gaze was currently trained on . . . me.

"Are you quite finished? Or would you prefer we all pull up a chair for the show?" His deep voice was calm but threaded with quiet danger. This was a man used to getting anything he asked for at the snap of his fingers.

The arrogance in his tone pulled me back to reality as I recalled the stories I'd heard in the tailor shop about our sovereign-to-be.

I set my jaw and squared up to him, determined that I would not be cowed or humiliated by this man.

"Nearly, sir," I gritted out, forcing myself to finish the last few notes of the song I'd been humming. It was foolish, and I don't know what made me do it, but I had always been a bit hotheaded.

Serena sniggered under her breath, Mellie elbowed me, and I dropped into a small curtsy, suddenly remembering that this man was not only our prince but also my employer. While I didn't put much stock in royalty, I didn't want to lose my position.

I swore I saw a hint of a smile playing at the left corner of his mouth, but it quickly vanished.

"Enlightening," he drawled. "Since your attention clearly isn't on your current task, perhaps you could be the one to tell me why my guests are upstairs sitting at an empty table?"

That was it? The crown prince came down to the kitchens to complain that they didn't have an appetizer? According to the clock above the chopping station, dinner didn't even begin for another seven minutes.

It took everything in me not to roll my eyes, which would have been a catastrophically bad idea after that stupid display of insubordination, which I was already very much regretting.

"My deepest apologies, your Highness." I forced my gaze downward in supplication.

"Yes, well, apologies aren't nearly as useful as action, are they? Please see that they're brought up now."

Jacques, who was tasked with overseeing the food as it was carried to the main dining hall, lunged for the tray of appetizers, his torso stretching halfway across the room. The poor man looked as though he might faint at any second.

"Not you. Her." The prince's eyes hadn't left my face.

I opened my mouth to protest that I wasn't even on the cooking or serving staff, but thought better of it when Mellie stepped on my foot without an ounce of subtlety.

"Of course, your Highness. Right away, your Highness," she answered for me.

"Good." Turning towards the stairs, he was gone without another word.

"Nice job, Quinny," Serena said, arching a blonde brow. "I was wondering how long it would take you to get yourself thrown out of here, but this surpasses my expectations."

Ignoring her, I turned to Mellie. "What in the hells was that? What should I do?"

Mellie wiped her hands on her apron, glancing around the kitchen to make sure no one could hear us. "I have no idea, Dumpling. I've never seen him down here before. The only thing to do now is follow his orders and keep your head down. The prince has no idea about our arrangement, and if we'd both like to keep our jobs we need to make sure he doesn't suspect anything. You just earned yourself a lot of attention that you shouldn't have," she reproached.

"He doesn't know?" I asked, incredulous. "Aren't you afraid someone else is going to tell him? Serena would be thrilled to get me fired."

"No, he doesn't, and he's not going to find out. He never comes down here and I doubt he's ever spoken to Serena."

Shoving the tray of miniature quiches into my hands hastily, she warned, "Just go up, hand this to one of the staff, curtsy, and come straight back down. Don't say a word."

I grabbed the tray with shaking hands, fear finally catching up to me after my ill-advised show of temper, and willed my feet to move toward the door.

"Quinn." Mellie stopped me. "You know I love you. But now is not the time to let that temper of yours get the best of you."

I nodded mutely and began my trek up the stairs, mentally kicking myself.

What had I been thinking? I just mouthed off to the *crown prince* for the gods' sakes. Taking the bait from my mother was one thing, but this was a whole new level of idiocy. Mellie had risked so much for me to be here, and it had only taken me one interaction to ruin her efforts.

Why hadn't I just held my tongue? Something about the man, his aloof haughtiness, sparked defiance in me. Perhaps it reminded me of my mother and I was doomed to spend my life pointlessly trying to riggle out from under the thumb of authority.

Determined to complete my task without incident, I used my back to push open the door of the dining room and turned to step inside.

Once again, I found myself in an eerily silent room. About twenty well-dressed young women sat listening with rapt attention to an older gentleman standing at the head of the table. A target painted on the northeast wall caught my eye. It seemed a strange addition to the royal dining hall.

A miniature cloud appeared over the table at the man's command, dropping a light snowfall that dissipated just before it reached the dinner guests. The room broke into polite applause. A Wielder, then.

Keeping my footsteps as light as possible, I tiptoed toward the waitstaff lining the walls, praying no one would notice me amidst his speech. Once I'd handed another staff member the tray of quiches, I began to creep back towards the service door.

As I moved, the cloud started to darken and crackle. With a flick of his wrist, the man sent shards of ice flying into the center ring of the target with a loud *thwack*. My eyes widened as a life-sized figure of ice crystallized in front of the target and pulled the shards out with a frigid hand.

I barely contained my gasp; a Gift that powerful was unheard of. This wasn't a simple cantrip to draw attention to a stall in the village square. This was a powerful spell. The amount of magical energy it must have taken . . . it was unbelievable.

The Wielder spoke to the assembled party. "In the Old Days, magic was abundant in this kingdom. Since the war with Falerin, much of our resources have gone to holding the wards, and Gifts have dwindled to an ember of what they once were. However, I can assure you that you will find your abilities far more powerful within these walls thanks to the special efforts of Queen Evalina."

What? I couldn't believe what I was hearing. The vast majority of Wielders in Enorias had no idea that casting that strongly was possible anymore. Hoarding this magic within the castle was selfishness on a level I had never even considered. If the Crown was willing to keep this power even from their fellow Wielders, what must they be keeping from Mundanes like me? I looked around the room to see if anyone else was as shocked as I was.

The prince sat at the other head of the table, seemingly unfazed by the Wielder's show of power.

"It is now time to strengthen the Rial line once more by choosing a bride for our own Prince Evander," the man continued. "In order to strengthen our great land, we have devised a series of tests to determine which contestants possess the appropriate magical skills and how strong they may be for each of you." He nodded at the contestants. "Three trials have been designed to determine which of you will make the most suitable bride for our crown prince. It is Queen Evalina's wish that she see him wed by the end of the year, so each task will be spaced one month apart, concluding at the Winter Solstice with a royal wedding.

"Participation is, of course, elective. For those who choose to continue, a word of warning:

"These events will test not only your magic, but your resourcefulness, preparation, and cunning, so I encourage you all to spend as much time working on your Gifts as possible. The first task will take place tomorrow morning and is designed to test whether you possess an appropriate affinity for the magical arts. No details will be given before the remaining trials, and you must be ready for anything."

The room broke into applause once more. Their adulation was punctuated with bursts of magic, colorful flowers springing up from one young woman's plate as a flock of songbirds circled the head of another. It seemed some of the ladies were already showing off.

I could feel my face heating in indignation as I blinked hard, trying to see how these vile people could feel justified in their actions. A firm hand encircled my arm and pulled me back towards the door, bringing me back to reality.

"Quinn," Mellie hissed, "We need to GO."

Panting in the stairwell, I put my hands on the narrow passageway walls to steady myself.

"What was *that?*"

Mellie caught up to me, closing the door behind us, and rubbed a hand over her eyes wearily.

"Come with me," she said, and swept by me towards the servants' quarters without another word.

As soon as the lock on Mellie's door clicked into place, I rounded on her.

"Mellie, did you know?"

My oldest friend in the world shifted uncomfortably, avoiding my eyes as she stared at the ceiling. I waited, but she gave no answer. The walls of the room seemed to close in as I grappled with the weight of the deception I had just uncovered. Not just from the Crown, but from Mellie as well. She had always felt like the healthy mother figure I'd never had, and the idea that she might be hiding her true self from me was too much to process.

"How can you possibly be all right with this?" I asked her. "These wicked people have been lying to *everyone.*"

"You weren't meant to hear any of that," she started.

"Unbelievable! I never thought I'd agree with my mother, but she's right. The royals are *evil.*" My voice sounded much too high, even to my own ears.

Mellie frowned; not the reaction I would have expected. Her quiet discomfort was enough to give me a second of pause as she began to explain.

"Deep breaths, Dumpling. As I said before, there are a lot of things about the castle you don't know yet. Things that I'm not at liberty to tell you. The queen–" she paused, choosing her words with care.

"The queen and I have known each other for many years. Trust me when I tell you that I wouldn't have asked you to come and work for a monster. There are larger things at play here."

I scoffed. "Oh, I'm sure she's told you a very convincing excuse about why they're keeping all this power to themselves, but I'm not about to be so easily fooled." Mundane or Wielder, I wouldn't let anyone stay in the dark about what was being held from them. "The people deserve the truth, and I'm going to give it to them."

Mellie paled. "You absolutely will not. Quinn, you can't just decide you want to be a vigilante without fully understanding the situation. Do you know the kind of unrest that would cause? You have no idea–"

"So tell me!" I shot back. "Tell what could possibly justify something like this, I beg you." My face burned with righteous indignation.

Mellie sighed. "Evalina is my friend, and she's a good woman. I don't want to keep you in the dark, Quinny, but I can't betray her confidence either. Let me find a way to help you understand. Give me a few days." Her pleading look cooled my temper an almost imperceptible amount, but it was enough.

Though I wanted to storm out, I couldn't turn off the tiny, rational part of my brain that reminded me that in nine years of friendship, Mellie had never betrayed my trust. There were so many things I had asked of her and so many of my secrets she had kept. If anyone deserved the benefit of the doubt, it was her.

"Fine." I snapped. Hurt flashed in her eyes and my tone softened. "This isn't like you, Mellie. You're a good, selfless person. I don't understand why you would be complicit in something like this."

"I haven't changed, Dumpling," Mellie said, and I could tell from the earnest look in her caramel eyes that she meant it. "Just let me figure out a way to help you understand without betraying my friend's trust."

Tears clouded my vision, though I wasn't entirely sure why I was crying.

"Oh, Quinny," she sighed, taking my hand in hers and patting it gently. "Why don't you take the rest of the day off? This must be overwhelming for you and I'm sure you need some time to yourself. Just promise me you won't repeat any of what you learned today."

Against my better judgment, I promised, "I won't."

Chapter 3

AFTER A FITFUL NIGHT of sleep, I returned to find the castle in a frenzy.

Mellie flitted around the kitchen, abuzz with nervous energy, while James stood in front of the oven, wringing his hands and refusing to take his eyes off his strudel. Even Serena had set aside her usual mask of snobbery and was working alongside me diligently to prepare the morning meal.

The sheer quantity of food was staggering; despite spending the evening stewing in anger over the premise of the contest, I had forgotten that the first trial would be taking place today. With twenty extra mouths to feed, it seemed we would have our work cut out for us.

The aroma of fat slices of bacon frying in the room next door made my stomach rumble as I tried to remain focused on the task at hand. Having arrived at the palace before sunrise to prep breakfast, I had already been working on this morning's pastries for almost three hours.

To combat my restlessness, I helped Mellie decorate her blueberry breakfast cake while I waited for my trays to finish baking. We worked in tense silence, trying to ignore everything unsaid between us. Now wasn't the time.

When we had finished, I pulled my custard-filled puff pastry out of the oven, sighing in relief that everything was ready in time, and set the baking sheet down on the warm wood of the butcher block countertop.

“All right,” Helga called, rounding up the kitchen staff. “I need everybody with a free hand to grab a dish and head upstairs. Our wait staff needs a bit of help with the extra volume and we’re all going to pitch in. I don’t want to hear any complaining about it.” No one challenged her, and I didn’t blame them. Helga ran a tight ship, and her years of service had hardened her into a machine of efficiency.

I reached for my tray only to find that James had already grabbed both his and my bakes, winking at me over his shoulder as he moved towards the servants’ passages.

There was a silver platter on the workbench next to me, so I grabbed it, careful not to upset the dome that insulated the food, and turned to follow him up.

Helga’s arm reached out to stop me just before I reached the door.

“Not that one.” She shook her head. “That’s the queen’s breakfast. The tray needs to be delivered directly to her quarters.”

I bit my lip, trying to spin the right words to get out of the task. I’d already made a fool of myself in front of one royal. Keeping a low profile would be best. “Can you give this to someone else? I’ve never met the queen before.”

“Meet the queen!” she laughed. “You won’t be getting so lucky today, Parry. Aurelie, her handmaid, will meet you at her door. Just curtsy, hand her the food, and come back down.”

“I don’t even know where her chambers are,” I said, a pleading note creeping into my voice.

My appeal didn’t sway Helga whatsoever.

“Keep going past the dining room entrance,” she barrelled on, "up the set of stairs on the left, make a right, then a left, and then take the second staircase on the right-hand side. Her door is the third on the right. You can’t miss it.”

I started to assure her that I most certainly could, but she marched away to chastise the poor boy delivering the scrambled eggs, who had upset half the tray he was carrying when he'd bumped into another chef.

"Can you repeat that?" I called after her.

Helga repeated the series of directives that still would not seem to stick in my mind, finishing with, "It's so simple a child could do it, and I don't have the time to baby you right now. Go!"

The passageway was cool and darker than I remembered. Perhaps it was only my anxiety as I begged my mind to recall her directions. Past the dining room entrance, make a left, then a right, then up the steps?

The winding staircase veered to the left and I adjusted the tray in my hands, careful not to drop it, as I continued my ascent.

A few paces further up, I began to hear faint scuffling sounds. Maybe the servant ahead of me could repeat the way, just to make sure I was remembering the directions correctly?

I opened my mouth to call out and nearly walked directly into the prince himself.

Not the right stairway, then. *Shit.*

He was seated on the steps, head in his hands, and when I met his gaze, I was surprised to note that his eyes were bloodshot.

"Oh." His voice was gruff and short. "You again. Do us both a favor and remove yourself from my presence. I'm in no mood for company at the moment."

More than happy to comply, I turned the way I came and began to bolt back down the stairs. In my haste to put as much distance between myself and the prince as possible, my foot lost purchase on the stone steps and I found myself slipping, the tray flying out of my hands and clattering on the ground.

Reality took a moment to catch up as I registered the pain in my leg where I had bashed it on the stone. Thankfully, it seemed to be a minor injury; the skin hadn't broken, but I would probably have a bruise tomorrow.

As I examined it, a large hand found my elbow and lifted me back up.

Caught off guard by the contact, I jerked my arm back.

"You don't have to break into a run. I'm not a dragon," came a baritone voice from just behind my ear.

No, just as selfish as one, I thought bitterly, *hoarding your magic like gold.*

This time I had the good sense to keep my anger to myself and settled on a polite, "Thank you," hastily moving away as I bent to gather the contents of the upset breakfast tray.

The porridge bowl was upturned all over the flagstone, the eggs and toast a mangled mess. I would have to go back to the kitchen for a new tray, and a rag to clean this passageway while I was at it.

To my surprise, the prince knelt next to me and began to gather the dishware off the ground.

"You don't have to do that, your Highness. Please allow me-"

"Well, I do take partial responsibility for the incident." *That must be a first.* "Besides, if I assist you in removing the spill, I can sooner go back to my solitude. It's been a very taxing morning."

My traitorous throat let out a scoff as I stood with the tray.

"Do you have something to say?" His gaze was piercing.

"No, your Highness." I forced myself to look at the stairs as I backed up, on the defensive once again.

"Your expression says otherwise. Though I applaud your attempt to keep your mouth shut this time. It's quite amusing, and I must confess I was in need of a diversion."

Bile rising in my throat, I turned toward him. How dare this man pretend to know me? To mock me so callously?

"If you must know, " the words slipped out of my mouth before I could stop them, "I was thinking about how truly *difficult* this must be for you." Sarcasm dripped from my words like honey. "To have two dozen young women throw themselves at your feet, begging you to take their power. I can see how that would be *taxing.* "

He took a long stride down the steps toward me.

"You think I want to be in this position?" he asked, his voice coming out in a low growl. "You have no idea what's at stake. What I have to find here, against all odds. Most of those women look at me and all they see is a crown." He was close again. Too close. I could see impossibly gold flecks in his blue eyes.

"A crown I somehow need to stabilize to keep every innocent Wielder in this kingdom safe from being hunted for their powers. A crown, mind you, that I don't even want," he continued, his volume rising. "If my mother wasn't dying–" The prince stopped, fumbling with his words as he found himself at a loss of what to say. His expression blanched, the color leaching from his face as he realized what he had just admitted.

My jaw dropped in shock, opening and closing like a fish as I tried and failed to come up with an appropriate response.

The queen is dying?

"I'm sorry," I said lamely.

"Dying to see me married, I mean. Of course." The words tumbled out too fast, a hastily wrapped bandage over a fatal wound.

The gears of my mind began whirring furiously, piecing everything together: the secret Mellie wouldn't divulge last night, the rush to get the prince to wed and assume the throne . . .

"Of course," I said. From his quick attempt at recovery, I was fairly sure I wasn't supposed to know any of what I was beginning to uncover, so I nodded furiously, all too willing to let him disguise his unintentional vulnerability. This was far above my station. "Your Highness, I apologize for my impertinence. I should be getting back to the kitchen."

I moved to go again and made it a few steps before he asked, "What is your name?"

Wonderful. I was sacked. Completely, absolutely, without a doubt sacked. I just hoped Mellie would emerge unscathed.

"Quinn Parry." The syllables tumbled from my lips before I had a chance to think about them. Why hadn't I made something up? Or said Serena? A total of five minutes in this man's presence and I had already made no fewer than three catastrophically terrible decisions.

I had no idea what I was going to tell Mellie. I reached the bottom of the steps, out of sight of the prince, and swung open the door.

As it closed behind me, I heard a soft, "I'm sorry, Quinn Parry."

Back in the kitchens, I searched for my friend. I had multiple apologies for her and I needed to be the one to tell her that I was about to be thrown out of the castle. She must've been upstairs, because I didn't see her messy bob weaving in and out of the bustling kitchen crowds.

My eyes caught on a well-dressed woman, likely in her fifties or sixties, speaking to one of the waitstaff by the door. Only a few words of their conversation were audible from here.

" . . .the queen's breakfast tray . . .?"

Oh gods. That must be Aurelie. I had completely forgotten about the queen's breakfast. The waitperson rushed to the staging area, assembling a new tray and pushing it into her hands.

As she turned to go, the door swung open, and Mellie rushed into the room. Her warm brown eyes found mine and she made her way towards me, nervous energy radiating off her. Did she already know?

"Mellie, I'm so sorry," I began.

"No time. You've been requested upstairs. By name."

Dread pooled in my gut. I needed to make her understand, but she was ushering me toward the door.

"Here, take this." She handed me a basket of scones.

"Mellie, I took a wrong turn in the hallway and ended up in this stairwell . . ."

She cut me off. "When the Crown calls on us, we do not make them wait, Quinny."

After a quick pat on the back, she shooed me out into the stairwell and closed the door behind me. Heaving a sigh, I started working my way up. It had only taken me a few days to lose my position here; it must be a record of some sort. Now I would have to go crawling home to Mother and endure her gloating about how right she had been . . .

Upon entering the dining room, I wasn't sure where I was supposed to report. Mellie hadn't said who had called for me, but I had a decent guess.

Prince Evander was already sitting at the head of the table, any trace of his earlier outburst wiped from his face. His mouth was fashioned into what I'd guess was meant to be a smile, though it came off more like a nervous grimace.

He glanced at me and motioned to the guard flanking him. The woman had warm olive skin and her dark hair was pulled back into a tight bun, not a strand out of place. An easy air of confidence identified her as a woman in charge. Despite looking to be about my mother's age, she had a strong build and I could tell that she could overpower me with half a thought.

When she bent down, he whispered something into her ear, his blue eyes once again finding me effortlessly in the crowded room. If only I had a Gift that could make me disappear. She followed his gaze to where I was standing and nodded once before resuming her position on his left.

Should I approach them?

My attention was stolen from my fretting as a burst of light flashed from the corner of the room. The ice-Wielder from yesterday rubbed his eyes as the woman in front of him bounced up and down with glee. He wrote something on the parchment he was holding, and she took her seat at the table, sending the woman on her left to take her place.

The second contestant picked up her fork, approached the man with all the confidence of a newborn fawn, and made a strained face as she stared at it in her hand. Nothing happened, so she tried again. It looked almost painful.

Finally, the utensil lifted off her hand an inch or so, hovered for a few seconds, and came back down. Her attempt to read what was being written about her was anything but subtle, and her shoulders slumped in relief when the man instructed her to return to the table.

A few more girls followed the same pattern; a petite dark-skinned woman with tight black curls produced a colorful bouquet from a salad bowl on the banquet table. Then a tall, lithe brunette woman conjured a small flock of blue jays. A sweet-looking redhead wasn't able to manage anything at all and was escorted out of the room weeping quietly.

This must be the first trial.

Not very dramatic or exciting, but a decent first testing point, I supposed. Demonstrate your magic and move on to round two. Fail, and you were sent home.

I was still standing there dumbly with my basket of scones, unsure if I should approach the prince and his guard, when I saw a familiar bob of short blonde hair approach the tester. The woman tapped the ice-Wielder on the shoulder and his uniform changed from its burgundy hue to a bright canary yellow.

I knew that trick. I knew that hair.

Marisol lived a few doors down from Mother's cottage and her father owned the tailor shop in our neighborhood. Though we had never been particularly friendly, she would certainly recognize me if she looked my way. I turned my back to her, praying I hadn't been spotted. Even if I was about to get fired, I didn't need my mother to know where I had been these past few days.

As if on command, the prince's guard marched over to me, every step of her confident stride a death toll.

"Quinn Parry?"

I nodded, heart in my throat.

The guard motioned me farther away from the table.

"Prince Evander informed me that you had an unexpected run-in this morning. From what I understand, there were aspects of the conversation that the prince wishes to remain quiet. You would do well to forget the encounter ever happened." She looked at me with an uncomfortable intensity, as if she was staring straight into my mind, and her eyes flashed. The woman was terrifying.

"Yes ma'am," I managed. I waited for my dismissal from the staff.

"Very good." She patted my shoulder in a bizarre change in demeanor. "You may return to the kitchens."

What? It took a considerable amount of effort to close my hanging jaw and compose myself.

Not willing to push my luck again, I did as I was told, resisting the urge to break into a full run towards the door. I needed to find Mellie.

Thankfully, I didn't have to look hard this time, as she was waiting for me at the entrance to the kitchens, the panic on her face veiled only by the thinnest sheet of gossamer.

"Quinn, what was that about?"

I glanced around the room. "We should probably speak in private."

Mellie's eyes widened, but she said nothing as she led the way to her chamber, locking the door behind us.

Not a second later, I blurted out, "Queen Evalina is *dying?*"

My friend let out a small gasp as her hand flew up to her mouth, shock carved into the lines on her forehead.

"Quinn, how . . .?"

The story spilled out of my lips, frantic and confused. "The prince told me. I don't think he meant to, but I was sort of baiting him a bit and it slipped out and he tried to recover but he *said it,* Mellie, I know what I heard–"

"Whoa," she interrupted, using both the tone and body language one might use on a spooked horse. "I'm going to need you to slow down. Let's start with the prince."

My face heated in embarrassment as I recounted our brush in the stairwell. Telling Mellie that I had lost my temper before knowing all the facts *again* was humiliating. A sigh of exasperation was her only reaction, but I knew she was disappointed in me. At least the knowledge I gained in the encounter shed light on one point of contention from the last week.

"Is that why they're having this competition?" I asked. "They need to find someone else to help Prince Evander hold the throne because the queen is ill?"

Mellie sighed. "Well, I suppose there's not much use in me hiding anything from you now. At least I wasn't the one who divulged Evalina's secret." After a deep inhale, she continued.

"Since the king died a few years ago, Queen Evalina has been bearing the weight of the crown on her own. I don't know the details, but from what I understand, it takes an immense amount of magic, and it became significantly harder after the war. She knew Prince Evander needed to find a bride and take the throne, but she loves her son so much that she couldn't stand the idea of him in an arranged marriage. What she and the King had was beautiful and rare, and she doesn't want anything less for Evander."

"So he's just been letting her suffer?" Though I could understand the queen's motivation, I still didn't know why her son hadn't assumed responsibility earlier, especially if his mother's health was at stake.

"That's the thing, Dumpling," Mellie said, taking my hand. "He didn't know it was draining her."

He didn't know? That seemed . . . convenient.

"How is that possible?" I asked.

"Evalina hid the truth from him for as long as she could to try to give him a chance to find a partner. She didn't want to burden him with the pressure, but she just kept getting weaker from the drain on her magic. I convinced her to come clean to him a few months ago, and he began the search for these contestants the very same day."

"Couldn't the queen just remarry?" I asked. If she was so set on her son finding love as she had, it would certainly be the easier option for her to enter into a political alliance.

"She should, in my opinion. But Evalina is a stubborn woman. I think she sees it as a betrayal of her late husband. And she was convinced she could do it on her own . . . until she couldn't."

Mellie's eyes welled up with tears, the sight shocking me out of my interrogation. I hadn't known she and the queen were so close, but with the secret visits to her bakery for the last ten years, I imagined they had spent more time together than I realized.

Reaching out, I squeezed my friend's hand. It seemed cruel to ask her more when she was barely maintaining her composure, but if I was ever going to get answers, now was the time. There was still one aspect of this that didn't make any sense to me.

I began as gently as I could. "So how does this tie into the strength of magic in the castle?"

Wiping her eyes with the back of her other hand, Mellie sniffled, closing her eyes tightly, as if she could shut the grief behind her lids.

"Evalina is concentrating as much power as she can here to allow Prince Evander to hold this competition. It's the best chance he has of finding a queen with enough power to help hold the throne in the little time he has."

I raised my eyebrows. While I still didn't like the man, I didn't envy his position. Having so little time to choose a wife, knowing that every day he delayed put his mother at more risk . . . that must be hellish.

As if sensing my thoughts, Mellie continued. "The prince has always been a mother's boy, named for her and everything, and he's outraged that she kept her condition from him. I've only met the man twice, but servants who've been around the castle for many years say he's a shadow of himself, short-tempered and on edge all of the time. I think he shoulders the blame for her decline. Even without the truth about Evalina's condition, everyone in the kingdom knew he needed to marry except himself . . . I don't think anyone had the courage to tell him."

Guilt settled in my stomach with the realization that I had inserted myself into a situation I knew very little about and had inadvertently kicked a man already down. Then I remembered his condescending attitude and felt a bit better. He didn't have to be such an ass.

Silence weighed down the room as I took in the impossible information and Mellie tried to compose herself.

"I owe you an apology, Mels."

"I understand, Dumpling. I was trying to find a way to help you see the truth without giving up Evalina's secret, but I kept a lot from you." She pulled me into an embrace. "Are you all right?"

My hand flew to my mouth. I had been so caught up in my line of questioning that I'd forgotten to tell her what happened in the dining room.

"Mellie, there's more. When I was called into the dining room, a guard asked to speak with me privately, told me to forget the conversation with Evander ever happened, and that was all. Why was I not sacked? I should be fired for speaking to him the way I did."

Mellie's brows furrowed. "A guard? What did they look like?"

I recalled the details as best I could. The whole morning was blurred with panic. "Medium height, strong build, warm skin, dark brown hair in a bun?"

Mellie's expression shifted from befuddled to flabbergasted as her eyes flared wide. "Quinny, that was Maddox," she concluded, punching emphasis into the last word.

I could tell from her tone the name was supposed to mean something to me, but it was entirely unfamiliar.

"The *Captain* of the Guard," Mellie said when I didn't react. "The woman is so efficient at her job it's like she's a machine. Maddox is not one to mess around." Her head shook slightly. Whether it was in warning or fear, I didn't know.

"So again, why am I still here?" My head was spinning with information.

"I'm not sure, Quinny, but I think it's best not to question your good fortune. Steer clear of the prince, keep your head down, and we'll make it out the other side of this."

I nodded, mute, as Mellie twisted her hands in her apron. Anyone else might have missed the tremor in her voice, but she couldn't hide her distress from me.

"The most helpful thing we can do for Evalina right now is to make sure this contest goes as smoothly as possible," she said.

"Of course, Mellie. Wherever you need, I'm here."

Sniffling one last time, she squared her shoulders and donned a protective mask of joviality. I suddenly wondered how often she had used it on me.

"Let's get back to the kitchen. I think we both need something to eat before the lunch rush begins."

Arm in arm, we headed back the way we came.

Chapter 4

SIXTEEN LADIES HAD PASSED the initial assessment and would be staying in the castle for at least a month. From the whispers I heard amongst the contestants while serving lunch, the second trial promised to be much more rigorous. The stressful atmosphere, it seemed, wouldn't be limited to the kitchens.

Wiping my hands on my linen apron, I leaned against the counter. To say it had been a long day would be a shadow of the truth.

A pile of dirty china loomed in front of me, the last obstacle between me and the comfort of my bed.

On days like this, I wished I could stay in the castle with everyone else, if only to avoid the journey home. I wasn't looking forward to the cold walk or the snide comments I knew Mother would make. That is, if she deigned to speak to me at all.

As I started to wash the goblets piled up by the sink, the warm suds of the water a pleasant sensation on my tired hands, James came bounding into the room breathlessly.

"Quinn!" The sound of my name startled me. We had worked together for over a week, so I supposed I shouldn't be surprised that he knew it, but I could count on one hand the number of conversations we'd held. The few words we had exchanged didn't go further than "Can you please hand me the sugar?" though he sometimes looked like he wished he could say more. Serena was always around, and she made it abundantly clear that he was *her* friend and she was not willing to share.

"Quinn!" he repeated, all but skidding to a stop. "The prince has decided to dine in his chambers tonight and he's asked for *you* to bring him his food. Any idea why?" My heart dropped into my stomach.

"None," I lied, my collar heating. I didn't know why he'd wish to see me ever again after our earlier confrontation, but I was sure that whatever his reason, it couldn't be good.

Serena snorted from across the room. She seemed to be a big fan of that noise where I was concerned.

"Just when I thought you couldn't get any more special treatment . . ." she seethed. "Then again, maybe this explains your 'special dispensation from the Crown.' Are you bargaining with the *pleasure of your company?*" The innuendo made me sick.

"For the gods' sake, Serena, what is wrong with you? I just met the man. I understand that you have an issue with me, but let's at least try to steer clear of treasonous accusations, all right?"

Raising her eyebrows, she affected an air of haughty superiority. "Yes, well, you've been here less than two weeks and you've had more conversations with the Crown than I have in five years. Most of us wouldn't have gotten away with the little *show* you put on the other day." With that, she sauntered away.

My pulse thundered in my veins until I took a few slow breaths to calm myself. Serena wasn't worth it, and I didn't need to get myself into any more trouble by fighting with her.

Fragrant thyme wafted to meet my nose as I piled a tray high with tonight's dinner, glazed mutton with buttery mashed potatoes and sauced carrots.

One positive thing about my recent revelations was that I was no longer worried about Mellie losing her position. From the sound of it, the queen wouldn't fire her because her assistant was a hothead. They had a personal relationship, and it seemed Queen Evalina likely understood all too well the struggle of having a child who was a bit short-tempered.

This time I had James write down the directions to complete my delivery and set out. With any luck, I'd be able to hand the food to a manservant and go on my way.

Maybe this is just a strange power trip to make me climb the four flights of stairs, I thought hopefully, trudging up and up and up.

By the time I reached the fourth floor, my heart was pounding. I told myself it was only because of the arduous climb and that I wouldn't let my nerves get the best of me again.

One, two, three, four, I counted the doors on the right as I walked down the hallway. This was the one. It was ajar, and I could hear the quiet rustling of pages within. My safest option was to knock, so I lifted a shaky hand, doing my best to avoid a second upset tray, and rapped on the wood three times.

The sudden sound of chair legs scraping across the floor was the most terrible noise I had ever heard.

Please let it be a manservant. Please let it be a manservant.

The door opened further, and I found myself at eye level with a white linen undershirt, its ties hanging loose. The result was a span of bare chest that, if I was being honest with myself, threatened to make my heart beat faster for reasons entirely unrelated to the climb or fear for my job.

The foreign thought shocked me, and I stepped back from the door, once again unable to meet the prince's eyes. This was absolutely not the time. In fact, I was fairly sure there *was* no time when it would be appropriate to ogle the crown prince, especially since every interaction we'd ever shared had been a disaster. I was sure he wasn't any fonder of me than I was of him.

"Your supper, your Highness."

His boots vanished from the floor in front of me.

"Yes, you can leave it on the table in my study."

I entered the doorway and thanked whichever god was looking over me as he continued straight through the antechamber, gesturing for me to turn right.

Stepping through the threshold into the dim room, a small gasp escaped my mouth. The walls of the study were at least twelve feet high and stacked to the ceiling with shelves and shelves of books. Gilded covers gleamed next to worn leather spines, and there were several volumes lying open on the dark mahogany desk

Moving one of the tomes on the workspace, I set the tray down, careful not to disturb any of the pieces of parchment that were strewn over the wooden surface. My eyes lingered on its title: *The Eriargen Encounter*.

I snorted. Not subtly, either.

"Another comment, Ms. Parry?" The prince leaned on the doorframe behind me, sleeves rolled up to his elbows.

"No sir."

"Oh come, don't start holding back now." A sparkle in his eyes dared me to speak.

"It's just that I finished this book recently and it doesn't strike me as your type of reading." I chose my words as carefully as possible

"And why is that?" he asked

"I just didn't think you would have time to read fiction, I suppose."

Pushing off the door frame, he took a few steps into the room. "We all need to escape our reality every so often. Better to do it with a tale of romance and selflessness than with drink."

"Romance?" I asked, raising my brows.

"I found Astrid and Galadaer's love to be honest and moving. To think that love can spur someone to take such great risks and triumph despite all obstacles is inspiring."

Try as I might, I couldn't hold myself back from refuting *that* comment. "But Astrid didn't do it for him! She did it for her kingdom. That's the real love story of the piece."

"You didn't care for Galadaer?" Now it was his turn to raise a brow. "I thought all young ladies loved a white knight."

"If the knight had a brain, maybe," I scoffed. "Astrid carried the weight of the entire plot. And she wouldn't have had to sacrifice her power at all if he had stopped to think for more than a second before running into battle."

"I hadn't reached that portion yet," he said, unsuccessfully attempting to hide his smirk at my tirade.

"Well, prepare yourself," I barreled on. "He's handsome and dashing, but the man doesn't have two thoughts to rub together. A typical spoiled prince, more interested in showing off and painting himself as the hero than in the actual result of his actions."

Stopping to consider my words, I quickly backpedaled.

"Not you, of course, your Highness. It's only that–"

Where I had expected anger, there was only a light chuckle and genuine warmth in his eyes.

"No, please don't apologize. I appreciate your candor. And your . . . spirit. Too many of the staff here are afraid to tell me what they really think. This has been refreshing."

I wasn't sure what to do with that. An awkward pause hung in the air before he changed the subject.

"About our earlier conversation . . ."

"What conversation?" Maddox had been very clear about acting as if our confrontation hadn't happened. I wasn't sure how literal she had been, but I wasn't taking any chances.

The line between the prince's brows softened in relief as he cleared his throat. "Nothing. Nothing. Well, I appreciate the meal. You are dismissed."

Another anticlimactic confrontation. Heeding Mellie's advice to keep my head down, I retreated toward the door.

I nearly made it before, unable to help myself, I blurted the question that had been plaguing me since I had received his summons.

"Why did you request me tonight?"

The prince assessed me, a strange look in his eye. "I just needed to confirm something," he said cryptically. "Although I must admit this was the most interesting conversation I've had in weeks."

With a contest for his hand and a crown he was about to inherit, I very much doubted that, but I nodded anyway. I shouldn't have asked to begin with.

My hand on the doorknob, I felt the energy in the room shift, as if deciding something pivotal before settling into place.

"Will you return with my tray tomorrow night as well?"

So close. I was so close to making it out of this conversation unscathed.

"Is that an order?"

He paused, tilting his head slightly before answering.

"No. A request. I haven't quite finished *The Eriargen Encounter,* but I'd be interested to get your thoughts when I do. It's been too long since I talked to someone who isn't afraid to disagree with me."

"Of course, your Highness." Fixing my eyes on the floor, I dipped into a curtsy. I couldn't refuse my prince, I told myself. That's why I'd agreed.

A small voice in the back of my head whispered "*Liar.*"

Chapter 5

THE FOLLOWING DAY, SERENA was even more unbearable than usual. She went out of her way to bump into me and took all three ovens for her one dish at breakfast. I swore she actually hid my ingredients on at least one occasion. Childish.

The ladies of the competition were set up in the grand ballroom for "training," which, from what I could tell, involved a lot of peacocking and apparently required a laughable quantity of food. I had a front row seat to their grandstanding, as Mellie had caught on to Serena's harassment and sent me upstairs to attend the refreshments. At this rate, I would be doing more serving than actual baking, but I had to admit I was thankful for the break from the tense atmosphere in the kitchen.

Satisfied with my work arranging the trays of pastries, smoked meats, and cheeses, I surveyed the training room. With its gilded walls and shining crystalline chandeliers, it was the picture of opulence. The floors were polished to such a shine that I imagined if one were dancing at a ball, they would see their partner's reflection in the marble.

The banquet table was pushed up against the wall, laden with dishes both sweet and savory; my job was to stand at one end with a pair of tongs and fill plates with whatever the ladies requested. Though it was dull work, it gave me the opportunity to observe the contestants at close range.

After a childhood of unfed curiosity about the Wielders, finally getting to watch them at work was fascinating. I tried not to stare too obviously as a tiny, mousy-looking girl sparked a flame on her fingertip and used it to paint the air in front of her, spelling her name "F-R-E-Y-A." The letters sparkled for a few seconds before fading.

Another woman stood on a patch of grass she had grown on the floor, using conjured vines to grab and release a ring of cups she had placed on the border of her area.

Meanwhile, the girl who'd levitated the fork the day prior had progressed to plates and was managing to lift them a few feet off the ground, the same unfortunate strained expression on her face. I stifled a giggle. It looked like she needed to use the lavatory.

My observations were cut short when the vine grower wiped the sweat off her brow and approached my station. She was petite, with warm brown skin and honest eyes. Dark, voluminous curls stood out against the sweetheart neckline of her long yellow gown, which featured gathered sleeves and a subtle gold floral print.

"Just water," she said, waving me off. "Don't trouble yourself. I'm happy to get it."

Despite her insistence, I reached for the silver pitcher, grabbing the ornate floral handle and pouring her a goblet. "It's my pleasure," I promised.

After several long gulps, she handed it back sheepishly for more.

"The maneuver you were working on over there looked impressive," I remarked as I refilled her cup. "Is it difficult?"

She perked up at the praise, hair swaying as she bounced on the balls of her feet. The woman seemed to radiate sunshine, and I had the strangest thought that if she were a beverage, she would be a glass of champagne, bubbly and crisp. I liked her immediately.

"This application is new for me, so I'm still getting the hang of it. My Papa, who owns a nursery in the village, is a green-Wielder as well. Until now, I've only used my Gift to tend to unhappy plants, but it's unbelievable how much stronger it feels in the castle. I thought I should try to turn it into something more useful." She shrugged.

"Well, you're doing an amazing job," I said. "Much better than most have been able to manage so far." At this, I nodded my head ever so slightly toward the levitator.

As if on cue, her plate fell to the ground with a loud crash.

"I'm sure she'll get the hang of it," the woman giggled. Turning back to face me, she extended her hand. "I'm Colette."

"Quinn," I said, reaching to return the gesture. "It's a pleasure to meet you."

Rather than shaking it, she took my hand in both of hers and gave it an excited squeeze. "Have you worked in the castle long?" she asked.

I shook my head. "Not at all. In fact, I arrived just before you did. I mainly work in the kitchen, but they're a bit short staffed with the extra guests, so I was called up to assist."

"Oh, I love cooking!" she squealed. "Although my cousin Lain always complains that I use too much salt." At this, she threw in an eye roll, inviting me to commiserate with her. I couldn't help but laugh.

"Actually, I mostly bake," I said. "So if anything, I might be accused of using too much cinnamon."

"No such thing!" she exclaimed. I cracked a broad grin; I agreed completely.

"Does this mean you're responsible for the amazing tarts at breakfast?" she asked. "I could kiss you!" Her enthusiasm was infectious, and I found myself giggling again.

Before I could respond, another figure sauntered over to the table. With thick, dark hair down to her waist and olive skin, she reminded me of somebody . . .

The all-black outfit she wore resembled fighting leathers more closely than the ballgowns that most of the other competitors had opted for. With a deep plunging neckline and gold detailing along the buttons that was mirrored on the bracers she wore on her forearms, she looked completely at ease with herself, boasting an easy kind of confidence that I envied. I wondered what her Gift might be.

"Nessa," Colette bubbled, "Quinn was telling me she's a baker down in the kitchens! Don't we just adore the breakfast tarts?"

The woman looked me up and down, as if taking my measure, and I tried not to shift uncomfortably in my plain baker's uniform. "They're very good," she said, no emotion leaking into her voice.

"It's nice to meet you, Nessa," I tried, holding my hand out once again.

"Vanessa," she corrected, "unless you're Colette." She made no move to raise her arm.

"Thanks for letting me know." I felt my cheeks redden and dropped my hand, letting the next few seconds pass in awkward silence. I was probably staring at her far too intently, but I couldn't seem to figure out who she resembled.

Noticing my attention, she saved me the trouble. "I'm Maddox's daughter," she said.

Now it all clicked. The looks, the intense demeanor. Her resemblance to her mother was striking.

"Are you practicing for the competition as well?" I asked.

She shrugged. "A bit."

Curiosity bloomed in my chest, and before I could stop myself I was asking her what type of power she Wielded.

"Family secret. It's a bit bothersome, but my mother wants to maintain an advantage over her enemies, and since Gifts are inherited a lot of the time . . ." she shrugged.

"I've got to get back to it," Colette cut in with an apologetic frown, "but it was so great meeting you."

"You too," I said, punctuating my words with a smile and nod for emphasis. I hoped she could tell I meant it.

Turning from the refreshment table, the two women went back to their corner and returned to their practice.

At least, Colette did. Vanessa just leaned against the wall about ten feet away from Colette's ring of flora, picking at her nails as though bored. She hadn't even taken any food.

A flash of blonde hair appeared at the far side of the room as another contestant entered the training space. Every time she took a step, her dress changed colors. It started an unobtrusive olive green, then melted into a shocking strawberry red. The colors flashed as she continued into the center of the room. Green. Red. Green. Red.

Marisol.

I ducked behind a potted plant that had been moved to accommodate the refreshment table I was manning, peeking out from behind the leaves to watch her.

She walked around the space, sizing up her competition, and finally chose a spot to practice, blessedly on the far side of the massive ballroom.

Although I didn't think she would be able to pick me out from so far away, I was still relieved when Jacques from the kitchen came to take my place and I was able to slip back into the kitchens to work on the baguette dough I had started earlier in the day.

As I turned it out onto my work surface and began coaxing it into long, even rolls, my mind wandered again to my encounter with Prince Evander the night before. His last words, in particular, nagged at me.

He'd said he needed to confirm something, but what?. If his goal was to verify that I had a hot head and exactly zero impulse control, he'd most definitely succeeded. I cringed thinking about how I had all but spelled out my opinion of his character and royals in general. Not my finest move, to be sure.

Tonight I would do better.

Tonight . . . when I was expected to return. A flush crept up behind the smattering of freckles on my face that Mother was always trying to get me to cover up.

A basic task really shouldn't be so difficult. I would take the tray up, keep my mouth shut, and leave as quickly as I could. Not a complicated plan.

Still, my anxious mind turned over every possibility in the few hours before suppertime. What if I spilled the food all over his very expensive-looking books? What if I put my foot in my mouth *again* somehow? I wasn't sure how many bruises his princely ego could take before he snapped and threw me out of the castle. He'd already been far more good natured than I'd expected.

The clock's ticking seemed to slow down by at least half as I vibrated with nervous energy. I itched to talk to Mellie and get her advice, but she was occupied with an endless bevy of urgent tasks to keep the kitchen moving like the well-oiled machine it had been before the extra guests arrived.

At last, the clock struck six, and I armed myself with a silver tray and every ounce of self-control I could muster.

Get in. Get out. I could do that.

I made it up the stairs more quickly this time, stopping to catch my breath at the top. *Who orders food carried up four flights of stairs? Someone used to getting his way,* I supposed, huffing out a breath in irritation.

When I was reasonably certain I no longer sounded like fireplace bellows, I repeated my three quick knocks on the door, which was fully closed this time.

A minute went by, then two. Maybe I had finally gotten a stroke of luck; I could set the serving platter on the ground and leave without incident. I squatted and was about to release the tray when the door opened. At first, all I could see was a large pair of well-made chocolate brown leather boots that looked as if they cost the equivalent of a year's income for someone in the village. Looking up, the figure of the prince stood high above me.

"My apologies, I was–" he stopped, raking his hand through his hair. "What are you doing?"

"I wasn't sure you were in, so I was going to leave it for you," I explained.

"Hm," he murmured, the sound deep and full. "Unlucky for you, I suppose, as I didn't forget our appointment."

I stood as gracefully as I could manage. Even when I had drawn myself to my full height, I was shocked by how far above me he towered.

Without another word, he swept into the room, this time turning directly into the study. I followed at a distance, counting my footsteps until I could set the tray on the desk.

An image of a frightened mouse flashed across my mind as I cataloged my own timid movements. It wasn't that I was afraid of *him* so much as I was of myself. I had shown a shocking lack of regard for my own interests of late and I had no desire for a repeat performance.

Task completed, I dropped into a stiff curtsy that was strangely juxtaposed with Prince Evander's comfortable reclined position in his chair. Hegestured to one of the seats on the opposite side of the table. "Please, sit."

With effort, I pulled the heavy wooden chair from its resting spot and perched uncomfortably on the edge of the tufted leather seat.

Rather than meeting his eyes, I focused on his maroon doublet, noting the decorative gold threading along the collar and shoulders. The cream shirt beneath was simple but well-tailored, and the thick fabric looked softer than my own puff-sleeved linen tunic. I self-consciously brushed a few crumbs off my wrinkled apron.

No doubt noting my discomfort at the disparity, the prince cleared his throat. "I must admit I didn't make it through the volume we discussed last night," he said.

I tried not to let the relief show on my face as I waited for his dismissal. To my chagrin, it didn't come. Instead, he held out a worn volume, its dark blue linen fraying in one corner.

"I wondered, though, if you had read *Son of the Marked One*," he asked.

The title didn't sound familiar, so I shook my head. "I can't say that I have."

"Based on our last conversation, I think you may enjoy it. And I doubt even you'll be able to find fault with the hero in this one."

It was definitely against decorum to take one of the palace's volumes home, and I started to say as much, but stopped myself, remembering that the prince didn't know about my *situation*. Instead of divulging the secret, I accepted the tome reluctantly.

"Thank you. I'm sure I won't."

"Then again, you may surprise me yet. You have a habit of doing that, I've noticed," he smirked. I didn't know how to reply to that.

"Why don't you return next week to discuss?" he suggested. "I should be free for dinner on the evening of the new moon."

I raised my eyebrows.

"Don't you dine with the contestants?"

"Usually. But there are some evenings, like tonight, when they're occupied by special training with General Finch. Truth be told, it's a bit of a relief to have an excuse to slip away occasionally."

Slip away? From the gaggle of googly-eyed young women who basically prostrated themselves at his feet? My confusion must have shown, because he expanded.

"They're all wonderful young ladies, and I look forward to getting to know them individually, but I've never enjoyed socializing in large groups. And the atmosphere is rather . . . tense." He rubbed the back of his neck.

Again, not what I would've suspected from him.

"Don't fret–I'm sure I'll have many opportunities to–how did you so charmingly phrase it? 'Show off and paint myself as a hero'?"

My face heated in embarrassment, but the prince's expression remained amused. He was teasing me. I didn't know what to do with that either.

"Of course, your Highness."

"Very good. I'm afraid I have some work that desperately needs my attention, but I shall see you then."

At last, I rose to go, curtsying before I turned toward the door.

"Have a nice evening, Ms. Parry."

"You as well, your Highness."

"Evander is fine."

"You as well, Prince Evander," I compromised.

The sound of his soft chuckle followed me out of the room.

I was late coming home that evening, a result of my extra excursion to serve the prince. Mother was waiting up when I arrived.

My heart skipped a beat when she looked up at me from the wooden table under the window. She stood, grounding her feet as if readying herself for a physical assault.

"Quinn. We need to speak."

"Of course, Mother," I said, feigning nonchalance as I moved past her and into the kitchen. Opening a cabinet, I searched for something to eat, but came out empty handed.

Though I'd eaten supper at the castle, it was always useful to have something to busy my hands and mouth when she was in a mood. Food was a kind of armor that allowed me a few extra seconds to calculate my response; that was probably one reason I'd gotten interested in baking in the first place.

"This needs to stop, Quinn."

"Excuse me?"

"You're gone practically all day, every day, and the neighbors are starting to ask questions. It won't reflect well on your father and me if it becomes common knowledge that you're out *working.*" Her face contorted at the word, as if it left a bad taste in her mouth.

Though I'd expected her to object to me spending so much time out of the cottage, this particular line of logic was perplexing. She'd never spoken negatively of my father for working, and it wasn't as if we were in the high echelons of Lilifel's upper class.

"Plenty of people on our street have respectable jobs, Mother," I said. "Honest work is nothing to be ashamed of."

Unable to refute that point, she changed tactics, her voice rising in both pitch and volume.

"Why are you always trying to escape this house? Is my company truly so tiresome? Is our family not enough for you?"

There it was. I should have known. It was never about the financial implications or even the reputation that my mother guarded so closely–it was about control. Her need to control my time, my opinion, and my affections had led to many an argument, and this was no different, regardless of how she tried to present it.

Mentally scanning possible responses, I tried to find the one that would draw the least ire. I could feign loneliness, but mentioning Father when he was away never went over well. And I knew I couldn't bring up Mellie for more reasons than one.

In the end, I settled on a simplified version of the truth. Over the years I'd learned that it was best to stay as concise as possible. Adding any extraneous details only offered more points of debate.

"I enjoy having something of my own to work on," I said, trying not to sigh outwardly.

Living this way was exhausting. I knew my mother loved me and acted as she did in a misguided attempt to keep me safe, but her comfort zone wasn't something I was interested in inheriting. Sequestering myself from the world might keep me from getting hurt, but it would be a lonely, unfulfilling existence.

"I just don't understand why you're wasting so much time away from home, Quinn. If you're truly so bored, why don't you focus your energy on assisting Father with his business? You know he has a wealth of knowledge on the merchant trade and he'd be grateful to have you help with the bookkeeping."

It took every ounce of self control I could muster to avoid rolling my eyes. Father was only home a few weeks out of the year, and he already had a company of full-time staff. Besides, if there was one thing I knew about my mother, it was that such a degree of absence from the family home would never be something she trusted me with.

An idea flickered to life as I realized I could spin that to my advantage.

"Oh, I could never be away from you for such long periods of time, Mother." I held my breath as I waited for her response. Either she would double down on her criticism of my work hours or . . .

The lines of her face softened as she strode over to me and pulled me into an embrace, stroking my hair as she did when I was a child.

"Of course not, darling," she crooned.

Hopefully my exhale of relief would pass as weariness after a taxing day.

"I only meant that perhaps we can find a way for you to assist him from home," she said.

"Perhaps," I said noncommittally, pulling out of the hug. "I should rest. Long day."

She nodded in understanding. "Poor dear. We'll put an end to those soon."

I offered no response, electing to trudge to my room in a show of faux exhaustion.

Sitting on my bed, I opened the worn midnight blue book and began to read.

Chapter 6

IT DIDN'T TAKE LONG for serving duty to become a highlight in my routine. Whether it was the absence of Serena's vitriol or the ability to watch the Wielders that made it so enjoyable, I didn't know, but I found myself looking forward to my shifts in the ballroom.

Every afternoon, some of the contestants piled in to practice their skills in preparation for the second task, which was now three weeks away. Queen Evalina's efforts to strengthen magic within the castle produced almost instant results, and within a matter of days, the Fork Girl evolved from shattering plates to flinging dinner knives into the wall with a satisfying *thud.*

The woman who had summoned the flock of birds at the first trial was in the process of training a rather wild-looking wolf to heed her commands, while the Wielder who utilized light had moved onto creating floating luminaries that followed her wherever she went.

Vanessa still showed up every day looking unimpressed, but she never seemed to do anything besides watch Colette, who was still working diligently on her vines. I observed, slack jawed, when she constructed an entire tower of greenery, complete with giant venus fly traps that snapped at anyone who got too close.

Thankfully, Marisol was rarely in attendance and hadn't approached the refreshment table on the few occasions I had seen her. From what I could tell, the maneuver she was working on was meant to utilize a long bolt of cloth to strangle one of the practice dummies, but it usually just ended with the mannequin draped in fabric reminiscent of a robe. I pitied her; her Gift was not a skill I imagined would translate well into the type of test the Crown had planned.

No information was given about the specifics of the trial, but the older ice-Wielder, who went by the name of Algernon Finch, dropped by every few days to remind the ladies to be "ready for anything." Their frustration seemed to multiply with his every appearance.

Towards the end of the week, Colette approached me to ask if I would help her with a new exercise she wanted to practice.

It wasn't as though I were doing anything important. The food went untouched most afternoons, but Mellie and Helga insisted on sending up the same quantity day after day. Whether it was a matter of pride or an instruction from the Crown, I didn't know.

When I agreed, Colette led me to a tile on the floor she had marked with a petal.

"This might be a little alarming, but I promise it won't hurt," she said. My expression must've betrayed my nerves, because she expounded.

"I've been working a lot with vines, but my specialty is actually flowers, and I need to see if I can find a way to make them more practical for . . . well, whatever is coming," she said, a line appearing between her brows.

She backed up a few feet, raising her arms into a casting position with her elbows slightly bent. As she concentrated, a ring of roses grew around my feet, bolting up about a foot before shriveling.

Colette deflated. "Those were meant to create a sort of web around you to keep you from moving," she said, shoulders bowed in defeat.

"Keep practicing," I encouraged. "It's only been a week."

The smile she offered was watery, and she was clearly dejected.

"Have you tried wisteria?" I asked. Her brows perked up at the suggestion. "If you're used to flowers, maybe it would provide a happy compromise?"

She darted forward and squeezed me without reservation. "Quinn, you're brilliant!"

"Happy to help." I chuckled and took a step back to watch her dive into the mechanics of her new medium. As I suspected, the wisteria offered her the confidence of working with her blooms and paired well with the utility of the vines she had been conjuring.

"The structure is sturdier too," she chirped excitedly as she tested the hardiness of the elaborate birdcage she had woven about two feet high. "Now I just need to work on scaling it."

Along the wall, the corner of Vanessa's mouth twitched in an expression that looked a lot like pride.

The heavy double doors groaned open and Jacques entered, beckoning me to switch roles. Thankfully, Serena had been roped into serving duty in another part of the castle, and Mellie had seen to it that our shifts were aligned so I had a few hours of reprieve from her constant irritability, which hadn't eased at all over the past week.

The kitchen was quiet, caught between the frantic preparation for lunch and the looming demands of dinner. I checked on my proofing dough and circled the room a few times, collecting spare whisks and bowls and bringing them to the washing station.

Turning the water on, I got to work cleaning them, resuming my old habit and humming a song I remembered Father singing when I was young. I didn't remember the words, but I could recall the way his face lit up as he sang it. He always loved music, and our home was full of it in my first memories.

When he began to travel to more distant ports, Mother said it was a blessing that business was so steady, but I wasn't sure. I just missed my father.

"Hello," came a tentative voice from behind me, snapping me out of my reverie. I turned to find a pair of soft brown eyes darting around, checking to be sure we were alone.

"Hello, James," I ventured, unsure what to say.

"I just, uh . . .well, I wanted to apologize for Serena. I've told her to lay off you but she's stubborn as an ox."

Well, that was putting it mildly.

"Oh," I replied lamely. "Thank you?"

"She's got some issues to work through, but you shouldn't bear the brunt of her anger when you aren't the cause of it."

He stood there for a moment, shifting back and forth on his feet as if there were something else he wanted to say but hadn't quite made up his mind on whether to say it. Something like resolve hardened in his eyes.

"I was wondering if you might sit with us at dinner tonight?" he asked.

"Us?"

"Jacques, Lucas, and Claire from the cooking side usually sit with Serena and I for meals since we work together and all. I know Permelia hasn't been around as much lately."

He was right. Mellie was constantly running around like a beheaded chicken, trying to keep all the literal and figurative fires under control. Since my mishap, she'd been the one taking the queen's meals up to her chambers every evening, and I could only guess that she was dining in her company as well, which left her spot next to me on the bench cold and empty.

"I'm not sure that's a good idea, James," I said, though part of me wanted to accept the offer. "I appreciate the gesture, but I doubt Serena would want me there, and I don't need any more drama from her."

James's eyes widened for a moment before he cast them downward. He looked like a puppy that had just been kicked.

"All right," he faltered. "I understand that. If you change your mind," he shrugged.

"Thank you, James, really."

He turned to go, but abandoned the motion about halfway through.

"For what it's worth, I think you belong here," he said. "I know some people aren't thrilled you jumped rank, but I can see why. Your glazed cardamom buns might be the best thing I've ever tasted."

I grinned at that. They were my favorite, too.

"Thank you, James," I repeated.

He returned to his work and I to mine, but the kitchen felt a little less hostile after that.

All too soon it was six o'clock and I was marching up the four flights of stairs, which hadn't gotten any easier in the last week.

The prince met me at the door, opening it before I had the chance to knock.

Prompt, I thought, even as my heart raced when he flashed me a dazzling smile and bade me to come in.

This time he sank into the settee in the antechamber, offering me a seat in one of the two brocade chairs opposite. A small marble table separated us. Once again it felt strange to sit in his presence, like I should be constantly at attention. After all, I was working.

"So," he began, holding up *The Eriargen Encounter.* It looked miniscule in his hand. It must be smaller than my copy, I reasoned. "I finished it."

Digging in the pocket of my apron, a sage green today, I retrieved my own copy. I wasn't sure why I had brought it, but it felt better to be prepared. If nothing else, it would be a useful tool for avoiding eye contact.

"And you're right. Galadaer is a foolish ass," Prince Evander said.

I barked a loud laugh; I certainly hadn't been expecting that.

"He doesn't stop to think about the tactical disadvantages of staging a battle at The Hold of Traitors, and the fact that he didn't even tell Astrid his plan before marching off in her name, well," he scoffed. "He would've deserved the capture had Astrid not unleashed her lightning on the field."

"I agree!"

The prince's expression turned thoughtful.

"In the latter half of the novel, he lacked the complexity that the author wrote so well in Astrid," he continued. "I understood that he was Good and Worthy, but he couldn't boast of much else. Edmund would've been a better choice for her."

"A more compelling one, surely," I said. "But I think the heart of the story was the love Astrid had for her kingdom, not a romantic love."

"Hmm," he hummed. "A love I know all too well."

Was that a hint of sadness? Bitterness, even?

Aware that he had left himself vulnerable, he changed the subject. "And what did you make of *Son of the Marked One?*"

Truthfully, I was loving it. Though I'd been skeptical at first, by about a hundred and twenty pages in I was truly enjoying the novel. A part of that may have been the dark-haired, morally grey sorcerer central to the story, but I wasn't about to tell him that.

"It's excellent," I said, a bit begrudgingly.

"High praise, coming from you," he teased.

Teased. Teased *me.* What world was I living in where the Crown Prince was cracking jokes about my literary taste?

Unable to back down from the challenge, I lifted my chin. "I know what I enjoy. It isn't a terrible thing for a woman to have an opinion." A bit combative, but not personally offensive at least. When had that become my bar for a successful conversation?

"Not at all." He shook his head earnestly. "We would be lost without the wisdom of our women."

"Indeed." There he went again, surprising me.

"And what," he asked, leaning forward with his elbows on his knees, "is your opinion of me?"

I swallowed. What was the right answer here?

"I'm sure you'll be a fair and just leader, your Highness," I postulated.

"Evander," he reminded me.

Uncomfortable, I shifted in my seat, turning my attention back to the book in my hands.

"The juxtaposition of Elara's Mark of the Ancients and Thorne's heritage with his father's mark was interesting. I thought it made for a compelling structure, especially since she spends the first few chapters subverting the audience's expectations about what being Chosen means about a person."

"What are your thoughts on Thorne's revelation about the spell?"

"I haven't gotten there yet," I confessed. "But I don't want to keep your copy from you any longer." I slid the book across the table, offering it to him.

He placed his palm on the top of the volume, gently pushing it back. Our fingers brushed for a moment and sparks shot up my arm. What was wrong with me?

"Keep it," he said.

"Thank you, your–Prince Evander," I corrected myself, "but really, it would be selfish of me–"

"The selfishness is decidedly on my side. There aren't many fiction readers in my circle and I need to speak with someone about the plot twist." A cheeky half smile lit up his face, and I found myself mirroring his grin.

"All right then. Thank you."

"Now," he said, as if getting down to business, "are we going to discuss Alastair?"

"*Yes!*" I exclaimed, my restraint failing. "I had absolutely no idea he was in league with the Eldorian King!"

"I don't believe he was the true Conspirator though. Doesn't it make more sense that he's being puppeteered by the Captain on the Dolinean Front?" Evander offered, arching an eyebrow.

The evening progressed as we swapped theories and argued over whether Edmund's protection of Astrid was justified. It was disconcertingly comfortable. I'd always wished to have a friend with whom to discuss my books, but I certainly hadn't expected it to be the crown prince. Nevertheless, I found myself smiling without reserve as he told me what he expected in the next volume. It wasn't until well after the sun had set that I headed home with a smile on my face and a promise to return that I gave far too easily. I was in trouble.

On my day off, I devoured the first part of the book Prince Evander had given me and tiptoed around my mother, who complained incessantly of how selfish I was to leave her alone in the cottage.

When I returned to work, it seemed Serena had backed off a bit. James must have spoken to her again after our conversation. The atmosphere in the kitchens improved markedly for everyone as a result of this shift, and I began to get to know my coworkers.

I was worried about Mellie, who was gone from the kitchen for several hours each time a meal was served, coming back with red-rimmed eyes. When I asked, she said couldn't discuss it, but it was clear from my friend's distress that Queen Evalina's condition wasn't improving.

The work hadn't slowed, but we had acclimated to the new volume and things no longer felt as frantic as they had in the past few weeks.

Almost a week after his offer, I finally drew up the courage to sit with James and his friends for a meal. Serena was busy upstairs, so it felt like a good time to test the waters. The little group turned out to be wonderful.

Jacques clearly saw James as a little brother and was always finding ways to bolster him up and teach him how to succeed in the castle. Lucas and Claire's preferred style of communication was good-humored quips at the other's expense, and it was nice to be included in the group instead of being the subject of the joke.

Claire was sharing a story about how Lucas had once made a whole batch of tomato soup with half a cup of sugar instead of half a tablespoon, and I found myself laughing out loud.

"What the hells?"

My head snapped up at Serena's voice, and I shrank into my seat like a child caught stealing sweets from the jar. Giving myself a mental shake,

I fought to remember Mellie's words and straightened back up. I had as much right to be here as she did.

"Quinn is part of our team, and I thought we should include her," James said. Serena glared at him until Jacques stepped in.

"Come off it, Serena. Lunch isn't going to kill you. Plus, Parry isn't half bad." He threw a wink in my direction.

"Fine," she huffed, setting her plate down on the opposite side of the table, as far away from me as she could get.

Claire rolled her eyes. "As I was *saying,"* she continued, "none of us caught it before it was sent upstairs. Jacques said the queen managed three bites before mentioning something."

Lucas's face turned red. "The writing on the recipe was smudged," he mumbled, bumping Claire with his shoulder.

"Besides," he drew himself to his full height, "it's not like you haven't made your fair share of mistakes. Remember the chicken stew?"

"Don't remind me!" Claire groaned, throwing her hands over her face.

"She put the chicken breasts in whole and they were still raw when she went to serve it," James filled me in conspiratorially.

"At least it was only a staff meal!" she defended herself, pointing her fork at Lucas.

I dissolved into a fit of giggles, earning me a pout from her.

"Don't worry, I've had my fair share of accidents too," I said. "When I was ten, I forgot to put the oven fire out for almost an entire day after I finished making some cookies. Everyone in the house was sweating and we couldn't figure out why for the longest time. My mother never let me use it again after that."

James's brows shot up. "Never again? That's a little harsh, don't you think?"

"That's my mother for you. She's very . . . authoritarian. She didn't allow me a lot of independence growing up," I managed.

"Then how did you learn to bake so well?" James asked.

"I wandered into Mellie's shop one afternoon about nine years ago," I said, smiling at the memory. "She just sort of adopted me, and I would sneak off to the bakery after school when I was supposed to be studying."

"That sounds like Permelia," James said, chuckling.

"Let's hope she doesn't decide to bring in any stray dogs next." Serena rolled her eyes. I chose to ignore her.

"She's been like a mother to me ever since," I said. "Things at home are . . . complicated." I winced.

Why did I just say that?

"Yes, well, at least you can go back and visit your home," Serena shot back.

"Sometimes I wish I couldn't," I admitted, more to myself than anyone else at the table.

The group settled into an awkward silence that was only interrupted by the ringing of the bell that announced the end of the meal. It was time to start preparing dinner. After clearing our places, we got to work on the foie gras bread pudding that would be served this evening.

The pang of disappointment I felt when I remembered there would be no visit to Evander tonight took me by surprise.

I had been summoned to serve the prince every few days for the last week, sometimes resulting in lengthy debates about our current reads, while other times he only had time for a few words of thanks. Apparently, my sense of self-preservation had gone completely out the window, because I found myself looking forward to dinner each night, and I was becoming irritatingly comfortable around him.

It was just as well, I told myself. Tonight's evening meal was a team effort that would have both the cooking side and baking side of the kitchen busy enough as it was, so I knew I needed to focus on my work.

The loaves of bread I had started this morning had been baking while we all ate lunch. Now I pulled one out, careful not to burn myself, and tested the crust. Crackly perfection. I turned over one of the boules and knocked on the bottom. The resulting sound was hollow, which meant the loaves were ready to come out.

They would need at least an hour on a cooling rack before we could cut them into cubes for the bread pudding, or else the texture would become gummy.

I inhaled deeply as I used the push-pull tool to move the rack so I could reach the rest of the loaves. The smell of freshly baked bread never lost its charm to me. It smelled like safety and love and *home.*

Once the bread was safely on the rack, I looked around to see who else might need assistance while I waited.

James was shaping a loaf on the center island, about an hour behind where I was in my bake, and Franc was sifting powdered sugar over the tops of the orange chocolate torte that would be served as dessert.

I didn't see Mellie anywhere, so I headed into the next room to look for her.

Instead, I found Serena, her head disappearing into the icebox as she balanced precariously on a small wooden crate.

Not so threatening now, are you? I couldn't help but laugh watching her struggle to reach the back contents of the rack, the tray in her free hand wobbling.

The sound must've startled her, because she hit her head on the top of the icebox, causing her to lose her footing and slip backwards.

Unable to stabilize herself on her makeshift footstool, she came tumbling to the ground, dropping her tray and raining unbaked dough onto the floor as she hit the ground with a thump. I cringed. That couldn't have felt good.

"What is wrong with you?" she yelled, turning on me.

"I didn't mean to startle you! Why weren't you using a proper stool?"

Instead of answering my question, she reached for one of the pastries that had fallen to the floor, wincing as she picked it up. From what was left of its original form, it looked like it had been a croissant.

"These are RUINED. And I landed on my wrist, so I have no idea how I'm going to roll out all the layers again in time to proof for breakfast." She glared at me. "You did this on purpose."

"Look, Serena, I'm sorry, but this was an accident.," I said, throwing my hands up. "We may not be on the best terms, but I'm not going to sacrifice a meal just to settle a petty grudge."

"Well it's going to be ruined regardless, so I hope you're satisfied. I'm going to get sacked."

I rolled my eyes. So dramatic. There was no way she was getting released for one missing pastry. Her wrist was already swelling, though, and I looked at it pointedly. "You've got more pressing problems right now. That needs a healer immediately."

"Absolutely not," she countered. "I have to start these over now, thanks to you."

"Serena," I sighed in exasperation, "stop being so stubborn and go get that fixed before it's beyond the healer's capabilities. We're too busy around here to be missing a baker indefinitely, and you're pretty useless in here with only one hand."

She shot me another glare.

"I'll make sure the croissants are ready for tomorrow," I promised begrudgingly. "Just go."

Ignoring my outstretched hand, she got to her feet. I didn't know why I even tried.

"Well, it's the least you could do," she huffed and stomped out.

I bent down to pick up the would-be croissants from the ground, now just sad, squashed lumps of dough. There weren't enough here to be the full batch, so there must be another tray hiding somewhere.

As I suspected, another bowl of dough sat abandoned on the counter outside the pantry.

"James," I asked, "do you know if this is Serena's?"

"I think so. Why?"

"It's a long story, but I'm taking over for her while she goes to the infirmary." His eyes widened in alarm and I clarified quickly. "Nothing serious, just a swollen wrist. Can you handle cubing my loaves when they've cooled? They're on the racks there," I said, pointing to my workstation.

He nodded, a trace of confusion lingering on his face.

I tossed the dirty dough in the garbage, cringing at the waste of it, and set out to determine where Serena was in her prep. I couldn't see a recipe card nearby, so she likely knew it by heart.

I should've asked for more details before she left. Maybe I could track her down in the infirmary . . .

No. It wasn't as if I hadn't made croissants before, and the gods knew I didn't need to give Serena any more reasons to mock me. I could do this myself.

If she was at nearly the same stage in both batches, I reasoned, she was about to roll out this dough and start laminating. Judging from how I found her, she must've needed something from the icebox to continue. Using a *real* stool, I confirmed my suspicions in the form of a thin sheet of butter in the back.

I got to work finishing the second batch so the dough didn't over-proof. I doubt she'd thank me if we ended up with dense, collapsed pastries.

After rolling out the dough, I added the butter slab I'd found prepared in the ice box.

Next came the lamination process. I folded the dough into thirds and rolled it out before repeating the process again and again and again. When the slab was appropriately layered, I cut it into long triangles and rolled them into shape.

Then I started a new second batch of croissant dough and set it aside for its first rise. Rubbing the back of my neck, I tried to massage out some of the tension from staring down at the workspace for so long and sighed. I was going to be here late again tonight. The small hand was already just shy of six. Almost time for dinner.

At least the two-hour proofing period the dough needed gave me plenty of time to help everybody get the foie-gras bread pudding and sides into the dining hall upstairs. It smelled delicious.

Mellie and Helga had outdone themselves on the dish. This was the first time since I had started working here that both teams had worked together on the same entrée, and judging by the aroma that was wafting its way to me, the collaboration had been worth it.

The staff had a simpler version of the same meal, made with pork sausage instead of duck liver, and it tasted just as good as it smelled.

It was nine o'clock by the time dinner cleanup had ended and I was able to get back to the second batch of croissants.

One good thing about being in the kitchen after hours was that you got your pick of all the best tools and utensils. Running my fingers along the contents of a cabinet below the workspace, I extracted a large wooden cutting board with no warping or cracks and began to flatten the dough, humming to myself.

As I was working, the hair on the back of my neck stood up and I got the unmistakable sense that someone was coming. Looking around the kitchens, I grabbed the largest rolling pin I could find, hiking it up to my shoulder.

A moment later I could hear heavy footsteps and the door opened to reveal–

Prince Evander. He froze in place, obviously not expecting anyone to be here at this time of night. It took a moment for him to shed his surprise as he looked me up and down.

"Were you going to hit me with a rolling pin?" he asked, a smirk on his face.

"Not *you,*" I floundered, embarrassed. "I just–I heard someone coming and panicked. The dark unsettles me a bit."

"At least you're armed," he joked, jutting his chin at my weapon of choice.

"I'm just going to die of embarrassment now," I declared with resolve.

"No need." His chuckle had my cheeks flushing even further. "I'll leave you to your–" he stopped, taking in the empty room and the ingredients on the counter. "What exactly are you doing?"

"Making croissants," I said. "One of the other bakers dropped a batch earlier today when I frightened her."

"Yes, you can be very intimidating," he teased, his eyes sparkling. "Is there any way I can be of assistance?"

My mind went absolutely blank. I didn't understand this man at all.

"Thank you for the offer, but I'm fine." I curtsied.

"If you're sure," he said. "Between the two of us, I'm a terrible cook anyway."

That at least made sense. The man had probably had a dozen chefs since before he could eat solid food.

"Goodnight, Ms. Parry."

I was returning his farewell when I realized he was retreating without getting whatever he had come for. "Wait!" I blurted. "Why did you come down here in the first place?"

He looked up at the ceiling as if I had caught him doing something he shouldn't. "I was hoping to find something to settle my stomach. I didn't eat much at dinner."

"And you didn't ring the bell for one of your manservants to get it for you?" I arched an eyebrow.

"Apparently not." The smirk was back.

Interesting. I waited to see if he would explain himself.

"Being royal does have its advantages, to be sure," he started, "but I often find myself wishing for something simpler. To have some agency in my day-to-day affairs. As it stands, I feel like an intruder in my own home's kitchen. I doubt I could make so much as a slice of toast without burning it," he laughed sadly. If he was hoping for pity, I wouldn't give it to him.

"That's ridiculous." I stood with my hands on my hips.

"It is, a bit."

"You can have as much agency as you take. It's not as if anyone around here is going to tell you *no,*" I pointed out.

"A sound argument. Though I'm afraid my own pride may be the obstacle at times. Princes aren't exactly lauded for showing their weaknesses."

"You just admitted to me that you can't make a piece of toast." I eyed him pointedly.

"You have me there." His hands came up, palms facing me in mock defeat.

Turning on my heel, I stalked to the pantry. Earlier in the day, I had left a loaf of bread to become slightly stale for tomorrow's cinnamon fried toast, but this was a more pressing issue.

When I reached the workstation again, Evander had his head cocked to one side and wore a slightly concerned expression on his face, as if he wasn't sure if I had stormed out and wouldn't be returning.

"Here," I said, sliding the bread across the countertop to him.

Now it was his turn to raise his eyebrows. "You want me to make toast?"

"Please," I scoffed. "Have some faith in yourself. At least try a cheese toastie."

He laughed, but to his credit, he took the bread and began looking around for a knife.

"Over here." I nodded toward a drawer by my left hip and continued to work on the croissants. The butter was still a bit too cold, but I knew Mother would already be livid that I was arriving home late, so I tried to wrestle it into the first fold.

I felt a hand reach for the drawer and swiveled around to make sure Evander found what he needed. My heart seized as I found myself only a breath away from him. He took up more space than Mellie, that was certain. Time seemed to slow as I had the disconcerting realization that I had never been this close to him before. I could count the individual eyelashes framing his sapphire eyes if I wanted to.

Where the hells did that thought come from?

His mouth parted slightly, as if he were about to say something, but he must've thought better of it, because he closed it slowly and began worrying his bottom lip with his teeth. Something in my core heated at the sight. I needed to get a hold of myself. He reached for the knife, his hand flexing in a way that I certainly did *not* notice.

I cleared my throat and stepped away, hoping he couldn't tell where my mind had gone.

Was I imagining that his face was flushed too? I noticed his gaze trail down to my mouth for a split second before his eyes snapped up to stare at a point beyond me.

Holding up the knife in silent triumph, he smiled tensely, pressing his lips together so they all but disappeared.

I watched as he swung back over to the other side of the worktop and earnestly began trying to crush my poor loaf of bread to death.

My loud laugh cut the tension in the room.

"You've honestly never cut a loaf of bread."

His only response was a sheepish grin.

"Use a sawing motion so it doesn't flatten." I instructed, miming the act to demonstrate the technique.

He caught on, and we worked in silence for a few moments. Four layers of lamination were finished before I realized he was watching me, his two slices of bread sitting contentedly next to the loaf.

"You're humming again," he observed. "You do that a lot."

"I didn't realize."

"Don't stop," he encouraged. "It's nice."

This, of course, made it impossible to continue. My pastry dough had suddenly become the most interesting thing in the world as I endeavored to hide my blush.

"I recognize that song. 'The Ballad of Brynne,' I believe,'" he said.

"Really? I didn't know the name or even the words. My father used to sing it when I was young."

"Is he a baker as well?" he asked.

"No, a merchant. He travels most of the year, so I haven't seen him in a long time. I miss him," I confided.

"It must be difficult to be away from him. Thank you for your sacrifice." With a start, I remembered that the prince was still under the impression that I was confined to the castle and unable to see my family.

"My mother . . ." he started, and for a moment I was sure he was going to bring up our conversation on the stairwell, but he continued on, "well, she loves the Head Baker's tarts, and from what I hear, Permelia wouldn't stop talking about you until you arrived here."

"I'm very lucky to have her," I said, still rolling out the dough. I didn't miss his use of Mellie's given name. She and Evalina must be very close for him to know it.

The silence stretched on before I realized he no longer had anything to do.

"Cheese!" I exclaimed, thankful for an excuse to run to the ice box. Returning with a wedge of cheddar, I handed it to him along with a paring knife.

"This bit I know how to do," he assured me, gracefully slicing off pieces of cheese with one hand.

"I miss my father too," he said, staring down at the countertop. The grief in his voice was deep and raw.

"I'm sorry," I said, wishing I had more to offer than the feeble words.

"Thank you." He blinked to clear his eyes, then held up his piece of bread piled with cheese shavings to steer the conversation in a lighter direction.

"You'll want butter too," I said. "Makes the outside crispy."

He nodded, heading into the next room in search of some, and I was grateful for a moment alone to gather myself. My croissants were almost done. The butter was still cold, though, and my arms were tired from all the rolling. I massaged my forearm and stared down the rectangle, willing it to behave.

When I went to pick up the rolling pin, I found Evander had made his way back and was already holding it.

"Allow me," he offered. "I don't wish to offend you by suggesting you're incapable, but it's been difficult to watch you wrestle that thing into submission." His laugh sounded like sunshine.

I nodded, my mouth dry. "Thank you."

He pushed his sleeves up in preparation for the task, and I watched the muscles in his forearms flex as he rolled out the dough. After making quick work of it, he handed back the wooden tool and finished up the preparation of his toastie.

"You can use this to get it in the oven," I said, grabbing a wooden paddle off its hook. "Watch it closely to make sure it doesn't burn, and flip it over after a few minutes."

I cut my laminated dough into triangles again, stretched and rolled them into shape, then carried them to the icebox, placing them gingerly next to my tart crusts from earlier in the day.

Poking my head through the door, I took my own moment of stealthy observation. The prince stood in front of the oven, biting his lower lip, his brow furrowed as he concentrated. It was . . . endearing.

My shoulders shook with silent laughter as I watched him pull out the toastie, smiling like a proud child who had just completed an art project. I handed him a plate and he slid the gooey, lopsided sandwich onto it and cut it in two.

"This requires your professional assessment," he said seriously, offering me half.

I took a bite and pretended to consider it thoughtfully. "The presentation could use some work, but I'll give this a passing score," I concluded.

He took a bite of his own, beaming from ear to ear.

"You know," he said when he finished chewing, "this might be the thing I'm proudest of doing all week."

"You're running a kingdom," I laughed, "and this is what you're proud of?"

"*This,*" he said, holding it up, "is the most useful thing I've done today. Besides, I'm fairly certain it might be the best cheese toastie known to man."

I rolled my eyes again at that. His eyes crinkled as he smiled and we stood looking at each other for a heartbeat.

Unable to sustain the eye contact, I took a bite of my sandwich.

"You'd better not put me out of a job," I warned.

"I wouldn't dream of it."

A few minutes passed in a silence that was far more comfortable than it should have been. When I glanced at the clock, I found it was nearly the next day.

"I need to get h–to bed." I caught myself at the last moment. "The kitchen wakes early."

"Of course," he said, rising from his stool.

I left our dishes in the sink, feeling too frenetic to clean up properly. Mellie might chastise me for it tomorrow, but I needed to get some distance from whatever this situation was and give myself time to think. I headed toward the door, unsure if I should wait for him.

"Thank you," he said earnestly, "for allowing me to do something. So often these days I feel useless."

"You're welcome, Prince Evander," I murmured.

When I arrived the next morning, the dirty dishes were gone.

Chapter 7

THE BALLROOM WAS QUIET the following day. A firm sense of competition had settled in amongst the contestants, and many of them had begun training in their rooms to avoid being analyzed.

This afternoon, Colette and Vanessa were joined by Fork Girl (whose real name I had learned was Lucy,) Freya the fire-Wielder, Anissa, who manipulated light, and, to my dismay, Marisol.

She was working diligently with her cloth, which she had finally been able to coax into wrapping around her mannequin to pull it towards her. It was actually very impressive and more practical than I would've thought tailoring magic could be in such generalized circumstances.

Liang, a contestant with long, shiny black hair I had seen in the training room several times this week, strode in and began to work on animating a chair in front of her. It stepped forward on its four wooden legs like a newborn colt, moving a few feet before stilling. Wiping her brow with an air of satisfaction, the Wielder reset her configuration and repeated the performance.

"Quinn!" Colette called from across the room, waving an arm over her head.

Avoiding Marisol's line of sight, I walked over to where she had stationed Vanessa on a platform made of vines with fragrant purple flowers. They looked like supersized versions of the blooms I had seen climbing trellises in the city, their shoots as thick around as my wrist. As

I watched, the platform rose several feet off the ground, stopping when it was about waist high.

"So sorry to bother you, but could I borrow you for a moment?" Colette asked.

"Of course!" Now that the newness of Wielder-watching had worn off, refreshment table duty was becoming a bit dull. I needed to track down Mellie tonight and talk to her about reducing the portions for these sessions. Maybe she would finally agree since so many of the contestants were keeping to their rooms.

"Wonderful," she bubbled, bouncing on her toes. "I need to test the weight of this. I know it can hold Nessa up just fine but I'm thinking with the improvements I made to the base structure it should easily lift two now. Will you be my test subject?"

I didn't love heights, but I liked Colette, so I agreed, stepping onto the platform beside Vanessa. A few feet wouldn't kill me.

"It feels solid," I said.

She beamed, raising her hands into a casting position.

The platform rumbled and started to lift higher and higher. I clutched Vanessa's arm, any self-consciousness I might have felt dwarfed by my fear, and tried not to look down.

"Is she growing the stem of this with us on it?"

"She's been working on it for days," Vanessa said, unperturbed by the fact that we were now a good fifteen feet in the air.

"Any chance your Gift is something that would help us out if this thing collapses?"

"No," was her only reply.

Great.

Though I was hyper aware of how awkward and stiff Vanessa felt under my grip, I couldn't bring myself to let go. I counted to ten, taking deep breaths in and out, and the platform slowly started to lower.

As soon as we were within reach of the ground I scrambled off, trying not to look as panicked as I felt.

"Oh, Quinn!" Colette exclaimed, worry in her eyes. "You don't like heights! I'm so sorry; I had no idea."

I thought about bluffing and telling her she didn't need to worry, but I was fairly certain I was turning a shade of green that would give me away if I tried to lie.

"It's fine," I said, still gulping down air. "No harm done."

She looked at me, doubt written all over her delicate features, and I gave her a weak smile.

Turning toward Vanessa, who stepped smoothly off the platform and stalked over to where we stood, Colette's face lit up once more.

"How was it? Did it feel stable?"

"Very," Vanessa promised, and Colette gathered her into a hug, which Vanessa returned with much more ease than I would've expected.

"Thank you again, Quinn," Colette beamed at me. "I promise I won't ever do that to you again." Her light laugh sounded like tinkling bells.

"It's fine," I said, the last of the tension in my shoulders dissipating. "Being out of my comfort zone is good for me. It seems as though we're both *growing.*"

"Booooooo!" she yelled at my terrible pun, smacking my arm.

The two of us dissolved into a fit of giggles that Vanessa decidedly did not join. In fact, the way she was looking at me made me feel uncomfortable. Like I had deeply offended her.

I extracted myself, making an excuse about needing to get back to work, and wondered what I had done.

Back in the kitchen, I found Serena waiting for me, her arms crossed. She was tapping her foot impatiently, as if she didn't know precisely when my shift in the ballroom ended. Resolved to ignore her, I started toward the pantry to gather the ingredients I needed for dinner.

"Quinn! Wait!" She followed me into the storeroom. I braced myself for more nastiness, but it didn't come.

"Thank you," she said curtly.

All I could do was stare at her.

"I got a lot of compliments on the croissants this morning," she said. "Apparently the prince said they were the best he's ever had." She rolled her eyes before narrowing them at me in suspicion. "When I left yesterday, I was half convinced you'd do them poorly just to spite me. But you didn't. And you didn't even take credit for them."

"That's not how I operate, Serena." How was I still the one on the defensive?

She huffed an exasperated breath. "I'm gathering that. At first, it irritated me. I spent ages trying to figure out what you were playing at. But I mentioned it to James and he told me I was being ridiculous."

I couldn't refute that, so I stayed silent.

"He said the fact that I thought you had a nefarious ulterior motive was probably a sign that you weren't the problem," Serena winced. "So . . . thank you."

"You're welcome," I managed. What strange alternate reality was I living in?

Serena sighed. "I know I've been hard on you, and that's probably my own shit I need to work through. It was just hard to see you come in here and take the assistant post with no formal experience, and then you got privileges to commute on top of it . . ." she trailed off.

I wasn't sure how to respond without apologizing for something I didn't have any control over, which seemed unfair. We stood there in tense silence for a moment before she continued. "When I was hired on here five years ago, I had to leave my family behind, and I can count on my hands the number of times I've seen them since. They only allow us to go back into the village on the Solstices."

Wow. That was . . . harsh.

"I'm sorry," I said. No wonder she was so bent out of shape.

"Yeah, well, that's the policy. And even if I could see them more often, I couldn't afford to take the time off. Money's scarce at home. I have four younger siblings and my father's not around, so I took this position to help support them."

"That's a lot to have on your shoulders, Serena." It was hard not to feel sympathetic, even if she had been horrible to me.

"It is what it is." She tossed her blonde braid over her shoulder, apparently at her limit of vulnerability for the day. "I'm doing what needs to be done. I just wanted to thank you for . . . you know."

"Serena, if you need me to take something to your family next time I have a day off, I'd be happy to."

Her lips parted slightly, then closed. "Thank you. I'll keep that in mind." She turned on her heel and was gone. When I returned to my workstation, everything looked exactly the same as it had before, but I had the feeling that something monumental had just shifted for our little crew.

At a quarter to six I started my trek up to the prince's quarters, trying to quell the jitters I was already feeling. I was working. Doing my job. That was all.

But after two weeks of swapping novels and developing a rapport, I had to admit to myself that the banter was feeling increasingly flirtatious. Which was a terrible idea, obviously.

Halfway down the hallway on the third floor, I was intercepted by a breathless Colette.

"Quinn!" She pulled me to the side of the hallway where we had partial cover from one of the carved marble columns that lined this stretch of the floor.

"Do you know what happened to Liang and Emory?"

"What do you mean?"

Leaning in, she dropped her voice to a whisper.

"Two girls went home today, and the rumor is that they both lost their magic. Vanessa was friendly with Emory, who was working on projection, and she said she just felt empty when she woke up this morning," she shuddered. "Liang was the same."

"Oh gods, that's awful. This is the first I've heard of it, but I'm headed up to deliver dinner to the prince's quarters, so I can ask if he has any information."

Colette raised her eyebrows. "You can just ask him something like that?"

Could I? The idea didn't make me nervous at all, and I hated how comfortable I had become around him.

"The good thing about being a servant is that you're not intimidating enough to withhold information from." *Mostly* true. "I'll try to get some answers for you."

"Thank you, Quinn." Colette pulled me into a quick hug. "Let me know if you hear anything. I'm scared. We all are."

A few minutes later, I was knocking on Evander's door, tray of now-cold food in hand.

I followed him back to his study and perched in one of the chairs opposite him in what had become a well-rehearsed dance.

"My apologies," he said without looking up, "I'm a bit distracted this evening, so I'm afraid you won't find me a very good conversation partner."

"Is this about what happened with Emory and Liang?"

He sighed, drawing his hands down his face in a gesture of weariness. "So you've already heard about that. Excellent."

"Do you know what's going on?" I asked.

"If I did, do you think I would be sitting here pouring over every book I can find on magical depletion instead of eating my dinner?"

It was a fair point, but I didn't appreciate his tone. I cocked my head and stared at him pointedly.

"Contrary to popular belief," he ground out, "having a crown does not mean that I have all the answers. I would think someone as smart as you would be able to come to that conclusion on your own." Ignoring the flutter in my stomach that accompanied his compliment, I focused on his less-than-cordial attitude.

"This isn't about me," I challenged.

The fire in his eyes extinguished when he looked up at me, the hard lines around his mouth falling as he sighed again.

"You're right. It's not."

"Would you like to try that again?" I asked. "Maybe I can help,"

He laughed bitterly. "Believe me, I wish you could. Because I'm at a complete godsdamned loss about what to do here." His hair fell into his face as he dropped his head, interlacing his fingers on the back of his neck.

"What's really going on?"

Evander assessed me for a moment, and I could see him arming himself with his best placations and excuses. *"It's nothing, the castle is well, all will be fine, don't trouble yourself."* It must be exhausting to carry all of that on your shoulders.

I met his eyes with as much kindness and understanding as I could muster, and something behind his mask cracked, his piercing blue eyes filling with tears.

"She's dying, Quinn," he whispered.

My heart sank. *His mother.*

I was under the impression he didn't want to talk about the queen, and given the threat from Maddox after our last conversation, I wasn't sure what I could say that would be safe. I don't know what made me do it, but I slid my hand across the desk and put my hand on his. Hoping it would communicate my support, I squeezed once and pulled it away quickly, blushing.

Evander grabbed it back like a drowning man who had been offered a life preserver. His grip was strong, palm surprisingly calloused.

"It's true that the Crown is stronger when there are two on the throne," he continued, "but there's more to it than that. A lot more that I didn't know until this year."

He took a deep breath, his next words spilling out as if he couldn't contain them any longer.

"The reason both a king and queen are needed to rule is that the monarchs channel the people's magic for the kingdoms's protective wards."

"Channel?"

"You're aware of how the Wielders of Enorias contribute to the protective wards around the kingdom?" he asked.

"Vaguely," I said, thinking of the woman I'd heard complaining about it in the tailor shop.

"Well, all that power needs to be melded and refined. The monarchs work as a kind of conduit to turn all the raw magic into the barrier," he explained.

"I've never heard that before," I said, trying not to let my surprise show. Had Mother truly sequestered me from magic so completely that I didn't even understand how our own government worked?

"The process is kept a secret so that we don't become targets for an internal attack. There are still some fanatics who support King Orobas even within our wards."

A stone settled in my stomach as I thought of Mother's tirades. What would Evander think if he knew my own mother was among those who prayed for his downfall?

"After my father passed a few years ago," Evander continued, "my mother argued that times were peaceful enough for her to hold the throne by herself, at least until I was old enough to find love." There was an undercurrent of anger in his voice that I understood all too well. Being controlled, even by someone who wanted the best for you, wasn't comfortable. Even less so when you were kept in the dark about it.

"But it's too big a task for one person, even without a war," he continued. "She's hung on much longer than she should have and she has almost nothing left."

"I'm sorry," I said, heaviness settling in my chest.

Grief and anger warred on his face with his next words. "I fear it may already be too late for her. The wards are already weakening. Every report I receive tells me Falerin is creeping closer to our borders." He rubbed his temples. "I can't help but fear the Time of Darkness is upon us."

"Time of Darkness?" One revelation after another had my head spinning.

"There's a prophecy," he explained. "It was made when I was young, but I only learned of it a few months ago."

He pulled a worn piece of parchment from his desk drawer and handed it to me.

In a hasty scrawl, it read:

"There will come a Time of Darkness when the kingdom is at its weakest. The fated halves of the Crown must find each other before the Deceiver seizes the Gifts of the people. Only the powers that sing to one another will be enough for the Protector to wipe The Evil One from existence and bring stability back to Enorias."

My breath caught as I read the words. So many vague, unfamiliar terms made it difficult to decipher, but what I understood right away was that I had been very, very wrong. All this time I had been worried about my employment status and petty squabbles with my coworkers while Evander was dealing with this. More than just the responsibility to rule, the fate of the kingdom had fallen on his shoulders, and he had been kept in the dark about it until things were dire. The stress he must be under was far beyond what I could imagine.

"Your mother kept this from you, too?" I asked.

He nodded, his mouth set in a grim line. "She convinced herself that the time the prophecy mentioned hadn't yet come, but the disappearances are ramping up again and now it seems that the magic of the castle is weakening as well. If my fears are right, that's why two Wielders were Extinguished today. The castle must've drawn on them to keep the inner wards up when my mother's power wasn't enough. It's my fault."

"It's not."

"It is!" The words were a barely-restrained explosion of anger, not at me, but at himself. "If I had been more focused on my duties I could've ascended to the throne long ago and she wouldn't have gotten to this point."

"You didn't know," I said, once again wishing I had more comforting words to offer him.

"It doesn't matter whether I knew. The result is the same." The self-loathing was thick in his voice.

"Even now, I can't do anything about it. I keep trying, forcing myself to attend endless dinners and pointless training sessions, making empty small talk and playing the part, but I can't make myself feel anything for any of them. It's as though the harder I try, the less success I find. In the beginning, I had hope, but now–nothing. It's maddening."

"Could you share the Crown with your mother until you decipher it?" It might be unconventional to have a mother and son on the throne at the same time, but at least she wouldn't have to channel power for the wards alone.

He shook his head. "I suggested that, but the two Wielders on the throne have to go through a tethering ceremony for their Gifts. My mother's magic is too weak to attempt it. Besides, it's a lifelong bond, so it's really meant for a married couple." He shifted uncomfortably in his seat.

"So your plan is to just wait until you feel something?" I hadn't meant to put it so indelicately, but it didn't seem like the most proactive solution.

"Well, that's not the phrasing I would've used," he glowered, "but yes, that is the general idea. My magic hasn't done anything unusual yet, but most of these women don't have a good handle on their Gifts. We're giving them access to our resources so they can hone them into something sharper. We'll just have to keep trying."

The logic didn't make any sense to me. It sounded as though he was thinking of the women and their magic as separate entities. Rather than trying to spend time with them one-on-one and form an emotional connection with any of them, he was relying on his magic to choose for him.

A cowardly strategy, I thought, but I kept the unkind observation to myself this time. Especially as the idea of him doing otherwise brought up an emotion in me that I'd rather not examine at the moment.

I scanned the paper again, moving on to the other words on the page.

"What do we know about this prophecy? Who are the Deceiver and the Protector?"

"I wish I knew. It certainly seems like we're entering the Time of Darkness, so I can only guess that I'm supposed to be the Protector. A great job I've done at that," he scoffed ruefully.

"What about the Wielder who made the prophecy? Could they tell us?"

Evander shook his head. "I don't know. The man disappeared shortly after he Saw this. No one knows where he is."

Well, that wasn't helpful.

"Let's break it down," I suggested. "Maybe a pair of fresh eyes would help." I didn't know what I of all people could do, but I couldn't just leave him dejected and alone. "Are we sure the Time of Darkness is now?"

"Our wards are failing, my mother is dying, and I'm completely unprepared to take the throne. My mother refuses to even speak about succession until I find a queen, hence this contest, but I don't even have a ghost of an idea of what I'm looking for." He pointed to the next line on the sheet. "The powers that sing together. What does that mean? The language is enough for me to narrow it down to another Wielder, but beyond that I have no idea."

"Could it be powers that complement each other, like fire and ice? What kind of Gift do you have?"

"That's not something I'm at liberty to share," he apologized. "Security and all that. Not my choice, but all I can say is that there isn't a simple foil to my abilities."

We spent the next four hours combing through the prophecy word by word, making guesses at who the Deceiver might be and what the imminent threat to the kingdom might look like, discussing how Evander might fortify the castle to take some of the burden off his mother, and how he would know when a power "sang" to his, whatever that meant.

Although we didn't get very far, having a new point of view seemed to help Evander feel less hopeless.

"You should spend some time with the contestants individually," I said, ignoring how my traitorous heart grew heavy at the thought of him taking my suggestion. "This connection you're looking for may not be purely magical. What about love? Surely that's a powerful force in itself."

Evander gritted his teeth but said nothing, and I pretended not to notice, moving onto the next part of the prophecy.

It was nearly eleven when he finally dismissed me, insisting I get some sleep before my shift in the kitchen started at sunrise.

"Are you going to get some as well?" I asked, already knowing the answer.

A sad smile appeared on his face. "I'll rest better when we've figured this out."

My chest warmed at the word *we,* and it was almost enough to make me forget that I was now actively helping him find another Wielder to wed.

I paused at the doorway, taking a moment to look back at the scene: he sat hunched over the desk, dark waves falling onto his forehead as he poured over the reference texts we had pulled. His left hand flexed and unflexed, as if grasping for the answers we couldn't find. There were dark bruises under his eyes; it seemed impossible that I had missed them before. My heart broke for him.

"Evander," I called. "We're going to figure this out. She'll be all right."

"I hope you're right. Truly. Thank you for your help."

"Of course."

He cracked a genuine smile.

"I just realized you called me Evander."

"I suppose I did." I couldn't help the corner of my mouth from listing slightly in return. "Goodnight."

I closed the door and then leaned against the other side for a moment.

Shit.

Chapter 8

"Excuse me, Quinn, can you please pass the butter?"

James gave me an enthusiastic thumbs up from across the room as Serena uttered what might be the first polite sentence she had ever directed toward me.

I rolled my eyes but smiled, completing her request and returning to the lemon meringue cookies I was preparing for dessert tonight.

After dusting the hardened peaks with a bit of powdered sugar to add aesthetic flair to the dish, I changed into a clean apron and headed upstairs for my serving shift in the ballroom.

As soon as I entered the room, Colette hurried up to me, eyes still full of worry.

"Did you find out what happened?" she asked.

I froze. In my concern for Evander, I had completely forgotten about my promise. Surely if the contestants were in danger of having their power drained, he would give them the chance to leave, wouldn't he? It wasn't my place to reveal that information. Not yet.

"They have a lead on something and they're working on it," I promised, "but I can't say much more than that."

Colette looked as if she were going to push harder, but before she got the chance, the doors swung open and Evander entered the room, distracting her.

First he greeted Lucy, who was practically slack-jawed at his appearance. He made his way around the room with a confident stride, listening as the Wielders told him what they were working on and smiling that dazzling grin at them. A dull ache in my hands altered me to the fact that I was gripping my serving spoons tight enough to leave marks on my palms.

I forced myself to look away. This was good. This was exactly what he needed to be doing.

When I glanced up again, Evander had made it to where Vanessa was leaning against the wall and slung his arm around her shoulders goodnaturedly. Freya glared at them from across the room with a vitriol so intense I was surprised Vanessa's clothing hadn't caught fire. I waited for the ugly jealousy to hit me again, but the way he touched her looked casual, even familial. If Vanessa had lived in the castle for most of her life, they had probably grown up together.

When she swatted him away from both her and Colette, he crossed the room to speak to Anissa, the light-Wielder. She batted her eyelashes at him in a way that made me recall his comment in the stairwell. I could practically see her mentally calculating the size of the tiara she would need. She leaned in closer and put a hand on his arm, right over his bicep. Evander smiled, putting his hand on the small of her back, and I swore the lamps glowed a little brighter.

I dropped the spoons.

The clatter as they hit the floor drew Evander's attention, and his eyes met mine, widening in shock for a moment before he schooled his features into the mask of composure he wore so often.

I turned my focus to Colette, who was now creating climbable bougainvillea vines on the ballroom wall, and didn't dare look up again until he left. Before I even heard the doors open, I felt his presence grow more distant, as if some of the warmth had leached from the room.

As soon as the doors shut, Vanessa strode up to me, crossed her arms, and looked at me expectantly.

"What was that?"

"The prince, I believe," I quipped. I wasn't in the mood to deal with her sour behavior. Even after several weeks, she still looked at me with a challenge in her eyes, like she was sizing up an opponent. The last thing I needed was for her to think that I was part of this competition.

"Don't bullshit me," she snapped. "I could see you clenching your jaw from across the room. You know him."

"Well, he is my employer," I said dryly.

Vanessa narrowed her eyes at me.

"I've known Evander since we were children, and he's never been flustered by a servant that way."

"Don't you have some training to do?" I asked, ignoring her interrogation.

"You cannot mess with this competition, Quinn. Let it be." She leveled her gaze at me and fire blazed in her amber eyes.

"I have no idea what you're talking about."

Unconvinced, she turned on her heel and stalked away.

That night I asked Serena to take Evander's tray to his quarters. To my surprise, she didn't even argue with me, and I got some desperately needed space.

In exchange, I was tasked with taking dinner up to a Wielder on the third floor who was feeling "under the weather" and would be dining in her rooms. I wondered if she had lost her magic, too.

On the third flight of stairs, as if summoned by my thoughts of him, I came face to face with Evander.

Deja vu.

"You didn't come tonight." He glowered down at me, unsettled.

"We have to stop meeting like this," I joked, trying to break the tension already building in the stairwell.

Ignoring the forced attempt at casual conversation, Evander tried again. "Why didn't you come?"

"I sent Serena with your tray," I explained. "It should be there any minute." With that, I tried to sidle past him, but he squared himself up on the steps, blocking my way.

"I wasn't asking about the food."

My heart stuttered in my chest. No. This wasn't fair to either of us. Wasn't fair to *me.*

"I know you had a *busy day,*" I said, hating the snide edge that slipped into my voice, "so I assumed you'd had enough female company for the day."

"Is that what this is about? My visit to the contestants?" He barked a laugh that made my chest seize up in anger.

"Of course not." I straightened my spine and forced myself to make eye contact. "I was the one who told you to spend time with them. And it isn't my business." I tried again to make it past him, but he took a step down, backing me into the curved wall and caging me in by leaning on it with one forearm.

We were close enough that I could feel his breath on my face. He smelled like parchment and ink and leather and . . . whisky? Had he been drinking?

"It didn't bother you at all?" he challenged, fire in his eyes. "Because it bothered me. It bothered me that there was only one person in that room I wanted to talk to, but I was stuck making small talk with half a dozen other women I wouldn't look at twice if it weren't for their casting abilities. I hated it. Didn't you?" His eyes bored holes into mine as he challenged me to admit something that I shouldn't. Couldn't.

"No," I breathed, willing myself not to shake.

"Interesting," he purred, pushing off the wall as if this were a game of cat and mouse.

"Glad to have entertained you." Finding myself again in my anger, I shoved past him, stomping up the stairs like a petulant child.

"If I didn't know better, I'd think you were jealous," his voice came from behind me.

I stilled. We couldn't go there. Especially when an ugly part of me whispered that he was right.

"Go drink some water, Evander," I said, still not turning around.

"I like the way you say my name." I dared a glance back and saw him sitting on the steps, eyes closed as he leaned against the wall, one corner of his mouth pulled into a smile. Setting my jaw, I pushed the image out of my mind.

"Goodnight."

I continued up the stairs and returned to my job. I only hoped he would do the same.

I'd barely begun the process of kneading my dough before Mellie pulled me aside, a concerned frown on her face.

"What's wrong, Quinny?"

"Nothing," I snapped.

"It looked like you were picturing someone's face on that dough," she observed with a raised brow. "Is Serena giving you trouble again? Because I've already warned her-"

"No. Everything is fine. I'm just going to finish this up and head home."

It was obvious she didn't believe me, but cornering me into talking about my feelings had never worked before so, to her credit, she gave me some space. I felt like an angry teenager again, hiding things from my mother.

When the rage softened and I could think a bit more clearly, I felt bad for taking my frustration out on my dearest friend.

Before I headed home, I made sure to give her a squeeze and a kiss on the cheek.

"Sorry, Mels. It's not you."

"I know, Dumpling. But who is it?"

"Nobody," I sighed, and I wasn't lying. Nobody but myself. I needed to get a hold of my emotions. My anger, yes, but also the *other ones.* The ones I didn't have words for and absolutely did not want to talk about.

I slipped out the kitchen side door, pulling my cloak around me to ward off the autumn chill as I headed home. As much as I tried to ignore it, a part of my mind lingered in that stairwell, wondering what would've happened if I had stayed.

Chapter 9

Rubbing my eyes, I tried not to fall asleep at my station. I had come home last night to Mother waiting up again. My attempt to bolt straight to my room hadn't worked, and we had been up into the early morning hours arguing with no resolution and nothing to show for it but the red rims around my eyes.

Mellie immediately picked up on my sour mood. She gave me the look she had developed when I was about sixteen that simultaneously said, "*I'm here for you,*" and "*You had better tell me what's going on right now and don't you dare lie to me.*"

"Just Mother," I sighed. With any luck she'd believe that's what had me on edge last night as well.

She nodded in understanding.

"What is it this time?"

"Oh, the usual," I said, as flippantly as I could manage. "Complaints that I'm selfishly abandoning my family and all that."

"For working?"

I didn't need to burden Mellie with my personal drama. Unwilling to delve into the tangled web again, I just nodded.

"Why don't you move into the castle, Quinny?" she asked. "It's not my place to push, but I don't understand why you keep going back there."

"It's complicated, Mels." How many times had I said that to her over the years? It was starting to sound stale, even to me.

"Complicated how?" she probed. "Talk to me about it. Are you holding on for your father?"

"Maybe partially, but I think more than that I'm hanging on to the possibility of what our family could be. I don't know . . . the whole thing is messy."

"It doesn't have to be," Mellie tried. "You can't change someone's heart to match the version you've dreamt up, Dumpling." With an affectionate squeeze of my arm, she returned to her pastries, giving me some time to think.

I was desperate for a distraction, but it seemed there would be no reprieve from my worrying; my mind took my desire to avoid ruminating on my fight with Mother as license to fill the empty space with thoughts of Evander.

I couldn't tell if I was hoping he would call for me tonight or dreading it. Would it be better to pretend last night hadn't happened or to discuss it and set some boundaries?

The smartest thing for him to do would be to cut me out of his life. After all, I was only a servant, and I should have no qualms about fading into the background.

Except that I did.

His missive came later than usual, just as I was about to ask Serena to deliver the tray for me.

All right, I steeled myself at the summons, *I can be an adult about this.*

Four flights of stairs later, a pink-faced and sheepish Evander opened the door.

"Thank you for coming."

"Of course, your Highness." I stepped back, putting space between us. Distance was good. If I got too close, I risked getting sucked into that gravitational pull.

"About last night," he said, running a hand through his hair. "I wanted to apologize. I shouldn't have put you in that position. I . . .wasn't feeling quite myself."

"No, I'm quite sure you were feeling the whisky," I said, arching a brow. "So much for turning to books over drink."

He had the good sense to look abashed for a moment and, against my better judgment, I found myself softening towards him again. He just looked so lost.

"Probably not the best way to manage your stress," I added. I fashioned the quip into a knife meant to carve through my sentimentality and force some emotional distance, but the words didn't have my desired effect. They came off too close to our usual banter, and a fire lit in his eyes again.

"Do you have a better idea?" He stepped closer, peering down through his lashes at me, eyes darkening in challenge. A powerful force in my gut told me to surrender, to lean into him. It would be so easy.

I imagined kissing him would be different than the few kisses I had experienced throughout my teen years in the village. They were sloppy things, born of rebellion and tasting of disobedience. None of them offered anything deeper than the momentary thrill of secrecy. But kissing Evander would be all consuming, I knew. The kind of precipice you only threw yourself off if you were at peace with the fact that you weren't coming back. I swallowed that feeling and took a step back.

"The apology doesn't count if you're just going to do the same thing again, Evander."

"Do what?" The hungry expression hadn't left his face.

"This." I gestured between the two of us, not daring to give voice to this dangerous game.

"What if I mean it?" he asked.

"You can't."

"Why?" The set of his jaw was stiff, as if bracing himself for the answer he already knew was coming.

"You know why. It will only lead to more heartbreak." *For both of us.* The unspoken words hung in the air. "You can't just do what you want to do all the time."

The floor took an assault from his boots as he took three quick, heavy steps away, turning from me and burying his hands in his hair.

"I can't do *anything!* I can't rule because my mother won't let me shoulder the crown alone, I can't help her recover, and I can't stand to be around those women. It feels like I'm awaiting a life sentence every time one of them bats their eyelashes at me and I feel nothing. I can't do it."

"Evander, that's what rulers have to do," I said, trying to keep my tone gentle, but firm. "You may not have asked for it, but you were born into this responsibility, and there's no use pretending you weren't. Have you considered using that authority to actually do something instead of avoiding it?"

He turned back to me, and hurt flashed across his face as he took in my words.

"You don't think I'm doing anything about this? Searching for these women, holding this competition even when it's the last thing in the world I want to do? I'm doing everything I can. And it's still not enough. I'm so sick of the performance, of showing up as the prince I'm supposed to be when all I want to do is lock myself up in here and scream. For my mother. For myself. For the little boy who never asked for this godsdamned crown or this useless power or this inane competition."

"Some of these women are working day and night for this *inane competition*," I shot back, thinking of Colette. "The least you can do is show them some respect for that."

"Respecting their hard work and wanting to marry one of them are two separate things," he ground out.

"Have you told them they're at risk of losing their magic?"

The shadow that crossed his face was enough of an answer.

"Is it 'respect' to keep them in the dark about what's really going on and let them stay here, risking their magic, while you wait for the right moment to pick one of them like a bonbon off a tray?" The ugly emotions I felt in the training room came flooding back to me, and I was no longer sure whether I was angry for Colette and the other Wielders or for myself. This was unfair to all of us.

Evander took two long strides toward where I was standing and towered over me, nearly spitting his next words.

"I'm not going to apologize for caring more about my mother's *life* than their powers. If that makes me selfish, so be it. They aren't in danger of anything more than losing a few parlor tricks. Tricks, might I remind you, that will become a very real danger to them if I don't assume the throne *quickly.* My mother can't hold the wards stable forever and without the protection of the crown those girls will be *hunted* for what they can do."

"So you don't even give them the choice?" I challenged. I was picking a fight, and I knew it, but fighting was safe. We were good at fighting.

"No. I don't." Too close again. I backed away.

"Then you're more of a self-important ass than I thought." I didn't wait to be dismissed, storming through the door and slamming it on my way out.

Almost a week passed without any word from Evander. Though I hated how we'd left things, I told myself it was good that I could focus on my job and my home life without any distractions. I had said my piece. Hopefully it would only be a matter of time until he found the other half of the "powers that sang to one another" and this whole competition would be at an end.

On the sixth day after the argument, Colette pulled me aside as I entered the ballroom..

"Prince Evander came in during breakfast," she said, her tone hushed. "He told us that Liang and Emory's powers are gone, and we're in danger of losing ours too. They didn't tell us why, but he gave us all the chance to leave. There are only nine of us left."

So he had told them. I swallowed, trying to push down the myriad of emotions that bubbled to the surface. For all his talk about selfishness, Evander had done the right thing. Though I was unsure why, the knowledge squirmed under my skin, making me shift uncomfortably. It was far easier to write him off as a spoiled princeling who didn't care about anybody beneath him in the aftermath of our fight. Instead, here he was taking a great personal risk to give others agency in their own safety. I told myself it had nothing to do with the argument we'd had. It was simply the right thing to do.

"Are you going?" I asked Colette, pushing thoughts of Evander out of my mind. Although I'd miss her, I would never blame her for protecting herself.

"No," she said, the word full of conviction. "I'm scared, but I'm where I need to be."

My stomach churned at the possibility of her winning this competition and marrying Evander. Did she already have feelings for him? Is that why she was staying? I wasn't sure I wanted to know the answer, so I didn't ask.

"Do you know who's doing this?" she asked, her eyes searching mine for an answer I couldn't give.

"No." I told myself it wasn't technically a lie, since it wasn't a some*one,* but a some*thing.*

"Let me know if you learn *anything*," she said, clutching my arm.

I couldn't get out of that one with a half-truth, so I squeezed her hand back by way of answer and tried to ignore the feeling of guilt that had settled into my stomach.

Chapter 10

My heart and feet were heavy as I made my trek back to the village that night.

When I opened the door, I found Mother standing in the middle of the room, hands on her hips and fury on her face.

"Is everything all right, Mother?" An alarm blared in my mind, telling me to choose my words very carefully.

Turning away, she started a slow prowl around the living room. She picked some pilling off the knit throw on the back of the settee and leveled her gaze at me again.

"I had a very interesting conversation with Sasha today. She visited the tailor this morning." *Shit.* "Did you know that his daughter Marisol has spent the last month at the palace?"

I said nothing. It was imperative that I found out exactly how much she knew before I built a defense. I couldn't afford to make this any worse than it already was.

"Strangely enough, Marisol was under the impression that she had seen *you* there as well," Mother continued. "I was convinced she was mistaken, and I told Sasha as much, but then she mentioned *Permelia* had been hired onto the royal staff." Her eyes narrowed at me, lips pursed together in a razor thin line of anger. "That's why you haven't been listening to me. You've been lying to me for a *month* because you've been with *her.*"

"I can explain," I started. I could only pray to the gods to help me somehow spin the right words to get out of this.

Mother advanced toward me, rage fueling every clack of her kitten heels. "And worse, you've been with *them.*" The snide edge she reserved for the royal family made its way into her tone. "Tell me, did you enjoy your time in their gilded castle? Did they charm you with their gaudy magic? I hope all their party tricks didn't make you forget that you're nothing more than dirt to them."

Of all the things she has said about the royals, that statement stung the most. I wasn't dirt to Evander.

Was I?

"You always were desperate for attention, Quinn," she sneered. "I bet you felt so important working for *The Crown*."

I fought to keep my tone neutral. "I was only in the kitchen, Mother. I've never even met the queen." True enough.

There was no jeering in her next words; all that remained was a hatred as cold as the metal of a blade plunged deep into snow. "You have no idea the kind of people they are, Quinn. No idea what you've gotten yourself into."

I hated when she talked down to me. I hated that she treated me like a rebellious child. I hated that she made me feel incapable of making decisions without her assistance.

"A job, Mother," I fired back. "A stable job that I actually enjoy. An excuse to be out of this living hell of a home."

She recoiled as if I had slapped her.

"How dare you speak to me that way after all I've done for you? I have put a roof over your head, clothes on your back, and have loved you more than you deserved."

More than I deserved? Those words, cruelest of all, were more than I could handle, and years of pent-up rage erupted from me..

"Love? Is that what you call this? Manipulating me into submission, not allowing me to have my own friends, my own life, trying to keep me compliant so you could turn me into a miniature version of you? That's not love, Mother."

"Oh, and I suppose Permelia loves you better than I do? A woman who isn't even blood, who schemes to take you away from us because she doesn't have children of her own? I bet you missed her, didn't you?" she asked, acid dripping from her words. "The mother you *wish* you had."

"YES!" I yelled at her. "Yes, I did! Is that what you wanted to hear? I am so sick and tired of the fighting and the melodrama and the echo chamber of this house! Working at the castle has made me *happy.* But you can't stand that, can you? You need me to be miserable just like you."

Without warning, her open palm connected with my cheek, the sting hot and angry.

"Get. Out," she ordered, her voice deadly quiet. "If you want to escape so badly, go. But don't expect me to take you back." It only took one look at the hard set of her jaw to know she wasn't bluffing.

My hand flew up to my face where she had struck me. I met her gaze. Her eyes held no remorse.

I fled past her into my room, grabbing the rucksack that hung on the post of my bedframe and filling it with as much as I could. Struggling to make decisions about what to take as the adrenaline surged through my system, I grabbed things at random: an extra set of clothing, my hairbrush, some books, and the stack of letters from my father I had hidden under my bed.

When I made it back to the parlor, Mother was holding the door open. Betrayal and wrath and righteous indignation swirled on her face. The sight threatened to make the moisture in my eyes overflow.

I would not let her see me cry. I was not going to give her the satisfaction.

Without a word, I pushed past her and held the tears that threatened to fall, even when her cottage was a speck of light behind me.

It wasn't until I was staring up at the iron gates of the castle that I realized I didn't know if I would even be afforded entry, but I didn't know where else to go. I needed Mellie immediately. There was a hole in my heart in the shape of a mother's comfort and guidance that only she could fill. But first I had to get into the castle.

It towered over me in the darkness, cutting an ever more intimidating figure than it did during the day. There must have been a shift change in the last hour, because I didn't recognize any of the guards walking just inside the perimeter. No one had noticed me yet, but it would undoubtedly be worse to be found lurking in the shadows.

Wiping my eyes with the back of my hand and summoning whatever courage I had left, I approached.

"Excuse me?" I called out. "I'm a baker in the kitchens and I need to be let back into the palace."

The nearest guard eyed me with the distrust I'd expected, advancing slowly but staying behind the gate.

"And why would you be out here at this hour?" he asked. "Staff live on the grounds."

"I've been given special dispensation to commute from the village," I explained, already knowing how this conversation would go. After all, I'd had it once before. Mellie wouldn't be coming to save me this time.

"Do you have proof of identity?"

I searched my mind frantically for something, anything that would help my case.

"This morning we served eggs benedict for breakfast?" A feeble attempt, but it was worth a try.

"I'm sorry, but that's not enough," the guard said, his expression equal parts pity and suspicion as his hand moved to rest on his sword.

My eyes welled up again and I turned away from him to hide my face. I had no idea where I was going to go. How had this happened?

"Let her in," came a rumbling voice from within the gate.

I whipped around at the unmistakable sound.

Evander.

He was breathing heavily, as if he had run here from the fourth floor, and looked disheveled in his nightclothes, his hair mussed.

"Yes, your Highness," the guard bowed, and I swore I could feel the ward ripple around me as I stepped onto the grounds.

The prince gave me a stern look and jerked his head toward the castle in a clear command to follow.

"Thank you, Your Highness," I said, making sure to use his proper title for anyone who may be listening. The castle would already be abuzz with gossip the next morning about the unkempt prince showing up at the castle gates at almost midnight.

"Follow me," he directed, not looking back. For the first time, I was thankful for the four flights of stairs and the time they gave me to figure out how to explain away what just happened.

Would he believe me if I said I'd lost my way and ended up outside the gates by accident? Unlikely. Should I pretend I had quit? Mellie may not get fired for my less-than-cordial attitude, but if Queen Evalina had asked that my working conditions be kept a secret from her son, I imagined a breach of that trust might get Mellie in some serious trouble.

Evander opened the door to his rooms, ushered me inside, and began pacing toward the window, looking down at the grounds near the gate.

"Do I even want to know why you were outside the wards?" he fumed.

"Probably not." My honesty likely wouldn't get me out of explaining myself, but it was worth a shot.

"If this is about what happened the other night and you've quit your post because of our conversation, I'd be extremely disappointed in you." He turned toward me and stalked my way. "You have more fire in you than–" he stopped short, training his gaze on my right cheek.

"Who is responsible for this?" he growled.

I glanced behind him at my reflection in the glass of the windows. An angry red handprint stained my face, and I cringed as I saw what looked to be a burst blood vessel marring my undereye, though it was hard to tell without a proper mirror.

"Quinn," he said, holding my jaw in his hand and turning my face towards him. "Who did this? I can promise you they will be out of the castle tonight." Carefully restrained anger simmered just beneath the surface of the vow.

"No one," I lied, already aware of what an unbelievable excuse I was about to make. "I fell asleep with my head on my hand. It must've left a mark." I laughed, the hollow sound unconvincing even to my ears.

"And this?" he asked, running the pad of his thumb gently under my eye.

I didn't have an excuse for that.

"Quinn," his eyes softened. "You have to know I can't let this go. Tell me."

"It wasn't anyone here," I said, hoping the partial truth would pacify him enough to drop it.

"So it was someone outside the gates," he said. "Why were you outside the grounds?"

"I don't know how to answer that," I hedged.

"Honestly, preferably."

"I'm not supposed to tell you." As soon as the words left my lips, I was aware of my mistake.

Evander took a step back, betrayal in his eyes. "And who ordered you to keep quiet?"

Shit. From the fear on his face, he probably thought this was an assassination attempt.

"No, no, it isn't like that," I hurried to interject. "I just don't want my friend to get in trouble. I have a . . . special arrangement."

He didn't seem convinced.

I had no choice but to be honest and hope that he would continue to surprise me with his leniency. After all, I had given him reason after reason to fire me over the last month, and in spite of my attitude and insults we had somehow ended up . . . friends?

I sighed. "I've been commuting from the village by special permission from your mother. You're not supposed to know."

Relief showed on his face for a heartbeat before the worry took over.

"How long?" he asked, caught somewhere between anger and frantic concern.

"Since I started working here."

"Oh, gods." He rubbed his brow. "Is there anyone else?"

"Not that I know of. I've been so careful, I promise. It hasn't been a security risk."

"That's not–" He rubbed his temples. "The reason we limit people coming and going from the palace isn't a matter of security. Not directly, anyway. Every time someone enters or leaves the palace, the wards do a check on the person's intent," he said. "It takes a drop of the Crown's power, my mother's power, power she desperately needs right now, and she's been doing it twice a day for a month? Why would she risk herself like that?"

The guilt was suffocating. All this time we had been working to help Evalina, and I had been one of the factors draining her.

"Evander, I'm so sorry. I had no idea."

His anger gave way to weariness as he sat down, running a hand through his hair.

"I believe you. I only wish you had told me. She has no right to keep things like this from me."

"I'm sure she just doesn't want you to worry," I said.

"Yes, because that strategy has worked out so well." He laughed bitterly. "I have to speak with her . . ." he trailed off, focusing his gaze back on me, eyes lingering on my face thoughtfully.

"You still haven't answered my question."

I joined him in the sitting area, sinking into one of the chairs opposite the settee.

"My mother," I admitted quietly.

"Your mother?"

"She didn't know I was working here. Our relationship is . . . complicated. One of the contestants who went home this week lived in our neighborhood and my mother found out I'd been lying about where I'd been employed. She . . ." I couldn't finish the sentence.

Evander waited patiently while I gathered myself.

"Doesn't want me to come back," I finished, sealing my emotions away behind a door and shutting it with as much force as I could muster. "So I suppose in one way your problem is solved. I won't be leaving the wards anymore." A horrible thought struck me. "That is, if I'm allowed to stay?"

Evander sighed. "Of course you can stay. I can't fault you for my mother's deception, and as angry as I am, I trust that she had a reason to do what she did."

"Thank you."

A muscle ticked in his jaw.

"I can't do much about your mother's actions since she's not within my employment. If I were sovereign, I could have her tried. I'll speak to my mother about it."

"No!" I cut in. "Please don't. It's not that big an issue." I didn't think I could bear the shame or the scrutiny if this escalated.

"You would defend the woman who struck you?" I didn't deserve his grace or the tender way he was looking at me.

"As I said, our relationship is complicated. And I shouldn't have lied to her."

"There is nothing complicated about abuse, Quinn. Lies or not, a woman who would harm her own daughter is not someone who deserves your protection. Or your love."

At a loss for words again, I just stared at my shoes.

"I need to go speak to my mother," Evander said, getting up. "We'll find you accommodations in the morning. The bedroom and washroom are through there." He pointed to the door in the back of the antechamber.

Absolutely not.

"Evander, I can't take your bed," I protested. "For about a dozen reasons."

He rolled his eyes at me, the ghost of a half-smile on his face. "Don't make this difficult, Quinn. I understand that may be a challenge for you, but this makes the most sense as a temporary solution. Unless you have something else in mind?"

I knew Mellie would let me stay with her, but she only had a single bed. And besides, I wasn't sure I was ready to tell her that I had let Evander in on our secret quite yet. There had already been enough contentious conversation for one night. I shook my head.

"Do you have anyone else offering you their bed tonight?" he challenged. A spark of something flashed in his eyes quickly at the thought, but it was gone before I could decipher it.

"No," I whispered.

"Good," he said, turning toward the entrance. "I'm not allowing you to sleep in the kitchen. I'll sleep in my mother's quarters; she has a spare room."

He narrowed his eyes at me and didn't look away until I'd opened the door he pointed out. When I turned to thank him, I found he was already gone.

Cautiously, I took a step into his room. Though I'd been in these chambers almost a dozen times already, I'd never set foot in the bedroom. The first things I noticed were the stacks of books that covered almost every surface.

I knew Evander liked to read, but this room was a veritable library. Organization didn't seem to be his strong suit, and I saw several of his vests and coats draped over the chair and the end of the bed. The cobalt blue of his coverlet matched the heavy curtains, currently tied shut with thick golden cords. I recognized a familiar scent, like old books and new leather boots.

Being here felt like trespassing, but the adrenaline had faded out of my system, and the night's events were beginning to catch up with me. I was so tired.

Climbing into the blankets felt far too intimate, so I lay down on top of the coverlet and almost immediately fell into a dreamless sleep.

Chapter 11

THE GOLDEN MORNING SUN peeked into the room through a slit in the curtains, turning specks of dust into enchanted snowfall in the beam of warm light. I rubbed the sleep from my eyes, disoriented. It only took me a moment to realize where I was and sit bolt upright in shock.

I cannot be here.

Swinging my feet off the bed, I was horrified to note that my boots had left dirt and debris on the luxurious fabric of the coverlet; I had never taken them off last night. Frowning at the space I'd just occupied, I smoothed the covers until no ident of my form remained.

Then, as quietly as possible, I crept out of the room and into the antechamber. A wave of relief washed over me when I found the entire wing empty. If Evander was still in his mother's chambers and no servants presented themselves, there was still a chance of getting out of this unscathed.

I tiptoed into his study to look at the grandfather clock just inside the door and gasped. It was already ten o'clock–far past the time I was expected to report for duty in the kitchen.

My frantic escape was interrupted by a piece of parchment stuck to the warm wood of the door.

Take the morning off and get settled in. I've already alerted the kitchens. Georgette will help you find your new chambers.

-E

So he had come back into his rooms. Or had asked a servant to place this where I would find it. I didn't know which was more mortifying.

I snatched the note off the door, tucking it away in the pocket of my skirt, and checked to make sure the hallway was empty before hurrying to the stairwell.

Sticking to the servant's passages, I made it down to the main floor and opened the door into the grand foyer. Because the kitchen had its own entrance, I hadn't seen it since the first day I arrived, and it was just as breathtaking the second time. An oil painting on the west wall caught my eye. A swath of grassy plain stretched across the canvas, the picture of serenity. In the distance was a small cottage and a windmill, framed against the soft pinks and oranges of the setting sun. Something about it filled my heart with quiet longing.

"Can I help you?" came a voice from behind me.

I swung around, embarrassed, to find a chambermaid waiting expectantly for my answer.

"Do you happen to know where I can find Georgette?"

The woman cocked her head as if she wasn't sure what to make of me.

"I can take you to her. She's usually in the greenhouses at this time of day."

The chambermaid led me to the most breathtaking garden I had ever seen. The entrance connected to the castle via a huge dome of paneled glass, under which thousands of vibrant blooms were nestled, spilling out the other side and into the sunshine.

It had an air of being unplanned, wild flowers dancing whimsically along the paths, but was so pristine that I knew a great deal of work must go into tending it. I couldn't believe I had never been here before. Had Colette seen this? She would adore the whimsical foxgloves swaying in the wind, the sweet scent of jasmine climbing up the walls, and the sea of colorful aster surrounding the marble fountain in the center.

We found Georgette a slender, elegant-looking woman in her mid-sixties snipping some yellow roses from a bush. Every grey hair on her head was immaculately placed, and the color only served to make her look more distinguished.

She glanced up from her work, looking me up and down with a critical eye.

"You must be Ms. Parry."

"I am," I confirmed, schooling myself into stillness. I had a feeling squirming under this woman's gaze would not endear me to her, so I resisted the urge to flatten my curls or run my hands over the creases in my clothing. After the events of last night, I must look atrocious.

"Follow me," she ordered. Taking care to ensure I didn't track mud into the castle, I trailed after her into the foyer. She led me up the main steps, but instead of turning to enter the servant's stairwell, we made our way up to the third floor–another space I'd never seen.

The long hallway was lined with dozens of beautifully-carved double doors. Between each set was a burgundy velvet bench, and miniature versions of the chandelier from the grand entrance hung about every fifteen feet. Why were we here?

Georgette stopped two-thirds of the way down the hallway. She stood in front of a set of doors on the right and pursed her lips.

"It would seem that these are your new accommodations, Ms. Parry."

I stared at the fleur-de-lis chiseled into the doors in front of me and fought to make sense of her words.

"I don't understand. We should be below the main floor. Isn't that where servants are housed?"

"Apparently not all of them," she said curtly, opening the doors and striding into the giant, sun-drenched room. Along the northern wall was a massive four-poster bed adorned with a canopy of the softest pink satin. A tufted sofa sat at its foot, and the floor was covered with a massive Gondorean rug. On the eastern side, there was a carved writing desk with a chair and a small pianoforte. I even spotted a door to what looked like a private washroom.

"I'm so sorry," I hesitated, looking at Georgette apologetically. "I think we're in the wrong place."

She dragged her gaze from my head to my toes and I prayed I'd managed to wipe all the mud off my boots.

"You are Quinn Parry?" she asked, with an air of tremendous exasperation.

"Yes."

"And we are on the third floor, are we not?"

"We are."

"Then we are in the right place," she huffed. "For reasons unbeknownst to me, the crown prince has seen fit to house you with the ladies of the royal competition. I am not one to question our future sovereign, but I will issue you a warning." Her steely eyes filled with suspicion and something that looked a lot like malice. "Do not mistake this for anything other than a show of our good prince's generosity and kindness toward his subjects. Put any designs you may have on him out of your mind. There is far more at play here than you know."

"Oh, I wouldn't ever–"

"Good." Without another word, she strode out of the room.

After hearing the door click shut, I turned around slowly, taking in my surroundings.

The coverlet on the bed was the same pale pink satin as the canopy, embellished with beads and tassels, and silk sheets lay underneath.

My fingers danced over the keys of the piano, plinking out a few sparkling notes. While I'd never learned to play, even I could tell it was a fine instrument.

I walked over to the desk and found a large envelope with my name written on the front.

Inside were four pieces of parchment, which I extracted as carefully as possible. It was sheet music. Reading the title, I let out a shaky breath.

"The Ballad of Brynne."

After an all-too-brief inspection of my new accommodations, I made my way back to the kitchen in a daze. It was the middle of the lunch prep chaos, but I needed to talk to Mellie.

I found her working on a batch of Monte Cristo sandwiches modified with a bit of Maddreccian flair. The scent of thyme and lemon wafted through the air, calming my heart.

"May I speak to you, Mellie?"

"One moment, Dumpling. I've just got to finish assembling these–" turning to face me as she worked, her hands stilled as she saw took in my appearance. I could only imagine what I looked like, still in yesterday's clothes and with a bruise blooming under my right eye.

"Franc!" Mellie yelled back without breaking eye contact with me. "Take over here, please."

Mellie grabbed my hand and led me to her quarters, closing the door behind us once again. Once inside, I sat down on her bed, running my hand over the quilt.

"Quinn, what happened?" My friend's eyes were wide with worry.

All the tears I had been keeping at bay released at once, and I was suddenly wracked with sobs, my nose running and breath shuddering in my chest with each inhale. Mellie sat down next to me and wrapped an arm around my shoulders, waiting until I was able to overcome the vice-like grip of my grief and distress.

Then I told her everything: my unlikely friendship with Evander, my fight with my mother, being kicked out of the cottage, and the room Georgette had led me to this morning. I left out the part about where I had slept last night, letting her believe I wound up on the third floor earlier than I had. That part of the story was still too much for me to face.

"Oh, Dumpling," Mellie comforted, draping an arm around my shoulder. "I'm so sorry."

And that was that. She would've been within her rights to say "I told you so," or to warn me about how foolish my actions had been, but she just sat with me, not trying to fix or diminish the experience.

I cried until there were no tears left and was about to straighten myself up so I could get back to work when James came skittering into the room.

"Permelia," he bleated, "you need to come now! Something's wrong with Serena."

We rushed back to the kitchen and found her bent over the counter, breathing rapidly. She vomited into the sink and crashed to the floor.

"Serena! What happened?"

"I don't know. I don't know," she repeated, clutching her head. "I was working on my mousse and got hungry, so I grabbed one of those cookies and started feeling strange. I'm lightheaded and nauseous . . . something's wrong, James." She clutched his hand.

"Who made these cookies?" Mellie asked, picking up the tray carefully. There were only about a dozen, and I didn't recognize the serveware.

No one answered.

"Does anyone know where they came from?" she tried again. We all shook our heads.

I picked up one of the cookies and sniffed. It smelled like browned butter and amaretto.

"We need to send these to Maddox immediately," Mellie said.

Walking over to Serena, I crouched down to where she was slumped against the lower cabinets.

"How much did you eat, Serena?"

"I don't know. Half of one? I got distracted because I thought my chocolate was burning." She pulled the half-eaten cookie out of her apron pocket, and I carefully set it on the counter.

"We need to get you to the healer," I said. "These were laced with something."

James paled. "Laced with something? How do you know?"

"I read a book where a character was poisoned with ground peach seeds," I explained. "It said they smelled like almonds."

"We're basing this on a *book?*" he asked warily.

"Obviously I don't know for certain, but the healer should be able to figure out what it is. But we need to act quickly. Serena, can you walk?"

She shook her head dismally and I knew how hard it must've been for her to admit her helplessness.

"James, you take her right side. Franc, take the left. I'm coming with you to the infirmary to let the healer know my suspicions." On our way out the door, I grabbed the half-eaten cookie and wrapped it in a napkin.

Mellie was frozen in place, her hand over her mouth in a mute gasp.

"Where were the trays on this table headed?" I asked her.

"The ballroom," she whispered.

A few hours later, Serena was sleeping soundly in the infirmary. The healer had confirmed my theory and provided an antidote quickly enough that Serena wouldn't have any lasting effects on her health, but it could've been so much worse.

Something like this didn't happen by accident. Someone was targeting the contestants . . . but why? Whoever it was didn't want this competition to continue, that much was certain. Could it be possible that Falerin was behind it? News of the contest hadn't been made public, so I don't know how they would have found out across the border.

I puzzled over it as I rolled out my dough later that night. It was late, and again I was the only one in the kitchen. While I'd told Mellie I needed some time to catch up from this morning and afternoon, I really just needed to keep my hands busy. What happened to Serena had shaken everyone in the kitchen, and I knew the Crown had been made aware as well. Mellie had already taken the cookies to Maddox by the time I had returned from the infirmary.

A small voice in the back of my mind whispered that I was also avoiding returning to my room, which I knew I needed to do eventually. There were just too many unanswered questions for me to face right now.

So for now, I would bake.

I had just popped the tart crusts in the oven when I heard a noise by the door; Evander was leaning against the frame with my rucksack hanging from two fingers.

"You left this last night," he said. "I tried to bring it to your room, but you weren't there."

"You didn't need to come all the way down here. You could've left it there."

He sighed. "I suppose I could've. As it turns out, I'm horrible at keeping my distance from you." Something in my chest fluttered at the words, and I tried to tamp it down.

He advanced, coming all the way around the island to hand me my bag.

"How are you holding up?" he asked, his voice raw and full of concern.

"All right," I lied. "The healer said Serena's going to be okay."

"I heard we have you to thank for that," he said, keeping his voice low.

"Who would've thought that reading so many books would actually help save someone's life one day?" I offered a watery smile.

Do not cry, I warned myself. *Do not cry right now.*

My useless eyes didn't seem to get the memo, and silent tears started rolling down my face.

Evander reached up to swipe them away, his hand lingering on my face. His next words were quiet, as if he were afraid of frightening me away.

"When I heard that it was a baker that had been poisoned, I was terrified it was you. It took everything in me to stay and hear the rest of the information instead of bolting right here to you. When they told me about a redheaded colleague who identified the poison and brought the affected girl to the healer, I nearly fell to my knees in relief."

He was still cradling my face, and his eyes flicked down to my mouth for a split second, his gaze darkening.

"Evander, you can't say things like that." My voice came out breathless and shaky.

"Because you don't want me to?" He shifted a few inches closer and my skin felt like it was going to catch fire.

"No, but–"

"Tell me you don't want this." He searched my eyes for an answer he didn't want to find.

"I can't."

He leaned forward, the gold flecks in his eyes sparkling as his lips barely brushed against mine, asking the question again.

No more lying. I had no fight left in me. Even if we couldn't have tomorrow, we could have this moment.

My lips met his with my answer, and the way he captured my mouth was all protection and possession, like a light went on in some dark corner of his soul long abandoned. He poured reverence into every movement of his lips against mine and it felt *delicious.* I tilted my head to deepen the kiss and ripped a low groan from his throat.

Something shifted and our movements became frantic. His hands left my face to slip under my thighs as he hoisted me onto the counter. I lost all capability of rational thought at the first stroke of his tongue behind my teeth. Only a small whimper escaped my throat. I had no idea a kiss could feel so good. So *right,* even when it was most assuredly wrong.

His hands traveled back up my body as if memorizing every curve, ending their pilgrimage in my hair. He found the leather tie I used to bind my braid and unraveled it, plunging his hand into my hair at the base of my newly freed waves.

When I pressed my body flush to his, needing him closer, needing *more,* I found him already hard underneath his trousers.

"Gods, Quinn." His voice vibrated against my lips as my hands tangled in his hair. The smell of parchment, ink, and leather was a heady cocktail that dared me to take what I wanted without considering what came next. But there was something else too. Something . . . smoky?

Shit.

I broke the kiss, mourning it already as confusion bloomed in his eyes, and hopped off the counter, racing to the oven. By the time I yanked out the tray of tart crusts with the push-pull, they were already blackened to a crisp. I stood there, facing the oven, breathing heavily for what felt like an eternity, too terrified to turn back to face him.

"Quinn," he called, his voice still heavy and full of desire.

If I turned around, I wasn't sure what I would do. I didn't know if I had the self-control to stop whatever would come next, and it would only hurt us both.

Ignoring every muscle in my body that begged me to stay, I did the only thing I could think to do at that moment and bolted for the door.

Chapter 12

Desperate to have some space to sort myself out, I hurried down the hall of the guest quarters on the third floor.

What did I just do? The slimy feeling of guilt had taken up residence in my chest, unpacking as if it planned to stay there for the foreseeable future. I kept searching for the regret that I thought would inevitably join it, but it was nowhere to be found.

Which is part of the problem, I reminded myself.

I wrenched open the gold handle of the door on the right and took a step inside before freezing. The layout was similar, but this was undoubtedly not my room. Colette and Vanessa sat on the settee at the end of the bed, an emerald green instead of the pink in my quarters, their heads together bent over a book.

Vanessa looked up first; her eyes flared in alarm but simmered down to annoyance when she took in my form.

Colette had no reservations as she jumped up and ran over to embrace me.

"Quinn! Hi!"

My arms felt heavy as I hugged her back, mortified that I had just burst into one of their rooms unannounced.

"Don't take this the wrong way: it's so good to see you, but what are you doing here?" she asked.

"I–um–wrong door . . ." I stuttered. "I must've counted wrong. This hallway is so long and everything looks basically the same." *Great, now I was rambling.*

"Were you looking for another contestant? We know where everybody is so we can point you in the right direction!" She beamed back at Vanessa.

"Actually, um . . ." How could I phrase this without it sounding ridiculous? "I was looking for my room. I moved up here this morning." No other information that might help my case presented itself, so I left it at that.

Vanessa's eyebrows shot up to her hairline and she rose and stalked over to join us.

"Seems like a strange place for a baker to be housed," she observed. Colette elbowed her sharply in the side. "No offense meant," she added begrudgingly. "I just thought everyone who worked here was down on the kitchen level."

"So did I. To be honest, I'm not sure why I'm here. Evander–" I froze as I caught my mistake but couldn't figure out how to recover the rest of my sentence.

Now it was Colette's turn to gawk at me. She hurried over to the door, which I had left slightly ajar, and shut it behind her.

"Evander?" Vanessa said, one eyebrow still cocked. "I've known the man since I was in diapers and I can count on one hand the people he allows to call him that."

And here I was thinking I couldn't mess up this situation further, I thought dryly.

Colette took my hand and led me to the four poster bed, sitting criss-cross atop the satin coverlet and patting the spot next to her.

"It's . . . complicated?" I winced. I was beginning to hate that word.

But what else was I supposed to say? "*Oh, by the way, I just kissed the man you're all competing to marry and then ran away because I have no self-control and I would've gone a lot further if I hadn't been saved by my own godsdamned tarts*"?

I was sure that wouldn't go over well.

I buried my face in my hands, both in frustration and to hide the blush that crept into my cheeks at the memory of what just occurred.

Vanessa didn't waste any time. "How long have you been sleeping with him?"

"Oh my gods, *Nessa!*" Colette shrieked, giggling, at the same time as I blurted "No, no, I swear! I would never!" *(Lies. I would.)* "He's the prince, and I'm a baker, and you're–"

"Oh gods," Vanessa said, rolling her eyes, "That's so much worse. You're besotted."

"You don't hate me?"

"Why would we hate you?" Colette asked, her eyebrows furrowed.

"Since you're all competing to marry him, I thought–"

"Evander is like my brother," Vanessa cringed, shaking her shoulders to rid herself of the phantom germs. "I'm here because my mother says I'm required to be, but he and I both know there's no way in hells that would ever work."

I turned to Colette, who shrugged her shoulders noncommittally. "Between you and me, I'm just staying for the tarts." She winked conspiratorially, making me laugh.

"Sooooo . . .?" she prompted.

"He kissed me." I covered my face again.

Colette squealed.

"He kissed me and I didn't stop him," *that was putting it mildly,* "and that can't happen because . . . well, obviously." I grabbed one of the brocade pillows and pulled it tightly into my chest as if I could squeeze out all the confusion I was feeling.

"You're not a Wielder," Colette pouted, disappointed for me.

"*His Royal Highness*," Vanessa cut in, using the title as if it were some kind of joke, "has never given a shit about that."

"But the Crown does," I said, thinking of the prophecy.

"What are you going to do?" Colette asked.

"Do?" My head snapped up and I'm sure my confusion was plain on my face. "Nothing. Even if I wanted to, there's nothing I could do about it." I released the pillow and let it fall into my lap sadly.

No, I am not going to mope over this. Mourning means acknowledging something's happening, which I absolutely refused to do.

"It's nothing. Just a stupid, one-time mistake. It won't happen again," I finished, forcing flippancy into my tone and throwing in a shrug for good measure.

"Sure." Vanessa rolled her eyes again.

We lapsed into an embarrassing silence as Colette looked at me with wide, compassionate eyes and Vanessa smirked to herself.

"Anyway," I forced a change of subject, "I was just trying to find my room. Seven doors down on the right?"

"That means you and Nessa are neighbors!" Colette squealed.

I smiled halfheartedly at Vanessa.

"I'm only up here for the duration of the contest," she clarified. "Then I'll be down in the barracks again."

"But that's not for two more months!" Colette grabbed my hand and squeezed. "We're going to have so much FUN!"

I couldn't help but smile at her enthusiasm. It would be nice to have friends to talk to about this. Well, a friend and a . . . Vanessa.

In my actual room, I found a set of cotton nightclothes waiting for me in the armoire. Too exhausted to even bathe, I slipped into the silky sheets and gave into sleep.

Chapter 13

THE DAYS PASSED IN a blur of baking, helping Colette train, and dutifully ignoring all of my feelings about what had happened with Evander in the kitchen. He had sent a summons for me twice in a week, and I had flat out ignored both of them.

There wasn't anything I could say that would make the situation better, especially when I wasn't sure what I'd do if I found myself in the same position again. Though I'd like to think I wouldn't let it get that far, the pull toward him that night had been so strong that it felt like I was powerless against it. It was hard to regret something that had felt so perfect.

"Hellloooooo? Quinn?" Colette broke me out of my thought spiral.

I forced my glazed eyes to push the world back into focus. "Sorry, Colette. One more time."

She let out an exasperated sigh, but I knew from her gentle nudge at my side she wasn't really mad. Her impish smile told me she knew exactly where my mind had been.

"Again?" she asked.

"I'm sorry," I started.

"I meant the exercise," she laughed. "But that too."

"Oh. Of course." I picked up one of the leather balls we had been using and lobbed it at her. A flowering vine darted out and batted it away harmlessly.

"You're getting faster," I observed, and Colette beamed.

Most afternoons were spent helping her practice her green-Wielding skills. I had stopped manning the refreshment table days ago. No one ever ate from it anyway, and half the time it was just the three of us in the ballroom in the afternoons. Mellie kept insisting I come up on serving duty, but I wasn't entirely sure it wasn't just because she was so thrilled to see me making friends.

Vanessa strode over, three muffins held out in her right hand.

I was fairly certain I wasn't supposed to eat these, but I had made them myself and ego aside, they were *really good.*

When I bit into the pastry, a warm blueberry burst in my mouth. The streusel on top complemented the tart fruit perfectly.

"Thank you," I muttered around my mouthful of food.

"Well, someone's got to serve the food around here," she deadpanned.

"Oh yes. Thank you so much for taking time out of your busy *practicing schedule*," I quipped back.

She grinned at me, wide and unguarded.

Ever since I'd moved up to the third floor, Vanessa had become surprisingly tolerant of me. There was still a fair amount of eye rolling and sarcastic one-liners, but they were friendly. It felt less like I was being sized up at all times and more like I was in on the joke.

After polishing off her muffin in a few dainty bites, Colette brushed her hands on her skirt. "Word on the third floor is that they're designing a specific test for each of us."

Vanessa nodded in confirmation. "I've seen at least half a dozen closed-off rooms between the guest wing and here, and I'm willing to bet there are more," Vanessa said. "One for each contestant if I had to guess. I've asked, but my mother won't tell me anything. Honor and equity and all that," she huffed.

"Are you nervous?" I asked.

"A little," Colette said. "I've been working hard, and I doubt they'd put us in a situation that was genuinely dangerous, but . . ." she trailed off.

"Will all the trials all be held at once?" I asked. "Or are they staggering the times so the prince can attend them all?" I hoped Evander would take my suggestion and try casting with each Wielder to see how his Gift responded. I wanted him to find the right person to save his mother, even if I was ignoring the implications of what would happen after that. The idea of baking a cake for his wedding was like poison in my stomach.

"Nobody will tell us anything," Vanessa complained. "At some point they're going to have to let us know where to report, right?"

I shrugged and grabbed another of the leather balls off the table.

"Ready?" I asked Colette.

She groaned but took fifteen paces toward the center of the room and raised her arms in a defensive position.

"Let's go again."

It was my turn on the cleanup rotation that night. I stood in front of the washing station, my arms braced on the apron front sink, and hinged my hips backward to try to release some of the tension in my lower back. I was used to the physically demanding work of the kitchen, but adding training in the middle of the day had my body groaning in protest.

Still, the dishes needed to be done, and the sooner I did them, the sooner I could go back up to my room and collapse into my bed, which,

I had to admit, was probably the most comfortable thing I had ever slept on.

"Need some help?" Mellie's familiar warm voice came from behind me.

I waved her off. "Go rest, Mels. I've got this under control. Just taking a minute to breathe."

"You look exhausted," she said, looking at my wan complexion. "No offense dear, but I've seen more color than that on a raw turkey."

I laughed as she nudged me over to one side and we began to work in tandem. A few minutes passed in comfortable silence, the only sounds the clinking of plates and running water.

"Something going on, Dumpling?" Mellie asked after a while.

"Just tired." I smiled at her. I didn't like this version of me that lied so easily to my oldest friend, but if I started to think about it too hard, the carefully fastened armor I had erected around my heart would come clattering down, and I wasn't sure if I had the energy to build it back up again.

Still, Mellie's company was always a balm for my soul, and when we finished the cleanup early, I found I wasn't ready to be alone again yet. Colette and Vanessa had plans, so I invited Mellie up to my room for a cup of tea.

We trekked up together, and while my friend arrived on the third floor with her floral-pattern cup still full of steaming chamomile, I had managed to slosh mine all over the stairs no fewer than three times. Somehow, I avoided spilling on myself, which was lucky, as I was too tired to change.

I strode into the room and set my cup on the writing desk.

When I turned around, Mellie was gaping like a fish as she took in the room around her.

"Quinny, this is . . ." she spun around slowly, her eyes lingering on the ornate detailing of the millwork, the linens that looked as if they cost more than what I would make in a month, and the piano in the corner.

"I know," I sighed.

"But why?" She eyed me suspiciously. Mellie had always been a little too good at sniffing out when I was keeping something from her.

"Do I have to answer that?" My face contorted into a grimace.

She tilted her head to the side, trying to read my expression, and crossed over to me, taking my hands in hers.

"What aren't you telling me, Dumpling?"

Sure my voice would betray me, I shook my head at her. She pulled me into a firm hug.

"It's not my place to tell you how to live your life, Quinn, but please be careful. I don't want to see you get hurt."

Too late for that.

"I just need a distraction right now, Mels," I said.

Taking a brisk step back, she wiped her hands on her apron.

"That I can do." She strode over to the piano and sighed wistfully, running her fingers over the ivory keys. "This is beautiful. I used to play when I was a girl."

"Do you still remember how?" I asked, thinking of the sheet music that I had yet to attempt.

"A little," she said, sitting down on the bench. She scooted all the way to the left and patted the spot next to her. It was a tight fit with us both there, but the closeness made me smile.

"This is middle C," she said, tapping a key in the center a few times. It was loud. I looked toward the door, hoping we weren't disturbing anyone. It wasn't quite nine, but still.

"Don't worry, Dumpling," she waved toward the door. "All of the rooms are sound-warded."

My shoulders relaxed. I might've tried this earlier if I had known that. Then again, my shifts were ending so late these days that by the time I made it back I was either pulled into Vanessa's room by Colette for what she called "girl time," or too exhausted to do anything more than bathe, change into my nightclothes, and collapse into bed.

Mellie explained the rest of the notes to me, plinking out a melody with her right hand while she played basic chords with the left. My hands refused to work independently the way hers could, but we laughed at my mistakes and she encouraged me to keep trying.

"You'll get it," she promised. "It's mostly muscle memory."

I made another clumsy attempt, but the noises I coaxed out of the piano sounded more like an armful of pots being dropped down the stairs than actual music.

"This could be good for you, Quinn," Mellie said, squeezing my shoulder. "I'd love for you to have some hobbies outside the kitchen, especially when this contest is over and your friend leaves. It's certainly less destructive than," she raised her eyebrows knowingly, "whatever else you've been spending your time doing that has you so exhausted."

"I'm just helping Colette train, Mels." I rolled my eyes. "That, and shifts have been so long lately. I'm just a little extra tired."

"I know, Dumpling," she conceded, patting my leg. "I'm sorry I have you working so hard. It's not always this busy. As soon as the contest ends," she promised, "things will slow down."

As soon as the contest ends, Evander will be married, I thought bitterly. *I think I'd take the long shifts.*

Mellie rose from the bench. "You're right, though. Some rest would be good for you," she said. "I'll see you in the morning?"

I nodded and hugged her goodbye, then sat on the edge of my bed. I knew I should rest, but something told me I wouldn't be able to sleep even if I tried. Instead, I got up and padded to the other side of the room, removing the sheet music from its hiding place and setting it on the music rack of the piano.

In between the lines on the staff, Evander had scrolled "FACE" to indicate the notes. I chuckled quietly, and began writing the letter for each below the staff. After the first few bars, I found that I could predict where the next note would be because I knew the song.

I worked at it for hours, ignoring bed in favor of this simple, rewarding distraction. It took complete concentration to learn the new skill, meaning there was no room for thoughts of the contest, or Evander, or my mother. Every time I mastered a new section, I found myself smiling.

As the final note rang out into my empty room, a lump formed in my throat and I found that my eyes were misty. I closed the lid of the piano and slept soundly all night.

Despite my emotional turmoil, my routine remained much the same: my morning work in the kitchen was always followed by breakfast with James and his friends before I reported for serving duty in the ballroom.

One night after a particularly grueling day of training, Vanessa swiped a bottle of wine from the barracks and the three of us drank the whole thing, laughing until we cried at Colette's impression of General Finch.

"Be ready . . . for *anything*." She wiggled her fingers at us menacingly before dissolving into a fit of giggles.

"Seriously, though," she said, wiping her eyes, "what do you think they have in store for us?"

"I'm the wrong person to ask," I shrugged, looking at Vanessa.

"The prince didn't tell you anything?" Colette pressed.

"I haven't spoken to him since–well, you know . . ."

Colette reacted as if I had told her I was planning to lace my next batch of cinnamon rolls with azcaltan pepper. Her delicate mouth formed a comically large O and she made several strangled-sounding attempts at responding before she finally got a sentence out.

"You haven't talked to him? At all?" she gaped.

"It's what's best for both of us," I said, pulling my arms across my chest. "He needs to find a wife with magic who can shoulder the other half of the crown, and I need to . . . bake," I finished lamely.

"That's the dumbest shit I've ever heard in my life," Vanessa said.

I groaned, frustrated, rubbing my face. "I just don't want to talk about it, all right?"

Vanessa took my glass and refilled it with another generous pour of wine.

"Whatever you say," she conceded, offering it to me.

The sip I took was slightly too long to be casual.

Lowering the glass from my lips, I steered the conversation back to our earlier jibing. "What's with the constant snow that follows him around? Isn't he cold?"

To my extreme gratitude, Colette took the hint and picked up where we had left off, putting the uncomfortable topic behind us.

The day before the second trial, I reported to the ballroom only to find it empty.

Maybe they're taking today off to rest before the event, I told myself. Still, Colette would have told me as much when we saw each other last night.

Abandoning my post, I made the trek up to the third floor to knock on her door. I hadn't been in Colette's room very many times, as we usually met in Vanessa's chambers, but I was fairly sure this was the one. Vanessa opened the door, slipping out into the hallway and closing it quietly behind her.

"She's panicking," she said. "She's convinced she's going to fail and get sent home tomorrow."

"That's ridiculous!" I argued. "Colette's worked harder than anyone here and her magic has evolved so much."

"I know that, and you know that," Vanessa said, "but Colette doesn't. She won't listen to me either. Go ahead and try your hand if you want," she offered, gesturing toward the door.

I stepped around her, reaching for the handle, when something occurred to me.

"Vanessa, why does she want to stay so badly?" I asked. "As far as I know, she's not interested in Evander . . ." *Unless that had changed?*

"She has her reasons." Vanessa's glare was icy. "Don't worry, she's not trying to steal your boyfriend." Another eye roll.

"He's not–" I shook my head rapidly, reminding myself to stay on task. This was about Colette. Turning the handle, I crept into the room.

"Hey," I said softly.

Colette sat slumped on her bed, a mess of tears and snot, her warm brown eyes bloodshot. She looked at me and blew her nose into a tissue with a deafening honk.

"What's going on?" I asked, joining her on the bed.

"They're going to send me home."

"No they're not." As I patted her back, I wondered how she could possibly think that was true.

"I've been trying so hard, but I'm still not good enough. I've just been sharpening random skills that might have some practical application, but I have no idea what to expect." She burst into quiet sobs again, wiping her nose with the back of her hand.

"Colette, are things bad at home?" I asked, as gently as I could. "Because if you're really that worried about returning, I'm sure Evander could find a place for you here, even if you don't move forward in the competition."

"No, it's not that." She buried her head in her hands, muffling her next words. "I just–I need to be here."

I still didn't understand, but she clearly didn't want to discuss it, so, returning her earlier kindness, I didn't press the issue. As I sat with her, hoping my presence might somehow soften her panic, a semblance of an idea started to form in my head.

"Colette," I asked tentatively, "would you feel better if you had an idea of what you're going into?"

She nodded emphatically. "What I'm most scared of is being so surprised that I just freeze up and don't do anything at all," she sniffled.

"All right," I said, rubbing my hands on my thighs. "I can work with that."

Colette cocked her head inquisitively.

"Hold on. I'm going to try to get some answers for you."

"The prince?" she asked.

"No, no." I shook my head. "I'm just going to poke around some of the rooms they've sectioned off. A servant shouldn't draw too much notice and I'm still new enough here that I can always pretend I'm lost if someone questions me."

Colette threw her arms around me and squeezed. I embraced her back, hoping this would be as simple as it sounded.

The hallways seemed to stretch to twice their normal length in the eerie shadows of the night. Every time I heard footsteps, I suppressed the urge to jump behind the nearest planter. There was nothing amiss about a servant walking through the hallway, and it would only serve to make me look more suspicious. Confidence was what I needed right now.

This wasn't even the difficult part.

Following Vanessa's direction toward the highest concentration of testing rooms, I found myself on the west wing of the second floor.

The corridor was eerily quiet; there didn't appear to be so much as a single security guard to keep the testing conditions a secret.

I approached the first door adorned with a sign reading *"KEEP OUT: Contest preparations in progress."*

Unlike the invisible wards around the castle, I could see the magical barrier they had placed around the entrance of the room. If I squinted, I could make out a slight blue-grey shimmering net strung between the sides of the door jam.

Shit. Not as easy as I'd hoped it would be.

I reached for the gold handle, expecting to be bounced back. To my surprise, my hand passed right through the ward and made contact with the cool metal. Gripping the lever, I twisted my wrist and pushed the door open.

Hmmm. Maybe it's keyed to the contestants?

I slipped into the room and shut the door behind me. The space had been rearranged for the task, heavy wooden furniture dragged towards the walls. In the center of the room was a clear box, perhaps eight feet in height and three feet across.

Keeping my footsteps light, I crept up to it and touched the glass to see if anything would happen. If every testing room were different, I could see this one being for Colette. Some type of greenhouse?

The surface was smooth and cold and didn't respond to my touch. I circled it once, looking for a switch or a lever.

When I pressed the right side of the front panel, it depressed slightly before springing open like a door hinged on the left, though there was no hardware.

Maybe you had to get in the box to figure out how it worked?

I took a tentative step in and waited, but again, nothing happened. When it felt safe, I brought my other foot inside the box and started feeling the walls for another push point.

Suddenly, the door I had come through snapped shut behind me.

Don't panic, I thought. *If it works the same inside as out, I only need to find the right spot to press.*

Then the tank started filling with water.

Shit. Shit shit shit shit.

The frigid water rose up to my ankles, though I couldn't see where it was coming from. There didn't seem to be a tap, but it continued to rise as if seeping in through the floor.

My hands shook as I searched for an entry point I could block and found nothing. I tried to keep my mind sharp even as my panic rose in tandem with the water; losing my faculties would make this situation even worse.

All right, I coached myself, *it makes sense to start from the bottom up while I can still reach the floor without submerging my head in the water.* It was now up to my knees. I pushed against every surface I could reach but didn't feel so much as a tiny budge.

No wonder Colette had been so nervous. What kind of sick, sadistic test was this? It clearly wasn't designed for a green-Wielder. Whose Gift would help in here? If I could figure that out, maybe I could find a way to mimic it non-magically.

I continued my assault on the glass, the water now reaching my chest. Gods, it was cold. Despite my best efforts, the terror started to creep in. If the aim was for this to fill the entire tank, I was going to drown.

The liquid reached my neck and I kicked, using the water below me to reach the top corners, the only places I hadn't tried yet.

Please, please, please.

As it lapped at my throat, I pressed my face into the top panel of glass, trying to take in as much air as I could before diving down to where I had opened the door.

Though I had never been the religious type, I prayed to every god I had ever heard of as I started banging my fists against the glass. The water slowed the momentum of my fists, turning my desperate efforts to free myself into something like a toddler throwing a tantrum.

My lungs started to burn. I wouldn't be able to hold out much longer.

I will come to your temple every week if you get me out of here, I promised no god in particular.

The edges of my vision began to go dark and I felt my lungs seize up. I closed my eyes and prepared for the water to flood into my airways. This was it. I was going to die in this room.

A pantomime of a life full of lukewarm choices flashed before my eyes. I'd been angry about so many things, but what progress had I really made? In the end, did my paltry rebellion against my mother amount to anything other than a thinly-veiled attempt to feel as if I was doing something to control the trajectory of my life?

As my body fought the inevitable, I remembered all of the kindness Mellie had shown me, and how heartbroken she would be when I was gone. I prayed Colette wouldn't blame herself for this, her sweet, innocent soul marked by the shadow of my death forever. Then, in the final moment before my lungs gave out, I thought of Evander.

Faced with the end of my life, I finally allowed myself to experience the full force of how I felt about him. I had tried again and again to tell myself that my emotions were complicated, but in truth, there was only longing. Longing, and love I had tried so foolishly to fight. Though I couldn't feel the tears on my face under the water, I was certain I was weeping.

No longer able to help myself, my burning lungs desperate for air I knew I would not find in the tank, my mouth flew open.

Then, two things my panicked brain couldn't make sense of happened in rapid succession: First, Evander burst through the door, as if I had summoned him with my thoughts. Panic in his eyes, he ran up to the glass, drawing his fist back like he meant to punch it open from the outside.

Second, I took a breath.

Evander's fist made contact with the glass and it spiderwebbed rapidly before shattering into thousands of tiny pieces.

What the hells just happened?

The water flooded the room and I fell to the ground in the remains of the tank, glass cutting up my hands and legs as I sputtered and began to sob.

Evander knelt beside me, grabbing my arms to lift me to standing. Blood dripped from his knuckles.

My knees buckled beneath me again at the sight, my frantic mind trying to find some logical explanation for what had happened.

I could've died. I should've died.

"What in the hells were you doing, Quinn?" he shook me by my shoulders, eyes frantically searching my own. His expression was pure panic.

"I-I'm sorry-" the tears came heavier now. Shock, I imagined.

"Sorry? No, Quinn, no. Shhhh." His brows creased in concern and he pulled me in close, rubbing calming circles on my back, his lips pressed into my hair. I melted into his embrace, allowing myself comfort in the wake of the trauma I had just experienced.

A whisper, so soft I barely heard it, ghosted the top of my head. "I almost lost you."

Evander said it with real fear in his voice, and when I looked up at his face, his eyes were wide with fear under his dark lashes.

He was drenched from head to toe, the fabric of his shirt and trousers cut in many places from the force of the glass breaking outward. The blood on his knuckles had crusted over shockingly fast. I pulled our joined hands toward me, brushing over his wounds with my other thumb.

Catching my shaky hand and raising it to his lips, he pressed a soft kiss into my skin.

"I'm all right," I promised.

"But you almost weren't."

The truth of that statement was terrifying. I should be dead right now, and I had no explanation for why I had been spared.

"Something strange happened," I told him, fighting to breathe in and out. "I don't know if it was real or if my mind was beginning to shut down, but just as you arrived . . ." I paused, realizing I still didn't know how or why he had come. "Evander–Why are you here?"

"I honestly don't know," he said, shaking his head. The tiny movement sent droplets of water flying from his wet curls. "I was lying in bed thinking about the trial tomorrow and I couldn't sleep. All of a sudden I just felt this tug in my gut. I don't know how, but I knew something was wrong," he swallowed, "so I got up and followed it here."

All I could do was stare at him as I tried to puzzle it out. It was impossible.

"Quinn, I know you don't want to see me right now. I've been trying to respect that, but I just need you to know that if anything happened to you . . ." he trailed off, tightening his grip on my hand. "It would break me, Quinn."

There was a cut on his cheek from the glass of the tank, and I reached up to trace it with my fingers without realizing what I was doing. Blue eyes met hazel, our gazes full of anguish and fear and something else I had been ignoring for weeks, and that armor around my heart came clattering down.

I could've died. I could've died without having made any choices for myself, always too scared of pain and failure to take any real risks.

A breath passed this way before Evander pulled back slightly and I watched as he began to build the walls back up between us. I couldn't bear it. Not again. Not tonight.

Raising my other hand to the side of his face, I searched his eyes for any hesitation before bringing our lips together in a bruising kiss that said all of the things I couldn't.

He met me with equal fervor, plunging one hand into my drenched hair while the other found its way to my waist, pulling me even closer. The kiss was a living thing, and we both surrendered to it, breathless and desperate.

His hands were everywhere, dancing along my body as if they ached to touch every spot. They trailed up my sides and into my hair, his thumb brushing my face before he wrapped his arms around me again.

I melted into the embrace as he anchored me, offering me something solid, something real to distract from the terror.

"I'm sorry," I said, pulling back. "I know this isn't fair."

Evander's lips coasted along my jaw before he lifted his head to meet my eyes.

"Don't you dare apologize for this," he ordered, his voice low and gravelly. "Don't think for a second that I don't want this. Unless you change your mind, I need you to stop putting barriers up between us and just take what you want."

I nodded, and his lips crashed into mine again.

"Say the word and we stop," he said into my skin, but I didn't want to.

A moan rose in the back of my throat unbidden. The sound seemed to snap whatever self-control Evander had been holding onto, and he let go of me only long enough to pull his shirt over the top of his head and lift me, carrying us both over to a settee pushed up against the wall.

I swung one leg over to straddle him as my tongue slipped into his mouth. Who was this woman controlling my movements?

Evander had told me to take what I wanted and right now my body was screaming for *more, more, more.* The title, the competition, the crown, the magic all faded away and it was just *us,* drowning in the chemistry and want I had been so desperate to ignore.

Why? I thought fleetingly as I felt his hands grip my thighs. *Why would I ever deprive myself of this?*

Evander put one hand on my lower back and expertly rolled us over, his weight on top of mine a delicious sensation. I craved the feeling of his warm chest on my skin. As if he knew what I was thinking, he shifted back to give me space to remove my wet blouse. I threw the fabric on the floor and looked up at him.

The moonlight coming in from the window worshiped his torso, emphasizing his broad shoulders and the lines of his abdominals, the vee of his hip muscles disappearing into the trousers that I very much resented at the moment.

His eyes drank in my form at the same time I observed his, and he growled with approval, leaning down to kiss me again. I could feel the length of him pressed against me, and I guided his hand to my breast. His thumb circled my nipple lightly, making me shiver, before he replaced it with the heat of his mouth. When he flicked his tongue over the sensitive peak, I whimpered, my nails digging into the golden skin of his shoulders.

Chuckling lowly, he continued pressing open-mouthed kisses to my sternum, my chest, and up my neck.

Gods, I needed more. He nipped at my earlobe, toying with me.

"Evander, please," I breathed.

Lifting his head, he searched my face for a moment before closing his eyes and shifting back onto his knees, away from me.

"Quinn . . ." he started. "Gods, I can't believe I'm about to do this."

Do what? Had I done something wrong? I tried to keep the sting of rejection from showing on my face, but I must've failed, because he leaned in close to me, cradling my face.

"I want to be very clear with you. I would love nothing more than to give you anything and everything you want right now. To worship you the way you deserve and feel you clenching around me as you find your release." He steadied himself, taking a breath. "But you've just had quite a shock, and I wouldn't feel right capitalizing on the emotion of the moment without giving you some time to think this over first."

"Evander," I said, a hand moving up to touch his face. I wanted to tell him I was certain, so sure of what I wanted in this moment. It wasn't just adrenaline fueling my body. But I also knew he had a tendency to flagelate himself, and I couldn't bear the thought of him looking back on this moment and second-guessing anything.

His eyes closed again at the sound of his name. "Besides," he replied, "when I finally get to make love to you, I want to do it correctly, not on a tiny settee."

He flashed a devilish grin at me, and the last of my disappointment melted away at the sight. I ignored the part of me that warned that this may be our only chance, that things would feel much different in the light of day. Not yet. We could stay in this moment for a little while longer.

"Can we . . . can we just lie here for a while?" I asked.

His gaze softened as he shifted onto his side. "Of course. Anything you want."

I moved to make space on the cushions and he lay down next to me, pulling me over so my head rested on his chest and his arm around my shoulder kept me from falling off the seat.

The adrenaline was wearing off and my eyes felt heavy, my chest warm with the feeling of safety and complete satisfaction.

Evander stroked my hair as I fell asleep.

In that liminal space between sleeping and waking, I heard him mutter a reverent promise into my hair, but I was unconscious before I could process what he said.

The next morning I woke in Evander's arms. At some point in the night, he had taken the throw off the back of the settee and draped it over me, and now I snuggled into it, savoring the warmth for a moment before my brain woke up and my eyes flew open. Disbelief hit as I took in my surroundings. There was shattered glass all over the floor and standing water all over the expensive rugs. The pillows of the loveseat had been discarded onto the floor during our . . . activities.

A flush crept into my cheeks as I remembered everything I had done–and said–last night.

Oh gods. I squinted my eyes shut as tightly as I could. Was it possible to die of embarrassment?

I shifted as slowly as I could, careful not to wake Evander and speed up the uncomfortable conversation we were surely about to have.

He looked younger when he slept, the crease between his eyebrows softened and a serene expression on his face. It was impossible not to marvel at his beauty, a piece of his dark wavy hair falling onto his forehead, long, dark eyelashes kissing the tops of his cheeks, lips still a little bit swollen. The arm he had around my shoulder tightened in his sleep.

A small sigh escaped my lips. I could pretend to be asleep a little while longer. Trying to immortalize this moment, I let my eyes flutter closed and took a long, deep breath.

The peace only lasted a moment before my thoughts turned to last night. To that tank.

What the hells had they been thinking? What kind of test could justify locking a girl up in a magical aquarium of death?

The memory elicited an involuntary shudder. I had been sure I was going to drown, but at the last second, I could've sworn I took a breath. A full, regular breath. But there had been no air left in the tank.

Either one of the gods I had prayed to had taken pity on me, or my mind was distorting reality as I neared unconsciousness. If I had aspirated water, though, surely I would have known by now. I moved my hand up to touch my neck, feeling ridiculous as I searched for gills but found only smooth skin.

The movement must've woken Evander, because he opened his eyes, taking in our surroundings and beaming a groggy smile at me.

"Good morning." His voice was froggy with sleep. It was both adorable and, if I was being honest, incredibly arousing.

"Morning," I echoed, feeling sheepish. I took the blanket with me and pressed it against my chest as I sat up. My feet met water when they hit the ground.

"Did we sleep the entire night on the settee?" Evander asked, chuckling.

"It would appear so," I said, already dreading what I knew had to come next. "Evander, I am so, so sorry," I began, but he cut me off, raising an eyebrow.

"I seem to remember telling you to stop apologizing last night." My core turned molten at the memory. "Besides, I can't remember the last time I slept so well."

He pulled himself up to join me in a seated position and I kept my eyes carefully trained on the ceiling. Out of the corner of my eye I could see him pluck his shirt off the back of the settee and put it on.

There was no use delaying the inevitable, so I turned to face him.

"This can't happen again," I said, though my heart wept as I watched his beautiful face turn desolate. I would forever be thankful for the perfect night we had spent together, but I couldn't come between him and his kingdom.

"Don't say that."

"Evander . . ."

"I meant what I said last night. This isn't the end for us. Please, Quinn, before you box this up and pretend it didn't happen, give me some time. I'll find a loophole in the prophecy. There has to be something I've missed. Because this," he gestured between the two of us, "is the closest thing I can imagine to my magic singing. The pull I feel towards you, the way my magic seems to know when you're in danger . . . that's never happened before. It has to mean something."

Hope lit traitorously in my chest at his words.

"Your Gift . . ." I started, looking at the wreckage around us.

"Not much of a point keeping it a secret now, I suppose. My Gift is a sort of amplification," he said. "It usually manifests as enhanced strength."

That was putting it lightly. The man had punched through an inch-thick panel of glass. To get to me, I thought, heat creeping up the back of my neck.

"Mother found out when I ripped my crib in half after my nursemaid didn't come get me fast enough one morning," he said, chuckling. "It's useful in hand-to-hand combat but doesn't do me much good commanding an army." There was something maudlin in his tone that sounded a lot like disappointment.

"Evander, that's incredible. You realize that, don't you?" I pushed.

"The practical application isn't as great as you might think. I feel more powerless than I'd like to admit most days," he said.

"But," he added, raising my hand to his lips, "I was incredibly thankful for it last night."

"Thank you." No matter how much meaning and sincerity I tried to inject into my words, they still felt paltry in comparison to what he had done for me. Surveying the room again, I couldn't help but wince. I couldn't imagine what the cost of the damages would be.

"I *would* like to know what you were doing in here," he asked, turning serious.

"I was curious," I said, leaving Colette out of it, "about the contest. About what the challenges would be. But I had no idea . . ." My eyes pricked with tears thinking about how unprepared I had been.

Evander's eyes softened. Doing my best to hide my embarrassment, I turned away and tried to put myself back together. I scanned the room for my clothing and found it in a sopping pile at the base of the settee. Lifting my blouse between two fingers, I watched as it comically dripped water onto the floor.

"I don't think you can wear that out," he pointed out, one side of his mouth quirking upward.

A giggle bubbled up from my throat, so at odds with my surroundings that it only made me want to laugh harder.

"It looks like my clothing survived." He plucked his trousers off a nearby chair and stepped into them. Dumping water from one of his boots, he frowned. "Or rather . . . most of it."

Our eyes met and we dissolved into a fit of laughter that was decidedly inappropriate considering the damage we had caused.

"Let me get you something," he said, pulling on his wet boot to avoid the glass shards. He sloshed his way over to the remains of the tank, crouching down to inspect the base.

"Xavier's going to be furious," he sighed. "He worked on this for weeks. It was supposed to be for the shifter. Cora, I think?"

So I was onto something with the whole fish thing, I thought dryly.

"Again, I am so sorry," I repeated. I didn't know what else I could say to express the depth of guilt I felt.

"How did you get past the wards?" Evander asked, ignoring my apology.

"I don't know," I said, pulling the throw tighter around me. "I could see them around the door, but I was able to reach right through. Inadvisable, I know now," I clarified before he lectured me. "I assumed they were keyed to keep only the contestants out."

"It's possible, I suppose." He cocked his head, lost in thought. "I'll have Algernon check them all this afternoon. I don't want this happening to anyone else."

He trudged back through the water to kiss my forehead before heading to the door. Something in my chest warmed at the gesture and I found myself smiling like a schoolgirl.

"I'll be right back," he promised.

An hour later, he still hadn't returned.

I'm not sure what I expected. A declaration of love? Breakfast in bed?

It's entirely possible he was pulled into a meeting. Or he got sidetracked checking the wards with General Finch, I rationalized.

Or he realized what a terrible mistake this was, ran as fast as he could, and is hoping you'll get the message, my brain added unhelpfully.

Either way, I couldn't sit in this flooded room all day. Today was my day off, but I wasn't taking the chance of anyone discovering me in this state.

I drew the blanket around me, positioning the middle of the short edge over my head, hoping it could pass as some kind of hooded cloak. My shoes were nowhere to be found, but luckily the fabric was long enough to keep my feet obscured. Hiking it up, I waded through the water, trying my best to step around the glass and miraculously avoiding any cuts.

This is delusional, I thought as I opened the door slowly, but I didn't know what else to do.

The water had leaked out into the tiled hallway, which was blessedly empty.

The servant's stairwell was probably my best chance at making it up to my room without being spotted, so I navigated to the nearest entrance and began to climb. Everyone must've been busy with preparation for the trial, because I didn't encounter anyone on the way up.

I made it all the way to the third floor and was halfway down the hallway when Satoria, a contestant with the Gift of wind manipulation, opened her door. She stepped out, took a moment to steel herself, and began her march down the hallway, presumably to her trial. Was that where Evander had gone?

My mind raced with excuses for why I was barefoot, wrapped in a blanket with a soaked hem, and hiding the fact that I had no clothes on. What could I tell her? A slip into one of the fountains? She might not notice that I wasn't clothed if I kept the blanket around me.

My anxiety proved to be pointless, as she swept down the hallway without acknowledging me. Either she found a servant to be below her notice, or she was so nervous and distracted herself that she had tunnel vision on her destination. Whatever the reason, I was thankful for it.

Safely inside my room at last, I let out a sigh of relief. Abandoning the blanket in the sink of the washroom, I dressed myself in the one spare set of clothes I had, a deep berry blouse with long flowing sleeves, and a plain brown linen skirt. I would need to find out how to acquire new clothing around here the next time I had a day off.

As I was lacing up my spare boots, a knock came from the door.

On the other side was Mellie, her face bright red and puffy and her eyes full of tears.

I put my arm around her and ushered her inside, sitting her down on the bed.

"What's the matter?" I asked, panicked. I'd never seen Mellie so upset.

"It's the queen," she sobbed. "Evalina won't wake up."

Chapter 14

THE CASTLE MOVED IN a sluggish haze for the rest of the day. I knew the trials were still held, which made me furious for Evander. To have to sit through those when I couldn't even imagine how he must be feeling . . .

In order to give Mellie some much-needed time to process, I decided to forgo my rest day and jumped into work in the kitchen. I wasn't sure what the prognosis was for magical depletion so intense it led to unconsciousness, but it couldn't be good.

Maddox came into the kitchen that evening to make an announcement. She looked as stoic as ever, but I recognized the sadness hiding in the grim set of her mouth. I had seen it in Vanessa.

"As I'm sure you've all heard, the queen has fallen ill," she said. "The decision has been made to attempt an immediate transfer of the Crown to Prince Evander. Typically, the current monarch needs to be an active participant in the succession process, since the magic needs to be relinquished to the new reining party, but given the circumstances, we don't have much choice. I'm sharing this information with you because, should the transfer be successful, we will hold a formal coronation for Prince Evander–*King Evander*–in three days' time. I realize this is short notice to prepare, but we must do our best to pull off a show of strength for our kingdom."

And for Falerin to see. The unspoken words hung in the air.

I'd have to speak to Mellie about the menu and see what I could get started. Three days . . .three days and Evander would be king.

I knew what position that put him, put *us in*. It had never been more crucial for him to find another Wielder to hold the other half of the Crown. No matter how my heart felt about it, I wouldn't let him shoulder that burden alone and be drained from it the way his mother had been. The tiny spark of hope that had been lit in my heart since the morning sputtered and went out, and I tried my best to ignore how desolate it made me feel. I had to compartmentalize.

Someone needed to see how Evander was holding up, and I was willing to bet Maddox and General Finch weren't the touchy-feely type. So, half an hour later I found myself trudging up the steps again. I arrived at his door, raised my fist to knock, and paused. This was a horrible idea. Again.

I lowered my hand, but the door swung open anyway. By the time I got inside, Evander was already walking back to the sitting area. He slumped into a cushion, fingers interlaced behind his neck.

"I'm so sorry I didn't come back," he said without looking up at me. "Georgette found me in the hallway before I even got to my room and told me. By the time I made it back to the testing room, you were gone."

"I thought we weren't apologizing?" I reminded him softly. "And I would never hold that against you. I can't imagine what today has been like for you. How are you, really?" I sat beside him, but kept a few inches between us.

He looked up, eyes bloodshot and puffy. He still wore the same shirt and trousers from this morning, but had added an overcoat to look more presentable. A cravat was untied and draped askew around his neck and his hair stuck up at odd angles, as if he had been running his hands through it all day. I had never seen him look anything other than regal, but this . . . this was a man on the edge of a complete breakdown.

He opened his mouth as if to reassure me, but something in his expression shattered when he met my eyes. The soft sound he made as his face screwed up was raw and haunting.

Instinctively, I reached for him and held his head while he cried, stroking his hair but saying nothing. There was nothing I could say. othing I could do to make this situation better for him, and it was killing me.

When all the tears had fallen, he turned to face me, something like shame in his eyes.

"I'm so, SO sorry," I said. "This is awful and I'm sorry you're expected to put on a brave face."

"Thank you," he whispered. "Quinn–"

"I know," I interrupted. If I had to listen to him actually say the words, I would go to pieces too. "I understand what this means and you have to know I don't blame you for a second."

Evander shook his head vehemently, like rejecting the truth would change it.

"I just need more time," he said. "I can take the throne now and come up with a solution afterward. I *will* come up with a solution."

"Right now you need to do what's best for your mother, for your kingdom, and for yourself." He started to protest. "Yes. Yourself," I repeated. "If you won't prioritize your well-being for your own sake, do it for your subjects. The people need a strong leader. You can't allow yourself to be weakened by the weight of bearing it alone; I won't let you." My eyes filled with tears as I forced myself to finish. "I will always care about you, and I will always cheer you on, Evander. Please, for me: be happy."

The kiss I pressed to his cheek as I rose from the settee was the melancholy goodbye I had been putting off for too long. It felt wrong to leave him in this state, but I couldn't maintain composure for much longer, and Evander had enough burdens on his shoulders without feeling responsible for my heartbreak as well.

He said nothing as I walked to the door, but I made the mistake of looking back as I opened it. A silent tear rolled down his cheek and all I wanted was to kiss it away, to hold his face in my hands and promise him that it would be okay, that we would weather this trial together.

But I couldn't. I slipped out and closed the door.

This was the kind of heartbreak that needed someone else to witness it. I knew I could trust Mellie to keep my secret, but she had her own grief to work through.

Besides, selfishly, I didn't think I could stand the dismayed look on her face when she learned I had ignored her advice and gotten myself involved where I shouldn't. I knew Mellie would love me no matter what, but that didn't mean she wouldn't be disappointed.

That left me with one other option. I wasn't sure how honest Colette had been about her disinterest for the prince, but I knew Vanessa at least would give me the tough love I needed.

My footsteps became more frantic as I got close to her room. For some reason, it felt vitally important that I didn't cry until I was behind closed doors.

By the time I passed the first set of doors in our hallway, I had broken into a run.

Yanking open the door, I had to blink away my tears and clear my vision enough to understand what I was seeing.

Colette and Vanessa stood in front of the fireplace, locked in a tender embrace. Vanessa stroked Collete's face as if it were porcelain, fragile and precious. Hearing the noise of the door, they jumped apart. Colette covered her face as Vanessa's eyes flared wide.

"You two . . ." I started, flabbergasted. This explained so much. "YOU TWO!" Forgetting my own misery for a moment, I bounced toward them to share my excitement, but Vanessa crossed between Colette and me, her nostrils flaring.

"That was not what you thought it was," she said, her tone strangely intense, eyes flashing.

"No," I cut in, "I think it's great that you're–wait, is this why Colette needs to advance so badly? So she can stay in the castle with you?"

Vanessa leaned in very close to my face, her eyes turning an intense gold.

"You will forget that happened," she hissed.

"No, I won't." I didn't understand. "Why are you acting so strange about this?"

"Forget what you saw," she tried again, her eyes glowing an even more brilliant shade.

Recognition flared in my gut. I had seen that look before. Maddox's eyes flashed in my mind as she told me to forget about Evander's admission on the stairwell, and a horrible realization dawned on me.

"Are you trying to wipe my memory? Is that your Gift?" And if it was, why wasn't it working?

Colette hurried over to us.

"Nessa, she's not going to tell anyone. It's fine."

"It's not fine!" Vanessa roared.

"Of course I'm not going to tell anyone. What is wrong with you?"

"YOU WILL FORGET WHAT YOU SAW." She flung the words at me, eyes now frantic beacons of light.

"STOP," I yelled. "Whatever it is you're trying to do, stop! Do you have any idea how invasive this is? You can't just force your way into my head!" Even as I raged, I backed up toward the door.

"Apparently not!" she snarled.

"Everyone just needs to calm down. We can talk about this," Colette tried to mediate.

"There's nothing to talk about," I said. "And to think I thought we were friends." I flung the door open, breaking the sound ward, and Vanessa and Colette fell silent. Protecting their secret was more important than our friendship. As if it were in any danger in the first place.

Whirling around on them, I prepared to fire off a parting blow, but found myself at a complete loss for words. Vanessa stood as a buffer between Colette and me, as if I were going to attack her lover at any moment.

I met Colette's big brown eyes over her shoulder and found them filled with tears. Her lips parted as if to say something, but I didn't give her the chance. Instead, I slammed the door and ran into my own room, throwing myself onto my bed and finally giving in to the sobs that wracked my body.

Two days later, Evander was officially crowned king. His mother did not wake to attend the coronation.

Chapter 15

When Serena was finally well enough to return to the kitchens, she worked at a slower pace than usual, meaning that Permelia, James, Franc, and I were left to pick up the slack.

I didn't blame her at all, of course, but the extra hours were starting to wear on me.

They hadn't found the would-be poisoner and nothing out of the ordinary had happened since, but it had Maddox on edge. She frequented the kitchens, looking for any evidence she had missed. The kitchen staff had all been questioned, but the investigation seemed to hit a dead end and the captain was visibly frustrated by her lack of progress. The transition of power, she said, was a tenuous time, and if Falerin were to try anything, it would likely be now.

There were now tasters before every meal (a job that I did not envy) and the security at the gate had been doubled.

Still, I heard whispers around the castle that disappearances had picked up slightly in the outer towns of Enorias. Evander had no practice holding the wards. His mother was still unconscious, and though the healers had said that they hoped she would recover now that her magic wasn't being overextended, I could tell it was more of a wish than a medical truth from the way the servants walked around as if they were preparing themselves for the inevitable. Queen Evalina, it seemed, was deeply beloved here, and her condition had a deep impact on the mood around the castle, which had become somber and tense.

Mellie managed to remain bright and optimistic, clinging to the possibility that her friend would recover, but there were moments where I could see her facade crack as she leaned against the counter with both hands and stared down at the worktop for minutes at a time, whatever she was working on forgotten.

The few glimpses of Evander I had caught in the halls and while serving meals were enough to make me truly worried for him. In just a matter of days, his complexion had gone from healthy and robust to greyed and drawn. Though I was careful never to meet his gaze, the glances I stole when he wasn't looking my way were enough to see that the light was gone from his eyes.

Was anticipatory grief eating at him, or had the demands of the Crown drained him this quickly? I couldn't imagine his massive display of magic in the trial room left much in his reserves. Taking the throne when he was already so depleted . . . the guilt settled heavily in my stomach.

Lost in thought, I nearly missed the soft knock on my door. I padded over, expecting to see Mellie on the other side. To my surprise, I instead found Colette.

It had been four days since the incident in Vanessa's room, and we hadn't spoken since. I didn't have anything to say that wouldn't be hurtful, and as angry as I was, I recognized that Colette wasn't the one who deserved the brunt of it.

"Can I come in?" she asked, not meeting my eyes.

Stepping aside, I gestured towards the room in assent.

She paced for a few seconds, gathering up the courage to say what she needed to.

"Look, I understand that you're really angry right now, and you have a right to be. What Vanessa did wasn't fair and I'm furious at her for putting us in this position, but you have to understand that she was only trying to keep me safe. If people found out the reason I was really here, I'd probably be asked to leave. I know you trust the king, but there are a lot of other people in this castle that wouldn't take kindly to a woman choosing a guard's daughter over the monarch, or finding out that she hid it and took up castle resources to stay anyway . . ." She looked at me, her eyes pleading with me to understand.

And I did. I was still angry at the situation, but she wasn't the one who had tried to wipe my mind.

I sighed. I missed my friend.

"So . . . how did you two meet?"

Colette crushed me in a hug.

"Thank you, Quinn," she sniffled.

I pulled her over and we sat cross-legged on the bed as she told me the story.

"It was in the summer months. Maddox and a few other guards showed up at my house to let us know in advance that we'd be receiving a royal summons. They didn't say what it was about, and my Papa and I were terrified. He runs a little plant nursery in the village and would never hurt anyone, so we had no idea why they would want to take me to the castle.

"Maddox must've picked up on our panic, because she disappeared for a few minutes and came back from the carriages with Vanessa, saying she had been summoned too. I think they meant for her to be more relatable, sort of calm me down a bit. After a few minutes of chatting, she asked if she could write me, and we started exchanging letters after that . . ." Colette trailed off, a dreamy look in her eyes. "A few weeks later I came here, not knowing anything other than what Nessa was able to write me in code. I didn't expect to be competing to become a broodmare." She made a face at that.

I took the opportunity to ask what had happened in the last trial.

"Vanessa had it easy," Colette said, rolling her eyes. "They locked her in a room with her proctor and chained her to an interrogation chair. All she had to do was convince the guard to let her out. It took her two minutes at the most."

"And you?" I asked. Colette looked away.

"It was," she shuddered, "not what I expected." A few long seconds passed before she spoke again.

"There was another green-Wielder who wrapped me in vines, and I had to convince the plants to loosen and let me out. I spent so much time working on making the plants function as extensions of myself. I didn't anticipate them using them against me. They kept getting tighter and tighter and I couldn't raise my arms to cast." Her voice sped up as she spoke, reliving the panic. "Eventually, I managed it, but for a while there I wasn't sure I would. I wasn't sure how far they'd go." She swallowed.

"And Evander?" I asked, horrified.

"What about him?"

"What was he doing during all of this?"

She shrugged. "He wasn't there."

"He wasn't there? For any of it?"

"I mean, his mother . . ." Colette said.

Of course I understood if Evander needed some time to process the news of his mother's condition, but couldn't they have delayed the trials for a day?

"He needed to be there." He needed to cast with the women and figure out how his magic interacted with theirs, but he hadn't even had the chance. I prayed to the gods it wasn't because of what he'd said the night before; he must've known that things had changed.

"Well, he'll be at the next one," Colette said. "That's actually what I came to talk to you about." She braced herself for my reaction before continuing. "The final trial is being moved up to next week."

My face fell as her words registered. I knew I shouldn't feel shocked. I knew this was a good thing for him. But that knowledge didn't stop the tears from coming, hot and angry.

Colette took my hands in hers, comforting me without forcing me to acknowledge the ugly emotions I was feeling.

Perhaps it was wishful thinking, but as my mind turned everything over again, desperate for an answer that would help us both, I kept getting stuck on the handful of moments I couldn't explain in the last few months: my talk with Maddox, the breath I took in the tank, the way Vanessa's eyes flashed at me but had no effect. If she were powerful enough to convince a fully-trained guard to bend to her will in less than two minutes, why hadn't her magic worked on me?

"Colette," I asked tentatively, "do you think it's possible for magic to be dormant in someone? Hypothetically."

She cocked her head and narrowed her eyes. "I have no idea. Why?"

Finally, I told her everything. When I finished, she looked at me with a strange mixture of skepticism and hope.

"That does sound like some of the accidental magic manifestations I experienced when I was young, before I had learned to Wield my powers properly, but . . ."

"Don't sugarcoat it."

"It's just that all the instances were so varied," she began. "For me, everything was always about plants, you know? Every time I presented magically it had something to do with my specific Gift. And I've never heard of it manifesting in anyone older than ten."

I sighed. I'd guessed as much, but my godsdamned heart still sank as she said it.

It must've shown on my face because she quickly interjected, "I could be wrong!" She stood up and beckoned me to follow her. "Let's try something."

She demonstrated her casting stance.

"Feet wide, hands up. I like to imagine a beam of light coming down through the top of my head and out through my hands."

I mimicked her, feeling a bit foolish, but didn't feel anything.

"Give it a second," she coached. "Imagine the magic filling you up before it pours out. It takes some patience at first."

Another minute passed as I adjusted my arms awkwardly at various angles to see if it might make a difference.

"Still nothing," I said dejectedly, letting my arms drop.

"You could keep trying," Colette offered. "When you don't know what your Gift is and can't visualize what you want to happen, it's much harder. That's why Wielder children are taught to wait until they manifest fully."

I shrugged it off. "I prayed to every god I could think of when I was stuck in that tank, asking them to bless me and get me out. One of them must've taken pity on me. That's all it was, I'm sure."

"And Vanessa?" Colette asked.

I didn't have an answer for that, but I didn't want to get my hopes up.

"I'll keep trying," I promised, even as I doubted it would help.

Colette was silent for a moment before steeling herself and turning towards me with determination, her mouth set into a hard line.

"There might be another way," she said. "I need you to be honest with me, because I know this isn't a fair thing to ask of you, but I don't see a better option for either of us right now." She took a deep breath. "I want you to ask the king to choose me."

My mind went blank and I stared at her for a few long seconds, trying to process what she had asked.

"Think about it," she urged. "I could help him rule, put my powers to use, and stay in the castle, but the relationship would be just for show. I could be with Vanessa, and you and King Evander . . ."

What would that make me? His *mistress?* My stomach soured at the idea. But I also couldn't bear the thought of him in a real marriage, with a real wife and real love. It was unfair, I knew, but every facet of this situation was unfair.

"It's not that simple, Colette," I said, shaking my head. "Part of the reason this competition is being held is because there are certain . . . conditions they're testing for," I wheedled.

"What conditions?" she asked.

I took a moment to weigh my options. I didn't want to betray Evander's trust, but Colette had just as much a chance as anyone else here of being the match. Maybe we could outsmart this after all.

Finally, I let out a long breath and told her about the prophecy.

"Basically," I finished, "he needs someone whose magic is compatible with his."

"So we test it!" she urged. "We have to at least give it a try!"

It was far from a perfect solution, but it was better than any of the alternatives. Maybe removing the pressure of a loveless marriage would spark something new if he cast with Colette. Maybe magic would be enough after all.

I tried to tamp down that stubborn spark of hope.

"We should try," I agreed.

A handful of too-short moments later, I found myself at Evander's door again. If I didn't talk to him now, I knew I would lose my nerve altogether. A (large) part of me hated this plan, but at least with Colette, I knew he would be safe and respected. She would care about their people and work hard to ensure the safety of the kingdom. I was leaving myself out of it. This might be his best chance.

My familiar three knocks had never sounded so deafening. A few seconds passed with no reply.

He must be out, I thought, my shoulders slumping. I would have to convince myself to do this all over again.

But just as I turned to leave, the door opened. Evander met my gaze for a moment, his expression barely changing, and wordlessly invited me in.

He looked so tired.

The sight had a small intake of breath catching in my throat.

"Evander–" I gasped. "I mean, King Evander . . ."

"Back to that now, are we?" His forlorn smile lacked the playful bite I knew he was aiming for.

"Are you all right?" I couldn't help but ask the question, though I already knew the answer.

He let out a hopeless laugh that sounded almost hysterical.

"All right? No," he ran a hand through his hair. "No, I'm not all right." I was reminded of a caged animal as he paced the room frenetically.

It had only been a few days, and in many ways he was unchanged. His hair was still the deep brown of dark chocolate, his build still strong, but somehow he looked . . . *hollow* was the best word, I supposed.

"Days," he said. "Days, Quinn, and I already feel like I'm fading away. My mother did this for *years.*" He shook his head.

"You haven't had any training," I said, feeling the familiar urge to protect him from himself. "And she had years of practice with someone by her side first."

"She wasn't even there," he whispered. "At my coronation. She wasn't even there. It might already be too late." He stopped himself abruptly, stilling in place and turning to face me. "I'm sorry. I shouldn't be burdening you with all this."

"No apologizing, remember?" I said softly.

"There aren't enough apologies in the world to express the regret I feel about how all of this has turned out. I'm so sorry."

I didn't even have the heart to banter with him. Seeing him like this . . . it scared me. We needed to fix this as quickly as possible.

"Evander," I broached, "I have a plan, and before you say no I need you to listen to all of it."

He didn't miss a beat. "All right," he said, all the trust in the world bringing a tiny speck of light back into those cerulean eyes.

So I sat and explained everything. Or almost everything. It felt best to keep out the part about us, but I made sure he knew the truth about Colette's affections being engaged elsewhere. This would be a political alliance. He had to know that.

"Vanessa, huh?" he asked, amused. "Good for her. I don't know why she didn't come to me with any of this, but she's always been so stubborn. Never known how to deal with her feelings."

I relayed the plan, forcing my tone to stay neutral and unbiased. He deserved that much. When I was done, he stared me down for a moment, considering, before declaring, "I hate it."

"I do too," I admitted. "But do you have a better plan?"

Evander shook his head.

"I don't know if it works that way, though, Quinn. It's not just about the magic itself. I think there has to be a basic chemistry there." He paused a moment before continuing with an exasperated sigh. "I have to admit, though, I have about as much of a connection with her as I do anyone else in this contest."

"What about Vanessa?" I asked. I was sure he had already considered it.

"Gods, no," he said. "She's like my sister."

"Still," I coaxed, "if it were purely political . . . And I'm sure she could find an excuse to keep Colette and her father in the castle. Head of groundskeeping or something?"

"I'll have to cast with all of them in a few days regardless," he said. "We might as well try to get ahead of it."

"Then I'll go get them now." I jumped out of my chair and headed toward the door before either of us could change our minds.

"Quinn." He stopped me just before I crossed through the threshold. "I would never try to keep you hidden like a dirty secret."

I swallowed, not trusting myself enough to turn around and face him and remain neutral. "No, Evander, I wouldn't–"

"But," he cut me off, "I need you to know that whatever tiny pieces of you I can earn, I will take, and I will not be sorry. I would spend my life trying to make that enough for you, but I would also understand if you needed to walk away."

Swallowing down an emotion I didn't dare name, I nodded and went to retrieve my friends.

Colette had the even less enviable task of letting Vanessa in on our plan. Given how she acted toward me until she knew I was involved with Evander, I could surmise that she would not be happy to share.

As predicted, she fumed all the way up to the fourth floor, flinging Evander's door open with a sense of familiarity that I envied.

"Your Heinous," she shot.

"Rat," he threw back.

When they embraced, Colette and I shared a look that plainly said "*Freaks.*"

"Gods, you look like shit," Vanessa said, pinching his cheek like an overzealous aunt.

"Thanks, V," Evander responded, swatting her away. It was the most animated I'd seen him in days.

"Should we get this over with?" she asked, throwing in a signature eye-roll for good measure. It irritated me to no end that she was so cavalier about the whole affair. She and Evander had known each other her entire life. That connection could make a difference for him.

"What do you suggest?" he asked.

"For some reason Quinn," she shot me an unsure look as she said my name, as if acknowledging the fragile state of our relationship, "seems to be resistant to my mother and me. Maybe the echo of some magical ancestor way up in her family tree, I don't know. But I'm thinking if we add your strength to my persuasion, we might be able to crack her shields."

She rounded on me and I threw up my hands, interjecting defensively. "I'm not exactly comfortable having my mind wiped for this experiment."

Colette found something incredibly interesting to study on the ceiling while Evander came up to me and took my hands.

"No wiping, I promise," he said. "Just pick a memory and hold it in the antechamber of your mind. Focus on it, but keep it sealed off. All we'll do is see if we can find it."

I nodded. Even if I didn't trust Vanessa, I trusted him.

"Ready?" Evander asked. He searched my face for any trace of hesitancy, protecting me until the very last. "You don't have to do this."

But I did.

"No use prolonging it. Go ahead."

I focused on an afternoon in Mellie's bakery, many years ago, when I pulled a successful batch of tarts out of the oven for the first time. I bathed in the memory, recalling the smell of blackberries and butter, the snow falling gently outside, like a scene from a picture book, and the warmth in Mellie's eyes when she told me how proud she was of me.

Vanessa's eyes flashed that same intense gold color I had seen before. Evander came up behind her, pushing out into the room with his hands bracketing her body to amplify her skill.

A gentle knock on the door of my mind asked permission to enter. It didn't feel invasive or threatening. In fact, I wanted to let it in. But I held firm. The presence didn't push, though I could see the veins bulging in Vanessa's temples.

Finally, she let out a breath and her eyes returned to their normal amber.

"Anything?' she asked, panting.

I explained the experience as best I could.

"It's like it was a guest asking for entry, but I had complete control."

"That's . . . not what's supposed to happen," Vanessa groused.

"What about you?" I asked, turning to Evander. He somehow looked even worse, as if a strong breeze would blow him over. For someone well over six feet, it was disconcerting.

"Nothing," he panted.

"Colette next," Vanessa said over her shoulder as she moved to sit down.

"Do you need a moment?" I offered Evander my arm, but he waved me off, even as he swayed on his feet.

"I'm fine."

Liar.

Colette extended her hand, no pity in her face. Good. He would appreciate that.

"It's good to see you, your Highness. And I have to apologize for my forwardness with this idea. I know the idea of marrying me is likely not your first choice."

Evander shifted uncomfortably. "Don't apologize, please. It isn't you," he tried feebly, "it's only that–"

"It's fine," she waved him off. "If I were in love with Quinn, I don't think I'd pay attention to other women either." She winked.

My face heated when Evander made no move to correct her.

Vanessa glowered in the corner.

"I'm not," Colette clarified, rolling her eyes. Vanessa had rubbed off on her. "All I'm saying is that our girl is a good one." My heart swelled with pride as she squeezed my arm affectionately before continuing.

"Shall we try?" she asked.

Evander assumed the same position behind her and ugly jealousy turned in my stomach at the sight. I needed to get a hold of myself.

Colette swirled her hands around one another, and a beautiful golden daffodil bloomed from the ground. Evander raised his hands around her, and the daffodil shot up another inch. My heart leapt into my throat, but nothing else happened.

"Evander?"

He shook his head sadly.

"I'm sorry," Colette said earnestly, mostly to me.

"It's not your fault," I said, letting out a breath I hadn't realized I'd been holding. I should be upset, but more than anything else I felt relieved.

It made no sense; this only meant he would need to choose someone else to marry, but I don't know how I would've borne it if I had to watch one of my friends take that role.

Suddenly, something horrible dawned on me. Something I should've thought about weeks ago.

"What happens if none of the women are a match?" I asked.

The grim set of Evander's mouth told me he had been thinking the same thing.

"We start over," he exhaled.

"And in the meantime?" I asked. "You keep fading away until you're like your mother?"

He rounded on me, anger and hurt flashing like a storm on his face.

"I'm sorry," I apologized quietly. "I didn't mean anything against her. It's just hard to see you like this. I don't want you getting even more hurt."

"As much as I like to give you hells, I don't either," Vanessa chimed in.

"How were the contestants chosen?" Colette asked. "Is there another pool to choose from?"

"The scribes traced the lineages of some of the more powerful Wielders present at the founding of Enorias. There were over three dozen of them, so we called on the female descendants of everyone we could track."

And then he let half of a dozen of them go home. Because of me. I was going to be sick.

Evander trudged over to me, putting his hands on my upper arms and rubbing up and down to comfort me.

"It's going to be fine," he promised, even as his eyes betrayed his fear.

I refused to add my own stress to his, so I put on a brave face, twisting my lips into my best approximation of a smile. "I'm sure it will be."

On the morning of the final trial, I felt like I was going to crawl out of my skin. I couldn't stop moving, because if I stopped moving, I would start thinking, and if I started thinking, I was going to lose my mind.

I didn't know which was worse: the possibility that none of the castings would produce a viable result, or the idea that they would and I would have to stand there, smiling, as I watched Evander marry someone else.

It would be more selfless to say that the former was more frightening, but it was the latter that had kept me up all night, tossing and turning.

Regardless, I would do what needed to be done. I would remove myself from the situation, resign from my post if necessary, and let Evander move on. But it was going to absolutely shatter me. It was that possibility that kept me pacing the kitchen, starting a dozen projects but never finishing any of them.

Mellie had offered me the day off, but the thought of sitting alone in my room was worse than the idea of working. Still, I knew I was likely being more of a hindrance than a help to anyone here.

The trial was set to occur directly after breakfast, and meal prep had never gone more slowly. For the third time in the last ten minutes, I checked my egg and caramelized onion puff pastries to see if they were finished baking.

"Why don't you work on some pancakes, Dumpling?" Mellie suggested gently, coming up behind me.

I groaned like a hormonal teenager.

Pancakes. That's how far gone I am right now. All I can handle is pancakes.

I trudged to the pantry for flour but was intercepted by Jacques, who handed me a note. The tiny piece of parchment looked like a corner that had been ripped off a larger document, and I recognized Evander's hand.

Can you be there?

I traced the words with my finger, the corners of my mouth pulling down. If he didn't already know I was coming to support him, he was even more frazzled than I thought.

I worked up the pancakes, making sure they were light and fluffy and adding a pinch of lemon zest for some zing. Then I started on whipped cream to go with them. Anything to keep my hands busy.

The food was sent up to the kitchen and the staff all gathered around their communal table to eat before the trial. Everyone seemed to move around me in slow motion until I was the only one left in the kitchen.

I don't know how long I had been standing there, staring at the countertop, before I heard a throat clear.

Behind me, Serena was tapping her foot and holding out a plate.

"Eat," she ordered.

"Thank you, Serena," I said, "but my appetite seems to have a better place to be right now."

She set the plate on the counter and pushed it over to me insistently.

"Eat," she repeated. "I'm not going away until you do."

I stared her down for a moment before realizing I didn't have the energy for a battle of wills right now. Sighing, I shoveled some pancake into my mouth.

"Happy?" I asked around the mouthful of food.

Serena didn't bother to answer. Instead, she leaned on the counter next to me, watching to make sure I wasn't going to dump my plate the second she left the room.

"No offense, Serena, but why do you care if I eat breakfast? You'd better be careful, or someone around here might think you like me," I joked.

"I do like you," she said matter-of-factly. "Besides, you're about to watch the man you're in love with get engaged to someone else. You're going to need all the help you can get to get through it."

I started to sputter an excuse, but she cut me off immediately.

"Don't try to be sneaky about it. That's below you," she said. "You know, one of the things I admired about you even when I couldn't stand you was that you get shit done. Regardless of how you're feeling about it, you do the right thing."

"Feels pretty great right about now," I mumbled sarcastically.

"But you'll do it," she said. "You'll do it and you'll keep going and you'll be all right. Maybe not today, or tomorrow, or even a month from now, but you'll get through it."

"Thank you, Serena." I was more than a little confused at her praise, but her words made me stand just a little straighter.

At that moment, James stuck his head in the doorframe like a character in a children's picture book. Upon seeing Serena, his face lit up and he bounded over, kissing her on the cheek. Her mouth turned up in an embarrassed half-smile that looked a bit too girlish on her.

"Wait . . ." I gestured between the two of them. "When did this happen?"

"For me? Twelve years ago. For her? About three weeks," James laughed. The corners of his light brown eyes crinkled with pride.

"James visited me a lot when I was sick," Serena explained, blushing as he took her hand.

"It only took almost dying for you to notice me," he joked. "I've been trying to get her attention since we were in school. Didn't think I'd have to follow her all the way to the castle to do it," he shrugged, "but all's well that ends well."

She squeezed his hand and my gaze lingered on the tender touch.

"Oof," James grimaced, rubbing the back of his neck with his free hand as he squinted one eye. "Sore subject?"

I groaned again, my face in my hands.

"Does everybody know?"

"Pretty much," Serena confirmed. "Did you think no one would notice you disappearing from dinner every other night?" She raised an eyebrow.

Great. Not only was I going to have to endure this, but I was going to do it while everybody I worked alongside watched me with pity.

"No one blames you," James said. "I mean, the king is . . ." he waggled his eyebrows and tilted his head. "You know."

Serena elbowed him lightly, glaring up at him through her scrunched eyebrows.

He kissed the top of her head cajolingly. "I'm just saying that if I wasn't already so taken with Serena . . . I see the appeal."

Despite my somber mood, I let out a giggle.

"There she is," Serena smirked, raising her chin.

I did my best to mirror her posture, holding my head high, and we walked up to the throne room together.

The vast space felt suffocating and oppressive. Even the swath of dull grey sky visible through the domed ceiling window lent itself to the somber mood. The dark paneling on the walls was reflected in the polished floor, interrupted only by a long burgundy rug. Not yet feeling brave enough to face Evander, I counted the carved marble columns along each side to steady my breaths. My distraction was short-lived; as I reached a count of sixteen lining the way to the raised dais, I met his eyes.

Evander was sitting on the throne, silhouetted by the arched stained glass windows behind him. His doublet was a deep blue that should've brought out his eyes, but instead made him look even more pale and drawn.

Still, he held his head with a regal air. Atop it was a golden crown with sapphires inlaid on the band. Funny, I had never seen him wear one before. It suited him.

I did my best to project confidence and positivity as I mouthed "Good luck." In return, he gave me a sad, tired sort of smile, returning his attention to General Finch, who was explaining the rules of the trial.

Besides Evander and the contestants, there were about three dozen audience members in attendance. The group was composed mostly of guards and older nobles, likely friends of Evander's mother. I looked around for Evalina herself, comparing the faces of the women I saw to the few portraits of her I had found hanging around the castle, but didn't find her in the crowd.

Good, I thought sadly. *She would hate this.*

The Wielders were lined up in front of the dais, various degrees of petrification on their faces. Colette, calm and composed, looked back at me and winked. I covered my snort with a loud cough.

No one knew about our little experiment a few days ago, so Colette and Vanessa would be casting with everybody else. There were a little under a dozen women in the line, and I looked at their faces, wondering which one would be the kingdom's salvation. *Evander's* salvation.

I allowed myself one last pining look at him, breathtaking even when he was so tired and worn, then slammed the doors of my heart shut for good. In a few days, he would be back to his old self, leading his kingdom the way I knew only he could. Maybe his mother would even wake up for the wedding. This was going to be good. It had to be.

As Finch finished explaining the exercise, practically the exact same casting we had tried earlier in the week, the audience broke into light applause. The crowd was tense, as if everyone in attendance knew how important this moment was.

The room itself seemed to hold its breath as the first woman stepped up onto the dais. It was Satoria, the wind-Wielder. Finch showed her where to stand and Evander came up behind her. After they exchanged a few words, he nodded, assuming a casting position with his arms outstretched around her, careful not to touch.

She focused on a spot a few feet in front of them and a small tornado, only about a foot high, whirled into existence. Sweat began beading on Evander's forehead the moment he joined her. Satoria furrowed her brows, willing the tornado to grow, but it didn't even reach the height that I had seen her achieve in the training room.

Evander thanked her and she put on a good show of neutrality as she stepped off the dais and made her way to one of the open seats.

Anissa was much the same, her light burning as brightly as it did in the practice room, but no brighter.

By the third contestant, I started to panic. What if he didn't find the right woman? Would he really start the whole process over again? If not one of the descendants of the founding Wielders, who would be powerful enough to help shoulder the burden?

Freya the fire-Wielder approached the dais but didn't step up.

"Your Majesty." She sunk into a deep bow. "King Orobas sends his regards." Panicked sparked as I recognized the name of the Falerian king, but I didn't have time to discern her meaning before she smirked and threw her chest back, pulling her arms behind her, and whipped them in Evander's direction.

Flames burst out from her outstretched hands, engulfing him in an orb of fire. It was easily ten feet tall, larger than any casting I had ever seen.

That kind of power . . .

Maddox sprinted up to the dais, only to be met with a second wall of fire Freya cast without even blinking.

My heart seized in alarm as the orb began to shrink, caging Evander inside.

Finch. Finch wielded ice. He could fix this. I looked over at him frantically. He threw his arms out repeatedly, but not so much as a single shard escaped his fingertips. He was completely drained. Like Liang Like Emory. Freya had done this to all of them, and I was willing to bet she was behind the poisoned cookies as well.

I watched her in mute horror. Hatred twisted her face as she paced back and forth in front of the dais. She held the orb steady, toying with Evander as she gloated.

"Orobas thought you would be more of an opponent," she said. "The fated Protector of Enorias. To think all it took to weaken you was your own Crown." She tutted. Though I couldn't see Evander's face, I knew it must be excruciating inside her casting. Even if he wasn't burned by the flames directly, the ambient heat and smoke inhalation were just as likely to kill him.

"Not to worry, though," she crooned. "He'll be a much stronger leader for your kingdom. A visionary as well as a king. He has plans beyond what you could possibly comprehend."

She walked up close to the orb, peered in as if she were looking through a window, and sneered.

"Goodbye, King Evander." The orb began to shrink even faster. It must be close to touching him now.

"No!" I let out a scream, piercing and shrill, and threw my arms outward as if I could somehow reach him from across the room.

I couldn't lose him like this.

A life I could never have flashed before my eyes. One where we had lazy Sunday mornings and walks in the village, where I learned his favorite songs by heart and played them to him before bed. A life where we were safe.

Freya's head snapped back to me, her lips curled in a mirthless smile as she witnessed my devastation.

Then the world erupted.

The orb of fire shattered outward, knocking her to the ground, and her conjured wall collapsed as she hit her head on the dais and lost consciousness. My eyes flicked over to Maddox only long enough to see her jump to action, pinning Freya's unconscious body to the ground, before I broke into a run.

Smoke filled the air, and I couldn't make out Evander, couldn't see if he was all right. I ran straight into it, my lungs protesting, and groped around blindly to try to find him.

Not for the first time since I had come to the palace, something impossible happened. Evander stepped out of the smoke, a shimmering blue-grey orb, smaller than the fire orb and completely free of pollution, surrounding him.

His eyes found mine and he looked at me as if he were seeing me for the first time.

“Quinn,” he said my name so softly I could barely hear it. “Lower your arms.”

I slowly drew them down to my sides and the orb dissipated as if it had been waiting for my permission.

In seconds, Evander’s lips were on mine, the kiss bruising and desperate. I pulled him in tight, desperate to feel the solid form of his shoulders, his chest. He was alive.

Pulling his head back a fraction of an inch, he threaded his hands into the curls on either side of my face, drawing our foreheads together. I didn’t care who was around us to see or what they might think. Everything that existed outside our embrace faded from the room.

Evander’s eyes were glistening with tears. He held my face as if it were the most precious thing in the world.

“You’re a Wielder, Quinn,” he said. “You’re a Wielder.” The second time he said it, his face split into a dazzling smile. “It’s you. It’s always been you. That pull we’ve been fighting–it’s the music. Can you hear it too?” I nodded, breath catching in my chest as I remembered a dozen unthinkable miracles . . .

The uncanny sense he had that I was in danger, the breath I took in the evaluation room. Even my fight with Vanessa and the way I managed to remain hidden from Satoria just a few days prior. But I hadn’t dared to hope.

Now I could dream freely, not about using this power to remain hidden or protect myself, but about what I could create with it. The life it opened up for me, for us. A disbelieving laugh bubbled up from my throat as Evander beamed at me.

He kissed my forehead and took my hand in his, kneeling to the ground.

In a booming voice, he announced, "I have found my queen. The one whom my magic sings to and whose power answers in return. She is braver, fiercer, and more worthy than I could ever hope to be."

His next words were quieter, meant only for me. "I love you. I will love you until my last breath and I will keep loving you in whatever world comes next." The tears were coming in full force now, sobs wracking my body as I took in the impossibility of this man on his knees for me, proclaiming his love in a burning room.

"Quinn Parry, will you do the honor of marrying me?"

I was on the ground with him without knowing how I got there, his face in my hands as I kissed him once, slowly.

When I looked into his sapphire eyes, I found the old familiar sparkle waiting for me.

With everything in me, I threw my arms around his neck and uttered the easiest answer I had ever given in my life.

"Yes."

I had a vague sense that the room was cleared and Freya escorted to the dungeons, but I felt like a sleepwalker, disconnected from my body as I moved around in a dreamlike haze. Refusing to let Evander out of my sight for any length of time, I clutched his hand tightly in mine even as the healer assessed him for injury.

All the while, he beamed at me, stopping every few moments to press a kiss to my knuckles.

Years seemed to pass before everything was settled and we retired to Evander's chambers at last. Once inside, he closed the doors and turned to meet my eyes. It was the first moment we had alone since before our experiment with Colette and Vanessa.

"Quinn," my name tumbled from his lips as he strode over to me, twining his arms around my waist.

"Is this real?" I whispered into his chest. "It feels like a miracle."

"It is," he said. "Because of you. If it weren't for your bravery, I wouldn't be here now. The kingdom would be floundering, poised for Falerin to invade at any moment. But instead, I get this. I get you." His tone became more emphatic with every word as he searched my eyes for understanding. "I couldn't be more grateful."

"I'm afraid to believe it," I admitted, casting my gaze downward again. "It feels impossible."

So much had happened at once, one unbelievable event after another, and I couldn't reconcile the disparity between where I now found myself and what I had been bracing for. I had expected to spend tonight quietly trying to hold myself together as I helped prepare a feast to celebrate his engagement to someone else. Now, my mind struggled to absorb this new reality.

Would I wake up at any moment to find that this was all a desperate fantasy? It might break my heart in two. Evander must have sensed my anxious thoughts, because he held my chin, tilting my face up so I was looking into his eyes as he spoke his next words.

"If you're asking if my love is true, let me assure you: You are everything good in my world. No one has ever challenged me the way you do. I love your temper almost as much as I adore your incomparable mind. Every time I look at you, it feels as if my heart is beating for the first time.

You have made me an immeasurably better man and I will endeavor to improve still in an impossible effort to deserve you. I love you, Quinn Parry."

Tears blurring my vision, I lifted onto my toes, brushing my lips against his.

When our mouths met, I could hear that music again, sweet and tender. I pulled back to look at Evander's face and traced the line of his jaw, my touch featherlight. Life had never felt so fragile or so important.

I had come so close to losing him. So close to never being able to hold him like this again. A bit of desperation crept into my movements as I kissed him again, more firmly this time. I poured all of the longing, the despair, and the love I had been fighting for months into the embrace. Evander tightened his arms around my waist as he kissed me back, his movements becoming greedy and desperate.

"I am yours, Quinn" he said against my lips.

"And I yours." A twinge of nervousness stirred as I contemplated what I was about to say, but I pushed it aside. "In all ways."

Breaking our kiss, I looked at his bed before catching his eyes once more.

A fire lit in his gaze as he grasped my meaning.

"Are you sure?" he asked.

"Yes. Are you?" It was a challenge, and he knew it.

Without any hesitation, he swept me up into his arms, carrying me to the bed and depositing me delicately on the plush coverlet. Settling over me, he swept my hair off my face in adoration. The moment between his eyes flicking down to my mouth and the kiss drew on for lifetimes, but at last our lips met, and the last of my reservations melted away. The way his hand cradled my face was so soft, so reverent, but still the most real thing I'd ever felt.

Reaching down, I grabbed the hem of my shirt and pulled it over my head, separating us only momentarily. Evander's eyes widened and he shifted back, pulling me onto his lap. Deft fingers unclasped my undergarments and cast them aside.

His hand slid to my breast, thumb lightly tracing its peak, but the teasing sensation wasn't enough. He was being too gentle, and I wanted more. I wanted all of him.

Capturing his mouth again, I drew his lower tip between my teeth, and his answering moan had me grinding against him. The desire I could already feel underneath me lit a fire in my core.

"Take what you want," I reminded him.

A strong arm snaked behind my waist and guided me back to the bed as Evander paved a path down my body with his mouth. The sensation of his lips against my throat, my chest, my stomach already had me panting. He made quick work of his trousers, then slipped my skirt down past my ankles, laying me bare before him.

Leaning back to stare at me, an expression of pure male hunger overtook his face.

"Gods, you're so beautiful. I imagined this moment so many times, but nothing compares to the reality."

A blush crept up on my cheeks as I took in his words.

"You thought about me like this?"

"Gods, yes. I had to satisfy myself with fantasies every time I let you leave these chambers instead of taking you straight to my bed. You have no idea how much I've thought about this," he said. "Thought about you."

"I've thought about you too," I breathed, thinking of nights when, even in my denial, my hand had slid under the covers as I thought about what it would feel like to feel his touch.

He growled in approval, kissing me hungrily. The muscles in his shoulders strained as he lifted himself over me.

"Are you ready?" he asked.

I nodded, shifting to spread my legs wider. Something clenched low within me and another whimper escaped my lips.

"Let me know if anything hurts, and I'll stop."

But it didn't.

He sunk into me slowly, giving me time to adjust to every inch, and the sensation of fullness that overtook me was like being consumed by my own pleasure from the inside out. I bucked my hips, begging for more, and he started to move within me.

This. This was transcendent. Our very souls collided as our gazes locked, sharing breaths of gasps and moans as our hips met again and again.

The sounds that came out of me were more animal than human as he whispered in my ear, "Oh gods, you feel so good. You're doing so well. Look how good you're taking me."

I tilted my pelvis, giving him even deeper access, and when he moaned, the sound threatened to undo me.

My release was building, and I searched wildly for his mouth again. Capturing mine with an equal passion, he shifted so his pelvis ground against that sensitive bundle of nerves as he took me.

"Come for me, Quinn."

My legs spasmed as I shattered into a million pieces, his name on my lips. I continued rocking my hips against him, wringing out every ounce of pleasure I could, until he buried his face in my neck and fell off the ledge with me.

Then he lifted his head up, searching my face.

"Are you all right?"

I nodded and kissed him again, softly this time. It was a lazy morning kind of kiss. The type of kiss that feels like a soft space to land. One that relays all your feelings without the need for words, full of passion but unhurried. For once, we had time. So much time.

PART TWO

Chapter 16

PREPARATIONS FOR THE WEDDING were well underway a week later.

Evander and I sat in the sunroom, taking some much-needed time away from our endless list of urgent royal tasks to tackle some of the planning together. Truth be told, I would have preferred we spend our time doing *other things,* but he insisted.

"Remind me again why we aren't just taking the oath tonight?" I complained, looking at my hundredth fabric swatch of the day.

"Because, my love," answered Evander with an amused smile, "I only get to marry you once, and I'm going to do it correctly."

He kissed the top of my head, cajoling me. "Besides, this is a reason for the people to celebrate. I wouldn't deny them that privilege, would you?" he asked, raising his eyebrows in challenge.

"The quicker we get everything taken care of, the sooner I can help you shoulder the burden," I argued. "Wouldn't it be better for *the people* to have their king in full health?"

"Already negotiating like a queen," he laughed. "Really, I am doing better." It was true that some color had crept back into his face, and though he looked like he might fall asleep at any moment, his spirits were high. Hope was a powerful thing.

I had been working on my own Wielding, too. Evander and I had officially hired Colette onto the staff to help me train, and he had even found a place for her father to stay as a groundskeeper until we could fortify the wards enough to keep the gates open for travel between the castle and village. That would be our first order of business after my coronation. I was so excited for Serena.

As eager as I was to take some of the weight off Evander, I had to admit that my control over my powers was weak at best. My Gift seemed to center around shielding, which Evander was optimistic would work well in supporting the kingdom's wards, but I had yet to gain any form of mastery over it.

Now that I knew what magic felt like, I couldn't believe it had taken me so long to realize I had been casting shields around myself my whole life. I was still subconsciously creating wards, and visitors to Evander's chambers found themselves flung from the door on more than one occasion while we were *occupied.* Unfortunately, I still wasn't able to cast one on demand by myself.

I could only hope something would settle into place during the tethering ceremony, which would be held directly after the wedding and coronation.

"Regrettably, I have a meeting," Evander said, standing, "but I fully support whatever choice you make." He gestured to the swatches, and I recognized a hint of the teasing tone he used only with me.

I groaned.

"Try to have some fun, Quinn," he said. "It is your wedding, after all."

He put his hands on the dark mahogany arms of my chair and leaned in to plant a brief, loving kiss on my lips. His eyes darkened as he pulled away a little too slowly.

"I'm sure the wedding will be wonderful," I said, trying and failing to hide my blush, "but I'm much more excited for the marriage."

"As am I, *fiancée,*" he purred, his face only inches away from my own.

Gods, I loved the way that sounded.

"Say that again," I whispered, somewhere between a plea and a challenge.

"You," he kissed my jaw, the touch featherlight, "my fiancée," his lips moved to the spot just behind my earlobe, giving me chills, "are going to be," he nipped at my earlobe, "the most incredible queen." He looked into my eyes, and I felt my soul shake with the sincerity of his words. "And I cannot wait to call you my wife."

I reached up and laced my fingers behind his neck, drawing him in until our lips met again. Gods, the taste of him was the sweetest thing I had ever experienced. Every time he kissed me, time seemed to stop entirely, reduced to the smell of leather and ink and the feel of his stubble on my lips. That bond between our Gifts shimmered brilliantly, and I could almost hear an actual song whenever we were in the same room.

Though the kiss started soft and slow, they never stayed that way for long. There was too much need between us, too much desperation to hold onto this precious thing we had almost lost forever.

Lowering himself to his knees, he slid me from the chair into his lap. His fingers wound themselves into my hair at the base of my skull, gripping it and pulling ever so slightly–not enough to hurt, but enough to elicit a breathy moan. I felt him smile against my lips.

I pulled away, kissing down the strong column of his neck and just inside the collar of his shirt. "You're going to be late," I muttered against his skin.

"At the moment I don't much care," he panted, eyes closed, head thrown back in want.

"I'm willing to bet Finch will, though," I teased, pulling away and placing one last chaste kiss on his lips as I stood up, offering him a hand.

"You'll pay for that later," he promised, winking at me as he adjusted his pants.

A saccharine smile lit up my face. "You started it. Now go! Let me finish this before I have to meet with Colette this afternoon."

Evander chuckled and headed to the door. I returned my attention to the swatches, trying to distinguish the difference between "Hunter" and "Fern," when I realized I could still feel him here, that cord that tied our magic together humming pleasantly at his proximity.

Looking up, I found him standing in the doorway, observing me with a serene smile on his face. He flushed slightly, as if he were a child who had been caught sneaking sweets from the larder.

"You're so beautiful," he said.

"Go!" I giggled, and he raised his hands in mock surrender, backing out of the door without breaking eye contact.

Looking out the window at the stunning gardens, I inhaled, holding the breath at the top before I let it come whooshing out, giddy. I wondered how long it would be before I stopped feeling like I might wake up at any moment.

Queen, he had said. I supposed that should've scared me more than it did. I had no experience leading and no education in diplomacy or politics, but with our Gifts dancing together, snapping into place like pieces of a puzzle, I felt like I could do anything. Deep in my bones it felt fated.

What I was less certain about was how my mother was going to react. I had foiled an assassination attempt, agreed to take on the throne of a country, and accepted the responsibility of protecting its people, but I still hadn't told my mother about my engagement. I wasn't even sure I wanted to.

That's a problem for another day, I decided for the fourth day in a row, and picked up a swatch called "Northern Blue." It reminded me of Evander's eyes.

I pinned it to the thick cream-colored card Georgette had given us to make our selection and tidied up the table before going to find Colette.

We met in the same ballroom where the contestants had practiced. How many times had I stood in this very spot, watching Freya sharpen her fire-wielding skills without suspecting a thing? The thought made me sick.

Schooling myself, I fought to remember that Freya was in the dungeons. She couldn't hurt Evander, or anyone, anymore.

Now, this room was mine to train in. Not much had changed except the absence of the refreshment table. I stared at the space it once occupied and let out a small sigh. I was no longer working in the kitchens. A necessary adjustment, but one I still mourned every day.

Sometimes I snuck in to help Mellie between training and my coronation preparation duties, but it was never for more than a half hour at a time, and I missed the meditative practice of kneading dough, watching as it went from scraggly and rough to smooth and elastic under my hands.

Mellie had no qualms about ushering me out of the kitchen–queen-to-be or not–when she knew I had things to do, snapping a towel playfully at me if necessary. Despite my grumbling, I secretly loved the normalcy of it. Maybe I would sneak back in tonight and make something easy, something I knew by heart. Cookies?

Right now, though, I needed to focus. Colette hadn't arrived yet, and I rubbed my hands together as I waited, willing them to cooperate so I could finally make some progress on my solo shielding today.

Sometimes I trained alone, and sometimes Evander was able to join me. The joint sessions were always more productive, his magic helping mine along and guiding it gently to where it needed to go. They worked in perfect harmony, a beautiful call and response that always took my breath away. Now that we had the answer to the prophecy, it seemed so *obvious.*

The sessions where I was on my own, however, felt like slogging through mud. I tried grounding my feet, imagining a beam of light, envisioning the ward I wanted to create, and two dozen other tips and tricks Colette, Evander, and even a disgruntled General Finch had given me, but whenever I reached for my magic, I hit a cold stone wall. But maybe today would be different.

Maybe today I would succeed.

"Good morning," Colette sing-songed, chipper as ever as she floated into the room, her pale pink dress billowing behind her angelically. She and Vanessa were no longer hiding their relationship and Colette was practically glowing with happiness.

"So," she began, bouncing lightly on the balls of her feet. "Today we're going to try something *fun.*" She punctuated the word with a wicked grin that made me nervous.

"What did you have in–OW!" I massaged my arm where the leather ball hit me.

"Sorry!" Colette winced slightly. "But seeing as what we've been doing isn't working, I thought we'd try something new. Do you remember helping me master vine blocking?"

I did. I scowled at her, suddenly making sense of the leather balls.

"You know, you actually asked me to do that," I pointed out. "This doesn't exactly make us even."

Rather than replying, Colette lobbed another ball at me. I stepped out of the way as it swished past my left ear.

"Well, it defeats the purpose if you just step aside," Colette pouted. "It's not actually going to hurt you, you know." She rolled her eyes in a manner very reminiscent of someone else I knew. Vanessa was a bad influence on her.

"So you want me to stand here while you throw things at me?"

"The way I see it, your magic automatically activates when it perceives you're in danger." she explained. "Maybe we just need to help it along a little."

A third ball flew through the air towards me, and I forced myself to stay still as it hit my thigh.

"All right," I sighed. I could see her logic, and at this point I was willing to try anything. Hopefully this would work. I refused to be crowned only to be useless.

"Another."

An hour later, we were both tired and sweaty, slumped on the floor of the ballroom dejectedly.

"We'll get it," Colette said, but I could tell that even her constant optimism was fading.

I groaned and lay down on the tile, throwing my forearm across my face in frustration.

"How can something that's supposedly fated be this *difficult?* What if this is all a massive mistake and I can't do it?" The heels of my hands conjured stars behind my lids as I pressed them into my eyes.

"The moment you convince yourself you can't do something, you've eliminated all possibility of growth, Quinn. You'll just keep looking to prove yourself right every time." Colette shook her head.

"But it's like my Gift is deliberately ignoring me. Why?" And how could I get it to *stop?*

"Honestly, Quinn, I don't know. Vanessa's been in the library every day looking for historical documentation of another Wielder presenting this late, but we can't find anything."

I knew firsthand how much time Vanessa had been spending researching. It was quite inconvenient, as I had a lot of studying to do on Enorias's political system before my coronation, and she and I still weren't on speaking terms. We each gave the other a wide berth any time we were roaming the shelves at the same time. Still, I was begrudgingly grateful for any help I could get.

"Your Gift has been running wild for so long that you don't know how to communicate with it," Colette continued, "but you have to stop thinking of it as something outside yourself that you have to wrangle. It's an innate part of you that's been there all along, fighting to keep you safe. Try showing it a little more appreciation."

"Or what, its feelings will be hurt?" I quipped. Stopping myself, I took a breath. "I'm sorry. You don't deserve me snapping at you." The pressure was setting me on edge, but that wasn't Colette's fault. "I'm just scared. Time is almost up and I can't get out of my own head."

"It's okay to be scared," Colette said. "But we can't let that fear freeze you. Acknowledge the feeling and let it go."

"That sounds a lot easier than it is," I grumbled. Planting my palms back on the cool, smooth surface of the tile, I pushed myself up to a seated position. "I do appreciate it, really. The magic. It's saved my life on more than one occasion and without it . . ." I shuddered. "But it still feels so abstract. Surreal, even. It's hard to come to terms with the fact that it's been with me my entire life and I had no clue. It's . . . a lot." I gestured vaguely with my hands.

"I know," was Colette's only reply. The seconds stretched into minutes as I reflected on her words. I was scared I wouldn't be the leader Enorias needed, yes, but on a more personal level, I was also afraid of the ground shifting under me again. I hadn't let myself get comfortable, lest I lose it all.

"Every night I worry that it will be gone when I wake," I admitted. "It feels like an impossible dream that might vanish with the dawn."

Colette squeezed my hand.

"You're going to connect with it," she promised with more resolve. "We'll keep researching to find a method that works. You're already making progress when the king is here, and the two of you will be holding the wards together. Everything will be okay." As always, her determination and positivity made me thankful to have her as a friend. Even if I were struggling, at least I wasn't fighting alone.

Colette got up and dusted off the front of her. "I'm heading to the library to join Nessa," she announced. "Take a walk, get some fresh air. The most productive thing you can do right now is rest, clear your head, and figure out what you're feeling."

I nodded. A walk in the gardens sounded nice.

Before making my way to the greenhouses, I went up to the third floor to change. While I had been spending most nights with Evander, this was still my official place of residence until after the wedding.

Seeing the stacks of boxes piled on the bed, I sighed. Georgette had gotten it into her head that I needed a more "royal wardrobe" and she would broker no arguments against it. I tried in vain to insist that I preferred my basic linen blouses and skirts, but she maintained that the people needed to see me as a queen, not a baker.

As a result, I was met with an array of pieces to try on every day. A slip of paper corresponding to each article was provided for me to detail my thoughts on the garments so adjustments could be made.

It seemed a trivial thing to spend my time on, but I supposed I'd burn out if I trained around the clock like I wanted to.

I opened the lid of a periwinkle box and was assaulted by the too-strong aroma of lavender.

Ignoring the tickle in my throat, I dove in and picked up a swath of fabric nestled within the tissue paper. To my surprise, it was unexpectedly lovely. The sage green dress featured a delicate floral print on the bodice, lacing that didn't look too restrictive, and full skirts that were accented by a delicate line of floral lace around the bottom. When I shucked off my training clothes and slipped into it, I still felt like myself.

I did a little twirl in the privacy of my room, taking a moment to appreciate the way it managed to be beautiful without being ridiculous or show offish. Smoothing the skirts with my hands, I found a small slit in the side.

Pockets! I smiled. Maybe Georgette didn't hate me after all.

I set out for the gardens, determined to give my mind rest from the constant worrying over what the next week might hold. Colette was right; I desperately needed a break.

The late autumn sun shone on my skin, and I turned my face toward it, basking in the warmth of its rays against the crisp chill in the air. As I walked along, I passed rows of white anemones with cheerful green centers and bunches of purple aster.

It was amazing what they could grow so late in the season. Colette's father Damian had big plans for the garden paths, and Colette would talk about them with a dreamy look in her eye, no doubt looking forward to the day she could stop babysitting me and return to her passion for growing things.

My sigh masked the sound of footsteps behind me. A woman cleared her throat and I whirled around, thankful to see only Georgette on the path.

"Miss Parry, I wondered if I might have a word?"

"Of course." Nervous, I followed her to one of the outdoor seating areas, where she had a bistro table ready with tea and cookies.

The formidable woman gestured for me to sit and waited until I was settled before taking a seat herself. Despite my best efforts to remain calm, I felt my pulse pounding in my temples as I stared back at her. If she was about to tell me I wasn't good enough for Evander or the kingdom, I wasn't sure I would be able to contradict her.

Georgette took a short breath in through her nose and closed her eyes only a fraction of a second longer than a blink before speaking her piece.

"I believe I owe you an apology," she said matter-of-factly.

"Excuse me?"

Georgette reached for the teapot and poured two cups of what smelled like rooibos. A slight tremor in her hands prompted the sudden realization that she had to be in her seventies.

"You have to understand that my intention in warning you away from the king was born out of care for Evander and his well-being." I didn't miss that she, too, used his first name.

"You don't need to apologize-"

"I do," she said, her tone unwavering and resolute. "I've seen the change in him over the last week, a change that has occurred even before having the full burden of the crown removed from his shoulders, and I want to thank you. I've cared for Evander since he was an infant, and when I saw how distracted he had become by your relationship this autumn, I was frightened. I knew he needed to focus on finding a partner that could support him, and I did not think that you were that person." Her gaze cut to me and I felt a pang of shame and embarrassment. Of course she didn't. Who would think an apprentice baker could be a part of the prophecy?

"But," she continued, "I realize now that I should not have spoken to you as I did, whether you were the future queen or not. Being someone that Evander deems worthy carries weight with me, and I lost sight of that. I am sorry, truly."

I resisted the urge to dismiss the apology again, settling instead on a simple thank you, which Georgette accepted with grace.

"I'm ashamed that I only realized my error after his proposal brought about such a transformation. I've never seen him with so much confidence."

She gazed into the gardens with a faraway look on her face before continuing. "I think a part of Evander didn't truly realize that he would be king one day. His parents were so beloved, and Evalina hid her decline well. At the very least, he thought he would have more time. To see him grapple with his new role as well as the absence of his mother the past few months has been nothing short of heartbreaking." Her face gave away none of the emotion she referenced, but her voice was clipped as she stirred her tea. "Something about you makes him feel ready to step up and lead, and I couldn't be more thankful for that."

I wasn't sure I could take credit for that, but I appreciated her candor. "I'm grateful to know that Evander has someone in his life who cares for him so deeply," I said. "That is truly a gift, and one I know he doesn't take for granted."

Georgette looked down at her teacup, blinking her eyes to will away any moisture. It was clear she loved him very much.

"What was he like as a boy?" I asked.

"Full of mischief, that one." The corners of her eyes crinkled as she chuckled at the memory. "I never knew whether I would find him with his nose in a book or up the tallest tree in the courtyard. He and Vanessa were always staging practical jokes on the noblemen. They once set General Finch's coat ablaze trying to light a firework under the table in the great hall. Finch was a Colonel then, mind you."

Her smile lingered for a moment before turning into something more reflective. "He was always very attached to his mother. Wanted to be just like her. His father, Roland, instructed him in matters of diplomacy, but Evalina was the one who helped him hone his Gift. I worry about him without her. I never thought I'd live to see the day he got married without her there."

My heart sank at the thought. We'd hoped she'd wake by now, but the healers hadn't reported any progress.

"I can't even imagine what this must be like for him." I said. I'd tried to talk to him about it, but he avoided the conversation whenever I brought it up, eyes going misty.

"Will your family be attending?" Georgette asked. I hadn't been expecting that question. My delicate porcelain teacup served as a shield, hiding my discomfort as I brought it to my lips.

"My father is away on business and likely wouldn't be here in time even if I could get the news to him. I've sent a letter, but I have little hope he'll be in attendance." It broke my heart, but I knew he would understand. And there would be plenty of time for him to get to know Evander when he returned. He'd never have to work again if he didn't want to. "My mother . . ." I shrugged. "I'm not sure if she would even want to come."

"If I may give you one last piece of unsolicited advice," Georgette said, "I'm sure she would be very grateful if you gave her the choice. I don't know the specifics of your situation, nor do I need to, but I can't imagine she would want to miss her daughter's wedding, whatever unpleasantness may be in your past."

At a loss for what to say, I took another sip and turned the conversation to more pleasant topics.

Later, as I headed up to Evander's chambers for the evening, Georgette's words echoed in my ears. I wasn't sure how I could simultaneously want my mother at my wedding and not want her anywhere near me, but my heart managed it nevertheless. More than anything, I yearned for the abstract concept of my mother, the one I imagined I might have by my side if things were different. But Wilomena was not that woman.

By the time I arrived at our rooms, I found myself wrapped in too many feelings to name. A decision needed to be made soon, but I couldn't extract one line of thinking long enough to follow it to its conclusion. It was all too muddied by emotion. And I needed to speak to Evander about it. After all, it was his wedding too.

I opened the door and his eyes widened at the sight of me, the passion in them starting to churn like wind picking up on a once-calm sea.

"You look–" His voice was honeyed and full of longing.

"Not too much?" I asked, looking down at my dress self-consciously. I had all but forgotten about it.

"Never. Never too much of you. Never enough of you," he said, wrapping his arms around me and nuzzling his face into my neck. I took a moment to breathe in the sweet, unhurried normalcy of it.

"One of Georgette's picks," I said. "It showed up this afternoon in my chambers."

Evander straightened up and rolled his eyes at the words. "*These* are your chambers, you know. I will be a very happy man when I don't have to sneak you in here to keep up this facade of living separately until the wedding. It's ridiculous."

"I'm inclined to agree with you," I muttered into his chest, "but I do see Georgette's point." Pulling away just enough to look up at him, I met his eyes. "I had a chat with her today."

"Oh?"

I hadn't told Evander about her earlier warning and didn't think it would accomplish anything now. Adding tension to their relationship seemed unnecessary. Instead, I took the opportunity to tease him.

"I asked her what you were like as a boy," I said, mouth already curling into a smug smile.

"I'm sure she had a fair few embarrassing stories to tell you." He tried to play it off, but I could see a hint of genuine self-consciousness on his face.

"A few," I said, laughing lightly. "But she also told me about your mother and how close you two always were."

That hadn't been what he was expecting. In the span of a heartbeat, he went rigid under my hands and the hard set of his jaw told me he had been doing his best to avoid thinking about his mother's absence.

I understood that, but I also knew the kind of partner I wanted to be, one who would check in with him even if he said he was fine. If he didn't want to talk about it, I wouldn't force him, but I did want to give him a chance to have the conversation.

When he didn't say anything, I pressed on. "I know how important she is to you. Are you all right?" A silly question. Of course he wasn't.

"Yes," he responded too quickly. After taking a moment to process what I had asked, he burrowed his face into my hair. "And no," he added. "I always thought she would be here for this, but I know we're running out of time."

"Do we need to postpone?" While I didn't like the idea of him continuing to live on the edge of burnout to stabilize the wards, not having his mother at our wedding might hurt him even more. Maybe we could find another way.

"No." His tone was firm and resolute. "Of course I wish she could be there, but I have a duty to the kingdom, to myself, and to you," he said, his voice getting more tender with each word.

"You know I would wait," I said, searching his eyes for any doubts. "I would wait as long as I needed to for you."

"But you don't have to," he reassured me. "We'll celebrate with her again when she wakes." Though his voice faltered, I could tell he was sincere.

"You know you don't have to be strong about this, don't you?" I asked, searching the gold flecks within the blue of his eyes. "I want you to feel safe with me."

"I do," Evander promised. "I just don't know how to process it all. The unknown is . . ." He shook his head. "I feel like I'm mourning her while she's still here."

I wanted to fix it. To take everyone and everything that had ever hurt him and lock them far, far away.

"That's heartbreaking," I managed, wishing the platitude could be more helpful but knowing there were no words that could rectify this wrong.

"What about your mother?" he asked. "Have you decided whether you're going to invite her to the wedding?"

"No." The admission was heavy on my tongue. "Georgette thinks I should. She said that she should have the choice, but–"

"No," Evander cut in emphatically. "Your mother lost her right to a choice the moment she laid hands on you. If you want her there, it needs to be for you. This is *your* decision, Quinn."

Shooting him a thankful smile, I started to think out loud as I walked. "If she's not there, I have a feeling I may regret it later. And not only because she'll hold it over me, which she will. I also know I'd spend the whole day feeling guilty, and that's not what I want for my wedding."

"What if we invited her, but minimized the contact as much as possible? You wouldn't even have to speak to her if you didn't want to."

I considered the suggestion and felt my shoulders relax.

"Honestly, that sounds ideal. Does that make me a horrid person?"

"No." Evander interrupted my pacing and smoothed my hair, gently tilting my chin up so my eyes met his. "It makes you far nobler and more forgiving than she deserves."

I nodded, tears in my eyes for the second time today.

"If you don't think it would drain you too much for me to move through the wards, I'll take a trip to the village tomorrow. I need to tell her in person."

"Do you want me to come with you?" Evander asked.

It was tempting. The thought of having his support and protection made the outing significantly less frightening. Mother wouldn't dare criticize our marriage in front of the king himself, would she?

But my gut told me I needed to do this by myself. If I were going to stand a chance as queen, I needed to find the courage to take charge of my life and move past my history.

"I'll be fine." The bluff was more for my own benefit than his. Evander would support whatever decision I made.

"You will," he said, sounding far more confident than I felt. "But I want you to know I'm here for you either way."

I did. And that alone gave me the confidence I needed.

Chapter 17

I woke before Evander the next morning, my body still on a baker's schedule. Golden light was just starting to pour in through the window, kissing the bump on the bridge of his nose and casting long shadows from his thick eyelashes onto his cheeks.

For a moment, I caught a glimpse of the boy Georgette had reminisced about so fondly. The lines around his brows softened, taking the last few months of stress and grief with them. I wished we could stay like this forever.

Unfortunately for me, I needed to go. The final fitting for my wedding gown was at two o'clock and I needed to be back from the village before then. Slipping from the bed as silently as I could, I dressed in the same sage green dress I had worn the day before.

I probably should have put on something new, but the memory of Evander's eyes when he saw me in this gown bolstered me with a foreign sense of confidence. Besides, Mother wouldn't know what I had worn the day before.

As I waited for my carriage in front of the gate, Vanessa emerged from the castle.

"Why do you have to go so godsdamned early?" she groused.

"I think my schedule is my business," I replied, training my gaze on the long landscaped drive rather than looking at her.

"Not when His Royal Heinous orders me to accompany you."

My eyes must've been wide as dinner plates, because Vanessa put her hands up in placation.

"Relax," she said. "I'll stay in the carriage. He just didn't want you going alone and assumed you wouldn't want a whole patrol showing up to your mother's house with you."

As much as I appreciated the gesture, did it have to be Vanessa? Evander knew we weren't on the best terms after the attempted mind-wiping stunt she had pulled. Though we'd settled into a tense truce over the past week, the ghost of our friendship loomed over us every time we interacted.

In fact, as I thought about it, I realized that was probably the reason he had asked her. Evander and Vanessa had grown up together and I knew she was important to him. I couldn't imagine he liked the all-too-obvious discord between us.

Well, I didn't have to trust her, but I could be civil. For Evander's sake.

The carriage pulled up and I gave the driver directions to the cottage. This time I felt the slight ripple of the ward as I slipped through it. I attempted painful small talk with Vanessa as we journeyed into the village, but she largely ignored me in favor of picking at her nails with the point of her knife until, at long last, we arrived.

"We're here, Ms. Parry," the driver called back, and I steeled myself as I opened the door and stepped onto the cobblestone street.

Nothing had changed since I had been here last, but I saw everything with a very different eye. The world outside the cottage, which had once seemed so foreign and exciting to me, suddenly looked small. The vendors down the road were opening their carts for the day, and I smiled as I watched the cobbler begin to enchant his shoes.

All the time I'd spent admiring Wielders and their Gifts made more sense in the wake of my manifestation. The defensiveness I always felt when Mother complained about the injustices of magical society, too. Perhaps a part of me had known all along.

My fist had hardly left the door before my mother opened it, her immaculate countenance showing no sign of early morning haze.

"Quinn!" She smiled when she met my eyes, her usual combative demeanor glaringly absent.

"Mother?" There was no hiding my bewilderment at the bizarre greeting.

Ignoring my confusion, she threw the door open wide to invite me in. No sooner had I crossed the threshold than my heart began to work harder, the memory of the place still fresh enough to feel dangerous. A strange feeling of emptiness came over me. Too many ghosts of the past in this place, I supposed.

After whisking us into the parlor, she sat across from me with her hands in her lap expectantly.

"I've been so anxious to see you!" she beamed. No trace of anger lingered in her words, as if our last conversation in this room hadn't been a screaming argument. None of this made sense. What was her angle? I was certain she had one.

"I've come to extend an invitation," I said, the words stiff as freshly starched crinoline. "I assume you've heard the news?"

"Of course I've heard the news!" she exclaimed. "My own daughter, queen of Enorias! Who would ever have guessed?"

I tried not to let the shock show on my face. I'd endured Mother's complaints about the royals for as long as I could remember, and now she was–what? *Excited* for me to become one of them? I had come here ready for an argument, but it didn't feel like a fight was on the horizon.

Which is good, isn't it? I thought, trying to ignore the pit in my stomach that told me to be cautious. I pushed the feeling aside and did my best to return her smile.

"Certainly not me," I confided, unable to help myself as I desperately grasped for the olive branch she seemed to be holding. Maybe I could have my mother back after all. "But Evander is a good man, and–"

"Oh I'm sure," she cut me off. "So when is the ceremony?"

"Four days' time," I told her, "at noon. I would be honored if you would come as my guest."

"Of course I will!" She accepted without any hesitation. "You think I would miss my own daughter's wedding?"

"Coronation too," I added, puffing with pride a bit.

Mother clapped her hands together.

"I'll have to meet with the tailor to have something suitable commissioned this afternoon," she stood up abruptly, "and I'm sure you have far more important things to do than sit here and talk to me. I must let you get back to the palace, but I so look forward to seeing you again."

Her wide smile looked plastered on her face. Usually I was an expert at judging her mood, but this was foreign to me. She gripped me in a hug for a moment before pulling back, a more serious look taking root in her eyes.

"I do love you, my daughter," she promised. "I hope you know that."

That was as close to an apology as I was going to get. She ushered me toward the door less than five minutes after I had arrived, and I spent the whole carriage ride home wondering what in the hells just happened.

That night I made good on my promise to myself to spend some time in the kitchen. When I knew the space would be empty, I tiptoed out of bed in my cotton nightgown, running through a mental list of recipes I could try.

I longed for something challenging that would take my mind off the thousand uncomfortable questions that had been swirling around in my head since this afternoon.

The pantry was fully stocked, and I began to pull out ingredients for macarons. Sugar? Check. Eggs? Check. Almond flour? Check.

I grabbed some lemon extract for flavoring and set my spoils on the counter, running through the steps in my head. The precision of macarons was exactly what I needed right now. A perfect distraction.

Once I began to mix the dry ingredients in a bowl, it didn't take long to fall into the meditative process I knew so well. Before I knew it, the batter was done, so I located a piping bag and began to make small circles on a sheet of parchment paper.

"We have to stop meeting like this," came a deep voice from the doorway. Evander chuckled as he strolled into the room, still in his nightclothes. I laughed softly as I recognized my own words from a few weeks ago. Had it only been weeks? It seemed like a lifetime.

"Everything all right?" he asked, snaking his arms around me from behind and settling his chin into the space between my neck and shoulder.

"Mhmm," I hummed, biting my lower lip in concentration as I tapped the tray on the counter to expel the air bubbles.

He began pressing hot, open-mouthed kisses to the side of my neck, and a hiss escaped my lips as I grabbed the counter.

Well, that's another type of distraction, I thought, leaning into his touch.

Evander huffed a laugh against my skin, moving upward to concentrate on my ear, drawing the lobe gently between his teeth as he let out a low sound of approval.

"Do you remember the last time I found you down here late at night?" he hummed.

"I remember you made me burn my tart crusts," I said, fighting to keep my voice at a normal pitch.

"Is that what you remember?" Evander asked, returning to my neck. "That's certainly not the impression that night left on me." His voice rumbled against my skin.

"No?" I didn't quite manage to inject the challenge I was aiming for into my tone. It came out breathy, all need.

"No." He breathed the word against my neck as if he were whispering a great secret into my flesh. "I remember the way you smelled like sugar and vanilla. I remember the way your mouth tasted exactly how I had imagined it would." My head lolled back as he drew his hands lightly over my shoulders and down my sides, making my skin prickle in goose flesh through the thin cotton of my nightgown.

"And I remember the way you let me lift you up onto the counter and that little sound you made when you realized just how much I wanted you. Gods, the noises you make . . ."

I spun around to face him, thrusting my hands into his hair hungrily and stealing his next words from his lips. Yes, I remembered that night, and I remembered all too well the hopelessness that followed when I thought I couldn't have this, have him.

This time, there were no pastries in the oven to call my attention away. Even if there had been, I would rather let the world burn than tear my focus away from the way Evander's mouth claimed mine. The shimmering string of our bond told me exactly how much he wanted me.

He hoisted me so my legs wrapped around his waist, and backed me up to the cooler. The cold metal was a sharp contrast from the heat of his body. Our tongues warred with each other, each fighting to gain ground.

My hands tangled in his thick, dark waves as he palmed one of my breasts. The sensation drew a sharp breath from my lungs, and the noise was all the confirmation he needed. Gently, he pushed the nightgown off my shoulders, one strap at a time, exposing my skin to the chilly evening air. When I was laid bare, he moved his lips to my neck, kissing down my throat, my collarbone, my chest, then to the sensitive peak of my nipple. My back arched when he drew it into his mouth, flicking his tongue in a way that made me shudder. It still wasn't enough.

"I need this off, now," I said, but Evander gingerly set me down and took a step back, his mouth kicking up at the corner in amusement.

"In your workspace, Quinn?" he tutted, toying with me. "Not very *professional.*" His goading smirk lit a fire in my core.

"I don't work here anymore," I tossed back. His teasing didn't have much bite when I could see his desire straining against his trousers. I let my nightgown drop to the floor.

"Hmmm, I suppose you don't," he mused, stalking back toward me. His hands landed on my hips, thumbs tracing light circles on my skin as he spoke. "Though if you're interested in that concept, we could certainly try this upstairs another time. I can think of some interesting positions I'd like to try on the throne with my queen." Eyes darkening, he slid his hands lower, lifting me onto one of the large counters in the center of the room. "My wife."

Climbing up to join me, he laid us down, his arms moving to bracket my face and he looked into my eyes.

"Evander," I breathed. That devilish grin returned to his face, but he only pressed a chaste kiss to my lips before sitting up and sliding off the counter.

"What are you . . .?"

"Shhhh," he cut me off.

So slowly it felt like torture, he slid my undergarments off and dropped them to the floor, all the while keeping his blue eyes trained on mine. I realized what he meant to do only an instant before he finally broke eye contact, lowering his head and dragging his tongue slowly through my center.

Oh gods.

Evander moaned. "Fuck, Quinn. You even taste the way I imagined you would that night."

At the sound of my name, I let out a little whimper.

"Tell me what feels good."

"Evander, you don't have to–"

He shushed me again, pressing a kiss to my inner thigh. "Let me take care of you." His hot mouth returned to its ministrations, and he tried a faster pace, finding that aching bud of nerves and flicking his tongue over it.

I cried out; there was no room for embarrassment as my skin caught fire.

"Like that?" he asked, momentarily stopping. I missed the contact immediately, shifting up to meet him again.

"*Gods yes.*"

With a low chuckle, he resumed, and I could only hope my shields were working, because the sounds I was making were enough to wake the whole castle.

His hands snaked up my thighs, ending above his mouth with a slight upward pressure to widen his access.

"I need-" I gasped. "I need more."

He dragged his fingers along my entrance, teasing me.

"Please," I breathed.

"Please what?" he rumbled. I could feel the ghost of his smile on my skin, and the sensation threatened to be my undoing then and there.

"Give me more," The huskiness in my voice came from someone else. "Use your hand."

That gravelly chuckle was going to be the death of me.

"That's my girl," he growled in approval, finally sliding two fingers inside me. When he moved them, I saw stars behind my lids. My toes curled as I rocked up into him.

Opening my eyes, I watched his dark curls between my thighs, and the sight was enough to push me over the edge. Wave after wave overtook me, my hips bucking off the counter as I found my release.

When I finally stilled, Evander lifted his head, and licked his lips slowly.

"Your chambers. Now," I panted.

"Excellent idea, my love."

Abandoning the macaron batter, we practically ran up the stairs, giggling, to finish what we started.

I didn't have a chance to tell Evander what happened with my mother until the next morning when we woke up in his four-poster bed, a happy mess of tangled limbs and sleepy smiles.

"Good morning, my love," he smiled down at me, brushing the hair off of my forehead before planting a tender kiss there.

I sighed contentedly and nuzzled down into his arms. "Good morning." Luxuriating in the downy covers, I took a moment of quiet gratitude. A week was not nearly long enough to have gotten used to the joy of a life with him. Truth be told, I didn't know if I ever would.

"What does your day look like?" he asked.

"Dull, if I'm being honest." Preparation for my coronation involved copious amounts of studying, so I'd likely spend the majority of my day in the library. I hoped Vanessa would be otherwise occupied so I wouldn't have to repeat yesterday's performance of stilted conversation.

Reminded of our strange sojourn into the village, I brought Evander up to speed.

"So I suppose my mother's attending," I finished in resignation.

"And how do you feel about that?" Evander asked, stroking my hair. I looked up at him and smiled. Bedhead. Despite my complicated feelings about my mother, my heart soared. Nothing she could do would ruin this.

"All right, I suppose," I said. "Her behavior made me feel . . . 'uneasy' might be the best word. But I don't think she'd be bold enough to make a scene at the wedding."

I hoped.

"We'll have someone keep an eye on her. Just in case," Evander promised, and I nodded my thanks.

"It's so strange to think about you meeting her," I mused, tracing circles on Evander's chest. "It feels as though my life is split in two, and both halves can't possibly coexist in the same space."

"Though I'd love nothing more than to let her know exactly what I think about her treatment of you," he said, "I promise I'll be cordial. I know avoiding tension on our wedding day is important to you, and I trust you to fight your own battles, as long as you know that I am a ready sword for you to wield as you wish."

"I know you are. But I want this to be a day of celebration, not confrontation." Besides, I didn't need protection from her any longer.

It was long past time for me to take the reins of my own life and decide how, if at all, she fit into it. At last, it would be my choice.

"Quinn," Evander began, "your visit to your mother got me thinking, and I'd like to ask something of you. If you have time today–the decision is yours, of course, but it would mean a great deal to me if you'd let me take you to meet my mother."

My heart sang in response to his request. I'd been hoping he would ask, but I didn't want to push or pry. Without knowing Evalina before she fell ill, I wasn't sure how she would feel about being seen in such a vulnerable state, and I wanted to respect both her and her son.

"She's still unresponsive," Evander continued, biting his lip, "but I'd like to believe she can sense my presence at the very least. It feels wrong for the two of you to be complete strangers." At this, he studied my face, eyebrows scrunched, and I realized he was waiting nervously for my reaction.

Placing a hand on his cheek, I reassured him. "I would love nothing more than to meet your mother, Evander. It would be an honor."

Relief flashed on his face before he kissed me, featherlight and adoring.

"I love you," he murmured.

"And I love you." So much that it felt impossible to communicate the feeling with words. Bringing his hand to my lips, I gave it a firm squeeze, and rose to dress for the day.

It was surreal to arrive at the chambers where I was supposed to bring Queen Evalina's breakfast all those months ago, this time with Evander's hand in mine. I recalled the contentious conversation we'd shared in the stairwell that day and smiled. I already had so much to thank his mother for.

"Are you ready?" Evander asked.

Truthfully, I didn't think anything could have primed either of us for this moment, but, like all important moments in life, it wasn't going to wait for me to be prepared.

Swallowing, I nodded to him, and he raised a hand to knock gently on the warm wood of the door.

The figure that opened it was a surprise.

"Mellie?"

My shock was mirrored in her eyes, which only widened as she took in Evander's form next to me. She dropped into a bow.

"Your Majesty," she greeted.

Evander bid her to rise, and she slipped out of the room to join us in the hallway, shutting the door behind her.

"We're here to see my mother," he explained. "I mean–of course we are. We're at her door, so . . ." he trailed off, words escaping him. His grip tightened on my hand. Was he nervous?

"It's all right," I laughed. "She doesn't bite."

Evander rubbed the back of his neck with his free hand. "My apologies. It's only that I know how important you are to Quinn, and I've heard so much about you."

Mellie quirked a brow. "And I you," she returned, smirking. "I've been lucky enough to call your mother a friend for many years."

Evander's face reddened as he realized the implication of her words.

"As a subject, and your head baker, I'm honored to meet you. As a friend of Quinn, even more so." She hesitated only a second before continuing. "You'll have to forgive an old woman for her protective nature, but I have to warn you: I've told your mother much about my darling Quinn over the years, and I'm sure she would protect her almost as fiercely as I would, so you'd best be good to her."

"Mellie!" I scolded, embarrassment creeping into my cheeks, even as my heart warmed at her words. She had told the queen about me. Perhaps we weren't complete strangers after all.

Now it was Evander's turn to chuckle. "It's all right. I wouldn't dream of hurting her, with or without a warning."

"Good man." Mellie patted his arm. Given all her talk about respecting Evander when I was first hired on, I loved her boldness with him now.

He flashed her a dazzling smile, but it wobbled when he turned his attention back to the door.

"Is she . . .?"

"No change, I'm afraid." Mellie shook her head sadly. "But she can feel us there, I know it."

Evander nodded, his lips a tight line.

"I'll give you some privacy," Mellie said, embracing me tightly and giving us a sad smile before leaving the way we had come.

Evander looked at the door but made no move to open it, worry and hesitation written in the furrow of his brow. While I hated to see him so grief-stricken, I cherished the opportunity to support him in this moment.

"Shall we?" I asked. He nodded and, taking his arm, I reached for the handle.

Though it was dim, I could tell that the room was well appointed. Lush, verdant hues of green could be found on the velvet couches in the sitting room, the papered walls, and the plush rug. Evander led the way to the bed chamber, opening the door as quietly as possible.

I took a deep breath as I stepped into the room, my heart heavy.

Though I'd seen her portraits in the castle, I was utterly unprepared for the reality of how much Evalina looked like her son. Though her hair, fanned out on her pillow, was a lighter brown, with waves instead of Evander's loose curls, there was so much of him in her face. I recognized her strong nose and high cheekbones, and long lashes that dusted the tops of her cheeks as she slept. If I didn't know how hard the healers had been working to keep her stable, I might've considered the sight peaceful.

The side of the bed opposite the queen was glaringly empty. King Roland's side table looked as if it had been kept as he left it, though there wasn't a speck of dust in sight. A pair of reading glasses and a thick leatherbound book sat next to an extinguished candle standing sentinel.

Evander cleared his throat softly. "Hello Mother." He moved to her bedside, taking her hand from where it rested on her sternum. His voice was thick as he continued. "I have someone I'd like you to meet."

My throat was tight as I moved to join him, placing a hand on his back.

"This is my fiancée, Quinn Parry."

"It's an honor to meet you, Queen Evalina." I dropped into a deep bow, though I knew she couldn't see. This woman deserved all the respect I could offer.

When I rose, I found Evander was struggling with his next words, tears shining in his eyes as he swallowed repeatedly.

"May I?" I asked him, gesturing to the chair that had been pulled up to her bedside. When he nodded in assent, I took a seat.

Giving him a moment, I began to speak, trying to keep my voice as steady as possible.

"I hope you can hear me, because I have been wanting to thank you for a very long time. You have raised such a kind and noble man. Evander has already been an incredible ruler to your people, and I can't tell you how grateful I am to have the honor of knowing him." I paused to look back at Evander, who had moved behind the chair, his hands gripping its carved wooden back, knuckles white.

Taking in a breath, I continued. "I know how important it was to you that he found a love like your own, and while I wasn't lucky enough to be a witness to your marriage, I want to assure you: I adore your son with my whole heart. We made our way to each other despite overwhelming odds, and I will never take his love for granted." Tears began to fall down my face as Evander's hand found my shoulder and squeezed. When I turned to him again, I found his cheeks shining as well.

Though Evalina couldn't react, I hoped she felt the sincerity of my words. There would never be anything I could do to repay her for the gift of her son, but perhaps I could bring her some comfort.

"Do you think . . . do you think we could stay a while and read to her?" I asked Evander.

His mouth dropped open for a moment before he responded, and I worried I had been too forward. Finally though, he spoke.

"I think she would love that." He picked up the volume from his father's side table, which turned out to be a book of Formerian poetry, and I began to read aloud.

Chapter 18

FINALLY, AFTER A DAYS-LONG frenzied blur of stationary, brocade, and frosting, I found myself awakening in my own bed for the first time in weeks. Out of habit, I reached for Evander's warmth next to me but found the space empty. Blinking my eyes open slowly, I realized I was in my room on the third floor. The morning of our wedding had arrived at last.

For all his complaining about Georgette's rules, Evander had been the one to insist we slept separately last night (to "build the suspense" he said with a wink.)

I would be sure to give him grief about it later. I hadn't slept so poorly in ages.

I kept having the same nightmare about being stuck in a fishbowl, my mother a giant looking in on me, laughing. I woke several times in a cold sweat, only to slip back into the same scene as soon as I fell back asleep.

Just a dream, I told myself. If I had already determined I wasn't going to let my flesh-and-blood mother ruin my day, I wasn't going to give that privilege to a distorted version of her in a nightmare.

I padded to the bathroom, splashed my face with cold water, and looked in the mirror. There were bags under my eyes, but they weren't dramatic enough that I was worried about them. The past few weeks of good sleep, good food, and more than enough time to recover from the stress of the competition had done me well. My face was pink and healthy, glowing with happiness I still couldn't believe was real.

Feeling like a schoolgirl, I giggled at myself in the mirror, the weight of the day settling into my heart.

My wedding day.

I hadn't been the kind of little girl who dreamed about white dresses and veils . . . Mostly because I didn't see a future outside Mother's cottage where I would get the chance to don them. But despite my lack of childhood daydreams about being a bride, I found myself looking forward to seeing how our selections for the day had all come together. I waltzed around my room by myself, too joyous to feel silly or self-conscious until the moment I heard a knock at the door.

Before I could even put my hand on the cool metal of the lever, the door burst open and Colette strolled inside, Vanessa a shadow behind her.

"Quiinnnn!" Colette exclaimed, taking my hands and spinning me around the room. "Happy wedding day! How are you feeling?"

"Excited," I said. "Nervous too, if I'm being honest. I just hope I can handle it all." We'd continued our practice, the hours getting longer every day, but hadn't made much progress on my solo work.

"You can handle it," Vanessa said from behind Colette, not quite meeting my eyes despite her vote of confidence.

With a tight smile, I nodded, grateful for her words even if I hadn't yet forgiven her. To be honest, I was surprised she was here at all.

Another figure cleared their throat and I raised my eyebrows to my hairline as I saw Serena standing in the doorway.

This was the first time I had seen her without her uniform. The grey dress she wore was basic, but flattering, and I saw a tan arm snake around her waist a second before I registered James behind her. She smiled at me, open and genuine, if a little unsure, and held up a bottle of sparkling wine I recognized from the castle's cellars. Winking at me, she nodded toward the bottle, and I laughed as I realized she probably hadn't asked Helga nicely for it.

"Are we late?" James asked. A mischievous grin lit his face as he took Serena's hand and pulled her into the room, his other arm laden with a tray of muffins.

"Not at all!" Colette bubbled, popping a pastry from the tray into her mouth and moaning happily at the taste. "The rest of those can go over there by the pianoforte." She flitted over to me and whispered, "Surprise! I hope it's all right that I invited them. I wanted to make sure you were surrounded by your friends this morning."

I nearly snorted; she clearly had no idea about the fraught history between Serena and me. Surprising myself, I realized that despite the rocky start to our relationship, she had indeed become my friend in a strange way, and I was glad to have her here.

"Thank you, Colette. I appreciate it. But where's–"

As if she knew she was being summoned, Mellie strode into the room, her smile all sunshine on a cloudless day, full of pride and joy. After enveloping me in a tight hug, she looked at me, tears forming in her eyes. The sight threatened to make my own overflow.

A moment passed in silence, rife with sentiment as we studied each other through blurry lenses, reminiscing on all we had been through together. If I could only have one person with me today, it would be this incredible woman who had wiped so many of my tears, celebrated each and every part of me, and given me tough love when I needed it. I smiled, wobbly and watery, hoping she could see all the love I held for her. The spell was only broken when Mellie laughed and waved the moisture away with her hands, sniffling loudly.

"Goodness gracious. It hasn't even been two minutes. I will not become a blubbering mess yet. Later, probably," she joked through the tears, "but right now it's time to celebrate."

On cue, James popped the bottle of wine and toasted, "To Quinn! Who makes the best tarts I've ever tasted and is also somehow about to become our queen. I'm still a little confused on the specifics!"

He yelled the last few words with the same enthusiasm as the first, and his laughter was contagious as we passed the bottle around, forgoing glasses in our excitement.

"Now," Serena said, all business, "let's see what we can do about this hair."

She sat me down at the desk where Evander had left "The Ballad of Brynne" all those weeks ago and started patiently detangling my copper curls.

I quirked an eyebrow at her. "I have to admit, Serena, this is not something I would have guessed was in your skill set."

"Everything is in my skill set, Parry," she quipped. "Besides, I have three younger sisters." She began to twist my hair into the beginnings of an elegant chignon when I shook my head.

"Leave at least part of it down," I said, thinking about how Evander had pulled it out of its tie the first night he kissed me in the kitchen. "Evander likes it that way."

Though she rolled her eyes at my blush, she complied, pinning up a small section at the back of my head and slipping white baby's breath into the remaining curls in a soft cascading shape. I craned my neck around to see the style in the small mirror above the desk.

"It's beautiful, Serena. Thank you," I said earnestly.

Feeling a bit nervous, I allowed Colette to unleash her cosmetics bag on me. I had nothing against it, but my lack of experience made me worry that I'd end up feeling like a clown instead of glamorous and sexy the way I'd seen other women look.

In the end, though, she did a beautiful job, dusting my cheeks with blush, adding a subtle raspberry-shaded stain to my lips, and brushing my eyelashes with mascara. She made no move to cover up my freckles.

I regarded myself in the mirror and took a small breath. I still looked like me, just *more.* Turning my head from side to side, I smiled, loving how confident I felt.

Colette squeezed my shoulders from behind. "Absolutely beautiful, Quinn," she beamed.

Opening the armoire, Mellie pulled out the garment bag containing my dress and removed the ivory-colored gown. It took her, Colette, and Serena to help me into it and fasten the dozens of tiny fabric-covered buttons in the back.

The dress was ethereal, with sheer bishop sleeves that extended to just below my elbows and intricate lace floral appliques trailing down from the sweetheart neckline to the hem of the full skirt.

Serena motioned for me to turn around, and I did a giddy spin. Mellie dissolved into tears in earnest, and I hugged her tight as she whispered, "I'm so proud of you, Dumpling."

I stared at my friends, these people who had seen value in me, in my heart and my company when I had nothing else to offer, and nodded to each of them, hoping the tears shining in my eyes would say what I couldn't voice.

Finally, my gaze made its way back to my reflection. I glanced from my soft copper curls to my smiling face to the luster of the tiny pearls sewn into my dress. Squaring my shoulders, I smiled, feeling more beautiful than I ever had, stronger and more sure of myself than I would have thought possible even just this summer.

Much to the dismay of the royal tailor, I had opted to forgo a veil. I had done enough hiding in my lifetime and now I wanted to walk down the aisle and into my reign obscuring nothing, with clear vision and all my cards on the table. The person I was, for all her flaws and hotheadedness, had gotten me to this moment, and I wouldn't do her the dishonor of concealing her. My eyes were fire and steel as I prepared for the moment I had unknowingly been barreling toward my entire life.

"I'm ready."

Soft music floated through the huge double doors in front of the great hall as I waited for my cue to begin walking down the aisle. I expected to be more nervous, but the fear I felt now was nothing compared to the hopelessness of a few weeks ago. The ceremony, I could get through. With Evander by my side, I would figure out the rest later.

Taking a breath and adjusting my posture so I stood as tall as possible, I promised myself that I would face everything behind the doors and everything that came after with courage and grace. I could do this. After all, I had as much experience ruling as any of the other girls in that competition. The self doubt had to go.

Warm, calloused hands slipped over my eyes just a second after my magic swelled in my chest, letting me know Evander was nearby.

"Hello, love," he whispered in my ear.

I rounded on him, searching the empty hall to make sure no one was watching us.

"What are you doing here? You're supposed to be inside!"

"Relax, love," Evander soothed, cupping my face in his hands. "No one will notice I'm gone. Maddox is making a speech about the unity of the kingdom and the importance of binding magic together before they start."

He pulled back to look at me and stopped before finishing his thought.

"Gods, you look radiant," he said. "You're like a dream, Quinn."

I blushed down to my toes. I already felt beautiful, but hearing him say so did something to me that I couldn't quite explain.

"You're not supposed to see me," I pointed out.

"Ah, right," he conceded. "I just came to give you this." From his outstretched hand dangled a stunning iridescent opal on a delicate gold chain. Tiny dewdrops of diamonds glittered every inch or so on either side, making it look like snow and ice, forever frozen in time.

"Happy wedding, my love," he said, slipping it around my neck and clasping it at the back.

My heart felt as though it would burst from the sheer volume of love I'd asked it to hold. "It's beautiful," I said. The words weren't enough to convey how I felt, but I knew he would understand. "Thank you."

"It's my mother's," Evander explained. "My father gave it to her on their wedding day, and I know she'd be honored that I'm giving it to you."

"I'm so sorry she's not here." I slipped my hand into his, trying to push all my support through our intertwined fingers.

"So am I," he smiled sadly. "But I have faith that this is one step closer to her being back with us. She's going to love you, Quinn."

He pressed a tender kiss to my lips before the smattering of applause started inside the doors. My stomach fluttered at the sound.

"That's my signal," he winked at me. "See you in there." He began to walk towards the side door he had initially slipped through before turning back to me.

"I love you, Quinn. I don't know if I'll get the chance to say that inside. These political ceremonies can be a bit dry. But I want you to know that I will spend every day of the rest of our lives showing you that you are the sun around which my world rotates."

"I love you," I echoed. "Now go!" I shooed him off with a giggle and waited several minutes before I heard the sound of the processional music begin to play. The double doors opened, and I stepped into the rest of my life.

The ceremony was as formal as Evander had warned, focusing more on the joining of the two halves of the Crown than on the union of husband and wife. An apology lingered in his eyes every time the officiant said "the king" in lieu of his name, but I didn't mind. There would be plenty of time for us to celebrate privately. This was for the kingdom. Our kingdom.

My friends' joyous faces shone from the audience. Even my mother smiled serenely from her seat in the middle of the crowd.

Around them, the room was overflowing with guests; the layer of extra wards around the palace had been lowered for the day to let in villagers and nobles alike. Maddox and her team had been manually searching every entrant and I could see the relief in the set of Evander's shoulders as he stood across from me, his eyes beacons of love and joy.

The wedding gave way to the coronation, a short affair in which I pledged my loyalty to the people of Enorias and promised to use my magic to serve and protect them. A golden and pearled crown was placed in my hair, lighter than I imagined, and before I knew it, we were standing at the front of the room, taking in the sounds of raucous applause as we were introduced as king and queen of Enorias. I even heard a wolf whistle, which I was fairly sure had come from James, and did my best to hide my amusement and look as regal as possible.

Lastly came the magic tethering ceremony. While the guests were herded to the ballroom for refreshments, Evander and I met with General Finch in one of the empty receiving parlors. I was thankful for the privacy, as Evander had warned me that this particular part of the day was both intimate and a bit jarring, according to what his mother had told him before she fell ill.

"In order to work as a joint conduit for the kingdom's wards, you need to merge your Gifts with one another," Finch explained. "Typically the dowager queen would perform the ceremony, but under the current circumstances . . ." he trailed off, meeting Evander's gaze with pity.

Evander's jaw clenched as he banished the emotion. I hadn't known that. My heart sank as I registered that he'd probably always imagined having his mother with him in this moment; General Finch, hard as he tried, was a poor substitute. I reached out and took Evander's hand, squeezing it gently.

Finch continued awkwardly, clearly uncomfortable with the emotionally-charged atmosphere.

"Join both hands–yes, very good. You'll have to have some patience with me as I attempt the process. I've found bits and pieces recorded from your mother and father's coronation, Your Majesty, but we'll need to fill in some gaps."

With this, he began chanting an incantation. I'd read about Wielders using them to magnify their power, but according to the history books I had been studying in preparation for the coronation, they hadn't been common practice in Enorias for several hundred years.

Finch's hands hovered above our joined ones as he began to cast. Rather than his signature ice, I felt a soft warmth where we were linked. There was a knock on the door of my mind, so similar to what I had experienced during his joint casting with Vanessa. This time, I flung the entrance open without hesitation.

Evander's magic swept into the space, and it felt so much like *him,* as if the essence of this man I had come to love so deeply was melding with my own. The harmony between our Gifts reached new heights as our powers mingled and the world narrowed to the space between us.

I could no longer hear the General's voice; the only sound in my ears was the echo of that beautiful music the prophecy foretold. Reading the prophecy was one thing; experiencing this felt nothing short of fated. From the awed look on Evander's face, I knew he felt the same.

After a moment, our magics stopped swirling and settled into a comfortable, intertwined calm. Evander gingerly released his hands, bringing them up to cradle my face. The kiss he pressed to my lips was so soft, so reverent that it felt like a dream.

Finch cleared his throat, bringing me back to reality, and I laughed, wiping tears I didn't realize I had shed from my face.

"I love you endlessly," Evander said.

"I love you."

Much more quickly than I would have liked, I was swept away by Finch, who decided that a few moments after the most pivotal experience of my life was the only time I would be able to make the acquaintance of every higher and lower noble in the kingdom.

Across the room, Evander was on a similar tour with Maddox. He shot me an apologetic smile and mouthed "Good luck" as he was pulled into the ballroom.

The first noblewoman I was wheeled to was introduced as Lady Garrison, the widow of a prominent metallurgist who, from what I could tell, had been running their foundry business with even more success than her late husband in the years since his passing.

Then there were the Viscount and Viscountess of Formere, a seaside province responsible for the majority of Enorias's fishing industry. My head reeled as I did my best to memorize names, faces, and occupations, suddenly regretting so much time spent on tasting cake flavors when I could've been studying for this. I left them with a vague promise to visit Formere in the future, which would've sounded lovely if it weren't for the pit in my stomach that was deepening with every encounter. Whether it was from nerves or the disconcerting new pull on my Gift from the Crown, I didn't know, but it left me feeling unsettled and on edge.

The next face I met contorted into a grimace for a moment too long before schooling itself into neutrality. The man in question stood tall and aloof, his expensive-looking suit tailored perfectly to his body. His long blonde hair shone in contrast to the dark fabric, and I could find no kindness in his eyes.

"Sir Calix is the Arch-Duke of Marione," Finch explained. I held my hand out to Calix, but he only sneered down at it before dragging his gaze back up to my face as if I had made some sort of lewd gesture.

"Charmed, I'm sure." The way his lip curled as he said the words made me feel like sinking into the floor, but I did my best to stand up straight as I returned the sentiment lukewarmly.

"I must admit," he said, "I wasn't sure if I should believe the invitation, but of course I had to come see for myself. A peasant girl from a merchant family no one has ever heard of wedding the crown prince?" He stopped just short of scoffing, and my fists clenched.

"King," I said, jutting my chin out slightly at him. "Evander is king, Sir Calix." I may not be comfortable advocating for myself, but I had no qualms about defending Evander and demanding he receive the respect he was due. After the hells he endured the last six months, it was the least he deserved.

Besides, I had a feeling that this man's first impression of me was going to stick, and I had no desire to play into his intimidation tactics.

"Ah yes," he said absently, "I forget that at times. Such a rushed coronation. Hardly anyone in attendance, I heard. Most of the nobles didn't even receive word until after the fact. Of course, from what I heard about the ceremony, I'm glad to have missed it." He raised his eyebrows as if rebuking a naughty child. "Still, it's hardly the most surprising thing that's happened in the kingdom this year. When I heard our new queen-to-be was a *servant,* I nearly fell out of my chair. "

"The queen was responsible for the apprehension of the assassin," Finch hedged nervously. It took me a moment to realize he was referring to me. "Her power shows great promise, I assure you."

"I'm sure," Calix said, looking down his nose as if sizing me up and finding me wanting. I met his eyes and raised my chin slowly, quirking my eyebrows ever so slightly in challenge. He scoffed almost imperceptibly as he registered the gauntlet I had thrown, and excused himself, feigning concern about "taking up too much of my time."

As he walked away, I couldn't decide if he simply thought me below his notice or if he was retreating in his own way.

"Forgive Sir Calix," Finch said. "He favored his daughter for the throne many years ago, but she never manifested a Gift. His wife is quite talented with scrying, but he isn't a Wielder himself and I suppose that won out. Always had a bit of a chip on his shoulder about it, if I'm being honest."

I could hear the explanation as we started walking toward the next group, but Finch's voice felt far away as panic began to rise in my chest.

My earlier nonchalance about ascending to rule felt so foolish. Love was a mighty force that could overcome many challenges, but it wouldn't do me any favors in the fields of diplomacy or politics.

Who was I to think I could manage this role? I thought I would have more time to adjust, though I wasn't sure why. I was assuming the throne during the most fraught climate Enorias had experienced in the last few decades–had I thought that would be simple? Easy? Effortless, even? Of course no one was going to accept me as a ruler. I was stupid for not seeing it earlier.

I fought to keep my breathing regulated as I smiled and nodded at something the man in front of me had said. Another general of some sort, I thought vaguely. A general in an army that I was now in power to command. The idea made me feel dizzy.

Enorias was a small kingdom, but I was quickly realizing that the inner workings of the realm were far more nuanced than I could hope to understand. My mind was stuttering with the sudden realization of how much I didn't even know I didn't know, and I felt a strange tension in my chest, like a bowstring pulled taut.

If these brief social interactions left me spiraling, what would I do in my first meeting? When the people I had just vowed to serve and protect needed me to make hard choices and trusted me to make the right ones?

My eyes wandered to the far side of the room, and I saw my mother chatting with a spectacled woman along the perimeter. I caught her eye and gestured to have her join me. Though I was sure she had seen, she returned her gaze to her companion, paying me no notice.

I tried to focus on what the general in front of me was asking, and when I flicked my gaze back to the spot where I saw my mother, she was gone. The man kissed my hand and I was swept away again.

The introductions were endless, a merry-go-round of posturing and vying for dominance. It felt like a personal welcome tour designed to torture me.

Suddenly, I was slammed with the force of something pulling at my magic, like a thread that had been pulled too tightly and finally snapped. An alarm was blaring in my mind, alerting me to a wrongness I couldn't name.

I reached for logic, something that would explain the way the air was suddenly gone from my lungs, why the edges of my vision began to darken.

The painful burning in my chest gave way to a hollow emptiness that had my heart in my throat. I broke from my conversation without warning or explanation, scanning the room for a face I knew I wouldn't see.

It was my bond with Evander. And he was gone.

Whirling around the room frantically, my mind stumbled over itself as I tried to figure out the best course of action. Maddox. I should find Maddox. I pushed my way through the crowd, ignoring the bewildered looks from guests. Tunnel vision made it impossible to process anything that wasn't Evander or the captain.

I hardly noticed when I barreled right into Vanessa, who grabbed me by my upper arms and steered me off to the side of the room, scanning my face with concern.

"Quinn, what's going on?"

"Your mother," I gulped down air, hoping it would lessen the phantom feeling of asphyxiation gripping my throat. "I need to find your mother."

"Okay. Okay, I can help with that. But first I need you to take a breath and tell me what's wrong," she coaxed.

"Evander's gone," I managed.

"Gone where?"

"I don't know, but I don't think it was his choice. I can't explain it; I just have this feeling in my chest . . . like his magic was stretched thin and then disappeared."

"All right, I'm going to go find my mother." She guided me to a chair. "Sit down and take some deep breaths. I'll bring her back here and you can tell her what you just told me."

I nodded again numbly as Vanessa squeezed my shoulder before turning and striding into the thick of the celebration.

Calm. I had to remain calm. It had been a long day, and the sudden tethering of my magic to the Crown was disorienting, to say the least.

I tried to tell myself that everything was fine, that Evander would emerge from around the corner at any moment, even as I knew he wouldn't. Though I couldn't explain why, I had never been more certain of anything in my life. Something was very, very wrong.

Counting my breaths, I scanned the crowd again for Vanessa and Maddox. It had already been longer than I anticipated, and the wait wasn't helping my rising fear. But I couldn't fall apart now. I had to be coherent to help.

A familiar face came into my line of sight. My mother's eyes creased with concern when she saw me sitting alone.

"Darling, what are you doing over here? Is everything all right?"

I smiled weakly at her, trying to swallow the lump in my throat. Something about the slight softening in her gaze weakened my resolve, and I found myself cracking around the edges, vision going blurry.

Mother rushed over to me, pulling me to standing and placing her arm around my shoulders.

"Let's get you out of here," she said. "You don't want to give these vultures another reason to pick you apart." I looked around and noticed for the first time how many eyes were on me, witnessing me panic. Dancing couples had stopped twirling to watch me, and I heard whispers behind hands all over the room.

Ushering me toward the door, Mother cast a quick glance over her shoulder.

"Vanessa is coming back," I managed to get out. "I need to wait for her."

"She sent me," Mother assured. "We'll go somewhere more private, and she'll meet us there."

I nodded, hoping my shields would do something to hide us from the crowds as we headed to the door. Mother was right. No one could see me like this.

Her grip on my shoulder tightened uncomfortably as she steered me down the hall. We passed one, two, three, four doors before veering into a small parlor I didn't recognize. There were so many rooms in the vast castle I'd never even entered; yet another way I was underprepared.

When I crossed the threshold, Mother released her grip on me, backing up toward the door and locking it behind us.

"Mother?"

She ignored me entirely, focusing her gaze on the other side of the room.

"I did as you asked," she said, her posture rigid.

"Excellent work, Wilomena," came a rough voice from the shadows. "Now we can begin."

Chapter 19

The man stepped forward, clad in leather armor so dark it seemed to disappear into the night. Age had weathered his face, and I could see pale white scars on every exposed inch of skin.

Fear seized in my chest as he took a step forward, the steel at his side clanking as he moved. I shot a panicked glance at my mother, the reality of the situation not quite catching up with me.

"It's all right, Quinn," she smiled saccharinely. "Helmund is going to help you."

"Help me?" I echoed. "Where's Vanessa?"

"Don't worry about that now, dearest," Mother dismissed. "We have more pressing matters to attend to." My eyes darted back and forth between her and the man, unwilling to turn my back on either one of them.

"Now, I understand the last few months have been quite trying for you," she continued. "I can't blame you entirely for falling under the king's spell. The castle, the riches, the magic . . ." She gave me a pointed look. "But these things are simply not for you. Helmund is going to help us . . . reset, shall we say? I've been assured he's one of the most talented Siphons alive."

"What are you talking about?" I backed toward the door only to find that pulling the lever did nothing. The man, Helmund, smiled smugly.

"We're going to sort out your little magic problem," he sneered, prowling toward me with a predatory look that had the hair on the back of my neck standing up. "Don't be scared, girl. Extracting it will be painless."

Extracting it? It sounded impossible, too horrifying to be true.

He held up a vial, no bigger than a hummingbird, and wiggled it between his fingers. "And after we Siphon Captain Maddox's Gift as well, you won't remember any of this."

Making sense of the words, I blanched. Terror pounded her fists inside my rib cage, begging me to run, but there was nowhere I could go. My mother's eyes watched me in cold indifference.

"Mother," I pleaded, "don't do this. I know you hate magic, but only because you don't understand. It's *life,* Mother. It's part of me. If you rip it out, it will take a piece of my soul with it."

I scanned her face, praying for any sign of softness or understanding, but she only rolled her eyes.

"Gods, you sound just like your father," she spat. "Tiernan was always going on about the power of magic and its 'oneness with life.'" Her words were cruel and mocking, but I could have sworn I saw a flash of hurt in her eyes as she spoke the unfamiliar name.

"Mother," I started slowly, suddenly worried she wasn't in her right mind, "Father's name is Otto."

The look she gave me was one of pure disdain, as if she were looking at me but seeing someone else. Perhaps she was bewitched. The thought was terrifying and, strangely, slightly comforting. If she was being controlled, maybe it wasn't really my mother trying to rob me of an intrinsic part of who I was.

"Who is Tiernan?" I probed gently, flicking my glance to Helmund, who was now grinning at me as if he was in on a hilarious joke.

"You were always a smart girl, if a little too romantic for my liking. I thought you'd have figured it out by now," Mother said. "Of course, to be fair, everything we did to keep your Gift from manifesting worked so well that you didn't have much of a clue. A little chip of hyalperite stone in the front door frame of the cottage worked like a charm."

I took a sharp breath, piecing it together at once. Hyalperite–an ugly name for the horrifying stone I'd heard tales of Falerin using in interrogations during the war. It was real. Horror coiled in my gut as I realized the extent of her betrayal–of what she had kept from me.

"After all," she said, "I couldn't have you turning out like *him.*"

"Who. Is. Tiernan?" I ground out, holding her gaze with as much ferocity as I could muster.

"Your father," she sighed as if disappointed in me. "I just told you, Quinn."

"My father?" My heart was quicker to put the pieces together than my mind, and all the air fled my lungs as I took in the enormity of it.

"Your biological one, anyway. In the end, he was nothing more than a shameful mark on my history. So I erased him," she said matter-of-factly.

My face fell in abject horror as Mother put a hand over her eyes, massaging both of her temples as if I had vexed her.

"Now you've upset me by making me talk of him. He doesn't deserve my memory. Thank the gods you won't recall any of this and we can move on with our lives. Helmund," she gestured to me, urging him to begin.

Helmand's gaze widened menacingly as I pressed my back flat against the door once more. This couldn't happen. I threw up my arms and imagined a shield settling around my body, but my magic didn't move to make it a reality. Was there hyalperite here too? Or was I simply so inept that I couldn't protect myself in my most vulnerable state?

Panic threatened to take hold as I frantically took stock of my situation: Evander was missing and I was locked in a room with a strange man who wanted to take my magic. A Siphon, Mother had called him. I tried to calm down my racing heart so I could think clearly.

Someone would notice I was missing. Vanessa was looking for me. I just needed to delay them long enough for her to realize what had happened. Anger bubbled up, scalding and all consuming. For once, the fact that my Mother never backed down from a fight and never allowed anyone the last word felt like a blessing instead of a curse.

"How could you lie to me? For twenty-four years?" I baited.

"Oh, Quinn, I never lied to you. I simply omitted his existence. Otto adopted you when we married, so when I told you he was your father, I wasn't telling any untruths." The logic was twisted and wrong, but she wasn't worked up enough about it. I needed her to fight back.

"And what did Tiernan do to deserve this? Were you truly so narrow-minded that you cast him out for nothing more than having different beliefs than you?"

"Of course you would think the worst of me," she spat. Her face was reddened with righteous anger, as I'd wanted, but there was something else there, too. Something that looked a lot like grief.

"He abandoned us, Quinn. Your own father left you before you were even born. His magic and 'the greater good' were more important to him than his family. One summons from the Crown was all it took for him to walk out the door and never come back. In the end, his Gift was the only thing he was loyal to."

Each word was sharper than the last, filled with the vitriol of a woman scorned. He had deserted us? It was strange to feel rejected by someone I hadn't known existed only a few moments prior, but her words swirled around me like wasps, buzzing and stinging and disorienting me further. He had been called to the palace . . .

"My father was a Wielder." The force of the realization slammed me in the chest and I found myself unable to breathe. How? How had she kept this from me? Shock and betrayal and a strange feeling of calm, as if a final puzzle piece had finally settled into place, warred within me as I struggled to come to terms with this new reality. Mother ignored me; even saying the word was something she considered beneath her.

"I stood at the gates for days," she continued, "thinking they had done something to him. Surely he hadn't left me while I was with child. No one could be that cruel. I screamed until my voice gave out and then I just sat there, right in front of the palace grounds.

"Then you were born and thank the gods Otto was simple enough to fall for the idea of a damsel in distress with her baby in tow, or I shudder to think where we'd be."

"All this time you knew I had a Gift, and you hid it from me?"

"Magic isn't as strong as you might think, dearest. And when you know the right people, the people with real power, you can win against it every time." She nodded at Helmund, signaling she was done with the conversation.

On her cue, he crept toward me as if approaching a frightened animal, but the manic grin on his face told me this was a game he very much enjoyed.

"This won't hurt a bit, pet," he said, even as he grabbed me by the roots of my hair and dragged me toward a chair. I threw my arms into a casting position again, but no magic hummed at my fingertips. Thrashing against him had no effect; I was caught in his snare.

"Don't be dramatic, Quinn," Mother said, turning away from me as if whatever happened next would be distasteful to witness. "It really is for the best. You and I will start over somewhere new. Somewhere no one will recognize you and we'll never have to hear about those filthy royals again."

"About that," Helmund grunted, still trying to restrain me, "there's been a change of plans. You've been very helpful, Wilomena, but I'm afraid she'll be leaving here with me."

Mother turned, an argument already forming on her lips, but the words were stolen from her as a knife flew from a holster on his side and embedded itself into her chest.

Her eyes widened with shock and she clutched the weapon, falling to her knees. When she locked eyes with me, her usual sneer was nowhere to be found, and the cold indifference faded from her gaze. All that remained was fear.

It was then that I finally screamed. Though I knew the room was likely sound-warded, I had to try. I yelled for my friends, for Maddox, for *anyone* who could hear to help me. Even when no one arrived, I continued to scream, shredding my throat with my terror, for the injustice of it all, for the life that was stolen from me, for having come so far only to end up here . . . even for my mother, who was cruel and imperfect but whom I still found my heart aching for, watching her blood sink into the carpet as she gasped for air.

Helmund clamped his hand over my mouth, and I bit down hard.

"Gods damnit!" he yelled. "Little bitch." He shoved my head roughly under his arm as he rummaged around in his pocket.

"This will shut you up," he seethed.

A foul-smelling cloth clamped over my nose and mouth, and everything went dark.

Chapter 20

THE FIRST THING I registered as my brain clawed its way back to consciousness was the ringing. Its high-pitched whine was an alarm sounding, "Wake up! Something is wrong." A part of me wanted to ignore it, to give in to my exhaustion and aching head. A gentle rocking motion that took me a moment to identify as a horse's walk joined the effort to lull me back into unconsciousness.

A solid pressure against my stomach let me know I was draped against the beast that was carrying me.

Where was I?

The events in the parlor rushed back to me as my skull pounded, and I was suddenly wide awake. The air was bitingly cold on my chest and forearms, and I morbidly realized I must still be in my wedding dress.

Slowly, I cracked an eye open, barely a slit so as not to alert my captor I was conscious. My surroundings were dark, and from this vantage point I could only see a carpet of soil and pine needles. A forest, it would seem.

Tempting fate, I dared to look around and was relieved to find that I was alone on my horse, though the animal was tied to something ahead. Following the line of hempen rope, I saw the shadowy figure of a man on another steed ahead, hazy through the fog.

I focused my energy inward to the glowing core of power I had been trying to pull from unsuccessfully all week. Normally I could at least sense it there, a warmth in my chest that, even when I couldn't access it, assured me that it was ready to strike if I could only figure out how to tap into it. Now, though? Nothing. A cavernous, dull ache was the only thing I felt when I reached out to my Gift.

Was this how the Mundanes felt all the time? Though I'd gone most of my life without knowing I had magic, the glaring discomfort of its sudden absence made me wonder how I had ever overlooked it in the first place.

I tried again and again, growing increasingly panicked as I threw myself at the block until I had a hard time concealing my panting from the effort.

It wouldn't do me any good to exert myself so much that I alerted Helmund I was awake, so I forced myself to breathe soundlessly. The fact that he assumed I was still unconscious was the only slight edge I had, and I clung to it tightly.

Think, Quinn. If I couldn't access my power, Helmund must've already done something to me while I was unconscious. My stomach roiled at the thought of him picking through my mind, finding that string of power, and pulling on it. How had he done it?

Wracking my brain, I recalled his words back in the castle. *"After we Siphon Maddox's power."* That must've been what he had done to me. After he had thrown that knife.

Oh gods, Mother.

I began to panic anew. The look on her face as the blood spread through the bodice of her dress was something I knew I would see in my nightmares for the rest of my life. I hadn't gotten a good look at the wound, but anything in the chest couldn't be good. Would anyone find her in time, or had she bled out on the carpet of that room?

As complicated as my relationship with my mother may be, I didn't want her lying cold and lifeless in the castle. I had too many questions I needed her to answer.

My heart warred between primal fear for my mother and an ugly emotion I didn't dare name that whispered she had brought her fate upon herself. The things she had plotted to do to my magic, to me, to Evander . . .

Had he gotten away? Or had he been dealt the same hand I had? Or worse? I didn't let myself dwell on that thought even for a second. If I started thinking about the worst-case scenario, I would lose any semblance of rational thinking. My mind was my only weapon right now and I couldn't afford to lose it.

Still, the questions swam in my head, threatening to drag me into their undercurrent. Had they gotten Vanessa too? Colette?

My breathing began to pick up again, and I counted my inhales through my nose, holding for a few seconds before blowing out my mouth as slowly as I could. Shoving all my fear and grief into a tiny box in my mind, I slammed the lid shut. I was going to get out of this, and I was going to help my friends. My chosen family.

Helmund shifted in his saddle and grunted as he turned to scan our surroundings. I closed my eyes, schooled my face into immobility, and prayed to every god I could think of that he hadn't realized I was awake.

Thankfully, it seemed at least one of those old deities took pity on me, because I heard nothing but the hooves of our horses as we trotted along for several more minutes. By the time I found the courage to open my eyes again, Helmund had directed his attention to his saddlebag, rummaging around hastily, nodding once, and closing the flap without removing anything.

Our horses picked their way through the forest for what felt like several hours, and he repeated this ritual at least four more times. Each time, he breathed a sigh of relief before closing it back up.

Either he was too concerned with whatever he was carrying to worry about me escaping, or he grossly underestimated me, because he only turned around to look at me once during the journey, his face curling into a sneer in the light of the lantern fastened on his belt.

At last we reached a small clearing and he dismounted, pausing to remove the bag from his horse and attach it to his person before coming to deal with me.

Grumbling, he tossed me over his shoulder.

Resisting the urge to strike out, to scream and rage and thrash at this man who had taken the best day of my life and turned it into this monstrosity of terror and injustice, was one of the hardest things I'd ever done. I forced myself to stay still and limp, praying he would keep his guard down and give me an opening to free myself.

Unfortunately, I had no such luck, and my wrist restraints stayed in place even as he deposited me roughly at the base of a tree. With my eyes closed, I braced myself with every movement he made, fearful of what he would deem a fit way to incapacitate me for the night.

In the end, he simply produced an extra length of rope, looping it through the space between my wrists and securing it to the tree.

His overconfidence was a dangerous flaw, one for which I was profoundly grateful. The oaf didn't even bother to make sure my fingers were bound. While my wrists were tied too tightly to reach the knot that secured them, I was almost certain I could get myself untethered from the tree if he slept. Maybe there would be something in the forest I could wedge between the restraints to sever them. If I could just get away.

I waited as Helmund started a fire and sat in front of the flames, drinking deeply from a flask of something I strongly suspected was not water.

What felt like hours passed before he slumped onto his bed roll and his breathing evened out.

This was my opening.

Rising as quietly as I could from my position on the forest floor, I began creeping toward the back of the trunk where the rope was secured, waiting a few heartbeats between each step to ensure he wasn't stirring. My heart pounded in my throat as I began working at the knot.

While he may have been sloppy in his plan, his execution left nothing to be desired. The ligature was strong and tight, and I clawed at it until my fingers burned, nails snapping and shredding as I tried to pry it apart.

Fatigue plagued me, though whether it was from whatever Helmund used to incapacitate me, a lack of food, or the disconnection from my power, I didn't know. I tried to ignore the horrible sense of *wrongness* that I could feel emanating from that cavernous place inside of me. I needed to focus on freeing myself.

Finally, millimeter by millimeter, I felt it give way, and nearly cried in relief as I slipped the end through my wrists and took three careful steps away from the trunk.

I had done it. The treeline loomed only a few dozen feet away. If I got to it without waking Helmund, I could run as fast as my legs could carry me away from here. I wasn't sure how far away from the castle I was, but anything was better than wherever he was taking me.

The man lay gracelessly by the fire, his jaw hanging open, flask still clutched in his left hand. I regarded him with distaste, wishing I could grab the dagger on his belt and use it to end him the same way he had ended my mother.

The vengeful thought jarred me, even as I imagined the satisfaction I'd find watching the shocked expression dawn on his face as he realized underestimating me had been his undoing. It was a dark, ugly fantasy, and I knew that getting the dagger off his person was a far bigger risk than was wise when I had this opportunity to escape.

As I turned away from him, my eyes caught on his bag. The bag he'd checked compulsively as we traveled here. Surely it was foolish not to flee, but looking at the satchel, I felt a tug behind my navel. Leaving it behind felt impossible. Whatever it contained was calling to the very essence of who I was, and I had a spark of impossible hope as I realized that it felt like *me.* Like my power.

It was a gamble, but something in my gut told me leaving here without it was the wrong choice.

Half cursing myself and half praying I was right, I inched toward the bag as silently as possible. Helmund's other hand reached out for it, even in sleep, another indication that whatever it held was important.

When I got close enough to smell the alcohol on his breath, I sent another prayer up to the gods and reached for the saddlebag. My heart sank as I registered the strap grasped in his hand; I would have to remove whatever was inside rather than stealing the whole thing.

The leather flap was secured with a metal clasp, and I held my breath as I undid it. The soft clinking noise had the potential to become my death toll if I wasn't careful enough.

Thankfully, the alcohol seemed to have a sedating effect on Helmund, who stayed fast asleep.

I slid my joined hands inside gingerly, rummaging around a piece of cloth and a crust of bread until I made contact with a small velvet pouch. My blood sang in response to the touch, as if straining to get closer to it. My Gift. It had to be. My heart leapt at the possibility of ridding myself of this horrible, empty feeling. I undid the strings of the bag and reached inside.

The moment my hands touched the cool, smooth vial, Helmund's eyes flew open.

Faster than I could process, he snarled and launched himself at me, tackling me to the ground. The bottle rolled out of my reach as he pushed his forearm across my throat.

"You're not supposed to be awake, filthy little Wielder bitch," he seethed, pressing into my windpipe so hard I couldn't breathe.

Something in his gaze turned feral. "King Orobas wanted you alive, but he can't possibly blame me when he hears that you stole my knife in the middle of the night and slit your own throat to avoid capture," he mocked, every word drenched in alcohol.

My eyes pricked with tears as his hand slid to the dagger in his belt, and I thrashed helplessly as I realized what was about to happen. I should never have gone for the pack; I should have run.

I'd always thought of myself as a brave person, but I couldn't help closing my eyes as he drew the dagger back with his free hand, waiting for the killing blow.

I'm sorry, Evander, I sobbed in my mind, *I'm so sorry.*

Of course I was failing him, the man I loved most in the world, the first person who had truly accepted me for what I was and made me dream that I could be more. How foolish I was to think I could have everything I wanted, that my life would be a fairytale out of one of my novels. I should have known it would end unremarkably, with me alone, bleeding out on the forest floor in a cruel parallel to my last moments with mother.

The moment of impact drew on for lifetimes as I waited for the pain, the blood, for my breathing to get ragged until it stopped altogether. Gods, I would never see my father again. Mellie, Colette, Vanessa, James, and Serena's faces flashed before my eyes; I had already been given so much more than I deserved. Tears streamed down my cheeks, Helmund's arm still heavy on my throat as I braced for the impact.

But instead of the sharp pain of a knife at my throat, there was only a heavy weight on my whole body. Helmund was lying on me, his own breathing labored as he let out a guttural yell.

An arrow stuck out from behind his back and he frantically grabbed for it as we lay there for several seconds, my mind struggling to catch up with reality.

"Freeze," a female voice ordered.

A pair of smaller, warm hands appeared, shoving him off me before their owner kneeled by my side.

I looked up, dazed, into a pair of wide, panicked eyes I knew well. Colette.

"Oh my gods, Quinn, are you all right?" she asked. Vanessa strode up behind her, bow still in her hand.

"No time for reunions yet, my love," Vanessa sneered, making eye contact with Helmund. Blood was seeping into the forest floor, dark and sticky. "First we have to deal with this son of a bitch."

He gave her a glare of pure hatred as she leaned close to his face and snarled, "Where. Is. My. Mother?"

"And who would that be?" The words were labored, but he still spit them with as much vitriol as he could manage.

Vanessa took a step back and sighed as if she were only tremendously annoyed by the man's ignorance. Examining her nails, she spoke slowly, as if explaining something to a particularly difficult child.

"You know very well who I'm talking about, and I'd thank you not to insult my intelligence by feigning otherwise. Now, I'm going to ask you again, and I suggest for your own sake you answer me honestly: where is my mother?"

Helmund let out a laugh that turned into a wet cough.

"For my own sake? What exactly does a spoiled little palace girl think she can possibly do to make me talk? You're a good shot, I'll give you that, but it's going to take more than an arrow to the back to overpower me." He grunted but remained frozen on the ground. Vanessa's command had worked.

Realizing he was unable to rise, his expression widened for a second before he schooled it back into smug nonchalance.

"I don't think it will," Vanessa crooned, leaning down until their faces were only a few inches apart. "So I'm going to give you one more chance at this."

"I'm not telling you anything, Wielder scum."

Vanessa straightened, dusting off her trousers, and shrugged as if there simply wasn't anything else to be done. "All right then. What a pity."

"'Captain' Maddox is going to get what she deserves," Helmund boasted. "I just hope they make her suffer a little bit first. If anyone should pay, it's her. Propping up those Wielder oppressors in the castle . . . Who knows? Maybe the poor captain will have an accident on the road and won't make it to King Orobas in one piece." He sounded darkly hopeful.

Vanessa's expression shifted, and a terrifying, vengeful coldness overtook her amber eyes.

"Grab the arrow."

Helmund looked bewildered for a moment, processing the strange request, but a few heartbeats later his arm was moving to where the shaft protruded from his back.

"What are you doing?" he asked.

"Oh no," Vanessa tutted with a mocking smile. "The better question is what are *you* doing? Why would you twist that arrow into your own back?"

Another flash of gold and Helmund did just that, writhing in pain as the pool of blood around him expanded.

"Now pull it out," Vanessa ordered, dropping her grin. "And don't attempt to get up."

Helmund's tough exterior made way to true panic as he yanked the arrow out with a shout.

"Nessa," Colette began, but Vanessa's eyes didn't soften at all as she cut her off.

"This man isn't fit to breathe anymore. Let him reap what he's sown." She turned to us. "We should go."

Helmund's face was in the dirt now, his back moving up and down at irregular intervals. There was so much blood. I turned my face away, unable to stomach the gore of his open wound. A twinge of pity stirred in my heart, but this man had been about to kill me. Had already killed my mother and orchestrated whatever hells Evander was currently trapped in.

Vanessa stalked back to the edge of the forest, and Colette gave me an apologetic glance over her shoulder before hurrying after her.

There wasn't anything I could do to help Helmund even if I wanted to, and if I was honest with myself, I didn't. But it didn't feel right to leave him like this either.

I ran back to his pack and grabbed the vial of my power, slinging the bag over my shoulder for future investigation.

Returning to where he lay, I crouched down. "If you help me, I can at least ease your suffering. What do I do with this?" I asked, holding up the bottle of soft orange liquid. It was slightly luminescent, giving off a soft, swirling glow.

Helmund's eyes stayed closed, but he gave an almost imperceptible shake of his head.

"Where is King Evander?" I tried.

He didn't respond at all this time.

"Where is Evander?" I asked more forcefully.

His breaths were shallow and labored, and they got fewer and farther between as I squatted in the dirt, trying to ignore the stinging in my eyes as I forced myself to get any information that might help those who had been taken.

I asked question after question, but Helmund gave nothing. The arrow was still clutched in his hand, and his fingers only went limp around it when his back stopped rising and falling.

Standing, I willed myself not to cry as I took in the hopelessness of the situation. We had no idea where in Falerin they had taken Evander and Maddox. My power pulsed from the vial in my hand, but I had no idea how to access it. Drinking it seemed like the most likely option, but could prove disastrous if I were wrong.

Pacing to the treeline, I found Vanessa sitting on a stump, Colette's hand resting on her back.

"Is he . . .?" Colette asked.

I swallowed and nodded my head, the only affirmation I could manage.

Vanessa looked up, her eyes ringed in red as she gritted her teeth and ground out, "Good."

"How did you even find me?" I asked. Piecing together the narrative of the evening was a good place to start.

"We never found my mother," Vanessa said. "When I saw your bench empty, it didn't take us very long to realize something was wrong. We mounted up as fast as we could and picked up his trail without a problem. Bastard was sloppy."

"Did you find my mother?" I asked, afraid of the answer.

Colette tilted her head quizzically. "No. Why?"

I wasn't sure if it was better not to know, or to have confirmation that she was gone. Both options made me sick.

"I'm not even sure she's alive. I have a lot to tell you." I looked around, a phantom chill making me shudder. "But not right now. I can't breathe here."

Colette nodded in agreement, looking back to the campsite where Helmund's body lay.

"How is your Gift working so strongly outside the castle?" I asked Vanessa, registering her control over him.

My friends exchanged nervous, knowing glances.

"We're not sure," Colette said. "It could just be that we've been inside the palace grounds so long that whatever bolstering effect it had will take a while to wear off, but . . ." she trailed off.

"But?"

Vanessa cut in. "We think all of the wards in Enorias are down."

My vision swam as I tried to make sense of her words. "What do you mean 'down?'"

"From what I understand, the wards are powered by the magic of Enorian Wielders, but their power needs to be focused by the monarchs. Since you don't have access to your Gift right now and I'm guessing Evander has been similarly incapacitated, there's no one to keep them up."

"How does that affect you two?" I asked.

"Well," Colette began carefully, "the wards take a lot of power. Without that drain on our Gifts, we might be able to access them more strongly, the way Wielders were able to before the war . . ."

When the wards were erected to protect the people from Falerin's clutches, I realized.

"But that means our people will be defenseless if Orobas tries to invade," I said. I was going to vomit.

Vanessa nodded grimly in confirmation. "We need to find Evander and get the both of you back to Enorias as soon as we possibly can."

I nodded mutely. Colette met my gaze, fear for Enorias and pity at my disheveled state warring on her face. Vanessa must've followed her train of thought, because she threw me a leather bag that blessedly contained a change of clothes.

"This was all I had time to grab, but I figured it would be better than what you're wearing. Change, and we'll head out." Looking around, she made her way towards the trees where Helmund's horses had been tacked.

I whispered my thanks and shucked off my ruined wedding dress. Tears threatened to overtake me again as I looked at the creamy fabric in a pile on the forest floor, ripped and matted with dirt and blood. Remembering the joy I felt putting it on this morning, surrounded by my friends and about to marry the love of my life, was like a knife to the gut. Had it only been a day since everything had fallen apart?

I stood dumbly while my friends gathered our supplies. I needed to go through Helmund's pack, but it was too dark to conduct a thorough investigation, and I wasn't sure I was ready to face whatever I found inside.

When Vanessa asked me which horse I'd be riding, I froze. I couldn't ride the mare I had been tied up on. Just looking at the saddle threatened full-scale panic. But the thought of riding Helmund's horse made my stomach churn.

The anxiety must've shown on my face, because Colette walked up and offered me the reins to the sweet-looking Palomino they had ridden to my rescue.

"Here." She extended the reins toward me. "Ride Buttercup. She's Nessa's childhood horse, and she's gentle as a mouse." Nodding gratefully, I mounted up.

Scanning the forest helplessly, a small strangled noise bubbled up from my throat.

"I don't even know where he is," I said.

Colette trotted up next to me and reached across the gap between our horses to take my hand. "Let's start by getting to Falerin. We'll be able to plan better when we know what we're facing."

I swallowed, and she gave my hand a small squeeze of reassurance.

Turning in the direction Helmund had been heading before we stopped to make camp, my friends and I rode into the night, unsure of what the dawn would bring.

Chapter 21

We only rode a few hours before stopping to get some sleep. The journey was tense and we didn't make it far with only the torchlight to guide our path, but we all needed to get away from the campsite and its troubling memories.

Having left Helmund's bedroll behind, I lay on the cold, hard ground, my mind racing with questions I couldn't answer. I didn't know how late it was when I finally drifted off to sleep.

The next morning I awoke to the sounds of Colette and Vanessa's hushed voices a few paces away.

"What are we even going to do when we get there?" Colette was asking.

"Whatever we need to." The grim set of Vanessa's jaw was silhouetted in the golden sunrise, and I recognized the same steely resolve I felt in her words.

"Nessa," Colette whispered, reaching out to put a hand on her counterpart's, "I know you're angry. I'm angry too. But if we go in with only our emotions guiding us, we're going to get slaughtered. All three of us." She glanced over to me. "We need a plan."

Vanessa let out a sigh, long and weary. "I know," she said. "I'm just so out of my depth with this. My mother would know exactly what to do, but me?" She shook her head. "I'm not even sure we're going in the right direction."

I sat up and cleared my throat, making my presence known. "We are," I assured her. "I was conscious for a long time before Helmund realized. This is definitely the route we were taking." Vanessa gave me a bittersweet half-smile.

"Plus," I continued, pulling my captor's rucksack into view, "I have this."

"And that would be . . .?" Vanessa prompted.

Even touching the satchel made my skin crawl, but I pushed through the uncomfortable emotion and opened the flap. "Helmund's bag. I'm hoping whatever is in here might give us a better idea of our next step. I already found this."

I scooted closer to the couple and held the shimmering bottle aloft. Having it in my possession made the gnawing emptiness a bit more bearable, but I still felt that cavern where my power should be.

"A vial of my power, I think."

"Your power?" Colette's eyes widened, horrified.

"He drained it somehow. Whenever I try to access it, I hit a wall. Even when I couldn't cast before, I could feel it. Now . . . nothing."

"That sounds awful." Colette shuddered.

I nodded, lips pressed tightly together. I didn't want to tell them the depth of the discomfort, the horrible emptiness I couldn't get away from. Not when I still had to break the news about Maddox to Vanessa. Her expression gave nothing away, and I decided I should be straightforward with her.

"I think they did the same to your mother," I winced.

Vanessa's face paled as she realized the implications of Maddox's powers in the hands of King Orobas. The things he could do . . . A shiver danced across my neck just thinking about it.

"And they can use it somehow?" Colette asked, a hand over her mouth.

I nodded grimly.

Colette took the vial from my hands, holding it up to the light.

"There must be a way for you to reconnect to it," she said, squinting at the liquid inside.

"If there is, I need to figure it out quickly, because I'm going to need this for whatever comes next," I said. As I watched its contents swirl, the movement of the liquid an ethereal dance of light and color, another thought occurred to me.

"I wonder if they found anything like this on Freya," Colette mused. "If we discover how it works, maybe we could restore Emory and Liang's powers too."

If she didn't already get the vials out of the castle before the third trial, it might be possible . . .

But that was getting too far down a road I could barely see the first few steps of. Before we could be of help to other victims of King Orobas's schemes, we had to rescue Evander.

We spent the remainder of the morning going through the satchel, searching for anything that might help us on our path, but didn't find much.

Either Helmund had made the trip through the Dyminian pass so many times that he didn't need a map, or it was still on his body. Thankfully, we did at least find a compass to help guide us east.

The rest of the bag proved to be rather unhelpful. There was a notebook with an unfamiliar embossed symbol stamped into the leather that initially seemed promising, but it was written in a code we couldn't decipher. The geometric shapes of the emblem resembled a twisted, unyielding knot, and the edges of the design were worn, as if it had been traced many times. We kept it with us for further study on the road, but I wasn't optimistic about its practical use. The time it would take us to decode the symbols might not be worth it when every second counted.

The last item we uncovered was another vial with dregs of a shimmering golden liquid inside.

"It looks like he drank it," Colette hedged nervously.

I had to agree with her, but the thought of imbibing my own power without knowing with absolute certainty it was the correct way to restore it felt foolish.

"We should keep trying to translate the notes," Vanessa said. "If we miscalculate, Quinn could end up without any powers at all," she warned, "or worse."

Colette opted to ride with Vanessa, leading Helmund's horse behind them so she could study the journal more comprehensively as we traveled.

The ride was tense and quiet, Vanessa and I left to ruminate on what might be happening to our loved ones and whether we would get to them in time. Colette interjected every hour or so with a theory on the notes, but without being able to look at them, we couldn't be of much help.

When it was no longer light enough to travel, Colette and I made camp while Vanessa went in search of water for the horses.

As I worked to build the fire, I felt my friend's presence behind me. She shifted from foot to foot and opened her mouth as if she wanted to say something but couldn't find the right words.

Finally she settled on, "They're smart, you know. And strong. Even without their powers, Nessa told me Maddox has been training Evander in hand-to-hand combat since he could walk. If anyone can get out of trouble, it's them."

Swiping at the moisture in my eyes, I tried and failed to find the conviction to agree with her. I didn't doubt their strength or wit, but without their Gifts . . .

Vanessa came trotting back into camp, the other two horses in tow, and held out a flask of water to Colette.

"I'll take the first watch. You should both get some rest," she said, not quite meeting our eyes.

"You need it more than I do, Nessa," Colette argued. "Give yourself a break from worrying for a few hours."

"Really, I'm fine." Vanessa's voice sounded as empty as I felt.

Colette acquiesced with a kiss on her partner's cheek and whispered instructions to wake her if Vanessa changed her mind.

The cold crept into my bones through Vanessa's leather gear as I lay on her bedroll. I didn't have a proper coat, but at least the outfit was warmer than my ruined wedding dress would've been. The image of it trampled in the mud flashed in my mind as I willed myself to sleep.

An hour passed as I tossed and turned before finally giving up, rising and shuffling around in our things to find the notes. Once I located them, I sat in front of the fire and squinted to make out the symbols. They didn't make any more sense to me than they had hours before, but I had to start somewhere. I needed to feel like I was doing *something.*

"Couldn't sleep?" Vanessa asked quietly from behind me.

I shook my head.

"I know the feeling," she sighed, sitting down beside me.

The fire flickered in the darkness, warming my hands but leaving my spirit cold and wanting.

"I'm terrified," I said into the flames.

"Only a fool wouldn't be," Vanessa replied, emotionless. "We're outnumbered, overpowered, and we have very little to go on. But they have the people we love. I'd charge into the fire over and over again for my mother, even knowing I was going to get burned."

I nodded, my throat painful as I swallowed.

"That's what loving someone is," she said. "And I know Evander. He'll be fighting like hells to get back to you too. We just have to hope all that love is enough." I could hear the emotion threatening to break free in her words, and her eyes were red again as I turned to look at her, the last of the walls I had built between us crumbling in the wake of our shared trauma.

"Thank you," I said, "for coming here. For saving me. I know we haven't been on the best terms since . . . you know."

She shrugged it off. "Well, I wouldn't be a very good friend if I didn't rescue you from your kidnapper just because you were angry with me."

A few moments passed in silence before she spoke again.

"You're right to be upset with me. I understand. And for what it's worth, I'm sorry. I shouldn't have violated you like that. I should've trusted you."

"You should've," I agreed with a sad smile. "I never would've done anything that would hurt you or Colette."

Vanessa sighed, rubbing her hand along her brow. "I know that," she said. "But I was so terrified of losing her that I wasn't thinking straight. It was beginning to feel like being caught was an inevitability after sneaking around for so long. I half expected someone to jump out from behind a column and start shouting for the guards every time we walked down the halls."

"Was it your mother you were afraid of?" I asked. "Would she have been upset that you weren't interested in Evander?"

"No, she wouldn't care about that. She already knows I prefer women. It's pretty easy to spot, even if you spend more of your time in the training ring than you do at home.

"But I knew Colette wouldn't be allowed to stay if they knew she wasn't a real competitor, and I wouldn't be permitted to leave the palace to visit her. My relationship woes seem so small in comparison now, but

. . ." she trailed off. "She's the first person who's ever really made me feel like I'm enough, you know?"

"I do," I said, reaching out for her hand. To my surprise, she didn't shy away from the contact, instead giving my fingers a firm squeeze. "And I understand. If there was anything I could've done to protect Evander during those first few days of his reign, I don't think I would've hesitated, no matter who it hurt."

"That's not the same." Vanessa shook her head. "What I did was purely selfish. Even if she was sent home, it's not as if she would've been hurt or drained. I just–I was so afraid."

I squeezed her hand back. "I forgive you, Nessa."

She leaned the side of her head against mine and we sat shoulder to shoulder in the glowing light of the fire, drawing strength from the fact that although we were both terrified, we weren't alone.

"Just don't do it again," I joked, breaking the tender moment. Vanessa laughed, wiping her eyes.

"I won't, I promise."

"So, Buttercup, huh?" I teased, arching an eyebrow as I looked at the sleeping animal. "I thought you'd name your horse something a little bit more menacing."

"Oh, shut up." Vanessa batted me with her hand. "I was nine."

Both laughing, we sunk into a companionable silence; I didn't realize how much I had missed her.

After a while, I returned my attention to the notebook, tracing over the symbol on the leather cover.

"This isn't any language I've ever seen." Years of being a merchant's daughter meant I could recognize almost all the languages spoken on the continent on sight, but I still couldn't read the pages. Mentally scanning through all the different scripts I had seen on my father's ledger over the years, I still came up empty.

"There are too many repetitive symbols to be a full language," Vanessa agreed. "It's probably just some sort of code."

"The empty bottle we found in the bag makes me think the vials are supposed to be ingested . . ."

"But you don't want to be wrong about that," Vanessa warned.

"I don't," I agreed. "But if I can get more information from the journal, I might be able to find out for certain." My eyes were already feeling strained from staring at the writing in the low light of the fire, but I knew there was no hope for sleep tonight.

"Go to bed," I said. "I need to look at this for a while."

"Are you sure?" Vanessa asked. "You don't exactly look well-rested yourself."

I chuckled halfheartedly. After what I had been through, I was certain I didn't, but I knew my mind wouldn't give me any respite until I had made some progress.

"Go," I waved her off. "I'll wake Colette to take over in a few hours."

"If you're sure." Vanessa stood up, rolling her neck.

She started to walk away but turned back and looked at me with an open look of vulnerability that I had only ever seen her offer Colette.

"Quinn?"

"Yes?"

"I'm glad to have you back," she said tentatively. "I missed my friend."

"Likewise," I smiled, and her returning grin was the timid sun on a winter morning, ready to begin its work of thawing the frost.

She made her way back to the sleeping form of her partner and moments later I heard her breathing even out as they slept, limbs intertwined peacefully.

Time felt strange as I pored over the journal. There were moments of clarity where I felt I was close to an answer, but seconds later I couldn't remember what I had been thinking about. It was disorienting, like the liminal space between waking and sleeping, where whatever fantasy you had concocted suddenly slips your grasp.

By the time I finally woke Colette and took her place on her bedroll, I was so exhausted that not even nightmares could find me.

Chapter 22

THE MOSSY FOREST UNDER our horses' hooves turned to the drier, more arid climate of the Dyminian pass as we traveled. This was the point of no return. While it was still technically Enorian soil, rumor had it east of the mountains was a lawless place; Vanessa had even heard whispers amongst the guards that King Orobas had assassins prowling the corridor, ready to capture and execute Wielders on his command.

I tried to put that particular thought out of my head as we picked a path through the rocks, traveling more slowly as the previously well-worn trails faded to nothing and water sources became fewer and farther between.

Without many options to be productive while we traveled, we continued taking turns with the notes, breaking only for meals and to water our horses. By Vanessa's estimate, we were still about two days' ride from the Falerian border, and it would be another day after that before we reached the capital city of Valine.

Our working theory was that if Orabas was extracting power, he would want it brought back to him at the palace. Given the ruler's famed hatred for magic, I wasn't sure what he wanted with it, but Helmund had spoken as if they planned to use the Gifts they Siphoned. It was conjecture at best, but it was the most logical guess we had.

By the time we stopped to set up camp that night, we hadn't made any more progress on cracking the code, and I was ready to scream in frustration. Every time I reached for that bond between Evander and me, I was met with that same unyielding wall in my mind.

There was no way to know if it was my lack of magic, his, or both, but I was growing more tempted to down the vial of my Gift just on the slim chance I might be able to feel him again. Instead, I focused on my breathing and reminded myself that my choices needed to prioritize his best chances of rescue over my own peace.

At least we weren't going hungry. Between Vanessa's archery skills and Colette's ability to coax fully fruited vines out of the ground, food was one thing we didn't have to worry about. I thought of my father's tales of the hard crusts of bread and stale dried meat he relied on during his travels and felt even more thankful for the zucchini Colette offered.

By the third day, my inner thighs were aching more intensely than I had previously thought possible.

If we get through this, I promised myself, *I'm going to do nothing but lie in bed for a week.*

Hopefully it would be with Evander lounging next to me, teasing me over my choice of reading material. I'd swat him away with my book and he'd capture my hand, kissing it tenderly before his lips found their way to my neck . . .

I shook myself out of the fantasy before the longing cracked me in two.

Focus. I needed to focus.

Colette was putting up a brave front, chattering away about the different types of flora we passed, but I couldn't manage more than a one-word reply. Vanessa, even more taciturn than usual, must've felt the same way, and poor Colette stopped trying by lunch.

That evening we broke camp early, saving a few hours of daylight for a basic hand-to-hand training session that Vanessa had suggested earlier in the day. I didn't like the idea of delaying our progress for even a minute, but she had a point; I wouldn't be of much use to anybody if I were captured before I could make it to wherever Evander and Maddox were being held.

"A lot of this technique is the same as what Colette taught you at the beginning of your Wielding training," Vanessa explained, meeting my gaze with a fire in her eyes I knew matched my own. "Your priority should be your stance. Get your feet shoulder-width apart and bend your knees slightly." I mimicked her position.

"Good. Focus on small, purposeful movements to maintain balance and control." She turned to the green-Wielder at my side. "Colette, use your wisteria vines to disable your opponent as quickly as possible. Quinn . . ." she trailed off.

"Hit them where the sun doesn't shine?" My attempt at humor was weak at best, but the left side of Vanessa's mouth quirked up in an amused smile anyway.

"That, and know where your strongest points of contact are. Since you don't have your Gift," she winced, "your most powerful allies are going to be your elbows and knees. I also want you to focus on their most vulnerable areas. Some people say the heel of your hand up into an assailant's nose can force their nasal bone into their brain, but that's an old wive's tale. There's nothing wrong with going for the eyes, especially if you have fingernails. Biting is also very effective."

Colette blanched a little at that, but to her credit, with a little shake of her head, she set her jaw and rolled her shoulders back, wiping any trace of squeamishness off her face.

"Now," Vanessa continued, "I want you to come at me, Quinn."

I raised my brows, skeptical.

"Oh, don't flatter yourself." She rolled her eyes. "Remember who my mother is. You won't hurt me."

"If you're sure," I shrugged, and with no further warning, I charged at her. When I made a move to knee her in the abdomen, she caught my leg and had me on my back in the dirt within seconds.

"You're projecting your movements," she corrected, offering me a hand up. "Don't go for such big strikes. Use your size to your advantage. Focus on agility and speed."

I accepted her outstretched hand and pulled myself to standing, panting already. This was harder than I'd thought.

"Try again, and when I grab your arm, I want you to swing it in an arc backwards to break my grip. You're not going to defeat a trained guard after a few days of hand-to-hand lessons, so your main objective is to get yourself free in the event of capture."

She beckoned me forward with her fingers.

"Let's go again."

We practiced until we were sweaty and thoroughly exhausted, breaking only when our tired muscles had slowed so much that Vanessa declared any further work a waste of energy.

Sitting by the fire, massaging our stiff arms, we heard a male voice from the east, barely audible over the symphony of the forest.

Vanessa put a finger to her lips, eyes wide.

I smothered our fire, unwilling to risk drawing anyone toward us without knowing if we could count them among our friends. This close to the Falerian border, I was willing to bet we couldn't.

Following my lead, Colette moved to unhitch our horses as the voice got closer. As we worked, Vanessa cocked her bow and held it at the ready.

One moment I registered a flash of movement at the edge of the clearing, and the next, a man stood in the middle of our encampment.

When I threw a nervous glance at Vanessa, I was thankful to note that she already had an arrow trained on him.

The man put his hands up in placation, speaking with an unfamiliar accent.

"It's all right there, love. I ain't going to hurt you."

Vanessa didn't lower her weapon even an inch.

"Then leave." There was no flash of gold from her amber eyes. Smart. If these were Orobas's men, we didn't want them to know about our Gifts.

The man turned around, and I hoped that he would do as she asked, but instead he shoved his hands, laden with golden rings, into his pockets as he began to take a leisurely lap around our campsite.

He made a big show of nonchalance as he nudged one of the logs that lay by our fire.

"You misjudge me, sweetheart," he said. "My friend and I were hunting about a half a mile to the east when we heard you over here. I was only wondering what three young ladies from Enorias were doing unaccompanied in the middle of the pass. Dangerous out here, you know." He waggled an eyebrow. The man gave me the creeps.

"You heard us from half a mile away?" Vanessa asked, also dubious.

"Well not me, exactly," he said. "I'm traveling with a friend who has a talent for that sort of thing. She wanted to see if you were all right, so she sent me to check on you." He raised his eyebrows in a show of concern that felt insincere. A quick glance to Colette, whose mouth was drawn into a tight line, told me that she wasn't buying it either.

"I could get here faster, you see. I have a talent of my own," he bragged, puffing out his chest. He raised his foot to take a step, and suddenly he was at the edge of the clearing again. Repeating the motion, he stood in front of us once more.

The man looked around, clearly expecting some kind of shock and awe, but instead we stood silent, stony-faced and tense.

Sighing, he took off his flat brown hat.

"Where are my manners?" he chastised himself. "We haven't properly introduced ourselves, have we? Theophilus Narder, at your service." He sketched a bow. "And you are?"

"Not about to tell you anything," Vanessa said harshly. "Leave us alone."

"In the middle of the pass, defenseless?" he asked. "What kind of gentleman would I be then?"

Vanessa looked pointedly at her weapon, reminding Theophilus that she was not "defenseless" in the slightest.

"Make no mistake, love," he said, shaking his head, "that'll do you a fat lot of good in here. Can't use a weapon like that against *them.*"

"Them?" I asked, curiosity getting the better of me.

"The Wielders." His words were a whisper, as if he were sharing a salacious piece of gossip. "They roam these parts, waiting to thieve from honest, hardworking Falerians trying to make the journey to Enorias. Brutal, they are."

"You'd make such a generalization about your own kind?" I asked. "You obviously have a Gift yourself." I gestured to the edge of the clearing, referencing his little trick, but he shook his head gravely.

"Oh no, lovie, I ain't one of them. Those bastards are born with so much power they don't even know what to do with it. My Gifts are *earned.*"

I didn't miss the plurality of the word. What other powers did he have hidden? And how was it possible for him to wield multiple Gifts?

"Earned?" I asked, praying he might give away some information that would help me with my own Gift.

"My benefactor has a certain talent for . . . redistributing the power, shall we say?"

My heart skipped a beat as I realized the implications of his admission.

"Don't look so scandalized, sweetheart. They deserve it, I promise you. All of them. Overpowering, conquering, *taking*... that's all second nature to them," he said. "They think they deserve to rule just because they were born with a *Gift*. Well, we ain't going to let them stay in their golden palace, I can promise you that."

My chest tightened at the threat. How many just like this man were out there, fed propaganda by Falerin and itching for violence? If he knew who I was, I'd be dead on the spot without even having a chance to explain myself.

"You should watch how you speak about things you know nothing about," Vanessa gritted out. "Not all Wielders are like that. The Enorian King certainly isn't like that."

"Met him, have you?" Theophilus chuckled.

"As a matter of fact, I have." She said nothing more.

"Is it true what they say, then? That he's a self-centered piece of shite content to sit up in his ivory tower and let the Mundanes do all the work while he galivants around kidnapping women to come entertain him at his palace? Never met a good Wielder, I'll tell you that."

That, I couldn't endure.

"He's worth twenty of you," I spat. "You aren't fit to clean his boots."

But Theophilus only laughed in my face. "An oppressor's boots will be covered in blood no matter how many times his servants shine them."

My face flushed with anger. I opened my mouth to retort, but Vanessa must've sensed that I was about to say something foolish, because she shot me a warning glare.

"Time to go," she ordered Theophilus. There was more than a hint of violence in her tone, but he paid her no mind, instead strolling over to a bush of berries that Colette had grown in preparation for dinner.

"Well this is curious, ain't it?" he asked, rubbing a leaf between his fingers. "Never seen a berry like this grow in these parts before." He looked around, eyes settling on Colette, who had gone pale. I was reminded of an old folktale as he shed his sheepish smile, instead donning a wolflike grin.

When he extended a hand toward the bush, a purple flame slithered out from his fingertip. The instant the fire touched the leaves, Colette crumpled in pain. On her hands and knees now, she lifted her head and snarled at him, raising one hand to grow a vine that wrapped around his arm.

It only took one flick of his wrist to turn the whole shoot to ash.

"Wielders after all," he frowned. "I was afraid of that. Awfully sorry about this, my dears." Raising two fingers to his lips, he whistled a few notes, a strange mimicry of a bird call.

Just as quickly, Vanessa shot at him, but he stepped away effortlessly, reappearing on the other side of me to pin my arm behind my back. I yelped in pain as he turned and positioned me in front of him so Vanessa couldn't target him again.

"And what about you, love?" Foul breath tickled my ear. "What little *Gift* are you hiding?"

There was no time to answer before a woman with a shock of purple hair emerged from the outcropping of rocks to the south of us.

"See? I told you, Katriana," Theophilus called out, swinging me around him in a circle. "That one's got some kind of a green-Wielding Gift," he said, nodding his head to indicate Colette. "Not sure about the other two."

I dared a glance at Vanessa, whose bow was now pointed at the woman. Even without Colette or me here, I was fairly certain the captain's daughter could end these two with very little effort.

"Let her go or I'll shoot your friend," she threatened.

"Big claim from a little girl," the woman laughed, drawing my eye. She stood about twenty paces away now, moving toward us with a gait that was direct, but unhurried.

The clothing she wore was finer than I expected from a bandit, and she carried a leather bag with a symbol on it. I squinted to make it out and barely contained my gasp.

It was the same mark from the journal.

Making sure to catch Vanessa's attention, I glanced quickly at the bag, widening my eyes, and shook my head as much as I could without alerting Theophilus. She followed my gaze before flicking her eyes back up to mine too quickly for him to see.

Theophilus barked a laugh. "Nice try, girlie. Lower your weapon and I won't hurt your little friend here."

Gingerly setting her bow on the ground, Vanessa shot me a meaningful look that said, "You'd better be right about this."

The purple-haired woman sauntered over to where he held me. She reached into her bag, and my wrists met cold metal, the shackles feeling oppressive and wrong, wrong, *wrong*. Set into each cuff was a tiny chip of a stone, so dark that it seemed to suck in all the light around it.

I drew in a sharp breath. More hyalperite.

Wracking my brain for a plan, I watched as Theophilus made his way over to my friends, shoving Colette's hands roughly to her back and lazily flicking a knife up to touch the soft skin of her throat.

"In case you get any ideas," he winked at Vanessa. Colette's eyes shone wide with confusion and fear as she looked between Vanessa and her bow on the ground.

"Don't you dare hurt her." Gold flashed across Vanessa's irises.

I hoped Katriana was too preoccupied to notice when Thoephilus's grip momentarily slackened before he resumed his position, a blankness in his eyes that I recognized as Vanessa's thrall.

Well done, my brilliant friend.

The purple-haired woman was now circling me like a cat who had found an injured mouse and intended to bat it around before devouring it.

"This is the fun part," she grinned maniacally, gripping my shoulder. Her other hand went to a pack at her waist, from which she procured a small glass vial, strikingly similar to the one that was still concealed at my hip. Without further warning, her power swept through me, an unfamiliar tidal wave that reached the depths of my soul.

"*Dividere potentiam et aperire viam ad maiorem potentiam*," she chanted, her hand white hot on my skin.

An incantation, like the one General Finch had used during our tethering ceremony. I recognized the Old Language from the few sections of the coronation that used it ceremonially.

"*Potentiam*" stuck out to me. That one I knew–power. But what of the rest of it?

Her magic swept into the empty cavern where my Gift had been, threatening to make me vomit onto the dirt, but then it slowly retreated.

The woman looked at me quizzically. "No trace of a Gift. What are you doing with these two?"

I had to think quickly. Many years of tiptoeing around my mother had made me a decent liar, and though it wasn't a skill set I was particularly proud of, I was thankful for it now.

"I was forced to come with them," I said, making my voice as pathetic as possible. "They didn't want to do their own dirty work, so they made me come along as a servant. If I didn't, they said they'd cover my family's cottage in ivy so thick no one would be able to get out."

Katriana tossed a disgusted glare in Colette's direction before nodding sympathetically at me.

Thank the gods.

"Apologies for my mistake," she said, removing the cuffs. I couldn't believe my good luck.

Vanessa caught my eye, flicking her gaze to where I was concealing the vial of my power. I sent up a silent prayer that I understood her correctly.

"Is there the incantation to reunite a Wielder with their power?" she asked Katriana.

"Wouldn't you like to know?" the purple-haired woman scoffed, turning around to face my friends.

"Chant it now," Vanessa ordered.

"And why would I do that?"

Vanessa's amber eyes alighted, brighter than I had ever seen them.

Katriana's mouth opened up to shoot out another derisive comment, but instead what came out was "*Coniungere potentiam et adsumere summam potentiam.*"

They really should've restrained Vanessa first, I laughed humorlessly in my head.

My hand shot to my belt and my fingers closed around the vial, which gave a happy little zap, as if it, too, understood what was happening.

Uncorking it, I brought it to my lips, the split second of anticipation stretching out into what felt like an age. As soon as I tipped it back, I was overcome with the surreal feeling of a wave of light washing over me. It swept into that chasm until it was filled to bursting, a thousand-year-old song of power being sung throughout every inch of my body.

Praying for a response, I reached down the string of power that tied Evander and me together, but nothing answered.

"Time to go," Vanessa called. Turning to Theophilus, she issued another command to freeze, just as she had given Helmund.

Smiling sweetly at his rigid form, Colette stepped easily out of his grasp. A graceful movement of her arms sent her signature flowering vines shooting out from the ground to restrain both the bandits. These were the thickest shoots I had ever seen her conjure, and when I looked closer, I could see thorns.

Snatching the hyalperite cuffs, I bound Theophilus's hands so he couldn't disintegrate them again when he regained the ability to move. Taking my lead, Colette raised her hands again, and the thick green ropes slid to cover both bandits' mouths and hands, cutting Katriana off from any casting as well. Four eyes full of murderous rage glared at us, as we packed up our supplies and mounted our horses.

"You're lucky I'm not doing worse to you for putting your hands on her," Vanessa seethed, looking back at Colette as if to reassure herself she was unharmed. Colette put a hand on Vanessa's arm in a show of tenderness that made me smile.

"Tell me," Vanessa asked, "can we expect any more of this unpleasantness on this trip?"

Theophilus glared at her, looking down at the vines around his mouth and throat. On Colette's command, the vines retreated just enough to allow him to speak.

"Why would I tell you anything, you filthy Wielder scum?"

"Because," Colette smiled, "I can either make these vines shrink back at sunrise, or I can instruct them to hold you for a week." She tilted her head and shrugged. "Or more. Though I'm guessing you won't make it that long without food or water."

Fear cast a shadow over his face, his eyes widening for a moment before his brows set themselves into harsh, angry lines.

"This is our territory," he said. "No one else will encroach from here to Moiaria, a half day's ride East."

"Good boy." Colette patted him on the cheek, and the vines slid back into place.

"Let's go." Vanessa still looked unsure about her decision not to slice him open like a fish that needed to be cleaned.

"Hold on," I said, making my way over to the woman. It felt dangerous to leave the bandits alive, especially with the wards down. The knife from Katriana's belt sliced through the strap of her hip pack easily.

"Am I correct in assuming you can't perform your little trick without these?" I jiggled the pack, the sound of glass clinking within. Staring at me with a hate-filled gaze, she made no reply, but something in my gut told me I was correct.

If we came across them on our way back, I'd be sure to take the cuffs as well, but right now it was more important to ensure they were restrained and couldn't follow us.

No glass could be heard from Theophilus's bag when I removed it, but I wasn't going to take any chances leaving the bandits with anything they could use against other unfortunate Wielders who crossed their path, so I secured it to my mount and tipped my imaginary hat.

"It's been a pleasure," I grinned, and my friends and I cantered off to the east.

A few hours later, we were regretting our decision to ride through the night. The path was no longer covered in rocks and debris, so our horses were having an easier time of it, but my muscles ached and the lack of sleep was getting to me.

"Are we going to talk about Vanessa's badassery back there?" I asked my companions, hoping the conversation would keep me awake.

"Yes!" Colette exclaimed. "I've been dying to say something, but Nessa hates it when I compliment her casting." She pecked Vanessa on the cheek, and though Vanessa rolled her eyes, I caught the ghost of a smug grin on the edges of her mouth.

"The way you managed to make your commands sound like regular conversation so the woman didn't notice was seriously impressive," I said.

"I've never successfully controlled two people at once." Vanessa admitted, keeping her gaze trained on her horse's reins. "It was a gamble, but I'm glad it paid off."

"How are you feeling now?" Colette asked.

I took a moment to reflect. I hadn't had any time to adjust to the reunification with my power, but now I noticed a warm buzz throughout my body.

"Better," I beamed. "Whole. Being without my magic was . . . horrible." I left it at that.

"I'm so sorry, Quinn. Maybe it will be easier for you to access your casting now that you can feel the difference," she said hopefully.

I had been wondering the same thing. I was dying to test the theory, but my legs were too sore to keep me on my horse with my arms in a casting position and there was no time to stop. We needed to make it to town before nightfall.

Moiaria was only a half day's ride from Valine, the Falerian capital, and after our encounter with the bandits, I was more determined than ever to get to Evander before his power could be taken from him. I ignored the voice in my head that had been reaching out for that connection to no avail, which whispered to me that it was very likely it already had. We would make it in time. We had to.

Chapter 23

There was only one inn in the dusty trading town of Moiaria. A worn wooden sign hanging above the door identified it as The Cask and Crow, and it was about as welcoming as the name suggested.

A middle-aged woman across the counter of the check-in area eyed our battle-worn traveling clothes suspiciously as Vanessa asked for a room.

"And whose name should I put this under?" she asked.

"Beada Knox," Vanessa replied easily. The woman arched an eyebrow, as if she knew it was an alias, but didn't push further when Vanessa plopped a fat bag of coins on the weathered wood of the bar.

"One room with two beds," she clarified.

The woman weighed the bag in her hand and pulled the drawstring open with two fingers, making a poor show of neutrality when she realized how much coin was inside.

"Upstairs," she directed. "Second door on the right."

After giving our thanks, we turned to go.

"You'd better not be bringing any trouble to my doorstep," she called after us.

"Wouldn't dream of it," Colette said sweetly, and we headed to find our lodgings for the night.

The room was little more than a dingy wooden box containing two worn bed frames topped with lumpy mattresses.

Vanessa eyed the space with distaste. "I think I preferred the forest," she grumbled.

Privately, I agreed with her, but it was only one night. Half a night, really. It would be foolish to delay any longer than that, but we couldn't go into Orobas's stronghold as haggard as we were. At least here, we could get a few hours of sleep, our horses could rest, eat, and be watered, and we would set off with the dawn light.

One more day. One more day, and I would be with Evander again. One more day, and we would free him . . . somehow.

After setting the two packs from the bandits on one of the beds, I went to examine our door. The wooden bar meant to function as a lock offered little in the way of security. I supposed now was a good time to test Colette's theory.

"Can one of you go stand on the other side of the door?" I asked, biting my lower lip. "I want to try something."

Vanessa nodded, immediately picking up on my intent, and shut the door behind her.

All right. Here we go.

Raising my arms, I reached for that space inside me, skimming the surface of the pool of light I could now feel there. Concentrating my energy on the door, I imagined the shimmering web of a ward falling around it before slowly lowering my hands and clearing my throat.

"Anything?" I called to Vanessa.

"Let me test it." A moment passed, but the door didn't budge.

Colette squealed, grabbing my arm. I imagined the web lifting and dissolving into the air.

"Now?"

Vanessa opened the door and strode into the room, hands on her hips.

"Took you long enough, Red." She grinned from ear to ear. My heart soared as Colette tackled me in a hug. Vanessa even joined in, the three of us ending up in a heap on the floor.

"I knew you could do it," Colette said, giggling.

"So did I, obviously." Vanessa rolled her eyes. "Though I'm pissed that those assholes in the pass did a better job teaching you than we did."

I laughed, giddy. "I just needed to connect to the source of it. I couldn't visualize it properly before, but when that woman tried to Siphon me, I felt the empty place where it used to be. All I had to do was dip into that pool and it was waiting for me."

"Well done." Vanessa ruffled my hair, standing up and heading over to one of the beds. "Now, let's rest and go get our families."

The floor creaked as I strode to the packs and began digging through their contents. Katriana's bag was full of empty glass vials, each with a tiny chip of hyalperite embedded along the rim. Even dormant, I could feel a cold, leaching pull on my magic when I held them; the disturbing feeling made me shudder.

The rest of the bag was full of basic traveling necessities: another compass, a canteen, and some rations, but no clues as to who she worked for or why they were harvesting Gifts in the pass.

Theophilus's bag was much the same. One by one, I unpacked a few hunting knives, some dried meat, and a flask of something that smelled like turpentine. Finally, my hand found the bottom of the satchel and closed around cool, smooth glass.

I pulled it out and gasped. Another vial. This one was full of a rich, plum-colored liquid that felt like stepping into an orchard in the middle of summer.

Vanessa walked up behind me and peered at it over my shoulder.

"Shit," she exhaled. I nodded, passing the bottle to her.

"Can you identify the Wielder?" I asked. "Even when it was bottled up, my power felt like me, but I don't recognize this one."

After a moment, she shook her head. "There are hundreds of casters in Enorias, and I don't know how many more might be left in hiding in Falerin. It would be impossible to find the right person without more information."

Colette didn't have any better luck.

Knowing that whoever this belonged to was out there somewhere, feeling as helpless and empty as I had the day before, was heart-rending.

"Maybe we'll find them in Valine," I said hopefully. "It's possible they're being held in the same place as Evander and Maddox."

"Maybe," was Vanessa's only reply. The expression on her face was enough to tell me she didn't have much hope.

I tucked the vial carefully back into the bag and kept it within arm's reach of my pillow all night.

Mother's cottage loomed over me in my dreams. Entering, I swept through the empty rooms, searching for her in vain, shuddering as I realized that everything looked as it had before she cast me out, frozen in time. One of her embroidery projects sat, half-finished, on the couch, and a loaf of day-old bread from the castle sat on the kitchen counter.

Something caught in my throat when I reached my old room and looked at my bed, sheets rumpled as if I had left in a hurry just that morning. I ran my fingers over the spines of the books at my bedside. *The Chronicles of Eldoria, Knights of the Silver Blade*... Tears pricked my eyes when I spotted *Son of the Marked One*. The copy Evander had lent me all those months ago.

The loneliness was a deep ache in my core. For the last few days, I had fought to compartmentalize, focusing all my energy on the next task instead of how much I missed him, but for a moment, vaguely aware that I was dreaming, I let myself crumble. I sank to my knees on the floor of my childhood bedroom and sobbed at the unfairness of it all. All of my hopelessness, despair, and longing poured out of my eyes as my body wracked itself with sobs.

"Quinn!" The call sounded like it was coming from Evander, and I wept harder at the cruelty of it.

"Quinn!" it came again, more panicked this time. Looking up through my tears, I saw what looked like his form in the doorway.

Unable to stop myself, I stood up and bolted for his arms. Even in a dream, his embrace felt like coming home.

"Quinn," he repeated a third time, his voice thick with emotion. "Thank the gods." His chest felt as solid as it ever had. The dream version even smelled like him.

He gave me the briefest, most tender squeeze before placing his hands on my shoulders and pushing me an arm's length from him so we stood face to face.

"I don't have much time," he said, his eyes boring into mine as he spoke as quickly as possible. "I was in the dungeons at Orobas's palace, and they only removed the shackles long enough to–" he took a deep breath. "Quinn, they have a way to drain our power."

This part didn't feel like a dream. My heart skipped a beat as I wiped my tears away to really look at him. His face was drawn and tired and there was a bruise blooming on his right eye. This wasn't the version of him I would've conjured in a fantasy.

"Evander?" I whispered. "Is that you?"

Moving one hand up to my cheek to stroke it gently, he nodded.

I placed a hand over his warm, solid touch. "I'm coming to get you," I promised. "We all are. We're almost there."

Evander's hand stilled and he paled, shaking his head furiously.

"No," he blanched. "Quinn, you have to promise me you won't come looking for me. Go back to Lilifel and find someone else to help you hold the wards. Lead our people. I know you'll be brilliant." He squeezed my hands with such earnestness and force that any last reservations about the reality of this "dream" left my head.

"Promise me," he repeated.

Was he asking me to abandon him? To *remarry* and lead a kingdom I had only just begun learning about? The thought made me shake with fury.

"Evander, I can't. We're coming to get you.

"If you love me, Quinn, go home. Our people need you, and I can't stand him getting his hands on you here. I–"

His eyes flared wide and he fell to the floor, clutching his chest.

No. NO.

I sank to my knees alongside him, trying to hold onto him as he vaporized under my touch.

"Evander!" I swiped at the air furiously, but he was gone.

I awoke in a cold sweat, bolting upright. My face was wet with tears and my heart pounded so hard I feared it might beat out of my chest.

That was no ordinary dream.

"Vanessa. Colette, " I called into the darkness.

Vanessa was awake, sitting up in an instant as Colette rubbed her eyes blearily.

"What's wrong?" Colette asked, a small frown forming on her sleepy face.

"It's Evander. He's in trouble. He said he was in the dungeons but then–" The lump in my throat became painful.

No matter what he said, I wouldn't leave him. It would never be an option. Seeing him alive, even for a moment, even in a dream, was enough to overcome any hesitancy to act, even without knowing what I was charging into. My breaths came hard and fast as I scrambled to assemble what meager belongings I had with me.

"Slow down," Vanessa ordered. "What happened?"

"It was a dream," I gulped air down madly, feeling as if I were suffocating anyway, "but it wasn't. I think he's been in those hyalperite shackles this whole time, but he found a way to contact me when they removed them." Panic held me in its clutches as I said, "I think they just Siphoned his power."

"You're sure it wasn't a nightmare?" Vanessa asked.

"Absolutely. It was him."

She nodded once, grimly, and started to pack her things. Colette jumped out of bed without asking any questions, all traces of sleep gone from her angelic face, and began frantically stuffing her belongings into her pack as well. I had never loved my friends more than in that moment.

While they dressed, I made sure to grab the bag containing the little purple vial and swept the room one final time to make sure we hadn't forgotten anything.

Wordlessly, we were out the door and creeping down the creaky stairs of the inn within minutes. The morning light was barely beginning to peek over the horizon as we stepped outside, so it must be five or six o'clock at the latest. All the employees of the inn were still asleep, but we were able to navigate to the small stable in the back and find our horses without incident.

As soon as we were out of the town, I pressed my heel into Buttercup's side, urging her into a full run. The countryside passed in a blur as we traveled at breakneck speed, hoping we weren't already too late.

Chapter 24

I didn't allow myself to feel relief when the outline of the Falerian capital became visible in the distance. Instead, I forced myself into numbness, steeled my nerves, and sharpened them into weapons. I had spent as much of the ride as I could practicing my casting, and though I was still nowhere near as controlled as Vanessa or Colette, I trusted myself enough to be useful on this mission. We would not fail.

On the outskirts of the city, Vanessa held up a hand for us to stop.

"We need a plan before we storm in," she said. "My Gift should be enough for us to gain entry to the castle, but I have no idea what kind of defenses they'll have once we're inside."

"I'll cover our backs," I promised. "I can do it."

"I believe you can, Quinn, but I also need you to be mindful of your limits. When we find my mother and Evander and have to make our way out, your Gift will be even more essential, so try not to burn out before then."

I nodded. I would master myself. I had to.

"I don't think I can stretch myself to controlling three at a time yet," she continued, "and they'll have more guards than that, so keep those vines ready, Colette."

Vanessa distributed the hunting knives from the bandits' packs and checked her quiver. Only three arrows remained. It didn't feel like nearly enough, but I knew our Gifts were the only weapons that would really matter.

Vanessa grimaced as she looked over our inventory, having a similar internal debate. Coming to the same conclusion I had, she looked up.

"We're going in with a lot less intel than I'd like, but I don't see that we have a choice. If they've already taken Evander's Gift, or gods forbid both his and my mother's, they have no reason to keep them alive." Her voice cracked on the last word, and I watched her throat bobas she swallowed the emotion.

"We can do this," Colette said, ever the encourager of the group. "Orobas has no idea we're here, and he still expects Quinn to be powerless."

Fortifying myself with a breath, I nodded. She was right. Stealth and cunning were our allies; I just hoped they would be enough.

The morning sun warmed my skin as I reached out for my friends' hands.

"Whatever happens in there, find Evander and get yourselves out," I said. Colette looked like she was going to protest, but stopped when she registered my pleading eyes. Emotion was thick in my throat as I fought to continue. "There will never be enough words of thanks to express my gratitude for all you've done for me. I love you both."

"We love you too, Quinn," Colette sniffled, throwing her arms around me. Vanessa simply slipped her hand in mine and nodded once. I knew I could count on her to do whatever was needed to get Colette, Evander, and her mother back to Enorias safely, and for that I would be forever grateful.

So, with only our resolve and a skeleton of a plan, we rode into Orobas's stronghold.

From the stories I'd heard growing up in Enorias, I was prepared for the capital city of Falerin to be a dark and desolate place, devoid of life and joy and reeking of oppression.

Instead, to my surprise, it was so much like Lilifel that I found myself blinking back surprise. Men and women walked the streets, carrying ingredients they had purchased at the market for supper. A cobbler advertised a special for resoling old shoes at a discounted price, and I heard the sound of children laughing as they played marbles in the alley.

I couldn't see the familiar shimmerings of magic, but otherwise it seemed no different than any other town.

The only ominous landmark I could pick out was, unfortunately, the very place we were headed. Orobas's castle rose from the center of the city, the dark cousin of the Rial palace. Its black marble turrets shone above iron gates tipped with what looked like spearheads. We circled it once at a distance, determining the best place to gain entry.

Like our own castle, it seemed there was only one way in, and the gates were heavily guarded. Soldiers in full armor, weapons glinting at their waists and on their backs, controlled the flow of traffic in and out of the palace, turning away most carriages that approached. The few that were let inside, however, looked familiar.

I ducked into an alleyway, beckoning for Vanessa and Colette to follow.

"Every carriage they've let in so far has been a merchant or tradesman," I whispered. "I recognize their wagons–they're the same type my father uses to transport goods."

"All right," Colette said, the wheels in her mind turning, "so we find someone who's supposed to be making a delivery today and Vanessa convinces them to let us stow away?"

"It's as good a plan as any," Vanessa sighed.

It took us the better part of the afternoon and some well-placed bribes to obtain the name of a local blacksmith that made deliveries to the palace, and an hour after that to find her shop. Bypassing the worn counter in the front of her smithy, we headed straight to the forge, where we found her working on a curious set of gauntlets.

Barely straightening when she heard us enter, she called over her shoulder. "Sorry, smithy is closed to the public today!"

Ignoring her dismissal, Vanessa continued toward her work bench. The woman straightened up and made the mistake of turning around, meeting my friend's gaze.

"You're going to take us with you into the palace grounds today." Vanessa ordered. The blacksmith looked confused for a moment before a serene smile came across her face and she nodded.

"Of course I am!"

"I am your apprentice," Vanessa continued. "You will make no mention of the other two."

"You are my apprentice," the woman repeated in the same bland tone. "Of course."

No wonder Maddox took such great pains to keep her and her daughter's Gifts a secret. Just watching her cast was mildly terrifying. It was a good thing Vanessa was on my side. A shiver ran down my spine as I imagined crossing her path as an enemy, even as I thanked the gods for her help.

Twenty minutes later, Colette and I were stowed in the back of the blacksmith's cart. Vanessa rode in front so she could help with further persuasion if necessary.

As we rolled up to the spiked gate, I held my breath, listening to the conversation happening ahead of us.

"Checking in for my regular delivery," the blacksmith said absently.

"And who is this?" the gruff voice of a guard asked.

"An apprentice." I held my breath as I waited for his response.

Without being able to see them, I didn't know whether the guard accepted the lie without further questioning or if Vanessa had needed to convince him with her Gift, but I breathed a sigh of relief as we crossed the gates regardless.

The wagon took us to the barracks, where we managed to slip out without notice.

"You don't remember the last half hour," Vanessa told the dreamy-eyed blacksmith. She seemed like a nice enough woman, so I hoped for her sake that our infiltration was never traced back to her.

Then again, if she was supplying weapons to Orobas, perhaps she wasn't as innocent as she seemed.

The soldiers' quarters were massive. The series of interconnected buildings were at least five times the size of the barracks in Lilifel. That didn't bode well.

Thankfully, the enormity worked in our favor in at least one regard. We managed to find a few guards' uniforms in the sparsely appointed sleeping quarters, and made it past several soldiers undetected as we skirted across the grounds and into the palace.

Inside, dark stone walls lit with torches extended in all directions. Luxury dripped from every surface, from the tapestries on the walls depicting rather gruesome battles Falerin had won, to the thick blood-red carpets under our feet. Suits of armor stood guard beside heavy doors studded with iron, seemingly ready to jump into service at a moment's notice.

"Now what?" I asked, keeping my voice to a whisper.

"We make our way down." Vanessa's tone was grim, her posture rigid. "And we find the dungeons."

This turned out to be easier said than done. The passages between floors didn't present themselves to us as effortlessly as I'd hoped, and we had to look surreptitiously to avoid alerting any of the servants.

With every guard that passed, I held my breath and tried to look at ease, as if I weren't wary of the long shadows cast by gilded braziers on the walls. One of the most important parts of a convincing lie was to act as though you believed it yourself, so I tried to become a Falerian guard on another dull day of rounds. Thankfully, our first two encounters yielded nothing more than a few stunted nods of acknowledgment, and I couldn't believe our good fortune.

That luck seemed to fizzle as we turned down a wide hallway and were stopped by one of the armored guards we had seen at the gates.

"What unit are you from?" he asked, squinting his eyes at me.

"The third," I said, venturing a distinctly *un*educated guess. "We've been assigned to the dungeons this evening, so we're headed down now."

The man's hand moved toward his scabbard and I began to panic. "On whose authority?" he asked.

"Yours," Vanessa cut in, her Gift flaring.

The guard nodded.

Thank the gods.

"Of course. Allow me to escort you," he said, his gaze blank and amiable.

My shoulders fell from where they had taken residence under my ears, though some unease lingered. I'd never been more aware that a single misstep could be the difference between succeeding in our mission and being locked in Orobas's dungeons ourselves.

As we followed the guard down the hallway, I memorized each turn we took. Right, right, third door on the left, down a flight of stairs, then another.

The smell of freshly baked bread wafted past my nose as we passed a room on the ground floor. I could hear the familiar sound of clanging pots and pans within.

How strange to think that there was a kitchen in this place, probably as bustling and busy as the one back home, that baked bread and made meals. I supposed not everyone in the castle was as wicked as the king. Did they have a head baker as kind as Mellie? A sous chef as competitive as Serena or as loyal as James? It was entirely possible, and the eeriness of it sent a chill down my spine.

Down one more level, the air grew cold and stale. A rogue moan drifted out from the long hallway, silenced after a sickening thump.

"Backup from the Third," our escort introduced us to the two men guarding the entrance.

The men looked at each other warily before turning their gazes back to us.

"Captain Walmont," one of them began delicately, "we're not off duty for several more hours."

"Then consider this your lucky day," Vanessa interjected. The two guards opened and closed their mouths like gaping fish, and the man who had escorted us to the dungeons, evidently Captain Walmont, shook his head, disoriented.

"Shit," Vanessa said, just as Walmont blinked at us, his eyes clearing.

"I don't know who you are, but you aren't leaving this dungeon," he promised, drawing his sword.

Pouring everything I had into the casting, I created a ward around us as Colette planted her feet and raised her arms. Confusion barely had time to register on Walmont's face before her vines shot out, knocking the sword from his hand and pinning him to the ground.

The other two guards stood there stupidly as Vanessa breathed a labored sigh of relief and Colette flashed a brilliant grin.

"I can't hold them both for much longer," Vanessa panted. "Both of you go ahead." Sweat was already beading on her forehead. We needed to be fast.

Colette and I rushed into a dark hallway lined with bars. Most were empty, which struck me as odd, but a few housed inhabitants in various stages of stupor. Averting my eyes, I tried not to look at their bloodied faces or gaunt bodies as we walked past. As much as I wished I could free every one of them, our priority had to be Evander and Maddox.

The dark flagstone reverberated with our footsteps as we passed one cell that held nothing but a pile of what looked suspiciously like bones. With a shudder, I forced my gaze ahead.

My panicked heart beat erratically as we passed cell after cell, finding no trace of my husband, until a weary voice croaked behind me, cutting the unnatural silence.

"Your Majesty?" I turned to peer through the bars of a room a few paces behind us.

The figure was huddled in a corner, clutching a ripped cloak for warmth. A ripped *Enorian* cloak.

"Captain Maddox?"

Vanessa's mother rose to meet me, wobbling on her legs. It looked like she hadn't eaten in days, and I could see a nasty-looking gash, covered in pus and blood, on her left thigh.

"Where is Evander?" I hated myself a little for neglecting to ask if she was all right before questioning her, but I had to know.

"I haven't seen him since early this morning," Maddox replied, and my heart fell. "Six guards came and took him to the throne room. I couldn't stop them. Your Majesty, I'm so sorry."

Her eyes were filled with guilt and shame at her perceived failure. I interrupted her with a gentle hand on her arm. "There's nothing you could have done."

She started to protest, but there was no time. I turned to Colette. "I'm going to go see if the guards at the front have a key."

"Wait," she countered, coaxing another vine from the ground. A fragrant tendril of Jasmine, smaller and thinner than the behemoth plants she had created to hold the guards, snaked toward the padlock on Maddox's cell and wormed its way into the keyhole. Colette's face screwed up in concentration for only a moment before I heard a soft click.

"You're brilliant." I beamed at my friend, dreading what I knew had to come next.

"Take care of Maddox. Get her back to Vanessa, and then I need all three of you to get yourselves out," I instructed. "I'm going to find Evander."

Colette, loyal as she was, didn't like that idea at all. "You're my friend," she protested. "I'm not leaving you."

"The captain is in no condition to fight," I said, gesturing to Vanessa's mother, "and I'll be less noticeable alone."

"But–" Colette pleaded.

"I'm not asking you as a friend," I said softly. "I'm ordering you as your sovereign." Her soft brown eyes steeled, and she nodded once, the movement small but resolute.

I tried not to think about the fact that it was my first command as queen. Gods willing, it wouldn't be my last.

Retracing my way through the stairwells Walmont had led us through to the dungeon, I found myself back in the first-floor corridor, this time blessedly empty.

As I picked my way through the halls, I shoved all my lingering doubts about my abilities out of my mind. There was no longer any room in my heart for fear or insecurity, even as I made my way up the levels of the palace, preparing to face an unspeakably evil, powerful King. I knew it was madness to confront him head-on, but leaving Evander here would rend me in two. There was no other choice for me.

I had faced impossible odds before and had come out the other side intact, and nothing was more important than this. I would not fail Evander now.

The throne room couldn't be too difficult to find. So far, the castle's layout was more or less similar to the Enorian palace, and if that parallel held, Orobas's seat of power would likely be up the grand staircase after a series of receiving rooms. There would be guard rooms positioned strategically along the way, but I hoped my uniform would allow me to blend in.

At the top of the steps, I turned a corner and nearly ran into two palace servants. A squat, middle-aged chambermaid with raven hair and deep brown eyes shot me a dirty look.

"Watch where you're going, won't you?"

Her companion, a younger blonde woman, stuck her chin in the air and looked down her button nose at me, similarly affronted.

"My apologies," I said stiffly.

They didn't deign to acknowledge me, but I heard their gossip as they passed.

"They're saying Duke Bora is on his way, but his carriage won't arrive until this evening. That's why Orobas hasn't done the deed yet," the old woman chittered.

"I don't think I could wait if it were me," the younger woman said. "The king of the Wielders . . ." She shook her head, disgusted. "He must be rotten to the core. Though it does seem a shame to waste such a beautiful face . . ."

The dark-haired woman scoffed. "I doubt his head will be so pretty when it rolls on the floor. Serves him right. The bastard's getting exactly what he deserves."

I shook with anger at their words, resisting the urge to follow them as they strolled out of earshot. It was valuable information, even if it made me sick to my stomach, but I couldn't waste another moment. Evander was *alive.* That knowledge fueled me forward.

The heavy doors of the throne room were flung open wide, and I could hear yelling and jeering as I approached. I hoped the chaos would provide enough cover for me to slip in unnoticed.

Inhaling sharply, I slid inside the doors. Positioning myself with my back to the wall, I clasped my hands behind me in my best imitation of a soldier. Holding my breath for what seemed like an eternity, I waited until I was satisfied no one had noticed me before surveying the room.

In the center, a group of courtiers and nobles, bedecked in finery, shouted at something. There were so many bodies that I couldn't get a clear look at what they were clustered around, but I had a good idea. Iron bars rose above their heads in a cruel rendition of a bird cage.

My blood ran cold as the group shifted and I caught a momentary glance of the figure inside, confirming what I'd suspected.

Evander.

Cold fury overtook my body as the crowd laughed and jeered at him. They taunted and screamed filthy names that made my frozen blood begin to boil. The floor was littered with broken glass, and I watched as a nobleman threw a heavy goblet, still half full of drink, at Evander's shoulder.

Through it all, my lionhearted love stood stoic, staring at the ground, giving no reaction to their cruelty. His thick dark hair hung in his face, matted with blood, and one eye was swollen shut.

With effort, I tore my eyes away and looked up at the dais where Orobas lounged carelessly, a glass of wine in one hand and a silver crown askew on his head. Ink-black hair fell to his shoulders, expertly coiffed.

Though he looked to be in his mid-fifties, something in his green eyes spoke of a malice far older. I could feel waves of slick, otherworldly power radiating off him from here, even as he maintained a casual air, laughing with his courtiers.

His gaze was muddled with alcohol and the smug satisfaction of his capture, and his face, all hard lines and unrelenting brutality, sneered in satisfaction at the gruesome show. I had never despised someone more than I did in that moment. Not my mother during her worst moments. Not even Freya when she attacked Evander during the third trial.

This was not an isolated act of misdirected rebellion. This was a daily practice in this court, and from the looks of it, he found it to be *fun.*

A servant approached him to refill his goblet, but he waved them off lazily.

"Now now, everyone, play nicely," he drawled. "We needn't hasten the evening's activities. Besides, we've forgotten our manners. We haven't even welcomed our new guest."

His eyes snapped to me, all the haziness gone from them in an instant.

"I wondered when we'd be seeing you, Ms. Parry," he smiled, tipping his head. "I was beginning to fear you wouldn't make it in time."

There was that crazed look again, the one I had seen in Katriana's eyes–a cat toying with a mouse.

Bending my knees, I threw my arms up at my sides, a protective ward forming at my fingertips. I imagined that shimmering net falling over Evander as well, but I had no way of knowing if it worked.

Even if it had, it didn't stop me from hearing his anguished scream as he roared my name. The sound cleaved my heart in half. As the crowd parted slightly, Evander gripped the bars of his cage, his good eye frantically searching my face.

"No. No no no no no." Panic coursed through the words, reaching a crescendo as he turned to Orobas. "Please. Let her go."

Orobas simply laughed, rising from his throne and taking a few steps off the dais.

"You bastard," I spat.

"Oh, come now," he tutted. "Is that any way to treat your host? Especially one who has something you desire so dearly?"

I refused to take the bait he was offering.

"Let him go."

With a wave of his hand, Orobas's noblemen cleared the cage.

"Dismissed," he ordered, and they began to file out of the room dutifully, throwing intrigued glances over their shoulders until the doors closed behind them. The turn of events had me on high alert, but I was thankful for fewer adversaries.

"Best to have this conversation in private," Orobas said conspiratorially when the chamber had emptied. "I'm going to let you in on a little secret, only because I have no intention of letting you leave this room. The courtiers and my kingdom at large are skillfully kept in the dark about certain . . . *abilities* that I possess." He began to pace between the dais and the cage, gesticulating casually as if he were telling a story at a dinner party.

"You see, it's been necessary to maintain a bit of the old anti-Wielder rhetoric in Falerin. Much easier to unite them against a common enemy elsewhere than have them question everything *I* do. So it might be upsetting to some to learn that I've 'borrowed' a few Gifts."

Helmund's words suddenly made horrifying sense, and I found the air knocked from my lungs. All those Gifts he had stolen, the power he had collected– this was so much worse than anyone had feared.

Oblivious to my terror, Orobas abandoned his pacing in favor of prowling circles around the bars of the gilded cage. He moved closer with each lap, but Evander ignored him, looking through the bars to address me instead.

"Run, Quinn. I don't care what you have to do to get out, just *go.*"

"So dramatic." Orobas rolled his eyes, flicking a hand toward Evander. His mouth continued to move, but no sound came out. One of the many Gifts Orobas had stolen, I was sure. I wouldn't have thought it possible, but as I watched the brutish silencing, my hatred deepened further.

"Ms. Parry and I are just going to have a little chat," he promised Evnder with a wink.

"Rial, actually," I ground out, wishing for the first time my Gift was something that could destroy rather than protect. "*Queen* Rial."

"Oh yes." Orobas waved a hand again, his favorite gesture of casual cruelty. "How could I forget about that troubling little detail? I had plans for you too, of course, but I'm afraid they went awry. When poor Helmund never arrived with you in tow, I was left to puzzle out how I would track you down, but you've handed me such a neat little solution. I really must thank you." He dipped his head in a mocking approximation of a bow.

As he rose, the doors flew open and a flustered soldier came barreling into the room, out of breath as he nearly skidded on the polished floor.

"Your Highness." He bowed quickly. "There's been a breach in the dungeons. The guard from Enorias has escaped." He made a valiant effort to remain still as he braced himself for King Orobas's reaction. Even from here, I could tell the man was terrified..

"Your doing?" Orobas asked me, raising an eyebrow. Hiding the wave of relief that crashed over me at the news that my friends had escaped, I gave nothing away.

"Ah, well," he sighed, turning back. "Give chase if you must, but don't trouble yourselves too much. I have what I needed from her."

The guard was still frozen in place, unsure what to do with the apathetic order until Orobas dismissed him carelessly over his shoulder, at which point he fled the room.

"Quite a useful Gift, your captain," the king remarked. "Though I doubt it will work on you." He assessed me carefully, narrowing his gaze.

"Lower your shield," he ordered. The flash of gold in his eyes looked so much like Vanessa's, it was uncanny. Thankfully, my wards seemed to hold against Maddox's stolen Gift.

Oroboas hummed. "Just as I thought. I have a theory, Ms. Parry. Would you like to hear it?"

When I didn't respond, Orobas shrugged. "Humor me."

I only looked at Evander, who was watching in terror, arms shaking as he gripped the bars of his enclosure.

"I'm sure you're aware of the existence of a certain troubling prophecy–'The Deceiver,' I believe it calls me." He laughed lightly. "Not very flattering, is it? And what's worse is that it rather irritatingly predicts my demise, which simply won't do.

"I went through all the trouble of organizing the retrieval of Queen Evalina, only to learn that she had fallen ill and was passing the Crown to her son." His lips curled into a sneer directed at Evander. "Inconvenient, to be sure, but I'm a flexible man." Tilting his head, he raised his palms in a show of complaisance.

I very much doubted that, but I let him continue. If I could keep him talking, perhaps I could buy myself time to construct a plan. I scanned the room, a study in opulence, for anything that might help me.

Its dark carved walls, adorned with gold, rose to a high ceiling peppered with wood and iron chandeliers. The black marble floor had veins of white and red throughout, giving the chilling impression of rivulets of blood.

Even Orobas's throne, made of obsidian that rose to three jagged points over the seat, felt foreboding. This was what I had pictured when I thought of Falerin. But I didn't spot anything that looked like it would open the cage.

"Rather than taking the risk of transporting him," Orobas was drawling on, "I decided it might be best to dispose of him in Enorias. An able-bodied male, trained in combat since birth, would be quite a liability to me on the road to Falerin if he couldn't be properly subdued. My finest men, my most clever spies, and decades of knowledge and preparation were all deployed for the attack.

"Imagine my surprise, then, when I heard a mysterious peasant girl had foiled the whole thing." He looked at me disapprovingly, like a school teacher reprimanding a pupil, but I couldn't help but raise my chin, feeling a tiny spark of pride.

"A shame, too," he said. "I liked Freya. A gifted Siphon and quite adept at poisoning. From what I heard in my reports, she was doing quite well with the fire-Wielding Gift I gave her, too. That is, until you had your little *squabble*. Then that plan *went up in flames* as well . . . " He laughed, a hand over his belly. "You'll have to forgive my joke."

My face remained impassive, and Orobas looked disappointed. I wasn't sure what he expected, but if my mask were to crack, it wouldn't be amusement that seeped through, but rage, deep and unadulterated. As it stood, it was taking all my focus to maintain a blank expression that wouldn't give away the whirring of my mind as I tried to formulate a plan.

"So," he sighed, writing off my stoicism, "I was forced to adapt again. As they say, to have something done right, you have to do it yourself. At last, the prince was successfully brought to me, but once again things went adrift. Do you know why, Ms. Parry?"

"I couldn't imagine," I gritted through my teeth. There had to be *something* in here I could use. Anything.

"Well, you see," he continued, "this morning was quite eventful for both of us." He gestured to the enclosure, but I couldn't bring myself to look fully at Evander, whose mouth was still moving soundlessly as he urged me to abandon him and run.

"Before disposing of him and securing my rule, I thought I may as well extract his power to add to my arsenal. It is, after all, rather legendary. I even had one of my most talented Siphons perform the incantation. But the results were . . . not what I expected. A useful Gift, to be sure, but not *the* Gift. It doesn't seem poor Evander here was the Protector after all." Orobas frowned. "Do you know what that means, Quinn?"

The force of the realization was like being run over by a horse. We'd been so foolish, jumping to conclusions far too quickly. The prophecy wasn't about Evander at all. There had never been a chance for us to beat Orobas.

There was the only option left. Evander's Gift had already been taken because of our mistake, but maybe I could convince Orobas to let him leave with his life if he thought we weren't a real threat to him.

"If you have his power already, why not let him go?" My words were full of a bravado that I didn't feel. "If he isn't The Protector, you have nothing to fear from him. Surely it would only serve to strengthen your position if you were to send your fallen rival back home, stripped powerless at your hand. The Mundane in Enorias might even respect that enough to turn to you." I avoided Evander's eyes as I said it. I knew it was horrible, but I would say anything, promise anything, to get him out.

Orobas barked out a laugh. "Ruthless, Ms. Parry. I didn't know you had that cunning in you." He nodded his head in a show of respect. "Unfortunately, I think you've misunderstood my meaning. Let me see if I can help you along."

With no further warning, he reached for the cage and wrested it apart as if the thick iron bars were paper. Using Evander's own Gift against him, he forced him to the ground just outside the jagged opening.

"Any inkling yet, Quinn?" Finally, the mask of indifference was gone, revealing the madman underneath. With wide, crazed eyes, he took Evander's right arm, the one he always used to stroke my cheek so gently, and in one move, wrenched it out of its socket. Evander's face contorted in pain and his mouth opened in a soundless scream.

Orbobas's smile widened further, "Oh, I forgot– Better to have the full effect, don't you think?"

After waving his hand, he twisted Evander's now dislocated arm further behind his back. This time I heard his cry of pain, and it threatened to bring me to my knees. Desperate, I tried again and again to ward around him, but the power sputtered out at my fingertips when it met Orobas.

"Stop it!" I screamed. "Stop hurting him!" I had thought the uncertainty of his safety was torturous, but that was nothing compared to the horror of this moment, no greater anguish than watching my love double in pain as I found myself powerless to help him. Nothing I had ever accomplished could make up for this failure. If I couldn't protect him now, I would never be able to live with myself.

Orobas only yanked his arm again, and Evander let out another gut-wrenching cry.

"*You* could stop me if you wanted to, Quinn," Orobas goaded. "Haven't you figured it out yet? Perhaps I need to give you a bit more of an incentive."

From his belt, he pulled a jeweled knife. The tip was curved and wicked: a true instrument of torture. He held it to Evander's throat, one hand still on the injured shoulder, using his own stolen Gift to hold him in place. I was going to vomit.

"All it would take is one tiny movement," he demonstrated by flicking his wrist in the air, "and your poor prince would be bleeding out on my floor. Don't you want to *protect* him?"

Protect. Hope fluttered in my heart at the word. I recalled the language of the prophecy we had poured over, hunched over Evander's desk until my eyes were dry and my head aching.

"There will come a Time of Darkness when the kingdom is at its weakest. The fated halves of the Crown must find each other before the Deceiver seizes the Gifts of the people. Only the powers that sing to one another will be enough for the Protector to wipe The Evil One from existence and bring stability back to Enorias."

Every time my Gift had manifested in the last few months, it had been to protect me or someone I loved. The breaths I took in the tank, the shield that protected Evander from Freya's fire . . .

It was impossible. And yet I knew instinctively it was true.

"I'm the Protector," I breathed.

Evander's eyes widened in sudden understanding as Orobas grinned ear to ear.

"Very good," the mad king praised.

Keeping one hand on Evander, he withdrew a vial from his pocket. Gilded and ornate, it was larger than the others I had seen, but I had no trouble recognizing it for what it was. Instead of a tiny chip along the rim, a large stone of hyalperite was set into the stopper.

"Let's strike a deal, Ms. Parry, since you made such an excellent point earlier. It would be a rather delicious serving of irony to return you both to Enorias drained and weak. So I will let you live," he wiggled the vial between his fingers, "*if* you let one of my Siphons collect your Gift for me."

"Quinn, no." Evander barely choked out the words before Orobas silenced him again.

"Why shouldn't I just make good on the prophecy here and now?" I bluffed, trying to buy myself time to examine my options. I couldn't leave Evander here, but I also couldn't give this monster another ounce of power under any circumstances.

"Yes, that is a bit of a gamble on my part," Orobas said, pocketing the vial again. "But I'm fairly certain you can't." When he leveled his gaze at me, it felt like he was slicing through all my bravado, exposing the fear underneath. "You see, I wield your lover's Gift now. I confess I thought that line about 'powers that sing together' was sentimental drivel, but then I realized . . . your power cannot work at odds with his, can it?" The glint of his green eyes betrayed a hint of that otherworldly malice I had sensed when I first entered the room.

Abandoning all caution, I flung my arms out, allowing my own shield to fall, and tried to cast around Evander one more time. My stomach turned leaden when nothing happened; Orobas was right. As long as he was using Evander's Gift, I couldn't touch him. Judging by his satisfied chuckle, he knew it too.

"So," he urged, "do we have an agreement?"

"You're a monster." A monster I had no idea how to stop. My heart beat thunderously, darkness closing in on my vision as he drew the knife and placed it once again on the column of Evander's throat.

"What a shame. I'm afraid this isn't going to be pretty, and my courtiers will be so disappointed to miss the execution."

Orobas raised his thin, dark brows, giving me one last moment to choose. I fought through the nausea as I faced two impossible options: give this cruel madman what he desired, or watch the life leave Evander's eyes right in front of me. I'd likely follow soon after.

There had to be another way. Something I could do to draw him away, something else I could barter.

"Tick-tock, Ms. Parry."

Suddenly, his crazed eyes flared wide as something struck his right forearm. The knife he had been holding clattered to the ground as blood began to seep into his fine tunic.

"Step away from my brother."

In the doorway stood Vanessa, a dark avenging angel, her bow raised and pointed at Orobas, already notched with another arrow. She let it fly, striking true as it embedded itself in his other arm. Orobas's flinch was shorter than a heartbeat, but the split second his hand left Evander's shoulder was enough.

Every injustice I had ever experienced, every ounce of fury at what had been taken from me exploded out of my palms.

A voice I didn't recognize as my own snarled from my lips. "You will never take what is mine."

Pure power flowed through me, endless and ancient. The room turned a blinding white as the ends of my hair rose off my shoulders and my feet left the ground. It might have frightened me if I wasn't so desperate for a way to free Evander, but there was nothing I wouldn't do, no god or devil I wouldn't call on, to save him.

Pouring everything I had into the power, I coaxed it to obey my will. The very essence of my being poured through my outstretched hands.

It was only when I could hear my heartbeat in my ears and my breath had grown so labored I felt on the verge of fainting that the light faded, leaving chaos in its wake. My eyes flew to every corner of the room, taking stock of what remained amongst the splintered wood and pieces of marble rubble.

Orobas had been knocked back several yards, where he was lying on the ground, unconscious. Vanessa stood in the doorway, unharmed, a visible sphere of shimmering ward surrounding her.

Finally, I turned my eyes to Evander, still on his knees in front of the cage. No trace of blood marred his hair or face, and both his striking blue eyes looked up at me in wonder.

"Quinn . . .?" he breathed.

I ran to him, throwing myself on the ground in front of him in relief. Our arms twined around each other so tightly that I couldn't decipher which pulse was my own.

Pulling my face out of the crook of his neck, I moved my hands to his cheeks, wiping away the tears there. I kissed him once, softly but fiercely, thanking the gods for every bit of luck and fate they had blessed me with to be in his arms once again.

"We need to leave," Vanessa called from the door.

I nodded, though I was loath to let Evander go for even a moment.

"My Gift," he croaked. "We can't let him have it."

I looked back to Orobas–or the spot on the floor Orobas had occupied a moment before. Confusion and dread swirled on Evander's face as he took in the empty space; the wicked king was gone.

"We'll get it back. Together," I promised, squeezing his hand.

"We need to get out of the palace before the other guards realize what's happened," Vanessa cut in. "Judging by the barracks, there are hundreds of soldiers stationed here, and we can't fight that kind of manpower, Gifts or no Gifts."

I knew she was right, so I stood, offering Evander a hand.

"Don't think we're not going to talk about that little stunt later," Vanessa warned, raising an eyebrow at me.

"Don't think we're not going to discuss you defying a direct order to get the hells out of here," I shot back.

"You gave that order to Colette," she shrugged. "I didn't promise you shit."

My face broke into a wide smile that reflected her own shit-eating grin, and together the three of us fled into the night.

Chapter 25

Somehow Colette had managed to get Maddox out of the castle single-handedly. The story would surely be something out of an adventure novel, and I couldn't wait to hear it, but when we met at our rendezvous spot, all I could manage was to throw my arms around her in relief.

The journey back to Moiria was slower than I would've liked with two extra members of our party, one of whom was seriously injured. We needed to get back to Enorias to see if it would be possible for me to hold the wards alone as soon as possible, but it wasn't safe for us to split up. Not with what we now knew to be Siphons crawling all over the forest.

The mood was somber and tense as we picked our way back through the Dyminian pass to the east of the mountains. We slept in shifts, looking over our shoulders at every turn. Evander and I spent our watches holding onto each other tightly, sharing stories in hushed whispers about the harrowing events of our separation. I cherished those moments under the stars where we could be a husband and wife instead of monarchs with the weight of a kingdom on our shoulders.

But the night before we reached Enorias, I awoke alone on my bedroll, Evander's warmth at my back glaringly absent. I sat bolt upright, looking around desperately.

Not again.

Instinctively, I searched for the bond between us before remembering Orobas still had Evander's Gift. The thought made me sick, and the feeling only intensified when I didn't find my husband in our camp. Rising from the ground, I took care not to wake the others until I was sure something was wrong.

This is irrational, I told myself. *Leftover trauma from his disappearance at the wedding, nothing more.*

To curb the panic, I walked myself through the facts: his boots were gone, so it was likely he had gotten up of his own free will. Maybe he needed to relieve himself. Willing my heart to stay calm, I began to make my way toward the treeline. I counted my breaths as I drew the cold air of the forest into my lungs.

One. He's all right.

Two. What if a Siphon found our camp?

Three. We would've heard a struggle if someone had been here.

Four. What if the Siphon had a Gift that dampened sound somehow?

By five, I had broken into a run.

The trees rushed past me as I moved, my arms and legs battered by rogue branches and thorny brambles. I circled the camp as quickly as I could, becoming more and more frantic as I found no sign of Evander.

Finally, a few paces into the forest, I caught the first glimpse of his back silhouetted in the spotted moonlight filtering through the trees.

Hearing me approach, he turned, pulling his hands out of his pockets to reach for me as I closed the distance between us.

"Quinn? What's wrong?"

Though I tried, I couldn't hold the tears at bay.

"When I woke up, you were gone. I thought–"

"Oh, my love," he soothed, rubbing his hands up and down my arms before drawing me into his chest. "I'm so sorry. I'm safe. You're safe."

I held on tightly for a moment, breathing in his familiar scent before pulling away to scan his face.

"You're all right?"

"I'm fine," he promised, but there was a ghost of something in his expression I couldn't quite decipher.

"What's wrong?"

"I couldn't sleep . . . Nightmares," he admitted.

"I have them too," I said, resting my head on his chest again. "Do you want to talk about it?"

Evander pressed a kiss to the top of my head and sighed. "I keep reliving what happened in Orobas's palace," he said. "The dungeons, Siphoning my power, being trapped in that cage while I watched him toy with you . . . My mind is torturing me with what might've happened if your Gift hadn't taken over when it did."

I knew the feeling all too well.

"You're safe," I repeated back to him. "I'm safe. I'm not going anywhere."

He nodded, his mouth a firm line. Raising my lips to his, I tried to kiss away the fear I found there. As my hands ghosted over his jaw, the beginnings of a beard tickled my fingers. It wasn't as if he'd had the opportunity to shave in the past few days, but I'd never seen him with facial hair.

"I like this," I told him.

"Oh?" Some of the shadow left his eyes as he raised his brows.

I hummed in assent. "It suits you, *Your Majesty,*" I teased, raising myself up on my tiptoes to kiss him again.

My heart sang when he smiled into the kiss, his arm snaking across my lower back to pull me in tighter.

"Anything to please my queen," he laughed against my lips. He kissed me back hungrily, taking advantage of the rare moment alone together on our travels. All my fears melted away as he parted my lips with his tongue, and I groaned.

"Would you mind getting a little dirty?" I asked, looking at the carpet of leaves on the forest floor.

"With you? Never," he smirked.

"That's not what I meant, but now you're giving me ideas." I raised my brows, a smile on my lips as I guided him to the ground. Any trace of shyness had vanished with the threat of losing him forever. The last time I had passed through this forest, I was so afraid I would never be able to touch him like this again. I wouldn't take it for granted now.

His eyes became heavy with lust as I worked to unfasten his trousers and divested myself of my own.

Straddling him, I leaned down to his lips again.

"I love you," I whispered, and tears pricked my eyes as he responded in kind.

sank down onto him, adjusting to the fullness. His hands found my hips and he began to help me move in a rhythm that had us both breathing heavily.

"Gods, Quinn," he panted.

The sound of my name on his lips drew a whimper from me and I began to move faster.

"Yes, love," Evander moaned, "Oh gods yes. You're so good to me."

I leaned down to kiss him again, and we became a frantic mix of tongues and teeth as I rode him. When I could tell he was getting close, I leaned back to watch him shatter, his hands squeezing my breasts as he climaxed with my name on his lips.

Satisfied with myself, I slid myself off him and went to lay my head on his chest when his smile turned devilish.

"Not so fast," he ordered. "Your turn, my queen."

He settled between my legs, lifting my calves up onto his shoulders, and I thought I might die with the first stroke of his tongue. He found that aching spot, circling it until I was writhing, hips lifting off the ground as I gripped his soft curls between my fingers.

"Gods, Evander. Just like that. Don't stop." I felt him smile against me and lost all control, spasming as the pleasure overtook me. When I finally stilled, Evander crawled up the length of my body to kiss me again.

There was a gleam in his eyes as he pulled away. "I'm still shaving when we get back," he smirked. I swatted at him, laughing, and we dissolved into a heap of satisfied giggles on the forest floor.

We made our way back to camp as the sun came up. Vanessa watched us emerge from the trees together and raised her brows with a smirk, but said nothing as she tended to her mother.

Maddox sat on her bedroll, a shadow of the woman I'd met several months prior. The absence of her magic was affecting her deeply, and she had been quiet since we had left Valine.

Evander was also haunted by the loss of his Gift, I knew, and my chest ached when I recalled how empty I'd felt without mine. I promised him we'd retrieve it together, but in truth, I had no idea how. There were so many unknowns.

As we rode toward Enorias, we puzzled over Orobas's disappearance and how his plan would evolve in the wake of our encounter. I had no doubt he was out there now, planning his next move in a game neither Evander nor I understood yet.

The moment we crossed the border, I felt the ghost of the wards sizzle and crackle against my Gift, but no matter how many times Evander tried to coach me, I couldn't get them back up. My show of power in Valine had drained me too much, and he didn't have any magic to lend to the effort.

"I have no doubt that you can do this, my love," he promised me, but I could see the shadow of his time protecting the realm alone ghost across his face.

"Being in the castle might help," Colette offered.

I had to hope she was right, because the idea of our borders being wide open to Falerin was terrifying.

When we finally reached the Lilifel city limits, I nearly wept with joy.

People whispered behind their hands as we passed them on our way to the castle, and I saw more than one business boarded up as we made our way through the city. That couldn't be a good sign.

How many Wielders had been drained or kidnapped in the brief window when Orobas had managed to lure us out of the city?

Stepping through the doors of the palace felt more like coming home than returning to the cottage ever could. Just knowing I was in the same building as Mellie had me breathing easier. I even found myself wondering how soon I could see Serena and James.

But standing in the massive foyer, I found I didn't know where to start. Evander, Colette, Vanessa, Maddox and I were frozen in the entrance, looking at each other in quiet disbelief until a clatter came from the base of the grand staircase, breaking the trance.

Georgette stood, white as a ghost, her eyes taking in every inch of Evander as she scanned him for injury. The tray she had been holding was strewn across the floor, tea leaking over the carefully polished tiles, the porcelain pot shattered.

"Miss me, Georgie?" Evander grinned, once again the carefree princeling she had told me about.

Decorum forgotten for the moment, Georgette ran toward us, taking Evander's hands in her own wrinkled ones.

"Where have you been? We've all been worried sick, Evander! Disappearing on your wedding night? Thank the gods you've come home in one piece."

In a hushed tone, she continued, "There have been kidnappings all over the city. They're saying the wards have been broken." My heart sank at her confirmation. Orobas's plan had worked. All those innocent Wielders . . . where had they been taken?

"Evander, I'm terribly sorry to do this. I know you've just returned, but there's something you need to attend to right away," Georgette said.

That was putting it lightly. There were so many urgent matters to attend to that my head spun. The wards needed to be re-established, we had to figure out the extent of the damage Orobas had done to the city in our absence, and I should find out what happened to my mother. And oh, gods, I needed a hug from Mellie.

Even without our bond, Evander could sense my overwhelm. He took my hand as he encouraged me with all the earnestness in the world. "You can do this, and you won't do it alone. We'll figure it out together."

He turned to his nursemaid. "Our first priority needs to be the wards, Georgie. My wife needs something to eat, and we need to resume training straight away."

"I understand, Evander, but this really can't wait," Georgette repeated, more forcefully this time.

"Your mother is awake."

Acknowledgments

THIS BOOK WOULDN'T HAVE been possible without my incredible husband, who is my biggest support and best friend. I also want to give thanks to:

My children, Rowan and Juniper, for allowing me to write while we watched Bluey.

My mother-in-law, who provided many hours of childcare so I could write in peace and fixed all my errant commas.

My cousin Peyton, who made me laugh until I cried while editing this novel.

My critique partner Kristi, who encouraged me to keep going after my messy first draft.

My therapist, who pushed me to do the scary thing.

My beta readers: Steph, Jessica, Vicka, Amanda, Miranda, and Hannah.

And you. If you find this book in your hands, you are incredibly special to me and I can't express my gratitude enough. See you in book two!

About the Author

Megan Acuna is a content creator, mom, and lover of all things cottagecore. She began writing and binding her own fantasy novels at age 11, and finishing a full-length romantasy feels like a dream come true. When she's not writing, you can probably find her in her greenhouse or at the thrift store. She lives in Seattle with her husband, Matt, and their two toddlers, Rowan and Juniper.

@meg.acuna

/meganacuna

For a list of content warnings, a clean romance page skip guide,
and news about book two, visit
thecrownprophecy.com

Milton Keynes UK
Ingram Content Group UK Ltd.
UKHW030856051124
450766UK00005B/513

9 798218 513108